An Inconvenient Beauty

Books by Kristi Ann Hunter

HAWTHORNE HOUSE

*A Lady of Esteem**
A Noble Masquerade
An Elegant Façade
An Uncommon Courtship
An Inconvenient Beauty

*e-novella only

AN INCONVENIENT BEAUTY

KRISTI ANN HUNTER

BETHANYHOUSE

a division of Baker Publishing Group
Minneapolis, Minnesota

© 2017 by Kristi Ann Hunter

Published by Bethany House Publishers
11400 Hampshire Avenue South
Bloomington, Minnesota 55438
www.bethanyhouse.com

Bethany House Publishers is a division of
Baker Publishing Group, Grand Rapids, Michigan

Printed in the United States of America

Library of Congress Control Number: 2017942758

ISBN 978-0-7642-1827-9 (paper)
ISBN 978-0-7642-3109-4 (cloth)

Scripture quotations are from the King James Version of the Bible.

This is a work of fiction. Names, characters, incidents, and dialogues are products of the author's imagination and are not to be construed as real. Any resemblance to actual events or persons, living or dead, is entirely coincidental.

Cover design by Kathleen Lynch / Black Kat design
Cover photography by Richard Jenkins, London, England

Author represented by Natasha Kern Literary Agency

17 18 19 20 21 22 23   7 6 5 4 3 2 1

Prologue

The line between boy and man was never murkier than when a father died too soon, leaving his son to walk through the foibles of youth while shouldering the responsibilities of adulthood.

Though a part of Griffith, Duke of Riverton, knew that having to show his ripped paper to his housemaster wasn't the worst thing that could ever happen, the eleven-year-old part of him seethed in anger. He fingered the tear in the top of his paper that meant the master teacher found his work inadequate. The head of his house was going to be angry.

Not as angry as Griffith was, though.

It would be better if he knew where to direct his anger. While some of it was definitely reserved for the group of upper boys who ruthlessly attacked Griffith and his friend Ryland, Duke of Marshington, there was a good bit directed at himself as well. Because of the ceaseless taunting, the snide mutterings of "*As you wish, Your Grace*" that rang in his ears until he heard it in his sleep, and the teachers' delight in being able to discipline such high-ranking boys, Griffith was coming to despise the title

7

he'd been raised to love and respect. Unlike Ryland, who had been all too pleased to obtain the title, since it meant his grandfather couldn't torture him anymore, Griffith had adored his father and would have been more than happy not to be the duke.

He'd have given anything to be able to ask his father what he should do now, because what he wanted was revenge. The anger at the older boys, the teachers, and himself coursed through him, burning right through his normal, logical reasoning until all he wanted to do was prove that—despite his tender years— he was no one to be crossed, that he wasn't a boy but a young man to be reckoned with.

The paper in his hand crumpled further as his fingers curled into a tight fist. He'd had very little time to work on his paper this week, given the several hours a day he'd had to help the groundskeeper as punishment for an escapade in the headmaster's office. An escapade that he'd had no part in but the headmaster had been convinced he and Ryland had done.

Rearranging all the furniture was a fairly harmless prank, but the older boys had also riffled through the files, making changes to Ryland's and Griffith's marks, to make it look like they'd done it. Headmaster Heath hadn't been pleased. Griffith's hands were raw and his muscles hurt from the hours spent shoveling bat guano into the flower beds as fertilizer as well as from the additional household chores he'd been given.

Ryland was waiting outside the house, his arms crossed over his thin chest. Griffith towered over him, having grown enough in the past year to require having his trousers retailored twice and ordering new coats and shirts made. Another second-year boy nodded at them as he scurried into the house, not wanting to be seen with them and thereby become a target of the older boys.

"Did you find out who invaded the headmaster's office?" Griffith shoved his already crumpled paper into his satchel.

Ryland nodded, lips pressed together. "The fifth years."

Griffith nodded at the building behind Ryland. "From our house?"

"No. They were King's Scholars."

"I guess that takes care of your plan, then." Secretly, Griffith was relieved. As much as his anger was driving him toward revenge, the idea Ryland had come up with while they shoveled manure yesterday made Griffith more than a little nervous. Sneaking into the upper boys' room in one of the houses in town was one thing, but the King's Scholars house was on campus.

"I say we do it." Deep creases formed in Ryland's forehead, causing a shadow to fall across his grey eyes. "If I hear 'As you wish, Your Grace' one more time, I'm liable to do something that will actually get me sent down from school."

Griffith was inclined to agree. Though violence hadn't been part of his life, even he was feeling the urge to hit something. The urge frightened him as much as the idea of sneaking into the King's Scholars' boardinghouse at night.

"I'm doing it. Tonight." Ryland lifted an eyebrow. "Are you with me?"

Was he? He was fairly sure that his father wouldn't approve. But his father had left him to figure things out on his own. And if Ryland did what he planned, Griffith was going to be blamed for it whether he was involved or not. Was it better to be falsely guilty or truly guilty? Either way he'd suffer the consequences. "I'm in."

Thankfully, the trembling in his body didn't reveal itself in his voice. He stuffed his hand down into his satchel and felt around for his paper, tracing his fingers along the edge until he could feel the tear in the top. It was his third in as many weeks. He'd come to school to learn, and that obviously wasn't happening. No matter what he did, his life was at the mercy of the older boys, determined to have their own against a pair of young dukes while they could. Renewed anger rushed through him, trampling over his misgivings. He'd hold on to his paper until tomorrow. He might need the motivation tonight.

⌒

Sneaking around the grounds of Eton at midnight was wrong. Then again, so was making someone's life miserable just because you could. If he tried really hard, Griffith could convince himself that teaching these older boys a lesson now would make them better men in the future. Wasn't that what a duke was supposed to do? Lead the elite of England to be better?

Tension tightened his shoulders as he slipped into the darkened building behind Ryland. It was strange being on campus when everything was dark and quiet. It added to the sense of unreality. Was he really, finally, going to do something about his school difficulties? Ryland and Griffith had found each other early on, their mutual disdain for life at Eton bonding them quickly. Their first year had been horrible, with one of them still grieving the loss of his father and the other trying desperately to live down the reputation of his grandfather. Griffith had been able to convince Ryland and himself that things would be better if they just got through the first year.

But they weren't.

If anything, things were worse. Now that there wasn't a sanctioned way to make Griffith and Ryland do their bidding, the older boys were resorting to new and worse means of persecution.

After tonight, they'd think twice. Or at the very least, they'd stop saying "As you wish."

"You have the paint?" Ryland whispered.

Griffith silently held up the can of red paint he'd bought in town. Ryland nodded and slid two brushes from his pocket.

His other hand reached for the latch on the door of the fifth-year boys' dormitory.

Sweat coated Griffith's palms, making him clutch the paint tighter so he wouldn't drop it. His chest felt like it was churning like the waters of the River Thames during a storm. Were they really going to do this? Somehow it didn't seem right to slip in and face his enemies while they slept. But what else could they do? He couldn't stand it if the year continued on the way it had started. And what would happen next year?

"Keep it simple," Ryland said in a toneless whisper. Griffith wasn't even sure he'd heard it so much as sensed what was being said by the shape of Ryland's lips.

"Simple," Griffith whispered back. He winced at the sound of his voice and decided to nod at Ryland instead.

Ryland nodded back. "We get in, paint *As you wish, Your Grace* on the backs of their shirts, and get out."

A small grin touched Griffith's lips. They'd think about the dukes every time they got dressed for the rest of the term, unless they wanted to explain to their parents why they needed new shirts.

It would be a reminder that he and Ryland had managed to sneak into their presence and could have done something much worse.

There was a certain biblical tone to the prank that appealed to Griffith and made him feel a bit like David facing down Saul, even if it was probably more like taking on Goliath.

"Remember—backs of the shirts," Ryland whispered. "We don't want them to violate dress code."

At Griffith's nod, Ryland eased the door open, pressing it tightly to the hinges so nothing squeaked.

They crept in, taking care not to make a noise in the silent room.

Griffith frowned. The room was too silent. He couldn't even hear the boys breathing in their sleep.

The room was empty.

"Where are they?" Ryland whispered.

As if Griffith could possibly know the answer. "Should we do it anyway?"

Ryland nodded and the boys made short work of marking the shirts, a task made much easier by the fact that they only had to be quiet enough to avoid waking the boys in the other rooms.

As they eased back out of the dormitory, Ryland's grin glowed in the moonlight. "Let's find them."

Griffith frowned. "Why?"

"Because whatever they're doing is against school rules, and we can use it to convince them to leave us alone."

"What we're doing is against school rules." Griffith rolled his eyes at his friend, wondering, not for the first time, if they would've gotten along with each other if they didn't have a title in common.

"Then, we don't let them see us." Ryland pulled Griffith after him, running from shadow to shadow in search of the upper boys.

It didn't take long to find them, huddled on the far side of the chapel, away from the dormitory, passing two bottles of pilfered liquor among them. Another two bottles lay on the ground, already emptied of their amber-colored contents. Two of the boys tried to stand up and promptly fell down on each other.

"Are they drunk?" Griffith whispered.

Ryland grinned. "Three sheets blown clear away by the wind, I'd guess."

The boys were talking among themselves, occasionally forgetting that they should probably be quiet.

"Come on." Ryland pulled Griffith around the corner.

"What? Why?"

"Because you're bigger. You don't have to say anything. I'll hide behind you and do all the talking."

And then Ryland was pushing Griffith into the group. Careful to stay in the deeper shadows in order to hide his face, Griffith staggered and Ryland spoke from behind him, slurring his words like he was one of the drunken group. Griffith's heart pounded from fear but also a bit of excitement. He was the same size as some of these boys, despite the difference in age, and to walk among them unnoticed was a thrill.

"Care for a drink?" one boy slurred. "Toasting the fall of one of the young dukes."

Another boy laughed until he hiccupped. "Saw him slip in the manure pile this morning."

All the boys laughed.

Griffith angled his head until he could see Ryland's shadow behind him. Griffith hadn't fallen—that meant Ryland had. His determination to have his revenge tonight made a little more sense.

"Where'd you get the liquor?" Ryland asked.

One boy staggered to his feet, looking proud and unstable. "Headmaster's office. Imagine how mad he's going to be that those two upstarts broke in again."

"How much better if he praised us while condemning them?" Ryland cackled and stabbed Griffith in the ribs, making him jerk his arms like a puppet. "We should do something no one would expect."

"He'll send us up!" one boy nearly shouted.

"Or make us prefects," another said.

"This way!" Ryland said, lifting Griffith's arm into the air. "He'll remember us forever!"

The boys cheered until Ryland was forced to shush them

through his muffled laughter. How could he be laughing at a time like this? Griffith was fairly certain his heart was about to explode and leave him in pieces all over the chapel wall.

"Lead them this way," Ryland whispered in Griffith's ear.

Griffith didn't know what he was doing, but none of the boys seemed to notice when Ryland slid out from behind him and gestured for Griffith to follow him. Soon Griffith was leading his pack of drunk upper boys to the garden shed, where Ryland and Griffith had been reporting for punishment for the past week.

The smell of the large pile of bat guano hit Griffith as they approached and he thought surely it would be strong enough to knock some sense into the crazy band behind him.

But it didn't.

Ryland nudged Griffith forward, directing the boys where he wanted them to go. Soon all of the boys were grabbing buckets of bat guano and staggering down to the field below the main college.

"What are you doing?" Griffith hissed as they led the brigade away from the garden shed with their buckets in hand. Occasionally Ryland gave out a slurred *shhh* and they'd talk a little softer.

"This will be even better than the shirts," he whispered.

They returned to the field below the chapel, and the boys spread out with their buckets. In the chaos, Ryland came out of hiding, directing the boys where to spread their bucket contents and convincing them how proud the headmaster was going to be, how much he wanted a very special garden in the middle of the field. Griffith slid farther and farther back until he was pressed against the chapel wall, the cool stone rough against his fingers.

If he hadn't been confident in his friendship with Ryland, Griffith would have been terrified by the abilities he was seeing.

14

There was no question who was orchestrating the entire thing, but when it was all over, Griffith and Ryland would honestly be able to say they hadn't spread a bit of guano.

One boy got sick. Another passed out, thankfully landing with his head outside of the spread manure.

It baffled Griffith, how the same boys who had been so cruel to them in the daylight were following Ryland's orders with the enthusiasm of puppies. Occasionally Ryland would press a bottle into a hand, and the boy would take another swallow of liquor.

Ryland finally stood to the side, arms crossed and a sly grin on his face.

"We need to go. They'll check our beds soon," Griffith whispered in Ryland's ear.

"Yeah," he whispered back and then called the boys—the ones who were still standing anyway—into a circle. "We don't want those pesky dukes to get credit for this, do we?"

The resounding "No!" was loud enough to make Griffith cringe and consider running for his house in town.

"Right," Ryland continued, seemingly fearless about any chance of getting caught. "So we need to sleep right there on the edge of the field so that in the morning everyone knows who gets the credit."

The boys enthusiastically piled over each other and found spots on the grass.

While the boys were settling in, Ryland grabbed an open-mouthed Griffith and hauled him back up the hill. From the top Griffith looked down at the field. The letters were crude and uneven, but it clearly spelled *As you wish*. When they realized what they had been tricked into doing, combined with what he and Ryland had done to the shirts, those boys were going to be fighting mad.

Ryland and Griffith left the campus and crept through the streets of the darkened town until they got back to their house. They slipped through the doorway and pressed themselves against the wall as the head boy made his rounds. When he didn't raise an alarm, they knew the bundles of blankets and pillows they'd left in their beds had done the trick.

Griffith slid into bed, surrounded by silence that seemed to press onto his chest until he wondered if he were somehow drowning without water. He'd never done anything like this before, and with the thrill came more than a bit of guilt. Now that the anger no longer coursed through his system, his father's voice rang clearly through his head. This wasn't how he or God would have wanted Griffith to handle the situation. Harmless pranks were one thing, but those boys were going to get into a heap of trouble.

Of course, his father wasn't there. God had left Griffith on his own to figure out how to be a man, a duke, and he was trying to do it right. But was this really the best he could do?

Griffith slept in fits and bursts, and when a yell ripped through the house the next morning, he felt as if he'd spent those few hours wrestling with his sheets instead of sleeping in them.

Shouts and curses could be heard up and down the street as boys spilled from their houses to run to Eton's fields. Two first-year King's Scholars were running from house to house, calling sentences that didn't make any sense but letting everyone know something incredible had happened the night before. Griffith rode the excited wave of students, trying not to look guilty, praying he wouldn't be sick.

There was already a crowd when Griffith, Ryland, and the rest of the boys from their house arrived at the field. Utter chaos reigned as the boys held their heads and tried to defend themselves against something they weren't completely sure they even remembered. Ryland and Griffith were mentioned, with two boys swearing Ryland had convinced them to do it.

So the headmaster checked their shoes.

Griffith nearly swallowed his tongue as the man told him to lift one foot and then the other. He'd been working with the guano all week, but never in his own shoes. No one wanted the stuff tracked into the dormitories. He couldn't remember if he'd stepped in any of it last night.

Lifting his feet didn't faze Ryland, though. He managed to look somewhat resigned and a bit offended as his shoes were checked.

They were both clear, and the headmaster proceeded to lay into the boys with promises of beatings and punishments.

And he hadn't even seen the liquor bottles yet.

One lay on the edge of the field, seemingly unnoticed by anyone but Griffith.

The aftermath of his evening escapades boiled around him, with the older boys getting hauled off, holding their heads and throwing accusatory looks at Ryland and Griffith. Unease clenched Griffith's middle, making him glad that he had yet to eat breakfast.

If he'd taken more time to think about it, would he have followed Ryland's lead? Griffith knew that, had the boys last night not been drunk, they wouldn't have followed Griffith anywhere.

As much as he hoped the boys would now leave them alone, he wished there'd been another way. Surely they could have found a better way.

"I don't get it," Griffith whispered to Ryland as the boys were herded back toward their rooms to dress. "Why'd you make them do that?"

"That's guano."

"I know."

"Fertilizer." Ryland grinned. "Fertilizer that soaked into the grass all night. Fertilizer that they're never going to be able to clean up completely."

He chuckled as he threw a hand on top of Griffith's shoulder. "That field will read *As you wish* until those boys graduate. And they're the ones who put it there."

Griffith threw one last look over his shoulder. The older boys were still looking around with confusion and in pain. One held his head in his hands and looked one step away from crying. Boys that were supposed to be the best England had to offer, brought low by liquor and a quick-thinking, crafty lad.

As Griffith topped the hill, he made a vow to himself. His father had been the perfect duke, and Griffith had a lot to live up to. If he was learning anything this morning, it was that letting his anger drive him didn't leave him confident and satisfied in the morning. He made a vow—to himself, to God, and to his late father—that he would never put himself in such a vulnerable position again. Never would someone or something else take away his control of his own actions.

He took one last look at the crudely written words on the field. *As you wish*. For the past year and a half it had been a slur, a derogatory term designed to get under his skin. But now it would be his strength. He would be in control. Always.

Chapter 1

London, England, March 1815

While the limits of human ability prevented Griffith, Duke of Riverton, from being everything to everyone who depended on him for their livelihoods, he'd always assumed there was no limit to what he would do for his family.

His mother's current request was more than stretching those limits. "No."

"Miss Watters is a very particular friend of Lady Cressida. And as I am married to her father I feel obliged to ensure Cressida's ball is a success in every way." Griffith's mother, Lady Blackstone, arched a brow in her son's direction as he turned from his perusal of the crowd filling the ballroom. The former duchess may have voluntarily lowered her rank to countess when she remarried a few years earlier, but she had never released her position as matriarch of her family, despite the fact that they'd all reached adulthood.

It was a position Griffith respected. Not only did the Word of God command that he do so, but he'd seen what his mother had gone through to raise her four children, including teaching her ten-year-old son how to manage a dukedom. That respect did not, however, extend to breaking one of his personal social rules.

He looked away from his mother to note the girl in question— a plain young woman hovering near a doorway, her dress an unfortunate color that was remarkably similar to the ballroom wallpaper. Given her supposedly close relationship with to-night's hostess, one would have thought the near-professional wallflower would have known to avoid that particular shade of rose. "If there is a true need for a member of our family to rescue Miss Watters from the wall—a position which I'm sure you know she takes up at every social gathering—there are other male members you can appeal to."

Mother's lips pressed together into a thin line. "They are married."

Griffith slowly lifted his own eyebrow in a perfect imitation of his mother's earlier expression. "I had no idea the institu-tion affected a man's ability to dance. No matter. Up to now they've shown remarkable resistance to whatever marriage-related malady might inhibit a man's dancing talents. I'm sure they can hold it off for another night."

His mother said nothing, though he could tell from the crinkles forming at the corner of her eye that she wanted to laugh. Almost as much as she wanted him to dance with Miss Watters. As he only danced with women he considered family, her laughter was the only desire he was inclined to grant. One more sardonic remark from him should send her over the edge.

"It is a comfort to know, however, that public scrutiny of my lack of dancing finesse will diminish once I've married. Until then I shall endeavor to plant myself among the married men on the rare occasion that I join a dancing formation with a sister or cousin. Perhaps then we shall all be equally bumblesome."

A brief snicker sputtered between Mother's lips. Her rare

break in decorum was like a trophy to the one who'd done everything in his power to make his mother smile again after the death of his father. As always, though, she quickly contained the outward signs of her mirth. "Bumblesome?"

Griffith shrugged his shoulders. Their massive width, when combined with his considerable height, was one of the main reasons he didn't perform at his best on a crowded dance floor. He was simply too large to maneuver through the steps with much grace, and *bumblesome* seemed the most accurate description of how he felt on the dance floor.

She sighed. "Very well, I shall ask your brother. Despite his marriage last year, he is still popular enough to draw notice."

"And accomplished enough for the lady to actually enjoy her dance. If she is only to get one turn around the floor, let it be a good one."

Cool daggers shot from his mother's blue eyes as she glided off to find Griffith's younger brother, Trent. He could have told Mother that she was going in the wrong direction, but as his primary objective was to remove her from his side, he kept his silence. By his count, he had to stay in the ballroom for two more dances before his absence wouldn't draw comment. Over the years he'd perfected the art of being seen enough that everyone knew he'd attended but not so much that he was drawn into any interactions he'd rather avoid.

Such as dancing with a female who might even remotely be considered a marriage possibility.

"You can't avoid it forever, you know."

Griffith glanced to his left to find his good friend Ryland, Duke of Marshington. Their friendship had started at Eton, holding fast through years of change and upheaval. Now that the man had married Griffith's sister Miranda, they were family as well. "You do."

Ryland grinned, the slash of white teeth standing out against his darker-than-was-fashionable skin. "I'm married."

With a tilt of his head, Griffith acknowledged the implications of Ryland's true statement. "And where is my sister?"

The grin widened. "Dancing."

Griffith swung his gaze to the rows of couples weaving in and out of formation on the dance floor. He could easily see over the surrounding heads, though sometimes his sister's shorter stature still made her difficult to find. Within moments he'd located the familiar blond curls of the elder of his younger sisters. At that moment she was happily spinning around on the arm of Colin McCrae, Griffith's other brother-in-law. His youngest sister, Georgina, stood next to them, waiting for her turn in the dance.

It was still a surprise to see the sisters voluntarily sharing space. The friendliness had only come about in the two years since they'd married their respective husbands. Those marriages had taken a great load off of Griffith's mind. In truth, now that Trent had also settled happily into an initially awkward marriage, there wasn't anyone left for Griffith to guide and watch over. There hadn't been for many months now, but Griffith had put off acknowledging the fact.

"You really should consider taking a turn or two yourself, you know." Ryland rocked forward on his toes and clasped his hands behind his back. Given that the man was a former spy and a master at blending in, the falsely innocent posture was obviously intentional.

Griffith knew better than to take the bait. "I shall ask Miranda for the next set."

"She'll turn you down."

Two years of marriage had obviously not made the man an expert on his wife. Miranda would never deny her big brother. "She never has before."

"She wasn't limiting her exertions before."

The two men fell silent as Griffith considered the implications of Ryland's statement. Happiness and worry warred within Griffith. It was difficult for him to remember that Miranda was not his to protect anymore. "I suppose congratulations are in order."

"Indeed they are." Ryland nodded, one side of his mouth kicked up in a smirk. "We've a dukedom to provide an heir for, after all." Grey eyes cut from the dancers to pin Griffith to the wall behind him. "You have one as well."

Griffith didn't want to think about it. He didn't know if it was the fact that his childhood had been cut so short or the fear of having something so vulnerable dependent on him, but the idea of children frightened Griffith like nothing else. It was, however, part of his duty, and Griffith took his duty very seriously. His younger brother would certainly breathe easier when it was ensured that the title and holdings wouldn't pass to him. Griffith had never understood Trent's aversion to the title, except, of course, for the fact that Griffith would have to be dead in order for Trent to inherit.

That was a fairly decent reason not to want the title.

He looked to Ryland. "I've a plan."

"You always do." The last strains of the dance faded into the chatter of the ball's attendees, and the couples dispersed while new ones took their places. By unspoken agreement the men waited for the music to drift back over the crowd before speaking again.

Ryland inspected his fingernails. "Dare I ask what this great marriage plan consists of?"

"Getting married." Griffith had been formulating a plan for years. When he'd first hit London after graduating from Oxford, he'd marveled at the games society played. The scheming marriage-minded mothers and the calculating influence-craving fathers made a powerful counterforce to the desperate dowry-hungry sons and the fun-loving, attachment-avoiding bachelors. Somewhere in the middle, the debutantes drifted—each with their own level of mercenariness, but all with the same goal in mind. Griffith hadn't wanted to deal with any of them.

Still didn't want to deal with them.

His reprieve was fast disappearing, though, because Ryland had a point. Griffith needed an heir, and for that he needed a wife.

"Do you intend to follow the family tradition?"

Surprise at the question broke Griffith's normally controlled countenance. "Of course."

All of Griffith's family, for as long as anyone could remember, had built their marriages on a strong foundation of love. His own parents had been possibly the most notorious of the lot. Just because Griffith was approaching marriage in a logical manner did not mean he had no plans to involve love in the equation.

The skeptical smile on Ryland's face brought an extra stiffness to Griffith's back. His plan was going to work. Watching his mother and siblings find love over the past three years had only assured him that his plan was a viable one, and he couldn't resist the urge to rub it in Ryland's face, given the other man's chaotic journey to happiness. "Before my mother tried to steer me in an unsuitable direction tonight, I was narrowing down the candidates."

Ryland coughed. "Candidates? And I can't imagine your mother suggesting you socialize with anyone unsuitable."

"My idea of suitable and hers do not always align."

"Particularly since you've never seen fit to share your idea." Ryland straightened his shoulders and settled in to observe the room. He was tall, but still a good two or three inches shorter than Griffith, and possessed the ability to look like something other than a hulking mountain with legs. That didn't mean he couldn't be intimidating if he wanted to. His face hardened from easy humor into serious concentration. "Your target is in this room, I assume, for you to have been contemplating a campaign."

Griffith resisted the childish urge to roll his eyes toward the ceiling. "Target? Really, Ryland. We're not stepping outside for pistols."

"You called them candidates. I'm simply upgrading your status from prize to be won to the pursuer in control. Now, be quiet. I'm analyzing."

Griffith waited. He leaned his shoulder against the wall behind him and crossed one foot over the other. Sweat trickled down his neck into his cravat. He hated ballrooms. They were always too crowded and too hot for a man of his size and stature to retain any sort of comfort. Normally he positioned himself near the terrace doors or an open window, but the unseasonably cold weather had prompted tonight's host to close everything up tight. Right then Griffith would have welcomed a chilly breeze. Waiting for Ryland to make his guess wasn't doing anything to relieve his tension.

Minutes passed. Another song began and ended. Was Ryland still analyzing, or was he simply torturing Griffith now?

"You want someone from the edge of the dance floor."

Griffith had to admire the confidence of the man's statement. Despite the accuracy of the remark, Griffith wasn't willing to give in that easily. "You had a one-in-four chance of selecting the correct group of ladies. And as it is by far the largest of the groups, I'm hardly impressed."

When the two men had attended their first balls right after

graduating from Eton, they'd divided the unmarried women into four groups. The corner held the spinsters, while the walls included those whose social standing or lack of popularity kept them outside the action. The dance floor was for the most popular of women—Diamonds of the First Water, the Incomparables, the ones on whom everyone doted and who never seemed to be without a partner or two clamoring for the next dance. The edge of the dance floor, though, held most of the women. The women who danced sometimes but not always. They were popular enough but hardly fodder for the social pages.

Ryland cast a glance over his shoulder. "Anyone else in here—your own family included—would assume you wanted someone from the dance floor. You could certainly land one, if you wished. Even the lovely Lady Alethea."

He could probably land anyone in this room, even if they were nearly betrothed. Young, single dukes weren't exactly plentiful in England. Griffith had to concede Ryland's point, however, and inclined his head to indicate his friend should continue his guess.

It was easy to spot the woman he'd mentioned. Lady Alethea was skipping her way through the dance with a wide smile on her face and strings of jewels in her dark hair.

It was also easy to see why most people, his family included, would assume he wanted someone like her. Everyone thought her the most sought-after woman among the marriage-minded aristocracy. Griffith's interests lay beyond the benefits of a beautiful wife, though.

Ryland tilted his head and looked slowly around the ballroom, murmuring to himself. "She's too attractive. Draws too much notice. Good family, but maybe a few too many of them. You don't want them asking you for favors."

Griffith forced himself not to fidget. It was remarkable how quickly Ryland was walking the lines of Griffith's reasoning.

"She's too new to London. You probably spent all of last year debating the merits of various ladies."

"Not all of it," Griffith grumbled. "I had to watch over the disastrous beginnings of Trent's marriage, after all." Fortunately, that had all worked out and Trent was now fully in love with his wife, but it had taken up a good bit of Griffith's attention last Season.

Fewer than five more minutes went by before Ryland turned around and crossed his arms. "You're not going to fall in love with her."

Griffith raised an eyebrow and lowered his head until he was glaring down his nose at Ryland. The superior look that had sent more than one man into a cold sweat didn't even make Ryland blink. "How do you know?"

"The same way I know whom you've chosen. I get the logic—really, I do—but she's not what you need."

The noise of the crowd ebbed and swelled around them as Griffith narrowed his eyes at the other duke. "You're bluffing," he finally said. "You want me to say the woman I've settled on because you don't know who it is."

"Oh, I know. But mark my words—she's not the woman for you. You don't need someone as boring as you think you are. And trust me, old friend, she will bore you."

Miranda chose that moment to come bounding to her husband's side, wide smile and flushed cheeks indicating how much she'd enjoyed her set of dances.

Griffith nodded to his sister, marveling, as he often did, that the same shade of blond hair and green eyes that he saw in the mirror each morning looked so different in a feminine face. "I hear congratulations are in order."

27

She frowned at her husband. "This is a terrible time for you to suddenly become incapable of keeping a secret."

"Revealing my potential heir was a strategic move, I assure you." Ryland took his wife's hand and looped it through his elbow, pulling her closer against his side.

Her smile returned. "Oh, really?"

Griffith wanted to groan, but that would have given Miranda too much satisfaction. A man of eight and twenty should not feel the need to squirm when his little sister stared at him, even if her expression held the intensity of every headmaster he'd ever had, combined.

"Pray tell, then, who were we discussing when I arrived?" Miranda bounced on her toes in anticipation.

It didn't matter now whether Ryland pulled the right name out of the crowd. Whomever he mentioned would become Miranda's new best friend as she did everything in her power to help him marry the woman she thought he wanted. There would be no stopping her.

Ryland grinned as he joined Miranda in staring Griffith's direction. "Miss Frederica St. Claire."

Chapter 2

"I do wish you'd come last night. You could have taken your first bow along with everyone else. I think half of London chose the ball as their first event of the Season."

Miss Isabella Breckenridge shrugged her shoulders as she looked across the room at her cousin perched on the edge of the bed, inspecting the fans lying on top of Isabella's unpacked trunk. "That ball or the next one, I don't see as it matters. I'm sure to make a better impression when I'm not covered in road dust."

"As if you could make a bad impression." Miss Frederica St. Claire rose from her chair and fluttered a fan in Bella's direction with a lopsided grin. "You would have been the *belle* of the ball."

Bella groaned at her cousin's play on words before giving in to the desire to chuckle at the joke. "I don't know how you always know how to make me laugh. I think you were born ridiculous."

As opposed to Isabella, who had, according to everyone she'd ever met, been born with perfection. She could go the rest of her life without hearing another compliment about the excellent tilt and color of her eyes or the splendid way her high cheekbones framed her face or even how nicely proportioned her ears and shoulders were. Unfortunately, she was about to embark on her first London Season, where she wasn't likely to hear anything but increasingly absurd and disturbing compliments about such things.

Maybe she could turn it into her own *lotteria* game and keep a list of all the features commented on. If she collected her entire face, she'd buy herself a new hat. Maybe even one with a veil. She could bring them back into fashion. Of course, that would require that she have money of her own, and while her uncle would agree to buy her a new hat, he'd likely balk at the idea of a veil.

A scoff escaped Isabella's decidedly less symmetrical cousin as she dropped back onto the bed. Frederica had yet to dress for the day and had a comfortable grey wool dressing gown wrapped around her, but a mass of curls already perched atop her head. The thick dark locks threatened to spill out of their confinement no matter how tightly her maid pinned them. "No, I *made* myself ridiculous. If I didn't look for the levity in the situation I'd be forced to walk around glum and gloomy like my father does. And I really don't think a dark frown is going to distract anyone from noticing my nose."

Bella smiled at her cousin in the mirror. "It's not that bad." Although it was. It truly was.

While Frederica had spent three months on Isabella's family farm every year for ten years when they were children, it had been another ten years since Isabella had actually seen her cousin. During those years Freddie's unfortunate nose had shrunk in Bella's mind. Seeing her yesterday had been a bit of a start.

Freddie groaned. "You're lying to be kind. That's a good skill to have. It makes an evening with pompous windbags so much easier."

"And how do you really feel about the society men?" Isabella frowned at a container of fine powder before using a puff to lightly dust the milled starch across her own coiffure. Back home she'd have simply twisted her hair into a plain bun with a few curls to frame her face, but that wasn't going to do for a Season in London. And even though she'd waited until the eleventh hour to make the decision, she'd finally chosen to give this challenge her best effort. The starch had been a last-minute purchase, and she hoped it would do what she needed it to do.

"Who said I was talking about the men? The matrons are just as bad." Frederica lifted her head and frowned. "What are you doing?"

"Removing the red, or at least making it less noticeable." Isabella turned her head, checking all angles to ensure that her hair looked blond and the hints of red were limited as much as possible. She didn't want it to be too obvious that she'd powdered her hair, but blond was certainly more popular when it didn't look as if it came from someone distantly related to the lowland Scots. Which she was. Her father's mother had grown up there, and Isabella had spent more than one fine spring dancing through a field of heather.

Not this spring, though. This year she would be taking her turns in London, doing her best to attract as many well-connected, titled gentlemen as possible. The fate of her family depended upon it.

"As if you need to be any more beautiful. Their faces are going to melt off as it is." Frederica took the powder puff and dabbed lightly at the back of Isabella's head. "I can't wait to see Lady Alethea's face when she meets you. She's already declared to everyone that she intends to be the most popular girl of the Season."

Any other time and Isabella would wish Lady Alethea the

best of luck and leave her to it, but not this year. This year Isabella's very future was riding on her popularity.

Perhaps her perfect nose would finally be good for something.

Frederica leaned over and propped her head on Isabella's shoulder, looking in the mirror as she wrapped her cousin in a hug. "I've missed you. Letters simply aren't the same."

"No." Isabella tilted her head into Frederica's and squeezed her hands. "They aren't. Though I'm thankful for those letters. And that your father was willing to frank the postage on them. I could never have paid for them."

Frederica's nose crinkled. "It was the least he could do after refusing to let me visit you anymore."

Isabella stood in order to hug her cousin properly. "But I'm here now, and getting to see you every day for a few months is the only bright spot in this entire situation. So we'll make the most of it."

"That we will." Frederica smiled, looking quite pretty despite her large nose. Hers was a unique beauty, unappreciated by most of London, which was probably why she was venturing out on her fourth Season.

"And we'll start today," Isabella said decisively. "Go finish getting ready. We're going to take London by storm."

A short laugh burst from Frederica's chest as she moved toward the door. "You are, maybe. You forget—I've been down this road before. I doubt my entrance will be anything more than a morning mist."

Frederica went to her own room to dress for the day, leaving Isabella to inspect every inch of her appearance for her first steps in Town. With her hair done, her head weighed down with all the jewelry she owned, and her new dress fitted to perfection, there was no reason to stay in her room—aside from the fact that leaving it would mean she really had agreed to Uncle

Percy's demands. Demands that made her feel a little ill and a lot detestable.

Her uncle had been unhappy that the travel delay had made Isabella miss last night's ball, but he'd be downright angry if he knew she'd done it on purpose. She'd stayed behind at Uncle Percy's country estate for two weeks to wait on the completion of her wardrobe. What Uncle Percy didn't know was that the clothing had been delivered a week ahead of schedule. Isabella had spent the rest of the time asking herself if she truly meant to follow his plan. Was she really going to gamble her family's future on a straight nose and a creamy complexion?

Apparently she was, because two days ago she'd set her mind away from debating the merits of the endeavor and focused instead on how to make the absurd plan a success. It was going to take more than a pretty face and a sweet smile. She couldn't be the only beautiful woman in London. Society's curiosity, however, could make even a plain girl the center of attention. Imagine what it could do for her.

Today, and for as many moments as possible until her uncle took her to her first formal event, she was going to be seen. Seen, but not heard, or at least not introduced. Freddie didn't know it yet, but they were going to go for rides, visit shops, and drink tea until everyone who was at all out and about in London had a chance to see Isabella looking better than she'd ever looked before. She'd taken lessons from a traveling singer and a group of actors and learned discreet tricks, not only for powdering her hair, but for lightening the appearance of her lightly tanned country-girl skin and making her eyes appear even larger and her lashes fuller.

Her thick locks didn't really require any hairpieces to achieve a full and fashionable coiffure, but she'd obtained some anyway, in a light blond that would further distract from the red in her hair. They itched, but nothing about the next few months was going to be comfortable, so what did a little false hair matter?

The sun was shining and a light breeze whisked through the streets as Isabella and Frederica stepped out of the house with their maids and turned toward Bond Street.

Frederica sighed. "This isn't going to work, you know."

Isabella clapped a hand on top of her bonnet and tilted her head up toward the sun, soaking in the warmth after the chill of her uncle's house, only part of which was due to the drafts and his stinginess with the coal. "Whyever not? I've been reading your letters, and you've assured me that, despite approaching your fourth Season in Town, you haven't made a lot of friends. You don't really know anyone."

Freddie sighed. "That is true. But I *know* everyone. More to the point, everyone knows me. It's rather hard to forget meeting me, even if they can't manage to look further than my nose. They're going to request introductions."

"Only the women. The men will have to wait until we approach them, and they're the only ones I care about." Isabella adjusted the strings of her gold silk reticule. "Besides, if we look involved enough, even the women will think twice before approaching us. We'll simply have to stay very active in whatever we choose to do."

Freddie shook her head and sighed. "If that is what you want to do, we'll do it. It's your first day in London, after all."

Bella hooked her arm through Freddie's, the bright yellow of her spencer providing quite a contrast to the burnt orange of her cousin's.

A small smile tilted up one side of Freddie's mouth. "Sometimes it's hard to remember that you're a year older than me. You don't look it, you know."

"Praise God." Isabella closed her eyes and tried to ignore the pang of guilt that the casual praise caused her. It felt wrong to praise God while planning to do something that was less than upright and possibly could be considered sinful. "Can you imagine if people knew I was taking my first bows at twenty-four? I'd be shuffled off to the side of the ballroom without a second glance. Uncle Percy has decided to tell everyone I'm nineteen. I can pass for it readily enough, so I've decided not to correct anyone, though I won't speak the lie."

Frederica frowned. "I don't like this."

That made two of them, but Bella didn't have a choice, not if she wanted to save her family from near ruin. As a woman, her options were limited, but as the oldest of five siblings, she felt a certain responsibility to help. Marriage would have made the most sense, but her father's devastating injury almost five years ago had necessitated delaying her debut a year. Not that it would have been much of a debut. Everyone in their village already knew her, and there weren't funds or time to spend a full Season in one of the larger cities, but they'd been planning to spend a few weeks here and there. Mother had even been considering a short trip to London. But with her father trapped in bed, waiting to see if his leg would heal well enough to avoid amputation, leaving wasn't an option.

That yearlong delay had turned into two and then three, and by the time anyone noticed, Isabella had been practically running the family farm. Whichever local boys hadn't been terrified of her near legendary beauty had been scared off by her family's situation. No one wanted to saddle himself with a wife whose relations were on the verge of desperation, especially when none of them had the means to solve her family's problems.

Problems she'd become all too familiar with in the past few years. Their situation was dire. Her father did all he could on his poorly healed leg, but that wasn't much. Her mother did all she could to help her father. That left four children stringing along behind Isabella, staring into a future that looked downright bleak if the family farm didn't find a way to thrive again.

And Isabella was out of ideas. The only way left was to take Uncle Percy's offer. So she had, telling herself she'd eventually quiet all the voices in her head telling her it was a bad idea.

Quieting the voice outside her head might prove a bit easier. She gave Frederica a smile that she hoped was reassuring and confident. "It's going to be fine. You'll see. One Season of dancing around with your cousin from the north, and then I'll disappear. No one will ever see me again, and any dust I stir up will settle without your being any worse off than you were before."

"But what will you do if you actually fall in love?" Frederica gripped Isabella's arm tighter. "Not all the men in London are awful, you know. You could meet someone you genuinely like, and then what will you do?"

The very idea that Isabella would find enough in common with a London aristocrat to fall in love was rather laughable. While it was true Isabella's interaction with aristocratic men was limited to Uncle Percy, a neighboring baron, her village's ancient hermit viscount, and one very distant viewing of the Duke of Northumberland, she'd read the papers. Though they were nearly two weeks old by the time they circulated through the women of the village, time didn't really matter when one wasn't an intimate part of the happenings anyway. Her life was so far removed from the antics of the men in those articles, she was confident that walking away would be the one guaranteed success of this entire plan.

It was hard to remember that her mother had come from a life like the one described on the pages, a life filled with parties and lace instead of sheep and quilting by the fire. Bella reached one gloved hand up to rub her neck, where her mother's topaz-and-seed-pearl earrings were brushing against her skin. The kid leather felt equally foreign. "I don't see that happening. As much as I adore you, Freddie, I don't think this life would ever be able to hold much appeal for me."

"I don't want to see you hurt." Frederica frowned. "You've no idea what it's like to love someone and lose them."

Bella looked into Freddie's eyes, trying to convey comfort and sympathy without hugging her tight like she wanted to. A comforting embrace would be too out of place on the busy street, but the fact that Freddie was still pining for her lost love, whom she'd lost to the war more than two years ago, made Isabella more determined than ever to keep her heart away from all of her interactions this Season.

"I'm not worried." It was probably the only thing about the upcoming months that Isabella wasn't worried about. "I'll have a fine time this Season"—that part was a lie—"and then I can return home with a bit of polish and find a nice landed gentleman to settle down with."

Though she still didn't look convinced, Frederica dropped the subject and turned to the nearby milliner's window to discuss the merits of the bonnets on display. Isabella faced the window, but her attention wasn't on the plumes and ribbons. She watched the reflection. More than one person slowed to get a better look in her direction before whispering something to their companion.

Whispers were good. The more attention she got, the more access Uncle Percy had to the people he wanted to influence. She was bait in a trap, and while she tried very hard not to think about the fact that the bait was often eaten, even in a successful trap, it was difficult to convince herself that all would be well in a few short months. Her family would have the money they needed, her brothers would have a future, and she would be free to make their farm the best one in the county again.

The breeze carried pieces of a nearby conversation to her ears. A conversation centered on who she was and whether or not she intended to socialize this year.

Isabella hid her smile of success. While most of the time she didn't give a thought to her straight nose or wide-set eyes, she was grateful for them today. They were getting the job done.

Chapter 3

On a normal day, a large group of people gathered excitedly around a single thing wouldn't have merited Griffith's interest. After all, if the thing were actually important beyond its inflated social significance, he would learn about it soon enough. Most things were usually forgotten within a week, and he had better things to do than clutter up his thoughts with the latest furor to catch society's interest.

It was, however, very difficult to ignore a group of men trying so very hard not to be noticed. The nervous hush that fell over the room as Griffith passed in front of Brooks's gaming room door was louder than any ballroom bailiff could ever hope to be, and it drew Griffith into the room with a sense of foreboding snaking down his spine.

Had the men simply gone about their business, Griffith would have made his way happily to the morning room for a cup of tea and an open newspaper. But they hadn't, so he hadn't, and now they were all stuck in a moment of eerie stillness in the middle of the card room. Well, Griffith was in the middle of the card room. The other twenty men stood huddled in the corner. And anyone who'd spent any time at all in this room knew exactly what was in that corner.

The betting book.

It hadn't seen a great deal of action since the king had been declared incapacitated, leaving Prinny to run the country. The bets had flown like scattered pheasants then, with as many people claiming he'd recover as those who gambled that he wouldn't. It had all been a bit of nonsense as far as Griffith was concerned. There were much more reliable ways to increase a man's fortune, after all, and a bet in a book only let the world into your private business.

This many men gathered around the betting book was concerning because they didn't appear to want Griffith's attention. Which meant, of course, that they had it. Completely.

"Good afternoon, gentlemen." Griffith strode toward the corner, doing his best to make his large frame look relaxed.

"Riverton."

"Duke."

The men greeted him and shifted their weight. Twenty sets of eyes looked anywhere but at him. Something was definitely stirring in the betting book, and it had something to do with him. Or his family. For the sake of the men gathered around, Griffith certainly hoped it had to do with himself. His family may all be married and settled and moved out on their own, but they would never stop being his responsibility.

Perhaps it was the conversation with Ryland the night before, but Griffith couldn't rid himself of the feeling of being exposed as he stepped forward, the crowd easily giving way before him. He wasn't the oldest man of good title to still be single, so there was no reason for anyone to be expecting him to actively look to marry this year. Those other men didn't have a legacy of ridiculously happy marriages following them around, though, and someone was sure to notice that Griffith was the last unmarried member of the legendary Hawthorne family.

As he approached the betting book, a few men left the room altogether. Those who remained scattered about, doing their best to look involved in anything other than watching Griffith approach the book. The obvious fear of what Griffith would do when he saw the bets set his nerves on edge, causing a tightening across his shoulders.

Despite his size, and perhaps even because of it, Griffith wasn't prone to violence. He'd even deliberately avoided joining Trent in training at Gentleman Jack's so that he wouldn't instinctively resort to punching a man in an emotionally heightened situation.

The betting book lay open on a low table, several fresh lines inked across its pages.

Curiosity and a bit of growing trepidation spurred Griffith's feet on until he was close enough to see his own name mentioned in each of the new lines.

Ld. Farnsworth bets Mr. Crenshaw 50 gs. that the Duke of Riverton weds Prendwick's daughter, Ldy. Jane.

Mr. Godfrey gave Ld. Yensworth 5 gs. to receive 20 when the Duke of Riverton dances with an unrelated female at the Yensworth ball.

And on it went for the rest of the page—gambles and conjectures about who and when Griffith would finally marry now that all of his family was settled down.

His fingers itched to write his own lines, to take on all the bettors who thought they knew his life better than he did, knew what he needed better than he did.

The last line on the page nearly made him smile, as it confirmed what Ryland had said the night before about everyone's assumptions regarding the woman he would pursue when he finally decided to wed.

Mr. Harrop bets Mr. Godfrey that the beautiful, unknown woman spotted on Bond Street will induce the Duke of Riverton to dance.

No amount had yet been filled in, and the bet actually had a line drawn through it. Not surprising given the fact that the woman in question's name was not recorded and so the bet could never be verified.

A heavy silence filled the gaming room. Even the candle flames on the various chandeliers stopped flickering and held their flames steady. Griffith thought through his options quickly, knowing he had mere moments to decide how to handle the situation if he wanted to remain in control of it. Or take control of it, as the case may be.

They were all waiting for his reaction, probably making internal side bets on what he was going to do or say. Would he slam the book closed? Give the cut direct to those involved? Throw his considerable political weight around and make their lives difficult and their business endeavors less profitable?

All of those options left the control of the situation in the hands of the cabbages who had made the bets in the first place.

So he did nothing.

Later he would consider the ramifications and sort through his current turmoil of emotions, but not now. Now he would act as if the paper held no significance at all. Even though it did, though probably not the significance they thought it did.

Griffith turned to the men around him. "Anyone fancy a game of whist?"

He hadn't planned on playing whist when he arrived, but whist gave him something to do. No one would expect him to talk. He could blame any looks of concentration on his cards. It was the perfect façade to think behind. He would limit himself to his customary two games so as not to become mired in the excessive marathon gambling, but it would give him time to sort through his thoughts and keep the gathered populace from knowing what he was thinking.

The offer broke the tension, and men sorted themselves into various games at the scattered, green felt-covered tables.

Voices bounced off the walls and the drawn curtains, most of the men chattering about the upcoming Yensworth ball. Ladies' names were already being bandied about, everyone wondering who would be popular, who would get married, if any of the confirmed bachelors would fall into the parson's mousetrap this year, though Griffith never heard his name mentioned in the discussion.

Quite a bit of speculation was given to a particular woman some of the men had seen around town earlier in the day. Griffith felt a bit sorry for the woman. No one could live up to the level of beauty the gossip had bestowed on her.

Griffith shook his head as the tales continued to fly. He would put this group of tonguewaggers up against any drawing room full of ladies when it came to tossing gossip back and forth for no other reason than to hear whose life was worse than their own.

He refused to marry a woman whose name would drip from the lips of the gossiping hordes. Yes, some of the men in the betting book would soon collect a hefty sum, because eventually Griffith was going to have to dance with the woman he hoped to marry. It was part of the courtship ritual, after all.

But he was a duke. If anyone could get by with courting and avoiding the dance floor, it was him.

One thing he knew from having sisters, though, was that women enjoyed dancing. It would be boorish of him to deny his future wife such an expected enjoyment.

That he hadn't seen Miss St. Claire's name on the page was both comforting and distressing. He had no wish to marry a woman who sprang quickly to the minds of the gossipmongers, but an unexpected choice would yield a crop of speculation that might turn his chosen bride into the talk of the town. Momentary fascination, however, was better than a lifetime of hearsay.

"Not having much luck today, Riverton?" Lord Yensworth chuckled as he gathered up another trick from the table.

"I don't believe in luck." Griffith shifted his hold on his remaining cards. "But it does not appear that the cards have fallen in my favor this afternoon."

Lord Yensworth smiled. "Perhaps you'll have more luck at the ball tomorrow night. Shall I reserve you a spot on the dance floor?"

Lord Farnsworth tossed his card onto the table. "I know my wife would be more than happy to fit you in on my daughter's dance card."

Several men chuckled even as they watched Griffith closely to gauge his reaction.

He tossed his trump card on top of Farnsworth's before leaning forward to scoop up the cards. "I believe I can arrange my own activities tomorrow evening."

The exchange solidified what Griffith already knew. The moment he made a move that indicated he was contemplating putting aside his bachelorhood, the marriage-minded mothers would swarm. There would be no peace until he declared his preference.

Which was why he'd already done so much work selecting the woman. It irritated him that Ryland had taken barely fifteen minutes to shuffle through the same thought process that had taken Griffith nearly a year to complete.

His observations had begun shortly after Trent's marriage. With no intention of marrying a young miss out for her first tour of the ballrooms, he'd taken his time to watch and investigate. Now all of those women were in their second, third, or even fourth Seasons.

Since his future duchess would need to possess a good bit of social acumen while causing no more than a cursory stir in the gossip rags, he wasn't worried about missing out on the perfect woman because he delayed. It gave him time to make special note of the ones who seemed to enjoy the attentions of multiple men too much. He had no desire to have to battle another man for his chosen bride.

Any of them who were too socially attuned were ignored as well. He wanted a wife more interested in building a family than advancing her social life.

The requirements had narrowed his list significantly.

The game drew to a close with Griffith a mere five pounds lighter than when he'd sat down. He looked at it as an investment in social relations. Now he knew what the men expected, which meant he could consider how to handle their surprise when he did things a bit differently.

Tomorrow night at the Yensworth ball society would declare their favorites, and everyone expected him to be in line to kiss their feet.

Yet he would be on the other side of the room, talking with his future wife. Perhaps even settling the whole affair before the ink had finished drying on Brooks's betting book.

⌒

Isabella braced herself with a deep breath before knocking on the door to her uncle's study. When she'd agreed to come to London, it had seemed so simple—play a few aristocrats for fools and save her family. But now that she was here, it didn't seem like much of a game anymore. The prospect of being bait hadn't seemed so daunting until she was actually surrounded by the trap with no way out, no way home, and no other way to save her family.

Seeing the beautiful gowns, baubles, and women on Bond Street earlier hadn't calmed her down any either. For the first time she'd considered what would happen if she failed. If Uncle Percy didn't get what he wanted out of this exchange, what would he do to her family?

"Enter!"

She pushed the door open and stepped into the most masculine space she'd ever entered. Dark paneling covered the lower portion of three walls, while bookcases took up the fourth. Large furniture filled the space, and an enormous portrait of the previous Lord Pontebrook stared down from the far wall.

Isabella's grandfather.

She'd never met the man who had all but disowned his daughter when she chose to marry a half-Scottish sheep farmer from the north. This was the first she'd ever seen of him, and even though it was a painting, he looked like he disapproved of her very existence.

With difficulty she jerked her gaze from the painting and directed it to the current Lord Pontebrook. "You wanted to see me, Uncle?"

"Yes." He pointed his quill at a wooden box on the edge of his desk. "This arrived for you."

Curiosity propelled Isabella farther into the room. Who on earth could be sending her something? Lifting the lid didn't resolve any of the confusion. If anything, it increased. The box was lined with velvet and housed layer after layer of sparkling jewelry that put her simple garnet-and-gold pendant necklace and her small topaz earrings to shame.

Isabella swallowed, afraid to even reach out a hand and touch the glittering gemstones. "What is this?"

Uncle Percy looked up from his paper with a frown. "It's jewelry, girl. What did you think it was?"

"But . . . why?" She was too confused to take much umbrage at his brusque tone.

"For you to wear, of course. Men aren't going to believe your father is wealthy unless you show off a little."

Men needed to believe her father was wealthy? But that was the furthest thing from the truth. Isabella didn't even have a dowry, not really. She supposed they could claim to give the man the barn since that's what her dowry money had gone to rebuild, but that didn't seem like much of an enticement. "But my father isn't wealthy."

The sigh that deflated Uncle Percy's chest was nearly enough to ruffle Isabella's curls. "I know that, and you know that, but no one else can know that. Your pretty face isn't going to keep the men in my drawing room forever, you know."

"But how?" Isabella lifted a strand of diamonds and sapphires that took her breath away. "Are these real?"

Uncle Percy frowned. "Of course not. They're the best paste money can buy, and they're borrowed, so don't lose any of them."

So the jewelry was a lie just as she was a lie. "Won't people think you bought me the jewels? Just like you bought the dresses?"

"They don't know I bought the dresses, and since Frederica's most expensive necklace is her mother's coral beads, I hardly think people will attribute your finery to me. Besides, I've put it about that your father is a land owner in the north, with a very large estate."

Isabella winced. In some ways that was true. Her father was a land-owning gentleman, and the boundaries of the farm in Northumberland were quite large, even though half of it was all but unusable. "And have I a dowry?"

"Of course." Uncle Percy waved a hand in the air and looked back down at the papers he'd been working on. "Large enough to attract a man in need of funds but small enough to keep anyone from doing something rash, such as kidnap you and hie off to Gretna Green."

"And how much is that?" Isabella had to work to push her voice out through a suddenly very narrow throat. She had no idea that the game would become this tangled before she'd even started to play.

"I've kept the number vague since I'll never have to actually pay it. Let each man think it's whatever he needs it to be." He pulled a ledger book toward them. "I've also let everyone know there's a distant bit of royal blood in your veins."

The wooden box lid fell back into place with a thud as Isabella's hands started to shake. There was, if one wanted to squint and tilt their head sideways, a distant link tracing her father's family back to a Scottish king in the 1600s. That probably wasn't the sort of royal blood her uncle had implied she had, though.

"What if someone remembers Mother?" It was a possibility. She'd had one Season in London before marrying Father. What was supposed to have been a summer jaunt to Edinburgh had ended with a broken carriage axle in Northumberland. Mother had fallen in love with the young man who assisted them out of the wreckage.

"Your mother never had a lot of social presence, even during her single Season. Given the fact that she married quietly in the winter, running off to Scotland with your sheep farmer of

48

a father, I don't think anyone will give much thought to a girl they haven't seen in twenty-five years. Most of London probably thinks her dead."

Isabella's hands clenched into fists. "But they will care now that you've made them think she married a royal, wealthy estate owner!"

Her uncle's brown eyes were hard when he looked up from his paper once more. "And isn't it a shame that your poor uncle was taken in by the whole thing, fooled into letting you into his home while you schemed your way through London."

"This isn't my scheme," Isabella cried. "It's yours!" And she wasn't completely sure she understood how it was supposed to even work.

"And you agreed. Which hardly makes you innocent. So if you had any notion of convincing someone else to bail your father out of debt, let me absolve you of the notion now. I've set you up for success, my dear niece. If you do anything to ruin it, I will see that your father loses everything and your brothers won't even be able to attend the local parish Sunday school."

Sharp teeth digging into her lip kept Isabella quiet. This was why she had agreed to come to London, after all. Her uncle possessed the funds and the clout to see that the debts on the family farm were paid and her brothers sent to a proper school. Without those things, her family's future looked dismal indeed.

In Northumberland, surrounded by sun and sky and sheep, the price he'd asked seemed so simple. Take the face God had blessed her with and entice a few men to the house so that Uncle Percy could convince them of the merits of the Apothecary Act, a piece of legislation he'd dedicated the past seven years of his life to creating that was finally coming before Parliament.

She should have known better. Any deal with the devil had

more to it than initial appearances, and now she was swimming neck-deep in lies and half-truths.

She opened the lid and looked at the jewels once more. Glittering and winking and as fake as she was. They served a purpose, though, and so would she. With a decisive bang she shut the box and gathered it close to her chest. "I won't ruin it."

Chapter 4

Half of the people in her village could have fit into the front hall of Lord Yensworth's home. The village square could have squeezed into the ballroom. Isabella clamped her lips shut so she wouldn't gape as she was being introduced to the host and hostess for the evening.

"Yes, such a shame her father couldn't accompany her." Uncle Percy cast her a look of loving indulgence that almost made Isabella ill. "Fortunately Frederica agreed to oversee her young cousin's first Season in London. There's no better guide than age and experience."

Isabella cast a sideways look at her uncle. Did he not realize Frederica could hear everything he was saying? He was practically declaring her a spinster while singing the praises of his niece, who was actually a year older and a far less eligible match. Isabella tried to catch her cousin's eye to offer a bit of sympathy, but Frederica had slid behind Isabella's shoulder, taking her proper place as overlooked spinster. The act of solidarity sparked a burning sensation along Isabella's eyelids. Nothing would convince Uncle Percy to save Isabella's family until he had what he wanted, and Freddie was doing everything she could to help Isabella succeed.

The necklace surrounding Isabella's throat felt heavy and unfamiliar. She lifted a hand to graze across the jewels as she looked around the room, the reality and enormity of the task finally sinking in. There was no way her uncle's plans would work. If the men of England's Parliament were so easily swayed by a pretty face and a charming smile, then the fate of their country was as precarious as her family's.

"Lord Vernham, may I have the honor of presenting my niece, Miss Isabella Breckenridge? She's just come down from the northern counties for her first Season."

Isabella shifted her gaze and lowered her lashes as she smiled and bobbed a small curtsy. Lord Vernham's returning smile showed considerably more teeth than hers had. Though his teeth could certainly have used a bit more attention from his toothbrush, assuming he even had one.

"It is an honor to meet you, my dear. Your reputation precedes you, but your beauty shines even greater than those accounts."

Isabella bobbed another curtsy with a sigh. Another general compliment to her beauty. If the men didn't get more creative, soon it was going to become difficult to come up with new ways to say thank you. And she would never earn her new hat. "You are too kind, my lord."

His chest puffed up. "If you are not otherwise engaged, I'd like the honor of claiming you for the first dances."

Isabella glanced at her uncle from beneath her lowered lashes. His slight nod indicated that this was one of the men he wanted to influence, meaning this was one of the men Isabella somehow had to put in thrall.

"The honor would be mine, my lord." As would the dishonor,

but she was going to have to learn to live with that. Seeing her uncle arrange for the deed to be returned to her father would go a long way toward making this entire ordeal more palatable, she was certain.

They milled around for several more minutes, greeting people as they arrived, almost as if this were their gathering instead of Lord and Lady Yensworth's. They'd arrived at the earliest possible respectable time. Servants had still been scrambling to change the candlesticks in the corner candelabras when they entered the ballroom.

Finally the hour grew late enough and the crowd thick enough for the musicians to play and the dancing to begin.

She encouraged Lord Vernham in whatever way she could, thankful that he required nothing more than her soft smiles and frequent nods to believe she was fully engaged in what he was saying. When he asked if he could call upon her the next day, however, she felt the mixed emotions of accomplishment and shame as she demurely agreed she would be home. There was no turning back now.

That dance was followed by another and another until she declared a need for a private moment and dragged her cousin, who had yet to step onto the dance floor, from the ballroom to the ladies' retiring room.

Frederica was grinning. "You should hear the talk. Everyone is trying to find out more about you. I'm having to be incredibly vague, since I've no idea what you want people to actually know, but I've never been in such high demand at a ball."

Isabella fanned herself and perched on a settee that had been pushed back into the corner of the room. "I'm glad you are enjoying yourself."

Her cousin's grin slipped. "Aren't you?"

Was she? Should she be?

Freddie sat on the settee, her hip pressed against Bella's. She reached out her hand and wrapped their gloved fingers together. "Perhaps if you tried thinking of them as potential suitors, instead of voters for Father's cause, you would feel better about the situation."

Would she? There were an awful lot of lies that Freddie didn't know about. She could never expect a man to overlook the fact that everything he thought he knew about her was wrong. Not to mention all the other difficulties that would arise if said man wasn't wealthy enough to save her family. "Even if I found a man I could love, how could he possibly understand the need to keep all the other men around? Uncle Percy said the vote isn't going to be for several weeks yet."

Freddie shrugged. "You wouldn't be the first popular girl to make the men wait while she enjoyed her Season."

Bella frowned. It seemed so . . . so . . . mercenary. "I suppose."

"Besides, many of these men are quite plump in the pocket. Perhaps they'd be willing to settle the debt for you."

She couldn't admit that she'd considered just such a thing. But since any man Isabella could relate to wouldn't be of the aristocracy nor able to get her brothers into the schools her uncle could, any such thinkings were nothing but castles in the air. Much like the history her uncle had concocted for her. Not that Isabella had shared that part with her cousin. Frederica was already displeased with her father. There was no reason to make her hate the man. At the end of the Season Isabella would leave, but he would still be a significant fixture in Frederica's life.

So she smiled and said nothing.

With a squeeze of encouragement, Frederica rose. "We should return to the ballroom."

She couldn't. Not yet. Just a few more minutes to breathe, and then she would return to the glittering ballroom and gather as many suitors as she could—men who would come calling, giving Uncle Percy a chance to convince them they needed to vote for the new apothecary law. Just a few more minutes and this nagging sense of guilt would go away. "You go. I'll be along in a few moments."

"If you haven't returned by the end of the next set, I'm coming back to drag you out."

Bella grinned. "Fair enough."

Once Freddie left, Isabella took a moment to look around the retiring room. She wasn't the only lady needing a break from the dance floor. But whereas the men couldn't seem to wait for an introduction, the women looked like they'd be happy if she took the next mail coach back to Northumberland.

What would they think if they knew she agreed?

Of all the social events that played out in London, balls made the least sense to Griffith. They were always massively crowded, so the chances of finding the person you actually wanted to see that evening were small, unless you'd arranged a meeting prior. Talking was difficult, what with the music and the people coming in and out of conversations in order to join the dancing.

And for a man who was looking to court, they made even less sense.

With gemstoned bodices and jeweled hair clips scattering the light from the multitude of candles, the finery in the room was enough to blind a man. Even the plainest of women could look exquisite with such trappings, and when the artificial beauty collided with natural beauty, men tended to lose their wits as well as their sight.

Clusters of impaired men crowded the ballroom, each with a glittering jewel at their center, the men pushing themselves to outdo each other to win the attention of the fair maiden. Griffith frowned. How could a man possibly form and know true feelings and opinions in an environment like that?

Griffith listened as the bailiff announced his presence. After greeting his host he stepped to the side, allowing the flow of people to pass him and make their way farther into the ballroom.

He hadn't decided if he was ready to declare his intent to marry by escorting his woman of choice onto the dance floor tonight, but given the betting book at Brooks's, all eyes were likely to be on him to see if he would.

Except they weren't.

With his greater than average height, Griffith could see over the heads of most of the event's attendees, and there was no denying the fact that something in the back of the room was drawing more attention than he was.

Someone.

And that someone was a girl.

He supposed he should call her a woman, but she was most definitely young enough to be a girl. And she was lovely. Even at this distance, her beauty was unmistakable. The shape of her face and form, the way she tilted her head and gracefully lifted her arm to delicately fan her neck—Griffith was male enough to appreciate the picture.

And experienced enough to know that it wasn't a painting he wanted to be a part of. His younger sister, Georgina, had been an Incomparable. The most precious Diamond to ever grace the ballroom according to some. There was little doubt that his sister had just been dethroned.

The door gliding closed behind her indicated she'd only recently returned to the ballroom, which was probably the only reason Griffith had been able to get a clear look at her. Within moments men were making their way in her direction, drawn like ants to a dropped morsel of cake at a picnic.

Even some of the men around Lady Alethea migrated over to the newcomer.

Yes, Griffith had certainly been right to remove all the Diamonds of the First Water and the Incomparables from his consideration. He had no wish to make a scene such as those men were doing.

His pleasure was short-lived, however. In order to get to the place he wanted to be, he was going to have to wade through the lady's admirers anyway. Miss St. Claire was standing less than three feet away from the woman drawing everyone's attention, though the growing throng was likely to push her farther away soon.

He watched her, waiting to see how she would handle the situation, wanting verification that she was indeed the woman to quietly enrich and support his dukedom while presenting a social presence worthy of his standing.

The only daughter of the Viscount of Pontebrook, Miss St. Claire appeared more than capable of accomplishing Griffith's requirements. She stood near enough the dance floor to show she was inclined to participate but not so close as to appear desperate. She was smiling and talking to a young couple beside her. When the song ended, the couple left her and moved to the dance floor. Miss St. Claire didn't look around in hasty unease, trying to find someone else to occupy her time—she simply stood. A peaceful oasis in the midst of a ballroom of chaos.

He wouldn't call her beautiful or even striking, with a rather large nose and bland brown hair, but she was presentable and not unattractive, even though he didn't experience the same spark of admiration he had moments ago for the other woman.

The light orange of her gown did little for Miss St. Claire's complexion, but it was fashionable and tasteful. There were certainly worse choices in the room.

Yes, Miss Frederica St. Claire would do nicely.

If he could get to her.

Griffith worked his way around the edge of the ballroom, past the corner of spinsters and a cluster of recently arrived soldiers, a more common sight these days. Now that the war was over, everyone was inviting the officers to social events as an act of patriotic goodwill.

Miss St. Claire was turned in profile to him, watching the commotion beside her with a smile on her face, almost as if she found the entire spectacle as ridiculous as he did.

He cleared his throat as he came up behind her. "Good evening, Miss St. Claire."

She turned with a look of expectation that changed to astonishment as her gaze climbed up and up until it met his face. "Your Grace! Good evening."

For the first time in his life Griffith finally understood the inducement of dancing. Were he a dancing man he could simply ask Miss St. Claire to dance, and they would have something to do while they discovered common topics of conversation. Since asking her to dance would likely be tantamount to publicly proposing to her, he wasn't quite willing to do so yet.

That didn't mean, however, that he had a different question ready to ask her. He had obviously not thought through the potential difficulty of this part of his plan.

As the silence stretched she dropped her gaze to his left, still facing him but apparently unwilling to look him in the eye as the awkwardness stretched between them. He liked the courage that showed. Perhaps he could find a way to tell her so. Compliments always put his sisters in a better mood, but he didn't think Miss St. Claire would believe him if he expounded upon her great physical beauty.

There really was nothing for it. He was going to have to ask her to dance.

"Miss St. Claire?"

She returned her gaze to him with that serene smile, but then something beyond Griffith's arm drew her attention away again.

"Would you do me the great honor—"

He let his words stumble to a halt as he realized she wasn't listening. Her eyes fixed on a point behind him. They widened, and she turned paler than he'd ever had the misfortune to witness someone do.

And then she fainted.

Chapter 5

Griffith moved to catch Miss St. Claire when her eyes rolled back in her head. He took one staggering step sideways as she fell into his arms, and he couldn't help the self-deprecating grin that formed as he looked down at her. He'd known breaking his social stoicism would be a surprise to everyone, including the lady in question, but he hadn't thought he'd elicit such a shock.

A sharp cry rose from his left, and several young men stepped quickly aside as the beautiful woman he'd noticed before pushed them out of the way. She stood frozen at the edge of her group of anxious swains, mouth open and eyes wide as she took in the fallen Miss St. Claire now resting in Griffith's arms. Up close she was even more stunning than she'd been from across the room. Possibly the most stunning creature God had ever made.

If Helen of Troy had looked anything like this woman, the Trojan War suddenly made a lot more sense.

The difficulty Griffith had tearing his gaze away from her was a bit disconcerting, given the fact that his potential wife lay unconscious in his arms. He straightened, then tightened his hold on Miss St. Claire's body, fingers digging into the gauzy orange overlay and creasing the white silk of her gown beneath.

She needed air and space to breathe, neither of which she was going to get in a ballroom full of people who had broken free of their surprise and started pressing in to find out what exactly had gone wrong.

"Freddie!" The alluring young lady hurried forward and placed a long-fingered hand on each pale cheek of the woman in his arms. That she could even do so startled him into realizing that she was tall as well as beautiful. With her coiffure mere inches from his face, he noticed that her hair had depths of another color catching the candlelight, moving it from simple blond to a unique shade of gold. Was it a trick of the lighting? Would it look more blond or red when it was down?

The thought slammed through Griffith's body with the force of a running plow mule. He did not want to see this young woman's hair down, did not even want to consider being curious. Those were the sort of mind-numbing thoughts that drove men to pick unsuitable brides.

"She needs to get out of here." He yanked on the reins of his mind and brought it in to focus on the issue at hand. This fainting incident made him a little concerned in his choice of Miss St. Claire, but he would reserve final judgment until they'd had a few more encounters. If she fainted at every one of them, he'd have to avoid her for the sake of her own health if nothing else.

"Through here. There's a small parlor where Lady Yensworth's maid repaired my gown earlier." A hint of red touched the young lady's cheeks and she ducked her head as she realized she'd been discussing a wardrobe issue with him. She even blushed prettily, with none of the splotchiness that so often occurred on other ladies' faces.

The young woman opened the door and held it as Griffith ducked his head and swept through, careful to angle Miss St. Claire so she didn't bump the frame. The hall was lit up with candles, drawing a silent sigh of relief from Griffith. If the hall was lit, it meant people would be passing through. He couldn't afford to mar his reputation by being alone with a set of unmarried women at the very moment he'd decided to enact his plan to procure a wife.

A maid was just exiting the room the other lady was leading Griffith to.

As Griffith laid his burden on the settee in the small room, the beautiful girl who had led him there held a rushed, whispered conversation with the departing maid.

"She's going to bring water and a blanket and some smelling salts, if she can find them."

Griffith knelt by the settee and watched the woman cross the room, her entire regard focused on the insensate Miss St. Claire. Where his attention should be as well.

"Freddie? Freddie, are you all right?"

The woman, whose name Griffith should probably learn since he was practically alone with her and she appeared to be an intimate acquaintance of his potential bride, knelt next to the settee and started yanking at her glove. How many suitors had she turned her back on to be in here now? It was one thing to show concern in a room full of people, but now her audience was limited to him.

"I am the Duke of Riverton." He almost winced at the harsh and clumsy sentence. Introducing himself was not something he did very often. The rules of society said that mutual acquaintances should make the introductions, but in truth most of London already knew who he was, making the introductions a moot point.

The girl glanced up at him. Her smooth, creamy skin and light hair were set off by blue-green eyes rimmed with a darker, near black color. A straight, thin nose perched between her eyes and over a set of delicate pale pink lips. She was, in short, perfection. The sheer purity of her face and complexion spoke of her youth and inexperience, something Griffith didn't want to deal with. He'd already raised two sisters after the untimely death of his father. He did not want to have to raise his wife too.

The fact that he was drawn to her despite all the reasons he shouldn't be was rather irritating.

"Miss Breckenridge. I am Fred . . . er, Miss St. Claire's cousin." She brushed the ringlets off her cousin's face with one hand while clutching Miss St. Claire's limp fingers in the other.

"I was unaware that she had such close relations." And considering the amount of research he'd done on Miss St. Claire, that lack of knowledge was a bit disturbing. He knelt next to the settee. "She's breathing easily. That's a good sign."

Miss Breckenridge's grin was almost impish. The playful look on such a beautiful face had Griffith shifting his shoulders beneath his well-tailored coat. "You have experience with this, then? A lot of girls faint at your feet during balls?"

A returning grin spread across his face before he could stop it, and he ducked his head to hide his reaction. "No. I confess this is actually the first occurrence." He raised his gaze back to hers. "I've sisters, though."

"And they are prone to fainting?"

A small spurt of laughter escaped him at the very thought of his sisters having a fragile enough constitution to require a fainting couch in every room. "No. But some of their friends are."

"Hmm." She turned her attention back to her cousin, though her lips remained curved in that teasing smile. "I imagine a handsome, unmarried brother in the vicinity made them even more so."

"Probably. Though my younger brother never seemed to find it too much of an inconvenience." Griffith winced at the way the sentence sounded. It wasn't that he thought himself un-attractive—he was still in possession of his own hair and teeth, after all—but he'd always assumed his size and demeanor kept him from being handsome.

"You were too busy being a duke to catch the swooning masses, then?" Her words sounded almost like laughter, sucking away tension Griffith hadn't even known he'd been holding in his shoulders. It took a moment for him to realize what a relief it was that she wasn't going to offer flattery and platitudes.

His relief relaxed him enough to draw forth an answering grin. "Something like that."

The silence that fell this time was less awkward and more anticipatory as they waited for Miss St. Claire to awaken. It wasn't lost on him that while he'd been floundering earlier to say a single complete sentence to his intended wife, conversation with the cousin had been easy, even without his putting in an effort.

As disconcerting as that fact was, Griffith found himself craving that the conversation would return, because without it he had little to distract himself from watching her care for her cousin without regard for the disarray she was causing to her own pale yellow ensemble. The discarded glove was now being crushed beneath one of her feet as she pressed in closer to her cousin.

Griffith slid the accessory free of its trap. "Is this your first Season?"

"Yes. First time in London, even." She brushed the hair back from Miss St. Claire's face again.

"Welcome to London, then, Miss Breckenridge."

She turned her head and her gaze clashed with his. "Thank you, Your Grace."

Unlike his siblings, Griffith remembered seeing his father and mother together. And when his mother remarried, there had been no doubt that she and the earl were completely devoted to each other's health and happiness. While he was more than thankful that all of his siblings had found loving and happy marriages, none of them had taken the easy road to get there.

More fool them.

And since Griffith was determined to learn from their mistakes, he listened to the warning signs that told him he found this vibrant young lady a little too intriguing. He turned his attention back to Miss St. Claire. By applying a little logic to the situation, he would have no problem finding love with someone who wouldn't throw his life into utter chaos and put him through complete turmoil before finding his way to happiness. The key was not getting caught off guard. God had blessed him with a brain, and Griffith intended to use it.

The maid returned, and Griffith rose to meet her and take the blanket. He snapped it open and draped it over Miss St. Claire and the settee, careful to keep his hands from touching her. Miss Breckenridge waved the smelling salts under Miss St. Claire's nose.

After a loud snuffling sound, her eyes blinked slowly open, but she made no move to get up until her gaze focused on Miss Breckenridge.

"He's haunting me, Bella. His ghost has come to fill me with guilt."

Maybe Griffith hadn't done enough research after all.

Miss Breckenridge scooted one hip onto the couch, crushing her dress in the process, and wrapped an arm around Miss St. Claire's shoulders. "Shh, shh. We don't have to talk about it now, but I'm sure there wasn't a ghost."

"I miss him so much, Bella. My heart is making me see him places he can't be."

65

While Miss Breckenridge tried to comfort and quiet her cousin, Griffith caught a nearby table to maintain stability. With all of his careful thoughts and calculations, there was one thing he hadn't considered.

That his woman of choice might already be in love with another.

———

Isabella dipped her head and looked into Frederica's eyes. Her cousin was talking nonsense, which wasn't actually that unusual—except that right now they had an audience, a rather focused one. She refused to glance over at the duke, no matter how badly she wanted to. The last thing Freddie needed was to know this nervous collapse was being witnessed.

"Freddie! Freddie, listen to me." Isabella relaxed her shoulders as her cousin's brown eyes finally seemed to be looking in Bella's direction. "Good, good. Look at me. There's no such thing as ghosts."

"Then why did I see him? Because I did. Arthur Saunderson was there."

"Oh, sweetie." Hoping the duke possessed at least a modicum of discretion, Isabella settled more firmly onto the couch. "Arthur gave himself to the war effort two years ago. He's not coming home. Your father showed you the letter, remember? The one about the battle? His regiment didn't survive."

Frederica nodded and took a breath, shaky with unspent tears.

"Okay. Here's what we're going to do. We're going to sit here for a few more moments, and then I'll fix your hair and we'll return to the ball. We must act as if nothing untoward has happened."

Freddie nodded.

A slow movement on the edge of Isabella's vision drew her attention, and she turned her head in time to see the duke slipping out of the room and pulling the door nearly closed behind him. Good man, that one. And probably one her uncle would want her to entice. A duke's say would have a far-reaching impact, she was sure.

Her concern for Frederica had caused her to drop the caution she'd been utilizing all night and speak as frankly as she was used to doing at home. Whatever potential conquest she might have had with the duke was probably lost. She couldn't worry about that now, though.

"I can't go back out there," Frederica whispered.

Isabella sighed. Where was her quiet, confident cousin who lingered on the edge of ballrooms and didn't begrudge Isabella the attention of men who'd ignored Frederica for years? "Are you the first woman to faint in a ballroom?"

Freddie frowned. "No."

"No. In fact, you aren't even the first one tonight. I saw another woman in the retiring room who had to be nearly carried in by her friends, so no one is going to think a thing of it. They are, however, going to have something to say about you being carried off by a duke and never returning."

Instead of having a bolstering effect, Isabella's statement caused Freddie to lose what little color she'd managed to regain. "Carried off by a duke?"

Bella winced. "You forgot that part? The Duke of Riverton caught you and carried you in here. But I've been with you the entire time, so there's nothing to worry about."

"Except for why the duke was talking to me in the first place." She rose and began to shake out the folds of her skirts. "Do you think he wanted an introduction to you?"

"I think he wanted to ask you to dance." Bella made a few

tweaks to Freddie's hair, which had survived the entire ordeal largely intact.

Freddie snorted. "The Duke of Riverton doesn't dance."

Isabella stopped her fussing and lifted her eyes in surprise. "At all?"

"Not with females he isn't closely related to." Satisfied with her appearance, Freddie led the way to the door, her steps only slightly halting as she worried about the reception she'd find in the ballroom. Whether she was more worried that people would judge her or that they wouldn't care at all was hard to say. Frederica's acceptance of her near-wallflower status had been hard won, but it would probably still sting if no one cared that she'd fainted dead away in the middle of a ballroom.

Outside the door, her slow steps halted entirely. "It can't be."

Isabella wedged her way between Freddie and the door to ease into the hallway.

"I told you I was seeing ghosts."

Bella blindly groped for her cousin's hand and squeezed. "You're not seeing ghosts."

There in the hallway—one shoulder leaned against the wall and hands clasped behind him as he stood in his bright red coat with the blue cuffs and collar of a Royal Dragoons officer—was a man who looked very much like Arthur Saunderson.

He straightened from the wall and allowed his hands to fall to his sides, but he didn't say anything. Simply stared, a flash of unreadable emotion in his eyes before the mask of soldierlike stoicism covered his face.

Frederica shifted and slid one foot forward but didn't take a step. Her mouth dropped open, but no sound came out.

Isabella swung her gaze from one to the other. This was never how the meeting of long-lost lovers played out in books. There was usually crying, hugging—at the very least someone said hello. What was stopping these two? Shouldn't Frederica be ecstatic about the confirmation of Arthur's status change? Dead to living was rather a big deal.

Unless the other man wasn't actually Arthur. Isabella squinted at him. She'd never actually seen the man. Had only recently seen a small painting Frederica kept hidden in her dressing room. If she were to go by Frederica's reaction, this man was definitely Arthur Saunderson or could pass for his twin brother.

Someone needed to say something. Isabella pushed her way into the corridor, intent on getting one of them to acknowledge the other, but the nudge seemed to be all Freddie needed.

"I haven't married," she blurted out.

Isabella winced and cut her eyes to catch the man's reaction. His eyes widened, and he swallowed hard enough to make his throat move.

"They told me you were dead," Frederica continued, the blockage on her tongue apparently dissolved. She dropped Isabella's hand in order to wrap her fingers together near her heart. "Obviously you're not. I can't tell you how happy that makes me."

Pale blue eyes widened, his mouth slacked open, and his chest expanded, as if he were bracing himself to speak something monumentally important or difficult. All sorts of possibilities swarmed Isabella's mind. What if he hadn't waited? What if he'd married? What if he'd been horribly injured and was even now walking around in imminent death?

"Saunderson!" a voice barked down the corridor. "The colonel is waiting."

Beyond Arthur's shoulder, in the shadows at the end of the long passage, stood an older soldier, his decorated uniform similar in style to Arthur's.

Arthur looked over his shoulder at the man and gave a single nod before turning back to Frederica. Isabella wasn't even sure he'd noticed her presence yet. His eyes had been only for Freddie, even if they hadn't looked very happy to see her. Of course, he hadn't been living with the idea that she was dead for the past two years.

He cleared his throat. "I—"

"Lieutenant!" the older man barked again.

Arthur pressed his lips together before spinning on his heel and marching down the corridor.

Neither lady said anything until even the echoes of boots had disappeared.

Finally, Isabella looked at Frederica. She was pale, even paler than she'd been when she fainted, but there was a firm set to her mouth and a tightness around her eyes that belied any idea of weakness or a recurrence of her earlier unconsciousness.

Isabella swallowed. "What are you going to do?"

Frederica pulled her gaze from the end of the hallway and blinked Isabella into focus. "Do?" She nodded her head in the direction Arthur had gone. "I'm going to marry Arthur."

Chapter 6

The benefit of having close friends who took their responsibilities in Parliament seriously and family who enjoyed socializing was that at least once a year they all converged on London at the same time. Right now, however, Griffith wouldn't have minded a little less diligence on their part. The crack of the billiard balls as they crashed into each other was less jarring than the speculative questions and glances he was currently being barraged with.

"I understand waiting to see the girls settled, but why were you waiting on me?" Trent leaned over the table, his blond hair flopping over his forehead as he lined up his next shot. "There's four years difference between us. You could have been setting yourself up for a long wait."

"Not with the way you stumbled into trouble, pup." Anthony, Marquis of Raebourne, extended his cue to slide the marker over on his and Trent's scoring line. While Anthony wasn't technically family, he lived in the estate next to Griffith's and had married Griffith's ward. As far as Griffith was concerned, he counted.

Trent shrugged with his regular good nature, the smile on

his face a clear indication that, while he may have stumbled his way into a forced marriage, the couple hadn't stayed distant from each other.

In fact, it was Trent's marriage that had convinced Griffith he could choose the woman he would fall in love with. Trent had barely known his wife when they married, so his options had narrowed to one if he wanted to build a family with the woman he loved. Griffith intended to take the same path, only he would choose who that woman would be instead of stumbling his way into it.

"That's rich, coming from you, Anthony." Ryland stepped up to the table, head tilted to examine his possible shots through narrowed grey eyes. "Trent couldn't get into as much trouble as you if he tried."

Anthony frowned, not caring for the reminder of his multiple youthful indiscretions, but the laughter of Colin McCrae, the husband of Griffith's youngest sister, kept Anthony from scowling too darkly.

Colin leaned against the wall, booted feet crossed at the ankles. "I'm less interested in his reasons for waiting and more interested in the logic behind his choice. Miss Frederica St. Claire? I've been mulling it over, and I honestly can't see it."

Griffith glared at Ryland. "Is there anyone you didn't tell?"

One eyebrow rose as Ryland leaned on his stick. "Me? I didn't tell anyone. Do recall who else was standing there when I made my prediction."

Miranda. Griffith's lively, meddlesome sister. While he knew he could count on her discretion in public, all was fair when it came to family.

"There's nothing wrong with Miss St. Claire." Apart from her predilection to faint at his appearance.

"There's not much right with her either. At least not for

you." Anthony took his shot, then stayed leaned over, hands braced against the billiard table. "Her dowry can't be much above mediocre—not that you need it—and there's no way you can convince me it's her sparkling wit that's drawn your attention. If it weren't for her unfortunate nose she'd be utterly forgettable."

"Exactly." Ryland crossed his legs at the ankle as he leaned against the wall. "He intends to slide her into his life without disrupting a thing. We'll hardly know she's here."

The quizzical looks being sent his way irritated Griffith. They made him question his decision, something he refused to do. Ever. A duke couldn't afford to second-guess himself. He pushed his cue forward, but his unease with the conversation had him putting a bit too much effort into the strike, and the ball pinged off the end of his cue and bounced into the rail.

"Though your arguments don't matter, I may have to change my mind." Griffith straightened from the table, knowing his uncharacteristic declaration would keep anyone from mentioning his poor game play. "Her affections appear to be tied to another. An Arthur Saunderson."

Anthony frowned. "Who's he?"

"One of Baron Ebchester's younger sons, would be my guess," Colin said.

Now the men's wide eyes swung toward Colin.

"You know him?" Anthony asked.

"No. But if someone of Miss St. Claire's ilk was going to encounter a man named Saunderson, that's the most likely. Lord Ebchester owns the textile mills near Lord Pontebrook's estate, and he has a passel of sons. Bought commissions for three of them." Colin frowned. "I think one of them died a couple of years ago."

Well, that explained her talk of ghosts.

73

Ryland gave a low whistle. "You don't want to compete with a dead man."

"Whyever not?" Griffith rather thought such a man wasn't going to be able to give him much competition, being dead and all.

"Because he can't do anything wrong." Colin stood next to Trent, examining the table. "That's a tough shot, there."

Trent lined up his cue and shot. The men watched the balls clank against each other before the red one plopped into a corner pocket. Even though he had to acknowledge the skill of that shot, Griffith didn't like losing to his younger brother. It wasn't quite as bad, though, as the idea of losing to a dead man, even if he had been a soldier.

"I'm a duke." Griffith set his shoulders back and tried not to look too haughty. "Some say I can do no wrong as well."

Ryland, the other duke in the room, bent nearly double in laughter.

Anthony slid a piece of chalk against the leather tip of his cue. "If you're serious about getting married, you could have your pick of women. Could probably even land the hand of Miss St. Claire's cousin."

Colin's eyebrows rose. "She has a cousin?"

"A beautiful one." Anthony grinned at Colin. "Your wife will be jealous."

Given the fact that until now Georgina had been touted as the most beautiful woman to grace London's ballrooms in a century, it was a distinct possibility that his youngest sister would indeed be jealous, but that wasn't Griffith's problem to deal with anymore.

The immediate tension in his shoulders and accelerated heart rate that came with the memory of the beautiful cousin, however, were his problem. The image of her disregarding her own

74

appearance and the attention of her myriad of suitors to see to the welfare of her cousin refused to leave his head. It went against everything he knew about women of her ilk.

"I don't see why you feel you need to pick beforehand." Ryland potted two balls with one quick stroke. "All you have to do is ask a lady to dance and you'll have half of London competing for your attention."

"That is precisely what I wish to avoid."

As three of the men debated the possibility that he could manage a courtship without inducing the mothers of London into a chaotic and desperate frenzy, Trent propped his hip on the cue rack and stared at his older brother.

Griffith tried not to stare back, but it was hard to ignore his brother's assessing gaze. It had been wonderful to watch Trent mature and become his own man this past year, but part of Griffith longed for the days when Trent looked up to him with unquestioning adoration. Especially when he now looked as if he were about to slash through Griffith's logic with his fencing foil.

"It's not as easy as it seems," Trent finally said.

The good-natured debate fell silent as the three men looked back and forth between the two brothers.

Griffith wanted to reply with a cutting remark, implying that if Trent could do it so could Griffith, but even his sudden discomfort wasn't enough to make him hurt a member of his family that way. "I don't see why not."

"Because it's not the same. Even if you say you aren't giving yourself another choice, you'll know that you have options. And so will she."

"It's a choice." Griffith glanced at the other men in the room and set his shoulders back. Last year this same group of men had convened to help Trent study the Bible and learn how to love his wife, and the result had been discovering that a great deal of love was a matter of choice.

Trent stepped forward to brace his hands on the billiard table, leaning toward his older brother in an aggressive, almost challenging pose. "And are you willing to say, right here, right now, that you love Miss St. Claire?"

Was he? If love was a choice and he'd already made his selection, shouldn't he be willing to declare himself in love with Miss St. Claire and act accordingly? He couldn't. He couldn't bring himself to say the words.

His silence was Trent's victory, which the man acknowledged with raised eyebrows and a slow nod.

No one said anything for several moments. Finally Ryland bent forward to angle his shot. Griffith was fairly certain it wasn't his turn, but whose turn it was had completely escaped his notice.

After his shot, Ryland straightened. "I've a new landau that should be perfect for attending the races next month, if you're still interested in going, Colin."

Colin's gaze lifted from the rolling billiard balls to Ryland's face. "I thought you were only staying in Town for a few weeks."

Ryland grinned at Griffith. "I wouldn't miss this for the world."

Griffith leaned back against the wall and crossed his arms over his chest. When he'd risen this morning, he'd had a few misgivings over his choice of bride, but now he was more sure of his selection than ever. The last thing he wanted to do was wreck his life stumbling toward the altar like the men before him had done. So it stood to reason that anything they thought was a bad idea was a good indicator of a way to avoid their mistakes.

"Miss Breckenridge, you must allow me to tell you how brilliant your teeth are. Were you a horse I would bid until I won you."

Isabella blinked, straining to maintain her smile, even though her cheeks were starting to hurt. There was a compliment somewhere in that bizarre statement, but she wasn't sure she wanted to find it. All she could do was be grateful that she wasn't a horse, led out onto the auction block to be snagged by the highest bidder.

Besides, she'd already sold herself to the highest—and only—bidder. Her one consolation was that at the end of it all, she'd be able to walk away from every last one of them, her uncle included.

She'd had no idea it would be this difficult, though. The men had been swarming the drawing room for nearly an hour. They'd given up the pretense of politeness that dictated one man at a time require her attention. Arriving on each other's heels as they did meant no one had time to do more than deliver their flowers before the next man was attempting to claim his turn.

So they didn't leave.

Ever.

At least ten men were currently in the drawing room, gathered around the settee, clogging the air with the combined scent of their varied cologne waters and enormous bouquets. Each man tried to give her a more outlandish compliment than the last. It was going to be very difficult to top the horse comparison. At least Frederica was seated on the settee beside her, preventing any of the men from claiming the coveted position. They were left to kneel or stand or take one of the three armchairs that sat about the room.

Or leave. Isabella would be the opposite of devastated if they took it upon themselves to leave the premises. As long as they gave her uncle an opportunity to talk to them first.

"Dearest Miss Breckenridge, would you do me the great honor of riding with me tomorrow?" A man she vaguely recognized but whose name she couldn't remember knelt next to the settee. Finally, here was a request she could work with.

"I'm sure you understand, given my lack of knowledge of Town, that I'm directing all such requests to my uncle. I'm constantly forgetting appointments, and he's promised to help me manage my calendar." Oh, how it pained her to spin the words that way. The only appointments she'd missed since she left home with her uncle were the ones he'd forgotten to tell her about. As the person who'd held their farm together for the past several years, Isabella was more than capable of managing her social calendar.

She had, however, bargained away the right to do so.

"How wise you are to leave such delicate matters in the hands of men who know more." The man had the audacity to take her hand in his and pat it. As if her appendage were a small puppy.

She gently slid her hand free and reached for her teacup. It was the sixth tea tray delivered to the drawing room that afternoon. Neither she nor Freddie ever rang for them—they just kept appearing. Of course her uncle would want the mass of men to remain in the house for as long as possible. How else could he pick them off one by one and convince them the way to her hand was through their parliamentary vote?

The excess of tea did give her an excuse to escape the madness, if only for a few moments. She just didn't know the polite way to do it.

She leaned in Frederica's direction to whisper in her ear. "I need to retire."

Wrinkles of confusion formed between Freddie's eyes but cleared as she looked from Bella to the nearly empty teacup in her hand.

A moment of panic made sweat pool in Isabella's gloves

as Freddie excused herself from the settee and crossed to the door. Was Isabella supposed to follow? Did they just leave all the men in the room?

Frederica's spot on the settee was immediately taken by a man reciting poetry. It was by far the best performance she'd seen today, but it was the third time she'd heard the same poem. She'd probably be able to quote it herself by the end of the week.

In moments, the butler, Osborn, appeared to whisk away the remains of the last tea tray. Then, one by one, the men were met by Osborn quietly holding their hats, coats, and canes. No one seemed affronted by it, but they did start pressing closer to Isabella's location, as Osborn was approaching the men nearest the door first. They couldn't avoid the summons forever, though, and by the time the last man was escorted out the door, Isabella's fictitious excuse had become a real one.

She grabbed Frederica's hand and all but ran up the stairs to the water closet. There was one on the ground floor that she could have used, but escaping upstairs meant she could take longer, and that she could have a private word with Freddie.

Isabella took care of business and then paced the floor in her bedchamber, wondering how long she could claim it was taking her to refresh herself.

"Can you believe some of the outlandish compliments they've been giving us?"

Perched delicately on the side of the bed so as not to muss her gown or coiffure, Freddie emitted a quick bark of laughter. "Us? My dear, more gentlemen have passed through that drawing room this afternoon than have darkened my door in the past three years. Not a one of them is here for me."

"Not one?" Surely someone was desirous of courting her cousin. She was a good match. Her dowry wasn't large, but it should at least attract a younger son or two.

Freddie shook her head.

Isabella sniffed. "Well, I'm sure they're simply waiting for a less hectic time to call. Now that the drawing room is empty, you'll see. I thought surely we'd see your Arthur by now."

Small white teeth snagged Frederica's bottom lip. "I had hoped so as well. I didn't tell Father about seeing Arthur last night, so he hasn't had a chance to tell Osborn not to admit him."

Uncle Percy detested the officer that much? Simply trying to understand her uncle's thought patterns gave Isabella a headache, so she turned her efforts into cheering her cousin instead. "Well then, I expect you should still receive a visitor or two today. Perhaps even the Duke of Riverton. He did seek you out last night."

"And then I promptly dropped at his feet before babbling on about ghosts and soldiers. No, the duke won't be coming anywhere near me, unless it's because he wants to visit you."

Bella shook her head. "The men in London are fools."

"Be that as it may, they're fools who can earn you the deed to your family's farm back. How many votes did Father say you had to recruit?"

"He didn't." Oh, how Isabella wished he had. Then she would figure out a way to calculate how many she needed and how far she'd gotten. "If the Apothecary Act doesn't pass, I'm afraid he'll claim I haven't held up my end of the bargain. It doesn't matter that the number of voting men who are single and socializing is remarkably limited. How many sons hold sway over their father's political dealings? There's no way of knowing."

"So you have no choice but to play the coquette and pray that no one calls you on it?"

"There'll be no praying involved." Isabella studiously avoided the dressing table where her grandmother's Bible sat, unopened since Isabella's arrival in London. A necklace and two sets of earrings lay on the table next to it. "I can't ask God to have any part of this farce."

Frederica frowned. "You do know that isn't how it works, don't you?"

"He's God. What do we know of how He works? He can't possibly approve of what I'm doing, but He didn't provide another way out, either, so I'm doing what has to be done. It's the curse of living in a fallen world, Frederica."

Freddie looked as if she wanted to argue more, but she had never been very good at debate—and was easily distracted. "Mark my words," Isabella continued. "Riverton is going to call on you."

Freddie's nose scrunched up, and she folded her arms across her middle. "If he does, I'm throwing you at him. I don't want anyone but Arthur. I'm sure whatever called him away from the ball is the same thing keeping him away today."

The girls had spent the remainder of last night's ball trying to find out more information about Arthur's arrival. All anyone knew, though, was that there had been a group of soldiers recently returned to London, but then a missive had arrived for the colonel and they'd all left.

Despite this incredible lack of information, Freddie's resolve to wait for Arthur had been renewed as if the past two years had never happened.

Isabella remembered, though. She remembered well the pages and pages of tearstained letters that had arrived nearly every day after news of Arthur's regiment had reached Frederica. Then the whispers had begun, that he wasn't even supposed to have been there, that the mission had been doomed to fail from the beginning. The letters had turned angry and bitter then, and there was no consoling her, especially not from as far away as Northumberland.

Isabella had been afraid to try, afraid that her cousin might be having a good day, might be moving on, and then she would receive Isabella's letter and become sad again. So she'd kept her letters to other topics, asking about Freddie's second Season and London until gradually her cousin's letters had changed and it seemed Frederica had forgotten Arthur.

Until last night.

Isabella wasn't willing to entreat God on her own behalf, but she was more than willing to throw Freddie on His mercies. She sent up a quick plea that distraction would work once more.

"You know, it's been two years. It wouldn't hurt to give another man a chance." Isabella made a point of looking in the mirror and tweaking a false blond curl. "He's a duke after all."

"Can you imagine me as a duchess?" Freddie laughed and rose to cross to the door. "The caricature artists would certainly enjoy that."

"They'll have a farcical ball with whomever the duke marries." Isabella frowned at the door. "I suppose we have to go back down there, don't we?"

"You do, at least." Freddie slid Bella's book from the table beside her bed. "No one would know if I stayed up here and read for the rest of the afternoon."

"I would know."

Frederica dropped the book back on the table. "This wouldn't be so bad if I knew we only had to suffer this chaos until you chose a man and married. Knowing it isn't going away anytime soon and is, in fact, likely to get worse is disheartening." She sighed and stood. "It's going to be a very long Season."

Chapter 7

Osborn greeted Isabella and Frederica at the bottom of the stairs. "The Duke of Riverton is in the drawing room, my ladies."

Isabella's eyes widened. "You let him in while we were unavailable?"

The butler stared at her, his face a blank mask that somehow managed to convey that he thought her a simpleton. "He's the Duke of Riverton."

Well, there was that. Residing at the top of the aristocratic pile meant things like social graces were irrelevant. Especially in the home of a man desperate to gain the favor of as many of those vote-wielding aristocrats as possible.

Isabella blinked at the harsh thoughts going through her head. Less than a week in London, and already she was wallowing in an anti-elitist tirade that even her father would frown on. While he'd never suffered any lost love for his wife's title-bearing ancestors, he'd always maintained a respect for them and the system. Isabella had too, until she'd been thrust into the inner workings of it.

Knowing that her uncle, a member of the elite House of

Lords, was willing to trade for votes instead of relying on the merit of the bill was a bit disillusioning.

Frederica's cold fingers wrapped around Isabella's. "We'll go in directly, Osborn. Please have a tray brought in."

The thought of more tea made Isabella's stomach roil. She'd have to make more of a point to nibble on biscuits, despite the fact that it wasn't easy to do so with any real elegance.

The duke was standing at the window when Frederica and Isabella walked in—although considering his enormous size, it could be more aptly described that he was blocking the window. The man really was impressive. As the daughter of a farmer, Isabella could appreciate the strength and ability of a man of the duke's stature. It was a shame that all of that fitness was probably limited to riding horses and shooting billiards.

He turned from the window with a smile, and even Isabella's malcontent attitude couldn't find fault with the man's appearance. Perfectly smoothed dark blond hair and smiling green eyes weren't a common combination in England, but they were certainly an attractive one. If his brother was the handsome one, she wasn't sure she'd survive meeting him.

"My apologies, Miss St. Claire, Miss Breckenridge. Had I been informed you were indisposed, I'd have gladly returned at a more convenient time." He inclined his head in Frederica's direction before nodding toward Isabella.

"Not at all, Your Grace. It is such an honor to have you come call." Frederica curtsied before settling herself into her earlier position on the settee. Isabella followed suit with a bit of wariness. The duke was the first man all afternoon to acknowledge Freddie before Bella. Despite her earlier teasing, Isabella hadn't really been confident in the duke's interest. And now that he was here, she wasn't sure what she really wanted him to do.

Having him interested in Frederica would obviously be a

testament to his good sense and a boon to her popularity, but such an increase in status would dampen any hope Freddie had of getting her father to accept Arthur's renewed suit. Assuming Arthur was interested in renewing his suit. When had life gotten so complicated?

"Thank you. I trust you have recovered from last night? The room was quite crowded. I heard many people comment on how difficult it was to breathe." He folded himself into one of the armchairs, which brought him close enough for Isabella to catch a whiff of cedar and grass. The earthy scent was in such contrast to the rosewater and lavender she'd been smelling the rest of the afternoon that she had to fight the urge to inhale deeply.

"Yes, thank you." Frederica's calm voice helped Isabella get a firm hold on her faculties. "All I needed was a bit of space and air. I was feeling quite refreshed by the time I rejoined the party. Miss Breckenridge's attentions made the recovery much faster than it would have been otherwise." Frederica smiled sweetly in Isabella's direction, making Bella want to bash her cousin in the head with the decorative pillow at her back.

The duke glanced sideways at Isabella and swallowed. Was he uncomfortable that Frederica had forced him to acknowledge Isabella? Did he wish her removed from the room? It was enough to make Isabella consider the merits of a spate of fake coughing or even the claim of another need to retire. Despite what Frederica seemed to think, the attentions of the duke were not something to be sloughed off easily. Arthur had been gone for years and might be intending to disappear again. Isabella couldn't let her cousin toss a secure and vibrant future away on a whim and a memory.

"I merely saw to your comfort, cousin. It was the esteemed duke who truly set you on the path to a quick recovery." Isabella winced, afraid she might be laying a bit too much praise on the man. She didn't want to make Frederica appear desperate.

"Of course." Freddie glared in Bella's direction before smiling at the duke once more. "I am most appreciative, Duke."

He inclined his head, managing to look powerful and superior even while sitting in a delicate armchair.

Osborn entered silently, a laden tray in his hands. After setting it on the table for the seventh time that day, he leaned over and whispered something in Frederica's ear.

Isabella's eyes narrowed as Frederica's widened. Her cousin's skin paled, and Isabella was very much afraid that her cousin was going to faint away in front of the duke for the second time in as many days. If Freddie wanted to retain the duke's attention at all, fainting was probably not the proper method. Isabella didn't know much about the duke, but she couldn't see him wanting a woman with such a propensity. It would be terribly inconvenient to have your wife faint every time you talked to her.

But Freddie didn't faint.

She didn't do much of anything else either, leaving Isabella to lean forward and see to the tea.

"Have you a favorite type of biscuit, Your Grace?" Isabella asked as she passed a cup of tea to the duke.

He thanked her with a nod, even as he cast a skeptical look in Frederica's direction. "Yes. There's a particularly fine cinnamon biscuit that my brother's housekeeper makes. I've never admitted it to her, but I have been known to stop by his house on occasion to see if she's made any that day."

Isabella fixed Frederica a cup but left it on the table, since she wasn't sure Freddie was even aware of what was going on around her. "I don't believe I've ever had a cinnamon—"

"If that's your favorite, I should see if we have some." Frederica burst into the conversation while popping up from her position on the settee.

The duke fumbled his cup as he quickly rose to his feet. Aside from the slight bobble of china, the move had been rather graceful for such a large man. Isabella had assumed he didn't dance because he wasn't good at it. Now she wasn't so sure.

He cleared his throat and slid his teacup onto the table. "I don't think cinnamon biscuits are all that com—"

"I'll check."

And before Isabella or the duke could say a word, Frederica's skirt was swishing through the door.

Isabella had no idea what had gotten into her normally sedate cousin, but she knew if word got back to her uncle that the duke had a terrible visit, both the girls' lives would be miserable.

So she smiled at the duke. Her best smile. The one men had been falling over themselves to compliment all afternoon.

He paused in the act of resuming his seat but said nothing.

Isabella's smile faltered a bit. "Miss St. Claire is very attentive to her guests."

One thick golden brow lifted, and his head tilted to the side as he considered her. "An admirable trait."

"Yes." Isabella nodded, wondering how far she could get before her compliments of Frederica made her sound like a medicine show charlatan. "She's been the best of hostesses."

She hadn't really left him much room to respond. He could hardly agree that yes she'd make a man a wonderful wife someday and wouldn't it be fortunate if that man was him. Frederica really would faint if she knew Isabella had pulled such a confession from him.

"Perhaps. But I wouldn't think she'd be the most adequate of chaperons."

Isabella winced at the frank statement, although she was a

bit more surprised that he was the first to call them out on it. Would her uncle's claim of Frederica's spinster status falter if the duke started courting her cousin? What would that do to their plans?

The duke settled back into the armchair with care, as if he worried that the entire thing was going to break at any moment. Given his size and the delicate appearance of the chair, that wasn't a completely foolish notion. She considered offering him the settee, but there wasn't a way to do that without appearing awkward.

More awkward than she'd already appeared anyway.

"Oh. Well." Isabella took a sip of tea, trying to come up with a reasonable justification for the lack of an older female relation in the house. "My uncle says the maturity Frederica has gained in her several Seasons is enough to serve as a chaperon here in our home."

The questioning look returned to the duke's face, but this time one side of his lips tilted up as well. He ran his thumb along the edge of his lip before returning his hand to rest on the arm of the chair, his forefinger rubbing slowly against his thumb. "I had no idea we were declaring women spinsters at such a young age."

Isabella tried not to laugh, but it was impossible not to answer the slight smirk on the duke's face with a small smile of her own. Unfortunately the shared humor gave her nowhere to take the conversation except further into the ridiculous—and nowhere near the true reason her situation was not quite as proper as they were pretending it was.

She could hardly tell the duke that Uncle Percy didn't trust that any of his distant female relations would not try to discourage certain men from calling on her or that they wouldn't actually marry her off to one of them before the vote. Instead she repeated the line he'd been bandying about Town. "I believe the age of declaration depends greatly upon the female in question. Some are more trustworthy and mature than others."

His grin broke wide open for a moment, displaying an even row of teeth and charming grooves on either side of his smile. The curved lips were quickly contained, but in that one moment the duke had been the most handsome man she'd ever seen. "That would explain her excellent hostessing skills."

"It would?" Isabella fumbled with her cup, unsure of how the duke had managed to find anything reasonable in her bumbling statement but thankful that he'd bought it. "I mean. Of course it does."

"What with her being so matronly at such a young age. I'm glad you enlightened me of her status. I was unaware. Do you think she still considers herself open to marriage, or is she planning on seeking a small cottage in Brighton? I hear the spinsters there like to meet weekly for cribbage."

Isabella wanted to laugh—she really did—but whether out of mirth or panic, she wasn't sure. Where was Frederica? Was she making the biscuits herself?

Just then Frederica burst into the room, a slight blush riding her cheekbones and a small smile on her face. She crossed the room and sat next to Isabella, leaning over to whisper while she adjusted her skirts. "Arthur is in the kitchens."

Whatever Miss St. Claire was sharing had a profound effect on Miss Breckenridge. Her incredibly colored eyes widened, glancing between her cousin and the door before she dropped her gaze back into her teacup.

Griffith was beginning to think that, despite their small numbers, this family had entirely too much turmoil for him. In truth, the only thing keeping him in this uncomfortably tiny chair was the fact that he wasn't ready to admit that he had been wrong in his choice of Miss St. Claire. He absolutely hated being wrong.

He cleared his throat and reached for a biscuit, though not a cinnamon one. Despite her long delay, Miss St. Claire didn't seem to remember that was what she'd gone to see to in the first place. Not that he'd expected her to return with cinnamon biscuits—they weren't that common, after all—but he had anticipated a pretty apology about it.

"Oh." Miss St. Claire turned her attention back to him, red splotches riding high across her cheekbones and making her nose appear even larger. "We don't have cinnamon biscuits."

Griffith inclined his head. "Quite all right."

The three of them stared at one another, the girls seeming to communicate without words, while Griffith was left to wonder how other men did this every day. Of course, he hadn't had any problem conversing with Miss Breckenridge moments before, even if the propriety of the conversation had been questionable. They'd at least been talking. And despite what his family seemed to think, Griffith did intend to converse with his wife. He didn't expect her to be a silent fixture he had to remember to dust off every once in a while.

Only he couldn't think of the first thing to say to Miss St. Claire.

"We went to the Egyptian Hall a few days ago." Miss Breckenridge's glance bounced from Griffith to her cousin to the door and back again. "Have you had a chance to go, Your Grace?"

"I'm afraid not."

She smiled. "Not a great lover of art?"

"Of some art." He shrugged. "My youngest sister paints quite well. I have several of her pieces at Hawthorne House. Nearly every fire screen in the house has her touch on it."

"I do watercolours." Miss St. Claire's blurted statement had Griffith jerking a bit in his chair. He'd forgotten she was there.

He cleared his throat and reminded himself—again—that he was here to visit Miss St. Claire and not her younger, prettier, more personable cousin. "Do you enjoy them?"

She popped up, nearly as abruptly as she had before, and Griffith scrambled to his feet.

"I'll go get them for you."

Miss Breckenridge jumped up from her seat and grabbed her cousin's elbow. "No, I rather think your watercolours can wait."

The tightening of Miss St. Claire's lips made it quite evident that more was under discussion than amateur artwork. Griffith should probably care what it was since he was intending to marry Miss St. Claire, but he couldn't seem to drum up more than the mild curiosity that naturally occurred when one was in the presence of a potentially good mystery.

"But he hasn't seen my watercolours in years."

Miss Breckenridge's eyes narrowed. "*The duke* has never seen your watercolours."

The blush returned in full force as Miss St. Claire looked his way with an apologetic smile. It appeared she was suffering from the same malady he was—forgetting the other person was there. Again. Being overlooked wasn't something Griffith was accustomed to experiencing.

He should probably have cared more.

As this wasn't the first time that thought had occurred to him, he had to wonder if Ryland was right and he was going to find his choice of wife a bit boring. Could he love boring?

The butler appeared in the door. "Miladies, Lord Naworth has arrived. Shall I send him away?"

Miss Breckenridge closed her eyes and sighed. "No. Send him

in." She gave a pointed look to her cousin. "His Grace came to visit with Miss St. Claire."

Sharp footsteps echoed from the adjacent hall as the butler turned to depart the room, and all of the room's occupants swung their gazes to the open door to see an average-sized man with a slender build and pointy chin enter the room with an enormous smile on his face. To be honest, Griffith was surprised it had taken Lord Pontebrook this long to join them.

"Riverton! What honor brings you to my home?"

Griffith thought that was rather obvious, given the fact that he was in the drawing room with the ladies instead of in the viscount's study, but he refrained from the comment. The quickly covered burst of laughter from Miss Breckenridge likely indicated a similar thought had crept through her head.

"I wanted to take note of Miss St. Claire's health after—"

"What beauty is before me, in grace as well as face?" A wiry man in a bottle-green coat swept into the room, extending a bouquet of brightly colored flowers. He crossed to Miss Breckenridge and bowed low. "For a glimpse of just her smile, I have walked from Bruton Place."

Had his sisters had to put up with such nauseating nonsense? Where was this man's sense of pride? Griffith couldn't resist mumbling, "You live in Brook Street, Naworth."

"I should see to more tea!" Miss St. Claire stepped around the tea table and headed for the door.

"You could simply ring for it." Miss Breckenridge's voice was resigned, as if she knew that her suggestion would be ignored.

"Her hair is the golden sun in the blue sky of her eyes," Lord Naworth continued.

Lord Pontebrook clapped Griffith on the back. "Since you're here I'd love to discuss the prospects in Parliament this year."

Griffith had never seen a house so chaotic. If he was going to take control of this courtship, he was going to have to remove Miss St. Claire from these surroundings. He cast a glance around the room as the butler showed yet another gentleman into the drawing room, thankfully removing Lord Pontebrook from Griffith's side but adding to the noise as the man expounded upon his joy at being able to simply bask in the presence of Miss Breckenridge's beauty.

The first man was still reciting his poem, though. And after a particularly excruciating line about the curve of Miss Breckenridge's temples, Griffith could have sworn he heard her mutter, "Oh good, I get a new hat."

Chapter 8

Isabella poked at her toast, wondering what woeful miseries awaited her that day. It had been a week since her first ball, a week since Frederica had seen Arthur, a week since the Duke of Riverton's attention had somehow wandered their way, and a week since her uncle had first introduced her to a man he wanted to manipulate.

With such a foreboding start to the week, it had been hard to imagine it getting much worse, but it had.

Frederica's stealthy meeting with Arthur in the kitchens had been exciting, but not very satisfactory. He hadn't renewed his suit but instead had left Frederica with a handful of reasons why she should find and marry someone else. Freddie hadn't accepted any of them and was more determined than ever to find him and declare that her feelings hadn't changed despite the separation.

To that end, she sought for Arthur at every event they went to. The duke, however, was at those same events and making a point of seeking out Frederica, which prompted Frederica to guilt Isabella into being a distraction, though how Isabella had room to feel more guilty she didn't know. Isabella's herd of admiring menfolk, encouraged and added to by her uncle's lauded praises, followed Isabella into the presence of the duke.

It was like a bad play. Only she didn't get to walk out and leave it at the end of the evening. She woke up and it was still there.

"Mr. Emerson will be coming for a visit today." Uncle Percy set aside his paper and tucked into the breakfast a footman set before him.

Isabella sighed. She was already exhausted from avoiding Freddie while trying to entice every unmarried lord from London to Brighton. She refused to add flirting with members of the House of Commons to her plate as well. Besides, if the man was coming to visit Uncle Percy, who was in the House of Lords, about the bill, it meant he was already interested in it. Isabella's smiles were not required. As far as she could tell, the men elected to the House of Commons were considerably more interested in the proceedings than the aristocrats who inherited their House of Lords seats.

Still, she needed to establish to Uncle Percy that despite their deal, there would be boundaries. "We received callers yesterday and have decided to rest today, so you'll have no need to worry about noisy suitors in the front hall."

Frederica lifted her attention from her own plate. "Actually, Father, we will be returning calls today."

Uncle Percy frowned. "People can't visit you if you aren't at home."

What he really meant was that he couldn't campaign to people who didn't come to the house, but since everyone in the room knew the underlying implication, there wasn't much point in calling him on it.

"Yes, Father, but if we don't go out and pay our own calls, people will start to talk, and Isabella's popularity will falter."

It was all Isabella could do to keep her head down and her

face free of exasperation. While it was true that they needed to get out and return calls to the few ladies who had stopped by in between the influx of gentlemen, what Frederica really wanted to do was wander around in the places where the army officers were known to be. So much for a quiet day at home.

Uncle Percy sighed dramatically. "I suppose I can receive Mr. Emerson without you in attendance. You can delay your calls long enough to at least greet him in passing. Isabella, I expect you to give him a warm welcome when he arrives. Perhaps arrange for someone to bring us tea before you leave."

Isabella nodded, because she didn't have a choice. She would smile and make a great show of seeing to the needs of Uncle Percy and his guest before they left. It didn't matter if the thought of it made her stomach cramp—this was what she had agreed to do. She'd already seen the bank draft and the letters of recommendation that would save her family as long as she convinced Uncle Percy she'd done enough smiling and dancing to get every single man of title or influence to vote in such a way as to earn Uncle Percy's favor.

Then she would leave town and not marry any of them.

They finished breakfast quietly before retiring to the music room and leaving Uncle Percy to his paper. There were still a few hours before it was socially respectable to be out and about. And they had to wait for Mr. Emerson to come so she could bestow her apparently magical smile upon him.

It was enough to make her want to frown until she developed wrinkles.

Frederica wandered over to the window, but her attention was on her notebook. "It's a bit far to walk to the Pulsford Hotel, but perhaps if we said we were visiting Lady Farnsworth? She's at least on Piccadilly."

Isabella groaned and dropped onto the chair in front of the

piano. "If I hadn't seen Arthur with my own eyes, I'd be convinced that you made up this entire search just to have an excuse to avoid the Duke of Riverton."

And there was no question that her cousin was doing her level best to avoid the man. In addition to seeking her out in public, he'd been by the house twice more to call upon her. Once they hadn't been home, and for the other she'd insisted on Isabella's presence. Even though Isabella had attempted to sit quietly in the corner and work on her needlework, she'd been pulled repeatedly into the stilted conversation.

If those two ever did get married, she hoped they would have children quickly. Watching them alone was almost painful.

"I'm not avoiding the duke." Frederica looked up from the notebook. "I haven't had him turned away yet."

Isabella plunked a few notes, making them deliberately disjointed in response to Freddie's lie. "And what do you plan to do when he asks you to go riding with him?"

"Why would he do that?" Frederica asked absently. She turned from the window and propped her hands on her hips. "I still can't believe we haven't seen him on Bond Street."

Obviously Isabella's distraction tactics weren't working anymore, because Freddie's mind was quite obviously still stuck back on her previous conversation topic.

Isabella plunked a meandering tune from the piano as she tried to follow her cousin's conversation. "Why should Arthur be on Bond Street? London is full of officers right now. He could be anywhere, possibly even shipped back to another country." She tried to distract her cousin once more. "As for the duke, he'll ask you to go riding because that's what gentlemen do when they want to court a lady."

"For the last time, the duke is not courting me." Frederica dropped her attention back to the notebook, where she'd been listing every officer or soldier sighting since the Yensworth ball. "Besides, even if Arthur has left the city, he's alive. And as long as he's alive I'm going to wait for him."

Isabella twiddled her fingers between two notes, worrying her lip with her teeth. Should she say it? She didn't want to. But Frederica wasn't being at all sensible about this situation. Chasing after a man this boldly, and obviously, simply wasn't done. Even Isabella knew that. And to chase after a man who had told you to find someone else to marry seemed like running after heartbreak. She kept her voice calm and quiet, hoping to break through Freddie's obsession and at least make her think. "What if he hasn't waited? It's been two years. He could have married someone else."

There was a moment of silence. "He'd have told me."

Isabella couldn't stop the wave of sympathy for her cousin. Bella had never been in love—and after seeing what it did to Freddie, she didn't think she ever wanted to be—but it had to be difficult to have such a strong emotion and no way to express it. Still, facts were facts despite their emotional pain. "He told you to find someone else. Maybe he didn't have time to tell you why you should."

Isabella plunked a few more notes before settling into playing an actual song. She certainly wouldn't put herself up to exhibit for anyone here in London, but she enjoyed playing.

Frederica was quiet for several moments. These were the times when Isabella mourned their loss of personal contact for the last ten years. Letters didn't require knowing how to handle a person's moods or how to decipher their silent signals. What was Freddie thinking?

"If he asks to go for a ride, I'll tell him I'm allergic to horses and send you instead."

Apparently she was thinking of ways to continue avoiding

the duke's obvious interest. "Your father is already throwing me at half the aristocracy. I don't need you to finish the job."

Frederica put the notebook down and crossed to lean on the piano. "Don't you see? It's perfect! If we can get the duke to transfer his attentions to you without Father knowing it, I'll be able to come along with you and keep searching for Arthur! Once I find him it will be the perfect disguise for our secret meetings."

Isabella frowned and banged the keys harder than necessary. "And if I don't want the duke's attentions?"

"You're already miserable, so what difference will it make?"

Truth was truth, even if Isabella didn't want to admit it. There wasn't really a reason for both of them to be miserable. Frederica's possible delusions were making her so happy. Did Isabella really need to crush them under the bootheel of good sense? "Arthur will never go along with it."

"I can convince him." Freddie sighed. "Once I find him again."

For her cousin's sake, Isabella hoped the man was worth finding. What would it be like to care about someone else that much? She knew what it meant to love your family enough to sacrifice for them, but for someone else? Someone you chose? Someone who had chosen you?

Frederica pulled a chair over and sat next to Isabella, resting her head on Bella's shoulder. It hindered Bella's playing, but since they were the only two to hear it, it didn't matter much if her mediocre song got a little worse.

"Have you met anyone you actually like?" Freddie asked. "I mean, I know you can't declare a preference yet, but once the vote is over, what's stopping you?"

"Besides the fact that I'm living a lie? I can't afford to be myself with any of these men. They're all infatuated with a pretty painting and your father's devious misleadings."

Isabella shifted into a slow dirge, the gloomy notes fitting her mood as she thought about the moment at the Yensworth ball, in a side room with the duke and her unconscious cousin. She'd been herself at that moment, more concerned about her cousin than her ruse.

Despite their easy conversation the man had still called on Frederica. If that wasn't proof that London wasn't ready for her to put down the façade, she didn't know what was.

"Everyone's living a lie, Bella. It's London. Do you think all of those men who've brought you flowers have their life together?" She laughed. "At least one of them is barely holding on to his rooms at the Albany because he's gambled away so much of his allowance this quarter."

"All the more reason to return home before seeking to establish my future." Isabella ran a finger over the jeweled necklace at her throat. It seemed to choke her with the lies she was allowing her uncle to spread like unchecked weeds.

Frederica thrummed her fingers on the piano in time with the song. "What do you think spinsters do with their time?"

Isabella forced herself to grin at her cousin. "I hear they meet weekly for cribbage."

"Ew." Freddie's nose scrunched up. "That doesn't sound like much fun. I suppose I should try to adapt myself to it, though. In case I can't find Arthur again."

"Or . . ." Isabella drew the word out to get Frederica's attention. "You could grab the future that's practically landed in your lap, for reasons neither of us can fathom, and become a duchess."

Frederica sniffed. "The very fact that we have no idea why he's bestowed his attentions on me proves that he's not in his right mind. It would be difficult enough handling the pressure of being a duchess. Can you imagine being a duchess to an insane duke?"

Isabella's playing grew soft, but her voice grew even softer. "He's a nice man, Frederica. I don't think he's insane."

"You marry him, then." Frederica huffed over to a chair and plopped herself down with a book.

Heavy footsteps approached the door to the music room. Had Mr. Emerson arrived earlier than expected?

Isabella looked to the door to see Uncle Percy rubbing his hands together, a smile so broad it was almost scary.

"I'm afraid you'll have to adjust your plans, my dear. You're going to be at home today."

Frederica frowned while Isabella slumped at the pianoforte.

"But, Father, we can't be at home two days in a row. It would be strange. People might think Isabella is desperate." Freddie hugged her notebook to her chest, eyes wide.

Uncle Percy waved his hands around. "So don't be at home for anyone else. But the Duke of Riverton is coming to take you for a walk, girl, and you will be available when he calls." He adjusted his waistcoat. "I thought he was impossible to entice, so I hadn't even planned on sending Isabella after him. See that you keep his attention long enough to collect his vote."

He started to leave the room but turned around at the door. "And you"—he pointed to Isabella—"leave the duke alone. If it became known that he was bestowing favor on you, the other men would leave. And then where would your family be?"

Isabella resisted the urge to stick her tongue out at her uncle's retreating back. Just because she was starting to feel like a helpless child didn't mean she had to act like one.

⌒

Griffith waited in the drawing room of Lord Pontebrook's house in Ford Street for the third time in a week. This time, however, he had a plan. Obviously he hadn't thought through his earlier attempts to court Miss St. Claire. Simply showing up and expecting his title and presence to make it happen was not only arrogant but foolish in that it left entirely too much to chance.

So today he had a plan. A plan to remove the distractions and interruptions. To ensure his success, he'd made his plans through Lord Pontebrook and had been gratified to receive a positive response, that Miss St. Claire would be pleased to go for a walk with him. At least men knew how to conduct a straightforward business agreement. Every attempt he'd made to connect directly with Miss St. Claire had met with nothing but chaos, mostly at the hands of her cousin. Miss Breckenridge was nothing but trouble. Beautiful and intriguing trouble, but trouble nonetheless.

With his long legs, walking alongside most people was a nuisance, and he avoided it whenever possible. Courting Miss St. Claire without the presence of Miss Breckenridge had provided sufficient inducement, however, and he'd become willing to deal with a woman's slower pace.

The door behind him opened, and he turned to see Miss St. Claire strolling sedately into the room, a slight curve to her lips. Not enough to show an overabundance of enthusiasm but enough to make her the picture of beatific grace. Behind her was Miss Breckenridge, who looked as if she'd been dragged into the drawing room by her coiffure.

Griffith bowed. "Good afternoon, Miss St. Claire." He bit back a sigh. "Miss Breckenridge."

"Your Grace." Miss St. Claire curtsied and stepped closer, hands clasped at her waist. "We arc honored that you wish to take us for a walk."

Us? Surely she meant her and her maid. Because he had been very deliberate not to mention Miss Breckenridge in his communication with Lord Pontebrook. "Of course."

Her brown eyes widened. "It is agreeable if Miss Brecken-ridge joins us, isn't it? I'm very concerned about her health if she's forced to stay indoors for another day. I'm afraid she's accustomed to the fresh air of the country, and her constitution would benefit from a bit of exercise."

"Of course." He was repeating himself, although what else could he say when she'd couched her request in such a manner? If he were going to marry this woman—and he was starting to have considerable doubts in the wisdom of his selection—they were going to have to learn how to say more than two words to each other.

Now in addition to walking slowly he was going to have to find a way to ignore the distracting Miss Breckenridge.

As the trio stepped into the hall, two maids were waiting by the door. Griffith lifted his eyebrow at the abundance of chaperonage.

Miss St. Claire turned a stiff smile to Miss Breckenridge. "Father would insist we take both of our maids, you know. In case something should happen. Besides, this way they can visit with each other as they walk behind us."

Miss Breckenridge's narrowed gaze indicated she too was suspicious of her cousin's consideration of the servants.

Lord Pontebrook strolled into the front hall. "Off on your walk, I see."

Griffith inclined his head. "Yes, we shall make quite a merry party."

The man narrowed his eyes in his niece's direction. "You are all going?"

"Yes." Miss St. Claire spoke without meeting her father's gaze. "Isabella is in need of exercise as well."

"I am delighted to escort you both." Griffith gave a slight bow to both women. He wasn't, but he didn't like Lord Pontebrook's attitude. Did the man think that his niece's presence would keep a man from finding value in his daughter? Obviously Griffith was already aware of Miss Breckenridge's existence, so the very fact that he'd contacted the man about his daughter should have set the matter to rest.

"Yes, of course you are." Lord Pontebrook smiled, though it didn't look like something his face was accustomed to doing. "Who wouldn't want to spend the afternoon in such lovely company? Perhaps you can join me for tea when you return. We've some important issues up for vote in the House this term."

Griffith lifted a single brow in Lord Pontebrook's direction. The man's daughter and niece were about to become the first unrelated females ever publicly associated with Griffith's name, and he wanted to talk politics?

"All the issues are important." Griffith had to believe that. If he didn't, he'd hole up at Riverton and never come to Town. Duty to family and country were the only things that could entice him to live in the crowded and dirty city for even part of the year.

"Yes. Yes. Of course." Lord Pontebrook clasped his hands behind his back and rocked back and forth on his heels. "I think the votes are there for the Corn Laws."

"There are still some changes to be made to that resolution, but yes, I think it will pass." He'd rather it didn't, but he wasn't inclined to go into detail about that at the moment. Somehow Griffith had trouble believing the taxes on corn and wheat were Lord Pontebrook's highest priority.

He glanced at the ladies to see if he could escape yet, but they were still on the other side of the hall, tying the bows on their bonnets.

"They're drafting the apothecary law as well." The viscount's chest puffed out a bit. "High time we put some regulations around those people. We can't have just anyone telling people they know how to heal what ails them."

Griffith had seen early drafts of the proposal but had mixed feelings about the entire thing. Until he made his own decision, he wasn't about to discuss the merits and drawbacks with someone he didn't have complete trust in. Especially considering that the apothecary laws weren't scheduled to even be discussed in the House of Lords for several more weeks, much less voted on.

"I believe the ladies are ready to depart." Griffith inclined his head toward Lord Pontebrook and then used his ducal privilege to rudely walk away from the man. While he could never be anything but a perfect gentleman when ladies were present—his mother would have it no other way—he was more than aware of the entitlements of rank when in the presence of other gentlemen. To do otherwise would have left his life in havoc. Everyone wanted the ear of a duke.

Miss St. Claire said something that made Miss Breckenridge laugh, and the light, tinkling sound bounced off the walls of the cavernous front hall. This was why Griffith had wanted a sedate, seasoned woman. Young debutantes like Miss Breckenridge would leave his current peaceful routines in shambles.

He escorted them out the door. Miss St. Claire's earlier calm was replaced by a look of eagerness, even though she avoided meeting his gaze. Miss Breckenridge had no trouble leveling her gaze at him, though her expression looked as if a walk with him was the last thing she wanted to be doing.

Probably because it meant she couldn't receive any more callers this afternoon. Didn't girls such as she spend the first few weeks of the Season collecting as many admirers as possible before, hopefully, culling the herd down to a few select favorites?

The sun was bright, despite the haze of the city, and Griffith rolled his shoulders—simply escaping the confines of the town house in Ford Street gave him an extra modicum of freedom.

"Shall we walk toward Berkelcy Square?" Miss St. Claire's spirits seemed buoyed by the outdoors as well, and the park she wanted to walk to was no short jaunt. That boded well for his hopes that she would be satisfied with a life set mostly in the country.

Miss Breckenridge frowned, and her turbulent sea-colored eyes narrowed at her cousin. "Why would we want to go there?"

"Why, because of the trees, of course."

Chapter 9

Isabella made a conscious effort to keep from her facial features the thought that her cousin had a few attics to let. If the duke was interested in Frederica, he didn't need a reason to question her faculties.

"You wanted to see them, didn't you?" Frederica continued. "You said it was one of the things you wished to see the most on your first trip to London."

"Yes. The trees." While it was true that Isabella had expressed a great desire to see the trees while she was in London, there wasn't any real urgency to the desire. She was going to be in Town for weeks, probably months. There would be plenty of time to go to the park in Berkeley Square.

Apparently they were going to go today, though.

As they began to walk down the pavement, Isabella tried to separate herself from the potential couple. Frederica was determined to return to where she left off with Arthur Saunderson, and if the man returned her affections, Isabella would be the first to approve the match. But if he didn't, if life as an officer of war for the past two years had altered him, then Frederica needed an alternate plan.

Isabella's main goal for the Season was, of course, to get the money needed to save her family's farm, but she was quickly coming to care almost as much about getting Frederica settled and out from under the control of Uncle Percy.

"The weather is quite fine today, Your Grace." Frederica placed one hand on top of her bonnet and turned her face up to the sun. "Might we walk down Bond Street so that we can more fully enjoy it? Davies Street is so narrow. The sun doesn't reach below the attics there."

Isabella suddenly felt as if she were choking on her heart. The pressure in her chest and the burning sensation in her throat mimicked the worry and unease that filled her mind as the implication of Frederica's words came to light. This walk was a ruse.

"Surely there isn't a call for that, dear cousin." Isabella sped up until she was walking on the other side of the duke. What an odd set they must appear strolling down the street. "Davies Street may be narrow, but it is much shorter. We'll be at Berkeley Square all the sooner and in the unhindered reach of the sun and a spot of fresher air. There is *no benefit* to going down Bond Street."

Frederica wrinkled her nose at Isabella's protest. They both knew that the only thing Frederica cared about on Bond Street was the Stephens Hotel. Arthur was alive, in town, and his reappearance hadn't yet made the gossip pages. Of course, with it being the beginning of the Season, there were much more interesting arrivals to report than the third son of an insignificant baron, but it still meant that there was every likelihood he had not returned to his family quarters.

Which put great odds that he was staying at the Stephens Hotel.

The duke looked down the pavement as if visualizing his street options and then at each of the young women at his side.

He released a gust of breath that sounded almost like a sigh. "We can walk to Berkeley Square via Bond Street and return up Davies."

There was nothing Isabella could say that wouldn't cause the duke to become suspicious, so she fell back a step or two again and considered praying—though whether she'd be praying for Lieutenant Saunderson to be there or for every officer to have disappeared from the vicinity, she wasn't sure.

It didn't matter which she chose. God didn't have any reason to ignore Frederica right now, so she'd be better off without any entreaty from Isabella. Still, Bella couldn't help but wonder which option would be better for Frederica.

Bella lowered her head and watched her toes appear and disappear beneath her hem as she walked. In front of her the duke and Frederica's voices droned on, discussing the same inane, polite topics everyone had discussed at every other social event she'd been to. She frowned. It sounded like the exact same discussion the two of them had had the night before. Didn't they have anything else to talk about?

She kicked a pebble and sent it careening off the pavement and bouncing onto the cobblestone street beside her. Did God miss her as much as she missed Him? Her family prayed together every morning, read the Bible by firelight in the evening. Some of her first childhood memories included skipping along the rutted lane to the village church.

But now? Now she couldn't even bring herself to whisper His name. Amazing how one decision could drive a person so far from where they thought they'd never stray.

"Oh!"

The startled cry from Frederica drove Isabella's head to rise, but not in time to see that the couple in front of her had come to an unexpected halt. She barreled into the duke's back, bumping her bonnet brim against his shoulder hard enough to cause the hat to push painfully into her scalp.

As she fell back a step, she raised a hand to her head to rub the sore area.

Frederica was clinging to the duke's arm while she dug her fan from her reticule. "I'm afraid this fine weather has become a bit warmer than I'd anticipated."

A glance around the area revealed they were in front of the coffee shop across from the Stephens Hotel. At least half of the shop's patrons sported the eye-catching scarlet coats and important bearing of English officers.

Off to the side of the building, leaning against the wall by the door, with his narrowed gaze glued to Frederica's antics, was Lieutenant Saunderson. His light brown hair was pulled back into a queue, and his uniform looked as pristine as any gentleman could ask for. The high jackboots were polished to a mirror shine.

Isabella tried not to groan, even as she knew she was going to aid Frederica's cause. Never let it be said that Bella wasn't loyal. "Perhaps you are becoming ill. Your constitution has seemed quite delicate of late."

Frederica looked over her shoulder, her eyes considerably more alert than they should be for a woman on the verge of unmovable exhaustion. "Yes, I do believe that could be true. I've overexerted myself."

The duke turned halfway around. "Should we return? We've been walking but a quarter hour. Your home is not far away."

"Oh, we couldn't possibly!" Frederica grabbed Isabella's arm, and laughter threatened to burst from Isabella's chest and ruin the entire show. Frederica had always been prone to absurd antics in private, especially when she visited Isabella during the summer, but in public she'd always been the epitome of gentility.

If this infatuation with Arthur allowed her to be more herself, then Isabella was going to have to admit it was a good thing. As long as Frederica didn't end up hurt.

Isabella looked over her cousin's head, locking gazes with the man in question. His mouth was flattened into a grim line, but it was not a look of resignation on his face. In fact he looked a great deal like her brother did when they walked the village fair and he stood before the candy cart, knowing he couldn't have any but wishing for it all the same.

Isabella heaved a dramatic sigh, though not as dramatic as Frederica's. If she was going to be acting and lying her way through London, it might as well be for a noble cause as well as a selfish one. And she was going to do a cracking good job of it. Or at least better than Frederica. "I did so wish to see the trees. Do you think you will feel up to walking such a distance soon?"

"I don't know." Frederica turned wide eyes in Isabella's direction. "I'm so sorry, cousin. I know how badly you wanted to see the trees. I hope this doesn't send me to my bed for weeks. My recovery is sure to be hindered knowing how much I've disappointed you."

Isabella ducked her head and bit her lip. She dug her fingernails into her palm. Anything to keep from laughing. She so desperately wanted to take a peek at His Grace to see what effect Frederica's antics had on his esteem. Was he regretting his choice? What would Uncle Percy say if the duke retracted his attentions?

That was a thought sobering enough to get her impending giggles under control.

"Your Grace," Freddie pleaded, "please go on without me. My maid will stay with me, and I'm positive that these kind officers will see to it that I find a table in the shade."

Isabella glanced once more in Lieutenant Saunderson's

direction. He'd straightened from the wall, ready to step in before any of the other officers could do so. No one else seemed to have noticed their conversation yet, but they couldn't stand here for much longer without drawing attention.

The duke sighed, or rather his massive chest deflated a bit. He was probably much too polite to sigh at a lady's request. "It would be my honor to fulfill such a dear request as—" he paused and cut a look in Isabella's direction, one that questioned her sanity—"viewing the trees."

The man already thought she was addled, so Isabella decided to take more of the attention off Frederica. "Perhaps that officer there."

Lieutenant Saunderson stepped forward and bowed. The duke started to introduce himself, but Frederica made a show of wilting further onto Isabella's shoulder, distracting both men. Moments later, Frederica was walking into the coffee shop on the arm of Arthur Saunderson, her maid trailing dutifully behind, and Isabella was left standing on the pavement with the duke.

And she discovered that she hadn't met her capacity for feeling guilty after all.

Griffith wasn't sure what to think as he watched Miss St. Claire stumble her way into the coffee shop, looking very much like a woman who had imbibed too much wine instead of over-exerting herself. Perhaps she had simply been seeking a way to avoid trying to make more conversation. He couldn't blame her. Instead of wishing he could take this opportunity to sit and have a quiet cup of tea with her, he found himself relieved to cut their time short. They'd already exhausted the topics of the fineness of the weather, the dreadful traffic caused by the abundance of London construction, and even the interesting trends in fashion now that the war was over.

Along with the relief came another emotion—one that he wasn't sure he could or even wanted to identify. The fact that he was now going to have to spend time alone with Miss Breckenridge, something he'd been doing his best to avoid, inspired something that wasn't excitement but wasn't dread either. She held none of the qualities he was looking for, but all the qualities people assumed he wanted. Once he was seen walking with her, there were sure to be a few more lines added to the betting books around town. That realization must be causing the feeling of near trepidation he had.

Bond Street grew considerably more crowded as they continued walking. Miss Breckenridge's arm brushed against his, and he resisted the urge to offer it to her as they walked down the pavement. The stares they were getting were enough to ensure his uncharacteristic behavior was going to make the society pages the next day. He didn't need to add any additional tidbits for the wagging tongues to share.

This was exactly the sort of thing he'd hoped to avoid.

"Are you enjoying London?"

She tilted her head so that her bonnet no longer blocked her view of his face. Or his view of hers. The features truly were exquisite. This close he could see that her skin was smooth and clear, though not quite as pale as he'd originally thought. A touch of sun and health bloomed across her cheeks, making her eyes appear even more luminous than they had in candlelight. "London has definitely been an experience unlike any I've ever had before. I had no idea so many people and businesses could exist in the same place."

Griffith turned his own head to be able to look at her more closely. London was large, yes, but in some ways it was more like many towns smashed together. Surely she had seen busy streets and squares before. "Where are you from?"

She hesitated a moment as they made the turn onto Bruton Street, licking her lips and clearing her throat before turning her attention back to the road in front of them. "Northumberland."

Not the most fashionable part of the country, to be certain, but there was nothing in it to cause her any shame. He was a bit surprised at how much he didn't like the idea of her feeling sad. It must be a holdover from raising his sisters. Anyone as young and inexperienced as Miss Breckenridge was bound to remind him of his youngest siblings. "Do you miss it?"

"At times. London is very different than Northumberland. You're the first to actually ask me about it."

He cleared his throat. "It is a fine area of the country."

"Oh." She turned her head to face him with wide eyes. "Have you been there?"

"Er, no." He looked both ways before directing her through a gap in the traffic and into the edges of Berkeley Square Gardens.

One side of her mouth lifted in an amused smile as she looked up at him through lowered lashes. "The area's reputation has preceded it, I suppose, in order for the county to earn your esteem."

Griffith steered her toward the shade trees they'd walked this way to see. "Northumberland is a county in England. Therefore it is a fine county."

Silence fell between them as her feet tripped to a stop.

He took one step past her before turning around to see what had caused her to become still.

Her lips were curled inward, pale stripes of near white showing in the light pink areas, an indication that she was actually biting the insides of her lips in an effort to remain silent. She swallowed visibly, the lines of her delicate neck jumping with the effort and her eyebrows raised high as she tried to push down whatever her initial reaction had been to his statement. "That shows quite a loyalty to king and country."

One of his eyebrows shot up. His brother was constantly complaining about the arrogance of such an expression, but it was a habit Griffith had never been able to conquer, much to his chagrin. "Of course. I am a duke. If our loyalty does not extend to our monarch and our country, then what good are we?"

"Well, you're very good at sending the attendees of a social gathering into a mad tempest."

It was Griffith's turn to suppress an inelegant response, though he trusted that he did so with less obvious methods than Miss Breckenridge had employed. He swept his arm toward the grove of trees. "The plane trees, madam."

She shifted her gaze to look beyond him, and her mouth dropped open a bit in a soundless gasp as she nearly ran past him to lay a gloved hand on the unique mottled and peeling bark of the tree. "Fascinating."

Griffith clasped his hands behind him at his lower back, trying to see what she was obviously seeing. "Fascinating?"

"Have you ever seen a tree like this? I read about it in one of my father's horticultural books—how the tree was discovered in Vauxhall Gardens and planted here. When I learned I was coming to London I knew I had to see them. I could never understand how the bark was being described, but it makes so much sense now."

The last thing Griffith expected the woman already being touted as London's own Aphrodite to be fascinated with was trees. Dances, shops, perhaps the latest in horses or even sporting, but trees? No one could feign that level of excitement and knowledge. The request to see the trees had obviously been genuine.

Griffith followed her at a more sedate pace until he was standing just a bit behind her shoulder. He stretched his right arm out and flicked one finger against the smooth but fractured bark. A chunk of it peeled off the tree and landed at Miss Breckenridge's feet.

"Oh!" She bent to retrieve the piece of bark and turned it over and over in her hands, examining it with an attention he'd have expected to be reserved for gossip rags or an updated copy of *Debrett's*.

"I've never seen a tree do this before. It's rather strange, when you think about it." She let one hand fall to her side, the bark still clutched in her fingers, leaving specks of dirt and tree bark on her gloves and dress. The other hand moved toward the tree to poke at the recently revealed portion of the trunk. "Does this leave it vulnerable, do you think? For animals or some other sort of plant to burrow in?"

"I wouldn't know. The plane tree doesn't have a lot of value for me, given that it doesn't produce much of anything besides shade. And I've trees aplenty that do that already."

She tilted her head and looked up at him from the corners of her eyes. "And do you only give consideration to things that benefit you?"

His first instinct was to deny the accusation, but something about the way she said it made him stop to consider his answer for truthfulness. "I give a great deal more thought to things that matter to myself and my family. I think everyone does."

"Yes. I imagine they do." Something sad crossed her features before she gave her attention back to the tree. "How long do you think it will take for the tree to replace that bark?"

Griffith wasn't very interested in investigating the parts of the tree, but he was becoming increasingly curious about what made up the woman before him. Watching her while he contemplated these new attributes wasn't much of a hardship either.

And that worried him.

Chapter 10

The duke was watching her with narrowed eyes, but Isabella couldn't bring herself to care. This was one man she didn't have to worry about impressing enough to convince him to talk to her uncle. His Grace was more interested in Frederica.

She glanced at him to see his gaze still on her even as they conversed about the trees. Or rather she talked about the trees and he politely listened. Although hearing the story of their discovery piqued his interest for a moment, he didn't seem to share her fascination with the trees. His attention never wavered, though, and she never got the feeling that his thoughts were elsewhere.

An uneasy feeling tightened across her shoulders as she let her tree-related commentary fade into silence. He was still intending to call upon Freddie, wasn't he? It hadn't been a ploy to gain her attention, had it? She needed to know even as she felt like a pompous goose for thinking it. If she needed to turn what limited wiles she was pretending to have on him, there would never be a better time than now.

"Thank you for bringing me to see the trees. I don't believe this was how you planned to spend your afternoon."

He shook his head and looked out over the grove being circled by carriages and vendors, an oasis in the middle of the city chaos. "No, I confess looking at trees in the middle of London was not what I expected to do today."

"I feel I should apologize for Miss St. Claire's insistence. I'm afraid my cousin is concerned that I won't feel at home here in London." Isabella stepped away from the tree and started to stroll through the middle of the park.

The duke fell in step beside her. "It is admirable for her to put the desires of family above her own."

"Yes. She'll make a good mother." Isabella winced. That wasn't very discreet. "That is . . . I'm sure she'll, uh . . . Frederica is very considerate."

"Yes. She is." He cleared his throat and gestured toward Hayhill Street. "Shall we be considerate in return and go back to relieve her solitude? You can bring the bark as proof that I fulfilled my duties as guide."

Isabella laughed. It felt good to laugh without restriction or conscious thought of how loud it was or whether or not her slightly crooked teeth were showing. There was no need to impress the duke or string him along. That would be Frederica's job, assuming the duke hadn't decided she was too delicate to court. "Yes, we shall."

Bella casually slowed her pace under the guise of getting one last look at some of the park's trees. Frederica was not going to be happy with their quick return. The entire afternoon wouldn't be long enough for Frederica now that she had found Arthur again.

Of course, that was assuming the lieutenant was actually interested in having a reunion of any kind with his former love interest. He had come by the house for the express purpose of telling her to find someone else. What if he'd escorted her inside the coffee shop and then left her with the maid? Even now, Frederica

118

could be fending off the unwanted attention of a myriad of other officers, intent on practicing their charms on a lonely woman with features that some would consider less than fashionable.

Isabella sped back up, walking perhaps a little faster than they had as they approached the park.

The abrupt change in pace drew the attention of the duke. "Is something wrong?"

"Oh, no." Isabella forced a smile even as worry threw idea after idea into her head of all the agonies Frederica could be suffering. "I simply cannot be selfish with your attentions any longer. It is quite unfair, as you came to visit Miss St. Claire."

She cut her eyes in the duke's direction, peeking at him around the edge of her bonnet. "You did come to visit Miss St. Claire, didn't you?"

He turned his arrogant ducal expression toward her once more, the one that made her feel as if he were examining her and finding her wanting—a thought that disturbed her more than she liked. "Yes. I came with the intention of calling upon Miss St. Claire this afternoon."

"Oh." Isabella swallowed. "That's good."

They strolled down the less busy Dover Street, speaking amiably of inconsequential things until they passed an elaborate display of fine wooden items in a shop window. In the center was a quaich, the bowl of the small cup polished to a sheen and the two handles carved with Celtic knots and sprigs of thistle. Though of a much higher quality, it was similar to the one her family drank from on special occasions, and it reminded Isabella of home, of her parents. She stopped in front of the window and let the conversation lapse into silence.

"Miss Breckenridge? Are you well?" The duke's deep voice rumbled out of that massive chest and seemed to roll into her ears like water over rocks.

119

"Yes, I am well. Only missing a bit of home. My father has a quaich very similar to that one. He and my mother share a drink from it on their anniversary." Isabella tried to force a smile onto her face as she looked up at him. "I was not expecting to miss them this much."

He watched her a while, jade green eyes roving over her face as if looking for something. She wished she knew what it was so she could give it to him. At that moment, despite the fact that his interest was in Frederica—where it truly belonged—Isabella didn't want to give him a reason to find her lacking.

He shifted to the side and reached for the door without a word. As he disappeared into the shop, Isabella looked back at her maid. Until that moment she'd been doing a wonderful job of acting as if the woman wasn't there. Mostly because she had forgotten the maid was there. Isabella didn't have to be constantly shadowed back home.

The maid looked as confused as Isabella felt. Were they supposed to follow him in?

Movement at the window drew her attention, and she saw the duke waiting while the shopkeeper removed the quaich from the window. He dropped a few coins into the shopkeeper's hand in exchange for the small two-handled wooden cup, and then the duke was heading for the door.

Isabella couldn't have moved if she tried.

The duke walked back out onto the shadowed street and handed the quaich to her. "I know what it is to be away from home. Consider this a token reminder that you are not alone here in London. One thing I've learned over the years is that family goes with you even when you travel on your own." He tapped the quaich now clutched in Isabella's free hand. "A little reminder never hurts, though."

She stepped to the side and carefully placed the bark and

the quaich into her reticule. The duke waited patiently while she did and then took her arm to escort her down the crowded pavement. They walked on, turning the corner onto busy Bond Street and moving in the direction of the coffee shop.

His arm was solid under her hand, and the weight of her loaded reticule bumped her hip, both strong reminders that this afternoon had not gone as she thought it would.

Frederica was watching and departed the shop to meet them on the pavement. She didn't look happy, but neither did she look like her time in the coffee shop had been torturous. The duke slid his arm from beneath Isabella's and offered his other one to Frederica. His head was bent as he asked after her health and assured her they would return to the house at whatever pace she wished.

Was it gentlemanly honor or something else spurring his consideration?

As they began to stroll back down Bond Street, Isabella cast a glance back at the coffee shop, where Lieutenant Saunderson had once more taken up his position against the outside wall. His expression held the same shadow of sadness that Frederica's had. Whatever had transpired in that coffee house was not the happy reunion Frederica had hoped for.

As they made their way back to the house, Isabella fell back a couple steps. Not so far as to be walking with the maids, but far enough to distance herself from the strolling couple.

And they were a couple. He hadn't simply offered Frederica his arm. He'd placed his free hand over hers, where it lay against his forearm. Isabella had to consciously shorten her stride as their walk slowed to nearly half the pace it had been coming from the park. Obviously the duke was trying to make the most out of every moment he could get with Frederica.

That was good. It was good that someone in London looked

past her cousin's unfortunate nose and saw how wonderful she was. Someone who was actually willing to do something about it.

Any jealousy Isabella was experiencing could be considered her penance for sinking into a life of deceit. The agony of finding something she could learn to want but never have was nothing more than she deserved.

It was another hour before Isabella managed to get alone with Frederica to learn what had happened at the coffee shop. When they'd returned home, Uncle Percy had still been visiting with Mr. Emerson and cornered them into sharing tea in the drawing room.

But now they were alone and nothing was going to stop Isabella from getting the details.

"Napoleon is back."

That had not been the detail Isabella expected. "Well, that's not very romantic."

Frederica shook her head with a sad smile. "Arthur wrote me. I never got the letters, though. He said that lots of mail never quite seemed to make it back from the war. We both know that any letter that did make it through probably got thrown in the fire by my father."

Isabella opened her mouth to defend Uncle Percy—it wasn't good for a girl to think ill of her father, after all—but this was the same man who had forbidden his daughter from seeing Arthur before, had told her that Arthur had died in battle, and was now using his niece to convince the noblemen of London to cast their votes in a particular direction. No, it wasn't difficult to imagine the man destroying his daughter's letters.

"Arthur was going to come calling." Frederica somehow

looked sad and joyful at the declaration. "He planned to come right through the front door and tell my father how he would be a suitable match for me. But then they learned that Napoleon was back and the Royal Dragoons might have to return to France. He refuses to court me and leave me to mourn a second time."

"You have to admit there's something admirable about that." Isabella sat on the edge of Frederica's bed and wrapped her hands around Frederica's cold fingers. "It shows he cares."

"Does he think I won't mourn him all over again, regardless? Arthur is alive. And should that change, my heart will break all over again." Freddie turned and buried her face into Isabella's shoulder.

Tears pricked Isabella's eyes as well. Love like this, though painful, was beautiful. And Isabella suddenly felt the loss of it, even though she'd never had it.

But could she? Could she stay and try to find someone who could inspire half of the devotion Arthur inspired in Frederica? Perhaps reclaiming her integrity and grasping for love would be worth the gamble. Uncle Percy couldn't truly ruin her family, could he? If she got the money elsewhere, was there really anything he could do? Could she make a man fall in love with her enough to move beyond all the lies and pay her family's debts before her uncle figured out what she was doing?

No, she couldn't do any of those things, because to seek out a man of means would make her as cold and calculating as her uncle. Even if she could bring herself to accept that path, how could she know the man wasn't lying about his circumstances as much as she was?

She felt a dampness seep through her dress to her shoulder and realized that while she'd been wrapped up in her own musings, Frederica's despair had overwhelmed her enough to drive her to tears.

And Isabella could do nothing. Real life held heartbreak, and all the platitudes in the world couldn't keep it at bay. She'd cried buckets when her father first injured his leg, hoping by sheer will and emotion she could help him heal into the man he'd been before the accident. But he hadn't. The leg had healed, but it was weak and crooked and he'd never be able to get around the way he used to. Devastation for a farmer.

"You need sleep." Isabella tilted Frederica's face up and wiped a thumb beneath her cousin's eye. "Why don't you take a nap? If you're not feeling up to the musicale tonight, I'll make your excuses. Uncle Percy won't mind as long as I still attend."

Frederica nodded and gave a watery sniffle before crawling up the bed to bury her face in a pillow.

Isabella slid into bed next to her, telling funny stories about the animals back home and rubbing Frederica's back until the hiccups slid into an easy breathing. She waited a few more moments before rising and slipping out of the room.

Isabella had no illusions that her life would ever hold a passion such as the one she saw in Freddie. She knew all the young men back home. The few who hadn't been scared off by her legendary beauty weren't willing to take on her family situation. It was why she remained unwed at twenty-four.

It was why she hadn't felt like she'd be losing much to give Uncle Percy what he wanted.

The reason seemed so flimsy now.

She stepped into her room, feeling suddenly exhausted and wondering if she should have joined Freddie in taking a nap.

On her dressing table, however, beside the jewelry she'd worn the past two evenings, was a folded letter. Her mother's familiar handwriting scrawled across the front, and Isabella pounced on it with renewed energy. Uncle Percy had assured her parents he would pay the postage on any letter they sent, but considering Uncle Percy had also declared an intent to purchase Isabella a new wardrobe, she hadn't been sure her family would ever take him up on the offer of paying for postage as well. It was quite dear to send a letter from Northumberland to London, after all. But Mother could not have any idea how much money Uncle Percy had already spent on her, and how insignificant the postage for a single letter was in comparison.

The letter contained no news of great import, mostly tales of the same life she'd left behind when Uncle Percy had come to collect her, but every few lines her mother reiterated how much she missed Bella, even though she knew this opportunity was a good one. The close of the letter stabbed Isabella in the heart, though.

Her brother Hugh was considering going to work in the coal mines. They had to face the fact that the farm might not be around for him to inherit, and he was going to need to make his way in the world. Bella knew what he truly wanted was to join the church, but without schooling, without support and recommendations, that wasn't going to happen.

Isabella could make it happen for him, though.

She turned the letter sideways to read the last few lines her mother had scrawled up the side of the page in order to save paper.

My darling, I am so thankful to God for taking you to London. I know you will do well there and I won't have to worry about you anymore. At least one of my children will have a solid future. You have worked so hard. You deserve it. We pray for you every morning. Blessings, Mother.

The letter blurred as Isabella's tears welled up. Whatever thoughts she'd had before, she knew she'd be going to the musicale tonight, smile at the ready, waiting for her uncle to point her toward the next man he expected her to enthrall. Love might be a gamble that could gain her everything she wanted for her and her family, but as the sleeping woman in the next room could attest, it was a gamble that was all too easy to lose.

Chapter 11

Griffith liked order. He liked traditions and routines. He especially liked when those around him followed them, because predictability meant a minimum of surprises. Unlike every attempt he'd made to court Miss St. Claire, which had thus far been one surprise after another.

Never would he have guessed that he'd spend the afternoon strolling more with Miss Breckenridge than Miss St. Claire.

Or that he would enjoy it.

It didn't make sense. Even if Miss St. Claire's affections were already given—something he hadn't seen coming because her name had never been publicly linked with a suitor's—she had to know that marriage was something she needed to do. Since her father had not remarried and produced another heir to the title, Miss St. Claire would be at the mercy of some distant cousin after her father passed. Surely she was too pragmatic to leave her fate up to such questionable circumstances.

Why, then, did his attentions never seem to get him anywhere?

He took a hack—which reminded him why he so often avoided hiring hacks—across Mayfair to Pall Mall. He could have walked the distance, but the hour was approaching when people would start scattering for their evening festivities, and he wanted to catch his sister before she did the same.

And he needed to do it before he lost the nerve.

Ryland's enormous butler, Price, filled the doorway. "Your Grace," he said with a nod of his head. "His Grace isn't available, I'm afraid."

A twitch of the butler's lips drew a smile from Griffith's. This was exactly why the family left titles at the door when they got together. It tended to get a bit ridiculous. "I'm here to see Her Grace."

Price gave in and allowed one side of his mouth to kick up, pulling the scar that ran across his cheek. "Of course, Your Grace." He stepped back to allow Griffith entrance. "Her Grace is in the family drawing room."

Griffith nodded and didn't wait for Price to show him up the stairs. Had Miranda been indisposed, the butler would have directed him to the main drawing room to wait. The fact that he'd done nothing more than wave Griffith into the house meant Miranda was available for visitors or at least available for him.

As he approached the parlor, more than one feminine voice drifted down the passage, making him groan. It wasn't the fact that Miranda was entertaining that distressed him—it was that all of the voices he heard were rather familiar. Were all the feminine members of his family in that room? If so, there'd be no hope of getting Miranda alone. She could have dismissed a stranger or acquaintance, but family was another thing entirely.

He couldn't simply leave either, because Price would take great joy in making sure everyone in the family knew he'd been a coward about facing the ladies. Why couldn't his family have any normal servants?

Griffith stepped into the open doorway of the drawing room and waited for the conversation to quiet.

His sister Miranda, Duchess of Marshington, sat directly across from the door on a sofa covered in deep blue. Her green eyes widened when she noticed him, and a large, welcoming smile alerted the rest of the women.

Georgina sat with her back to the door, while Amelia, Marchioness of Raebourne, sat to Miranda's left in a delicately carved armchair. Trent's wife, Adelaide, finished the circle. At least his mother wasn't present. He had a great respect for the woman who had raised him and taught him how to be a duke, loving the land, the people, and the Lord as much if not more than he loved his country. That didn't mean he wanted to tell his mother about his romantic inclinations.

The urge to come to Miranda had been bad enough.

"Griff! Come sit." Miranda slid to one end of the sofa and patted the upholstered cushion next to her before frowning at the scattering of dishes on the tea tray. "I'm afraid we've finished the tea. Shall I ring for more?"

"Er, no." Griffith coughed as he settled into the seat next to his sister. Ryland's servants were nosy former spies and reformed criminals. He didn't need to call any of them into the vicinity.

"Overwhelmed any young ladies today?" Miranda asked with a cheeky grin.

The back of Griffith's neck felt tight and itchy against his cravat. If he was flushing from that simple statement, he would never make it through this conversation without contracting a full blush. Perhaps if he caught them off guard and shut down their teasing before it really got started he could avoid any outward sign of embarrassment.

"As a matter of fact, I did go visit a lady today. Two, actually." Two? What was he doing bringing Miss Breckenridge into the conversation? He hadn't meant to. She was simply Miss St. Claire's cousin. That was all he would allow her to be.

Otherwise he was afraid she'd become a major thorn in his side.

Miranda clasped her hands in her lap and bounced in her seat until she'd turned nearly sideways on the sofa. Georgina was more refined in her response, but her excited smile and rapt attention were impossible to miss. Even Adelaide and Amelia were intent enough to move their teacups aside and lean forward in their seats.

He really should have waited until he could have gotten Miranda alone.

"I called on Miss St. Claire this afternoon."

Georgina arched a thin eyebrow. Trent was right. The skeptical expression was arrogant and annoying. "To see after her welfare?"

"In part." Griffith adjusted the cuffs of his perfectly tailored coat. "I had arranged to take her for a walk."

Silence crept across the room for several heartbeats. Miranda cleared her throat. "Arranged?"

"Yes." He looked around at the faces displaying various levels of curiosity. "I've been by to visit her twice and tried to greet her at several functions this week, but there were always so many people about. So I contacted her father to make sure she would be available."

He fell silent again as some of the ladies shifted in their seats and two of them gave a series of small coughs. Had he done something wrong? Men went for walks with the women they were courting. He knew this to be true, even if he'd never done it before.

Miranda groaned and sliced a hand through the air palm up. "And was she? Available to go for a walk with you?"

"Of course." Hadn't he just said he arranged it with her father? Griffith looked around the circle, his confidence suddenly bolstered. What was he worried about? If Miss St. Claire wasn't amenable to his suit, she never would have left the house with him. A calm peace allowed his heart rate to quiet and his back to relax farther into the sofa. "She brought her cousin along as well."

Two gasps, a high-pitched "Eeep," and a quickly smothered laugh answered his statement.

Georgina, who had surprisingly been the one trying not to laugh, looked down at her toes to gain composure before meeting his eyes once more. "Maid too?"

"Of course." Griffith frowned. Why wouldn't they bring the maids? His sisters had taken their maids everywhere. "They both brought their maid."

Another round of sighs and groans circled the room.

"Please tell me she didn't turn an ankle. No one can ever effectively fake turning an ankle. They're too afraid of falling to make it look real enough." Amelia shook her head, causing the short brown curls at her neck to slowly sway in commiserating disappointment.

"No. Her strength gave out on Bond Street. She believes she's coming down with an illness and the walk overexerted her." Some of Griffith's earlier peace and confidence began to waver as he looked at four amused female faces. "She fainted on me last week. I should have known her constitution was delicate right now and avoided such a vigorous outing."

Three sets of eyes cast their gaze to the ceiling. Only Adelaide looked a bit sympathetic—probably because she hadn't been with this group of women long enough to become comfortable with censuring a duke. She and Trent had only been married a year, and they'd spent a great deal of that year at their estate in Suffolk.

Her smile was a bit sad as she cleared her throat. "Did she turn back?"

"No," Griffith said slowly, a thread of worry winding its way through his memory of the afternoon. "She asked to rest in a coffee shop."

"Oh." Miranda sat up straighter, eyes wide. "Well, that is good, actually. I've never understood why more courting couples don't go to coffee shops. The conversation is ever so much closer. Did you have a good visit?"

This had been a bad idea. He'd come to get Miranda's advice on how to most quickly win over Miss St. Claire, and instead he was dissecting a mere walk as if it were the latest measure to come before Parliament. "She insisted I continue my walk, actually, and return for her on the way back."

Amelia's head jerked back. "By yourself?"

Georgina wiggled her fingers at the other ladies. "No, no. With the cousin." One side of Georgina's lips tweaked in amusement. "Do remember Miss Breckenridge was there."

Griffith frowned, his thick brows lowering until he could see them in the edges of his vision. "Yes. Miss Breckenridge had been intent on seeing the trees in Berkeley Square, and Miss St. Claire was very distraught at being the reason her cousin would have to wait."

"Trees?" Amelia bit her lips together.

"Are they that remarkable? I've never paid them much attention." Adelaide looked around the room as if she'd missed something.

Miranda snorted. "That's because you're paying too much attention to Trent's ridiculous ice confection from Gunter's whenever you go to the square."

"I didn't know Miss St. Claire had that in her. Brava." Georgina gave three slow claps. "Rather clever workings for someone I've always thought a bit light in the head."

"Georgina, that's a terrible thing to say," Amelia cried. Then she bit her lip. "Griffith is a wonderful man, but if her affections are elsewhere . . ."

"Griffith is a duke," Georgina responded, "and if her affections lie elsewhere, the man has been deplorably slow in returning them and she needs to secure herself another future post haste."

Griffith cleared his throat. "I believe there was an officer. He died in the war."

Miranda swung her head around to stare at him with open mouth. "And you wish to compete with the memory of a dead man? My dear brother, I'm not sure even your perfect ducalness can overcome that."

"Ducalness isn't a word," Adelaide murmured.

"Everyone knew what I meant, though, so it should count." Miranda sniffed. "Besides, making up words should be a duchess's privilege."

Georgina frowned. "You don't get to declare duchess privilege just to get out of admitting you're wrong."

"I'm happy to admit I'm wrong. Ducalness is not a word." Miranda crossed her arms. "But it should be."

"I think Griffith is more interested in peace and practicality." Adelaide cocked her head to the side, her enormous blue eyes seeming to stare straight through Griffith from behind her spectacles. "I would think that of her as well, which makes the push toward the cousin interesting. Especially considering how much attention Miss Breckenridge has already garnered."

"Her collection does not yet include a duke," Amelia pointed out.

Miranda was shaking her head so hard the sofa shifted. "Griffith is absolutely looking for love over peace and practicality. He wouldn't dare break with family tradition on this one."

Griffith looked around the group as Georgina and Miranda

fell into an argument about the merits of love matches over practical ones, ironic given that Georgina's marriage was the most impractical one in the room. When had he lost control of the situation? Had he ever had it? He now had a better understanding of Ryland's insistence on always being somewhere other than the house on Tuesday afternoons, when the ladies traditionally gathered for tea whenever they were all in Town. Apparently they didn't limit themselves to Tuesdays. If only they were as committed to tradition and routine as Griffith was, he would be having a quiet conversation with Miranda instead of watching the downward spiral of his family's composure.

"Just because you're jealous doesn't mean she's mercenary." Miranda leaned forward to toss the verbal dagger at her sister.

Amelia and Adelaide sat silent, looking back and forth at the sisters as the verbal battle waged.

"I've nothing to be jealous of, Miranda. And I only said the fortune of her beauty increased the chances of her being mercenary. She asked Griffith to take her to see trees!"

Griffith cleared his throat. "Her interest in the trees was quite genuine."

All eyes in the room turned his way as if the ladies had forgotten he was there. Miranda often told him he was the size of a mountain, so he was rather amazed at the possibility.

Now that he had their rapt attention, he felt the need to defend his statement and defend Miss Breckenridge. "She took a piece of the bark home."

More staring, with an occasional quizzical glance at their own fingers.

Griffith shifted in his seat. "I pulled it off for her."

A slow smile stretched across Georgina's lips. "You like her."

Miranda narrowed her eyes and leaned in, as if she could smell the truth in his cologne. "You do."

The women in his family had lost their collective minds. He had to get this conversation back on course. "Yes, I like Miss St. Claire. However, while I had intended to conduct this courtship via casual outings, she is obviously of too delicate a condition for such a plan, so I was hoping you would have suggestions for how I could make this courtship happen in a method that is both expedient and effective."

An uncomfortable moment of silence ensued, and Griffith feared the women had no intention of following his conversational lead. Finally, Miranda cleared her throat.

"You approached her at a ball and she fainted—correct?" Miranda held up a single finger as if she were preparing to count.

Amelia nodded. "It was authentic. I was there. Miss Breckenridge assisted Griffith with getting Miss St. Claire out of the room."

Miranda held up a second finger. "And you went to her house?"

"Er, yes." Griffith shifted. "I had tea with her and Miss Breckenridge until she left to go see about finding me a cinnamon biscuit from the kitchens."

"I saw you both at Mrs. Crenshaw's card party. You sat down to whist with her." Adelaide sat a bit taller with a smile, as if she was glad to be helping. Then her lips fell into a frown. "But then she pled a headache and Miss Breckenridge took her place."

"Yes." Griffith rubbed his finger along his thumb, knowing this was why they only allowed men in Parliament. The women were rehashing everything but being of no help whatsoever.

"My first suggestion would be that you ask Miss Breckenridge to dance," Georgina said with a lift of one shoulder.

Adelaide came to Griffith's rescue by asking the question he didn't really want to voice. "How would that help him woo Miss St. Claire?"

"It wouldn't." Miranda scoffed.

"No, but it would declare his intentions toward Miss Breck-enridge, and many of her horde of admirers would scatter. Not all, of course, but enough to make them less of a nuisance. As we have already stated, Griffith is a duke, and most men aren't going to want to compete with such a quality."

Griffith sighed. "But I don't want to woo Miss Breckenridge."

"Yes, you do," four voices said at the same time.

"Dismissing part of the crowd should give you enough time to come to that conclusion yourself." Georgina used a finger to pick through the biscuits remaining on a small plate before selecting a ginger one.

"You might as well," Miranda said, snagging one of the biscuits Georgina had passed on. "Unless you've decided you actually do want a loveless marriage. Because Miss St. Claire is most certainly not interested."

⁓

The hinges of her bedchamber door emitted a soft squeak, pulling Isabella from the edges of sleep. A light rustling preceded a dip in the mattress, and Isabella shifted to the side to allow Frederica to snuggle in under the covers.

"I didn't get a chance to ask you earlier." Freddie angled her body so their heads shared a pillow, just like they'd done on those summer nights so many years ago. "How were the trees?"

Bella laughed and turned on her side to face Freddie. Sleep still tugged at her consciousness but she didn't want to miss these precious moments. Everything had been so strained since she came to London, but here, in the dark, she could pretend she was home, that things had never gone wrong.

"The trees were nice," Bella murmured sleepily. She gave a tired laugh. "The company was nice too."

"Handsome."

Bella smiled as her eyes drifted shut. "Yes."

Sleep had almost taken Isabella when Frederica spoke up once more. "Do you ever wonder?"

"Wonder what?" Isabella turned her head and yawned into the pillow. She was managing to stay awake, but opening her eyes again was impossible.

"What it would have been like? If things had been different? If this were really your first Season, our first Season?"

When they'd been thirteen they started making plans, dreaming of spending their first Season together. Isabella hadn't thought of those late-night conversations in years. Life had taken those dreams and blown them away like so much dust, trampling them under the death of Freddie's mother and brother and her father's subsequent refusal to allow her to visit a remote area without access to proper medical care. Burying them under a rock slide so much like the one that had crushed Isabella's father's leg.

"We'd have danced."

Frederica sighed. "You would have, anyway. And we'd have spent nights just like this, talking about all the men we'd met and whether or not they were worthy of our attentions."

Isabella eased one eyelid open, seeing for the first time what she'd never seen in Freddie's letters. She had been lonely. No one had taken the place of confidante that Isabella was supposed to have held.

"Lord Vernham trips over his feet whenever he has to cross the square in a quadrille."

Freddie's head jerked to face Isabella. "He does not."

Isabella nodded and snuggled deeper into the covers, cocooning their heads like they'd done as children. "Not always when he has to go left, but every time he has to go right. He trips."

"I heard Lord Ivonbrook has the breath of a horse, but I've

never been close enough to him to verify. Is it true?" Freddie's wide smile was interrupted by a yawn of her own.

Isabella laughed as her eyes slid shut once more. She wasn't going to be able to hold off sleep much longer. "Absolutely not. Or if he does, he uses tooth powder liberally to mask it. No, I'm afraid his physical appeal is genuine and thorough."

"Is he the most handsome man you've danced with?"

"I don't know." Isabella sighed. "I try not to think about it. What about you? Who is the most handsome man you've ever danced with?"

Silence fell between them for a moment. Long enough for the darkness to creep along the edges of Isabella's mind.

"Lord Trent Hawthorne danced with me once," Freddie said quietly. "Before he was married, of course. He was nice too."

"Handsome and nice," Isabella mumbled. "A dangerous and rare combination."

One his brother shared. She couldn't imagine any of the other men taking a woman they hadn't intended to go walking with on an outing to see trees. But the duke hadn't made her feel like an interloper or an obligation, even though he had to find the whole thing frustrating.

"I probably should have said Arthur, shouldn't I?" Freddie grumbled.

"I won't tell if you won't," Bella whispered, thankful her cousin had interrupted Bella's line of thinking. "Good night, Freddie."

"Good night, Bella."

Isabella drifted off to sleep, snuggled close to her cousin, dreaming they were running through the fields of Northumberland once more, with Arthur, the duke, and an enormous purple hedgehog running alongside.

Chapter 12

The days fell into a routine. Eventually Isabella stopped trying to remember what day it was or how long she'd been away from home. When things got too bad, she'd slip into Frederica's bed at night, talking nonsense about the day or sharing memories from simpler years. Over the past four weeks they'd come to know each other as they never could have when they were younger.

They developed secret signals to save each other from intolerable situations at parties and balls. Of course, Isabella never used hers, due to the fact that every situation was currently uncomfortable, but Freddie called on Isabella when she was trying to avoid the Duke of Riverton without appearing obvious about it, while at the same time trying to use him as a distraction for Uncle Percy so she could visit with a reluctant but cooperative Arthur.

While those weeks had brought peace to Freddie and Bella's friendship, they had brought agitation to Uncle Percy. The debates were dragging on longer than he'd anticipated. Raised voices coming from his study had become a regular occurrence, though Isabella had never heard him quite as unhappy as he seemed now, as she made her way down the corridor to take the stairs down to breakfast.

He hadn't even been this loud when Mr. Emerson brought word that the College of Physicians had stepped in and required more changes to the Apothecary Act, delaying the vote even more. Last week Uncle Percy had been forced to spread yet another enticing lie about Isabella to keep the men from sending their attentions elsewhere. Isabella wasn't entirely sure what the lie had been, but it had something to do with a lucrative mine on a piece of dowry property. While his other lies had been twists and stretches of the truth, this one had been an outright fabrication.

The masses of men had eaten it up like ambrosia.

Isabella continued toward the stairs, trying not to listen to the yelling from the study. When the door flew open, though, and a footman scurried through it, there was no missing the words ". . . worthless half-Scot can't even do this right."

The footman saw Isabella in the corridor and gave her a look of sympathy before he charged on down the passage.

Whatever her uncle was yelling about obviously had to do with her.

"And those worthless physicians think they can have whatever they want. Obviously they aren't seeing what really needs to be done here! Sacrifices must be made for the greater good."

Well, at least that part of it had nothing to do with her.

She continued down the stairs, trying not to care. She was doing exactly what Uncle Percy had asked of her. It wasn't her fault that the process was taking too long.

In the breakfast room, the sympathetic glances continued. Coming from Frederica, though, it caused a lot more concern.

"What has happened?"

Freddie frowned. "A lot of nonsense, if you ask me. Jealousy is the cause, I'm certain."

"The cause of what?" Isabella filled her plate in slow methodical movements.

"The papers." Freddie held up a sheet and waved it in the air. "Haven't you seen them?"

Isabella sat at the table and reached for the paper in Frederica's hand. "And how could I have seen them if they're down here? Snuck down and looked at them before dressing? I'm sorry to tell you I don't care what's going on in London society enough to do that."

"Well, that's good." Freddie snatched the paper back. "You can just continue not caring, then."

Now Isabella really wanted to know what was on that paper. As much as she hated to admit it, her curiosity could be piqued as well as anyone's, and after four weeks in London, she was fast learning that no one knew how to pique curiosity like the cream of English society. It was as if they had nothing better to do than try to make everyone else wonder what they knew.

And drat it all, it was working.

She snatched the paper back and turned so that Frederica couldn't reach it again.

The first article in the society column was about Isabella. And it wasn't very nice.

"A mystical coquette sent to London to fell the men not caught in Napoleon's cannon fire?" Isabella looked up. "That's rather harsh."

Frederica nodded toward another paper on the table. "That one says you are the bane of every mother of an unwed daughter."

Isabella winced.

"And there's a comic in that one that shows you dangling five men by puppet strings in front of St. George's."

"Truly?" Isabella dug through the papers to find the comic. That sounded like it might actually be funny.

141

She found it and snickered. The drawing of her was very flattering, but then again, her ridiculously fashionable and symmetrical features were what had gotten her in this position in the first place. The men in the puppet strings looked besotted, while the parson standing to the side of a columned façade was trying to placate a horde of crying girls in white gowns.

A giggle bubbled out of Isabella's lips, a bit of panic making it sound brassy to her own ears. It was actually quite funny, if one looked at it from an objective standpoint. Of course, she wasn't objective, and the idea that she was affecting so many people was distressing, as was the fact that until recently they hadn't even really been people in her mind.

"What could you possibly find amusing?" Uncle Percy stormed in and began banging plates around as he fixed his breakfast. "If this nonsense continues, we won't be able to convince them it's in their best interest to be on my good side."

Isabella set the paper down carefully, trying to contain her irritation at her uncle. "And how many men have you promised my hand to in return for a vote?"

"None. At least not in so many words." He dropped into a chair. "Nonsense, I tell you."

"It's rather odd, don't you think, that they've all decided to print such a story on the same day? I've been moving about in society with my—" she glanced down at the paper to make sure she got the wording correct—"'brood of besotted admirers' for weeks. Why now?"

Uncle Percy stabbed his fork into a potato and left it standing there while he pointed a thick finger in her direction. "Because you reached too far. I told you to leave the duke alone. But you had to commandeer his attention last night."

"I did no such thing." Except she had. Sort of.

"Isabella was trying to help me." Frederica shuffled the papers around, bringing them into something of a stack. "I'm afraid I get a bit tongue-tied around the duke, and I know how much you want to . . . to—" she glanced in Isabella's direction—"secure his cooperation."

"If you wish to retain the duke's attention—and you would be wise to do so—you should stay far away from your cousin." He retrieved his fork and pointed it in Isabella's direction. "And if you don't want your admirers to scatter, you'd best stay far away from the duke. No one wants competition the likes of him."

She would love to have stayed far away from the duke, but she couldn't bear to see Frederica suffer under his attentions. And she was suffering. Trying to have any sort of flirtation with the duke when she knew Arthur was alive and in London was driving Frederica to Bedlam. She could think of nothing to say to the duke aside from asking after his family, and in the unfortunate incident last evening, she'd snagged Isabella to save her from a conversation about the quality of his shoes.

"I spoke to him briefly last night. Surely that was not enough to elicit such a response." The truth was she'd spoken to him for much longer periods at other events since their strange walk through the park trees. Twice she'd distracted the duke so that Frederica could slip out and see Arthur in the gardens outside the home hosting the evening's event. And on one very memorable occasion she'd sought a dark corner for a moment's reprieve only to find the corner had already been occupied by the duke.

She'd meant to leave right away but somehow found herself staying through half a dance set, discussing nothing of more importance than the ratio of green dresses to blue and how even together they couldn't compare to the number of white ones.

"I've heard rumors of your being called a coquette at the

club, but this is the first it's been in print." He stabbed a piece of ham. "You'll have to be more careful."

Isabella choked on air. *She* would have to be more careful? What would he have her do? And were people really referring to her as a coquette outside of the papers? Guilt crept up her neck and whispered in her ear that she had no right to be outraged by such an accusation when she was, in fact, being the very definition of a coquette by flirting with such a number of men but not allowing anything further to develop.

She stabbed at the food on her plate. Just because she was one didn't mean she liked having it pointed out. And it wasn't as if she'd chosen such a role. Well, she had, but only because there'd been no other choice.

The little voice in her ear whispered again that she'd known it was the wrong choice to make even as she'd quietly agreed to her uncle's scheme. As she'd pretended her mother's excitement was her own, that her uncle's invitation was exactly what she'd been waiting for. Her mother was expecting Isabella to secure her future this Season, and she would. Just not in the way Mother expected.

Not in the way that was right.

She slumped in her chair, wishing her parents hadn't spent so much time drilling Bible verses into her head while growing up. Despite the fact that she hadn't opened the book since coming to London, she kept remembering verses about trusting God and having an upright heart. Not in detail, but in small snatches and phrases. Enough to remember the basics of what the Bible said.

It hurt more than a little to go against the teaching, knowing she was disappointing not only her parents but God as well.

But God wasn't on the verge of losing His home, and He wasn't there to help shear the sheep or assess which ones should be slaughtered or sold. She hadn't seen Him come down and miraculously heal her father so that he could take care of all of those things. And by the time her parents found out what Isabella was actually doing, they'd be too happy about the outcome to be mad at the method.

"I won't marry him, Father!"

Isabella broke out of her reverie to discover the conversation had continued without her.

"You'll marry him if I say you will!" Uncle Percy banged on the table.

The sound seemed to echo repeatedly through the house until everyone realized someone was knocking on the front door.

In silent agreement, the argument stopped. No matter that they'd probably been heard by all the servants and one or two neighbors—now that someone else was in the house, they were going to be on their best behavior.

Eating stopped.

They all turned to watch the door to the breakfast room.

And then chaos erupted.

"You! Who gave you leave to enter this house?"

"Arthur! Whyever did you come? I thought we agreed."

"You agreed? You've been seeing him? When?"

Arthur Saunderson stepped into the room, his light brown hair pulled back into a queue at his neck, emphasizing his deep-set eyes and long, narrow nose. Some part of Isabella's mind—the part that wished she could be removed from the scene, most likely—had a vague pang of sympathy for any children Frederica and Arthur would have. They were rather doomed when it came to prominent facial features.

Arthur's lips pressed together, and he took a deep, chest-raising breath through his nose. "I couldn't wait any longer, Freddie. He's bound to learn I'm in London sooner or later."

"Please hear him out, Father." Frederica clasped her hands together at her throat.

Uncle Percy jabbed a finger in Arthur's direction. "You aren't supposed to be in London. You're supposed to be dead."

And that declaration was enough to bring all the tongues to a halt.

"Well," Arthur said quietly, shifting to stand at attention. "I'm not."

"I see that."

No one said anything as Uncle Percy tucked back into his breakfast.

Freddie stood and slid around the table. "Would you like some breakfast?"

"No he would not." Uncle Percy looked up with a frown. "He's already departed."

"Not until you hear me out, my lord." Arthur cleared his throat. "I love your daughter, sir. And I'm a lieutenant now. I can provide for her."

He frowned. "She doesn't need you. She's got a duke near to offering for her."

"I don't want the duke. And he's nowhere nearer to offering for me than the prince himself."

Arthur cleared his throat. "Darling, the prince regent is married."

She arched one eyebrow. "Then he won't be offering for me, will he?"

"And what happens when you run off to war again?" Uncle Percy slammed his fork down, his eyes wide and a bit frightening, deep grooves bracketing his mouth like arrows to his pointed chin. "She ends up right back in the house—only she'd be no use to me then, bringing along a passel of children and noise to disrupt my life. That's assuming she doesn't follow you off to war and get herself killed because the men who pass for doctors there are more interested in hacking off body parts than practicing medicine."

Frederica frowned. "The war won't go on forever, Father."

He grunted. "We've been at war with someone my entire life, girl. Trust me. He'll be away more often than not."

"Then Isabella will marry the duke and I'll go live with her."

Isabella nearly groaned at being hauled into the mess.

The idea nearly sent Uncle Percy over the edge. His sanity looked to be a very tenuous thing. "She will do no such thing! She will be returning home to that forsaken sheep farm where they will all probably die of some dread disease because they have nothing but an apothecary to help them."

They didn't even have one of those in her actual village, but Isabella found herself wishing she could return to that forsaken farm sooner rather than later.

The butler stepped back into the room. "My lord?"

"What?" Uncle Percy banged a fist on the table, causing the dishes to jump and tea to slosh out of his untouched cup.

Osborn cleared his throat and extended a thick white envelope. "This just arrived. Delivered personally by the Earl of Blackstone's footman."

Finally, something that would distract her uncle. Whatever was in that letter, Isabella hoped it was good. They couldn't take any more distressing news this morning.

The smile that crept across his face, though, didn't bring Isabella any comfort. It made her stomach threaten to abandon what little breakfast she'd eaten.

"Leave us, *Lieutenant* Saunderson. Napoleon didn't stay put, and neither will you. I'll not talk to you now." He knocked the stiff parchment in his hand against the table and stared down the soldier.

Eventually, at Frederica's pleading, Arthur left with a promise to return soon.

Uncle Percy's smile didn't dim as they listened to Arthur's footsteps fade away. He ran a finger lovingly along the top of the parchment. "Girls, you are to pack your bags. We're leaving London for a while."

Chapter 13

"You are my brother, and I love you."

Griffith looked up from the ledger on his desk to see Miranda standing in the doorway of his study. "Thank you?"

She released a sigh and rolled her shoulders back. "Of course."

He rolled his quill in his fingertips, waiting for her to continue. It wasn't a very taxing trip from her house to his, but there didn't seem to be much reason for her to make such a trip in order to tell him something he already knew, even though they rarely mentioned it. "Is that all?"

"No. Mother isn't going to be happy that I'm doing this, but you don't deserve to be ambushed on a blind side."

"What are you talking about?" Griffith set his quill aside and stood as Miranda took a step into the room. The idea that his mother was hiding something disturbed him. She'd been honest to a fault with him since his father had died. What could possibly be so horrible that she would try to protect him from it now? "What is wrong?"

Miranda's eyes widened. "Oh! I didn't mean for you to

149

think anything was wrong. It's nothing like that. You're giving a party."

Years of practice kept Griffith's face devoid of surprise. As a young duke he'd learned early on that people would try to shock him into action or make him think he didn't know enough. Now he mulled over Miranda's statement in his mind, looking at it from every angle.

It still didn't make any sense.

"Are you well, Miranda? Is the baby making you ill?"

"Yes, a little. Mostly in the afternoons, though, which is rather convenient, when you think about it."

Griffith didn't want to think about it. He really didn't. With a gentle hand he guided Miranda to one of the chairs near the fireplace.

His lack of response, however, didn't deter her from going into detail about how the midday malady allowed her to accomplish her morning tasks and still go out in the evenings, for at least a little while longer.

Ryland entered without knocking. "Did she tell you? I've already made arrangements for us to stay with Anthony and Amelia. I'll not have her becoming overtired by a misplaced sense of responsibility for this event. We'll travel back and forth as needed."

"He, however"—Miranda pointed one angry finger at her husband while rubbing her other hand over her middle—"is very inconvenient. There is no reason why I cannot help Mother."

"Aside from the fact that she doesn't want your help."

"If I don't help she'll have him tied to a chair in the drawing room while the ladies take turns passing through for inspection."

Griffith liked to think he could normally determine what was going on with only a portion of the information, but this was something he couldn't quite follow.

Mother was giving a party, apparently, although Miranda had first said that Griffith was giving one. It had something to do with him, though, because Miranda was concerned for his well-being, and Ryland seemed to be in at least a bit of agreement.

"Whatever Mother is planning"—Griffith kept his voice even and slow, like when he talked to the animals at his estate—"I'm afraid I cannot be a part of it. I need to take a short trip back to Riverton. I shall be gone but a week. We can return to looking at this situation then."

With any luck they'd have all regained their senses and learned how to actually deliver a piece of apparently important news.

Ryland looked at his wife. "I thought you said you told him."

"I did!" She shifted in her chair. "But then we started talking about the baby."

The smile Ryland gave her as he brushed a hand through the curls at the back of Miranda's neck made Griffith feel intrusive. Should he be witness to such an obvious gesture of love? He never remembered his father giving his mother little touches, but he did recall the shared smiles.

Ryland's attention soon turned back to Griffith. "You're having a party."

"So Miranda said."

"Your mother has sent out the invitations. In some cases she's delivered them personally."

A heavy lump began to form in Griffith's throat. His quiet week at Riverton, his plan to find a way to think and pray through everything, was in definite danger. "The party is at Riverton?"

"Yes."

Griffith turned to his sister. "And she wasn't going to tell me?"

Miranda shook her head. "No. She didn't want to give you a chance to tell her otherwise. She already has a speech prepared for your argument that she has her own house in which to throw a party. There's even an answer if you are bold enough to tell her she's no longer mistress of Riverton."

"She isn't mistress of Riverton. No one is."

"Tell that to Mother."

As much as Griffith wanted to, they all knew he wouldn't. His mother had been encouraging him to host a house party in the country for years, claiming it was the fastest, easiest way to cull the best of the lot.

In the past the excuse had been to find husbands for his sisters. Now that everyone else was settled, the intent could only be his own matrimonial bliss.

"How many ladies has she invited?"

"At least a dozen. She wouldn't let me hold the list, but I did spy Miss St. Claire's name." Miranda paused a moment before grinning like the impish younger sister she was. "And Miss Breckenridge's."

She could tease him all she wanted. He wasn't worried on that front. "Miss Breckenridge would never tear herself away from all of her suitors to retire to the country for a week."

Miranda scoffed. "She will if it will land her cousin a duke."

Ryland leaned on the back of Miranda's chair and pierced Griffith with his grey gaze until Griffith wanted to punch the duke in the face just to get him to stop. "You could stop your mother easily enough, you know. Just ask Miss St. Claire to marry you. You've already decided it's going to be her."

The solution was as simple as Ryland stated, but Griffith found himself struggling to muster the same enthusiasm he'd had for the match at the beginning of the Season. That, more than anything, caused his heart to beat against his chest. Griffith never changed his mind. That was why he always thought his decisions through so carefully. Why didn't he want to march over to Lord Pontebrook's house and ask for Miss St. Claire's hand?

"No, this is good."

Neither of his guests looked shocked. Miranda smiled indulgently while Ryland merely twitched an eyebrow.

Griffith cleared his throat and continued. "I spend a lot of time at Riverton. It is best that Miss St. Claire see the house and how things get along there so she can best know what I am asking of her."

The excuse sounded good. Sort of. If he'd said it to anyone else he wouldn't be worried about it, but Ryland was capable of dissecting a statement as well as Griffith did. Probably better.

"A test of sorts," Ryland said softly. "To ensure her suitability."

"Yes." Griffith gave a single nod. "That's it precisely."

"Because you might change your mind."

Griffith said nothing. There was absolutely nothing he could say that wouldn't make the situation worse. "I must go tell my valet to pack some of my nicer evening clothes for the trip. Excuse me."

He bowed his head at his sister and her husband and then left the room in a measured pace that was at odds with his racing heart and the desperate need to breathe.

Praise God and all that was holy, perhaps Isabella hadn't been abandoned after all. There was no way to describe a sudden trip to the country other than as a blessing. Even if she had to spend the whole time avoiding the Duke of Riverton. Not that she wouldn't have avoided him anyway—interacting with the duke always left her feeling despondent—but her uncle had very nearly demanded it.

The carriage rocked as it turned from the road onto the long drive through the grounds of Riverton. She hadn't known what to make of the invitation to the duke's house party—or rather Lady Blackstone's house party at the duke's estate—other than the fact that its timing had been perfect.

"It looks like it might rain." Uncle Percy nearly clapped his hands in glee as he pressed closer to the window and looked up at the sky. "We'll be forced to stay indoors and converse. I should be able to convince at least two or three men of the merits of voting for the apothecary law."

Unless any of them had actually been helped by an apothecary. Knowing how much the people in her own village depended on the local apothecary—even though he lived in a village three miles distant—made Isabella a bit uneasy. The closest doctor was another six miles down the road from the apothecary. What would happen to the people of her village when this measure passed? And why hadn't she considered that aspect before? True, her aunt and cousin had died because of an apothecary's misdiagnosis, but couldn't a trained physician have made the same mistake?

She turned from her view out the other side of the carriage. "I thought you said none of the men would be here. You specifically told me I was to remain inconspicuous this week."

"These are married men. Come to get away from the stress of the city." Uncle Percy straightened his waistcoat. "You keep to your rooms and make your excuses. Frederica will have the duke well in hand, and there's no one else you need to bring to heel."

Isabella glanced at Frederica, who grimaced at the mention of the duke. She had to know that was why they'd been invited. The party was a thinly veiled attempt on his mother's part to see him finally wed.

"I don't want to have the duke well in hand," Frederica said quietly.

Isabella had to applaud the will of determination. Freddie seemed to have grown bolder since the fight between her father and Arthur, but it was making Isabella's life difficult. The more aggravated Uncle Percy got, the more demanding he became. And his bad mood only meant more demands on Isabella.

"You'd throw a nearly guaranteed future as a duchess away for what—a muddy tent, following around a bunch of soldiers? He's in the cavalry. He'll have to spend more money on the horse than he does on you." Uncle Percy looked as if he wanted to spit, but he'd rented the carriage they were riding in, and he wouldn't risk damaging anything. "You'll do as I say and entertain the duke this week."

Frederica set her mouth in a line and crossed her arms, but she didn't say anything. Isabella knew that wasn't an agreement, but her uncle seemed to take it that way, because he relaxed and rubbed his hands together while nodding.

"This is good," her uncle continued. "Frederica will have a week with the duke and you will disappear. A few days away from London, everyone having to do without your presence— that should put all those coquettish rumors to rest when they're knocked on their backsides once more by your beauty."

He frowned at her, glaring. "Take care not to get too much sun. I won't have you going back to town all tan and country."

"I thought you said it was going to rain," Isabella mumbled.

His eyes narrowed. "What did you say?"

She tightened her face into a smile that hurt everything from her forehead to her chin with its falseness. "I brought three books, so it should be easy to occupy myself away from the party."

It would be refreshing, if she were honest. Especially if she could sneak out of the house and go for a walk every day. Alone. Just her and the sunshine and the grass and the trees. Would the duke's lands carry the same scent as he did, that woodsy, earthy scent? She shook her head to clear the thought.

As they rounded a corner in the lane, Riverton came into view.

Air left Isabella's lungs in a rush as her mouth dropped open a bit at the beauty of the house before her. Behind an elaborate wrought-iron gate, intricately carved spires reached for the sky as the evening sun hit the rows of windows in a sea of sparkling, dancing lights. The closer they got to the house, the more detailed the carvings on the side became and the more house she could see. It stretched on in a series of turrets and alcoves until it gave way to the rolling lawns and decorative gardens.

It was glorious. She could certainly stand to spend a few days wandering around the grounds admiring the house from every possible angle.

They were greeted by a smiling Lady Blackstone and a grim-looking duke.

"We are so very glad you could make arrangements to leave London on such short notice." Lady Blackstone turned a serene gaze on her son.

Isabella had only encountered the countess a handful of times since coming to London, but all of those encounters had left Isabella feeling the slightest bit frightened of the woman. In a room of calm and collected people, Lady Blackstone seemed the most contained, yet she also seemed dangerous. The depth of her gaze indicated she was simply waiting for the right time to strike.

Even now, without a glare or a grimace, she seemed to be pulling her son, who had to weigh at least twice as much as she did, into line.

The grimace cleared from the duke's face, and he nodded his

head in a welcoming bow. "Welcome to Riverton. Enjoy your stay. We've readied rooms for you. The maid will show the ladies to their room. Feel free to rest and freshen up. We will have a late dinner to accommodate all of the travelers. My lord, there are men in the library, if you wish to join them."

Isabella was glad to leave both Uncle Percy and the nerve-racking duke behind as she and Frederica were led up the stairs and through rooms and passages, each more exquisite than the last. Wide corridors flanked with decorative tables and charming paintings were also lined with doors into clusters of bedchambers. It seemed the entire passage was bedchambers.

The room they were finally left in was draped in sumptuous, gold-colored fabrics. Pale yellow silk covered the walls, while a deep-gold brocade nestled behind gilded hooks on either side of the large window. Sheer curtains surrounded the bed, and paintings of angels covered the ceiling.

Frederica collapsed facedown onto the bed, her deep green traveling skirt billowing halfway up to her knees. "I hate traveling."

"You love traveling." Isabella crossed to the window and threw it open. The short burst of fresh country air she'd gotten between the carriage and the front door hadn't been enough. "You hate leaving Arthur."

Freddie propped her head on her fist. "You speak the truth."

Isabella leaned out the window and took a deep breath. "It's lovely. Isn't it?"

"Yes." Frederica looked around the room. "But are you really going to stay in here all week? Won't you get bored?"

Her cousin had a valid point. Isabella was going to see much too much of these golden walls over the next few days to stay cooped up here when it wasn't absolutely necessary. "I believe I shall see a bit of the house now, before the party truly starts.

The duke is occupied and the other women will be resting in their rooms, so I won't run into anyone."

Freddie cupped one hand across her mouth to cover a large yawn. "Do you want me to come with you?"

The offer made Isabella smile. "No. You rest. I'll retire early tonight, whereas you will have the responsibility of keeping the duke well in hand."

The frown that accompanied Frederica's stuck-out tongue was refreshing. Bella had missed the old Freddie—before she'd become worried and maudlin over the situation with Arthur.

Isabella left the room and made her way quietly down the passage. The house was beautiful. No matter where she turned, she saw another place where careful attention had been paid to details. A bird carved into the underside of a banister. A table angled into a corner so that the gilded vase caught the sun from a nearby window.

Whenever she heard voices, she turned the other way. She hadn't been alone in nearly a month. Hadn't been able to move without thinking about how her expression looked to other people, how flattering her posture was, whether the appropriate people were positioned to notice her. Her uncle's demand that she make herself scarce had, in truth, been a blessing, giving her permission to do as she wanted and hide away from everyone for a few days.

She turned the corner and gasped at the long gallery before her. Windows draped with sheer fabric lined one wall, letting the sunlight in without making the long room too bright and harsh to enjoy. Artwork covered the other walls. Brilliant tapestries flanked the doors on either end of the room. A glance at the one nearest her showed a large cross surrounded by blue-robed saints and holy artifacts. She'd have to find her way back here later in the week to examine it more closely, because it didn't come close to holding her attention right then.

Not considering the large figure standing perfectly still half-way down the room.

"I thought you were greeting guests," she said as she walked slowly toward him. She should leave. Not only because he'd obviously come seeking solitude but because he was the one man she'd met who made it hard to remember her goal. And here, away from the noise and pollution, it was even harder.

"We have people watching the road from London. They'll let us know when someone is coming." The duke stood with his legs braced and his hands at his back. In the large, high-ceilinged room he looked almost normal. The undeniable but understated elegance of the room seemed to suit him. Despite the simplicity of his outfit, he looked polished, dignified. It made her wish she'd taken the time to clean up and change out of her dust-covered light-brown traveling clothes.

When she was still more than an arm's length away from him, Isabella turned to see what he was looking at. Portraits marched across the middle section of the gallery wall. Large and powerful men dominated the settings they'd been put in. One stood in front of a glorious brown steed, his foot propped on a tree stump. Another sat in a throne-like chair, a chessboard at his right elbow. On and on it went, with enough remarkable family resemblance that there was no doubt she was looking at the previous Dukes of Riverton.

The painting in front of the current duke was different. It was a family portrait. A man with a Bible tucked against his side stood behind a younger version of Lady Blackstone, sitting on a swing with a small child in her lap. At her feet sat a young boy and a dog, while behind her other shoulder stood an older boy, one who was undoubtedly the current duke. He couldn't have been ten years old yet, but he already stood tall and proud.

"We have a portrait of him alone," the duke said. "It's hanging in the study. He had this one commissioned at the same time for this space, saying he'd rather leave this as his legacy than anything else."

Isabella thought of her own father, of the farm he'd worked so hard to make successful, of the way no matter what troubles the day had brought, the evening was always about family and faith. "It's a lovely family."

They stood for a few moments. The silence was pressing but not uncomfortable. Like a blanket that makes one feel protected on a cold night. Isabella nodded in the direction of the wall beyond the painting, where intricate scrollwork and large, ornate carvings took up space. "And is there a portrait of you somewhere?"

His eyes cut in her direction and one side of his mouth quirked upward. "A small one. In the study alongside my father. I've promised my mother I'll stand for a larger one when I reach the age of thirty."

Isabella took a step closer. The conversation felt too private, too intimate to have such a large space between them. "And will you do as your father did? Include your family in the painting?"

The question brought her an unexpected pang of hurt. She didn't know the duke that well, but what she did know was that he was a good man. A man she could respect. The kind of man she really hadn't expected to meet in London. She would never have thought that an aristocrat could draw her like he did, and it caught her off guard, leaving her vulnerable but unable to resist the pull.

"No." His voice was quiet but resigned. "Family is important, and I will pass that legacy along to my children. Perhaps my father had an idea that he would die young, that my mother would have to teach me everything he could not. But one thing

I learned at an early age, that I will make sure my son under-stands, is that at the end of the day the duke stands alone."

Before she could stop herself, one hand lifted and rested against his elbow. "That sounds lonely."

He glanced at her and then her hand before turning back to the portrait. "It can be. But that doesn't change how it is."

"Perhaps it will change when you marry." Isabella flushed at the whispered words. Would he think she was flirting? That she was asking for the position?

He turned to face her, the movement forcing her to drop the hand she should have pulled back to her side ages ago. "I hadn't thought it would, but now . . ."

Their eyes met as his words drifted into nothing, their implications floating on the air if she wanted to reach for them.

She didn't. If she did, she might start to think things she couldn't afford to think.

"It should, I think." She swallowed and nodded toward the portrait. "Your father thought it did."

The duke turned his head to look at the painting again. "So he did."

His green eyes slid back in her direction. "And what about you?"

"Me?" Was he asking what kept her from feeling alone? Asking her to stop his loneliness? Neither were topics she could risk, so she fell back into the light teasing that always managed to distract her father. A grin tipped her lips, and she tilted her head to the side. "I'm not a duke."

A flash of an answering grin fed her triumph. "No, but are you lonely? Here without your family?"

"I have Frederica."

His brows drew together, leaving him looking a little lost. "Is it the same? A cousin?"

Emotion threatened to choke Isabella at the full implications of the statement he'd made about the duke standing alone. Beyond his siblings, was there anyone who didn't want something from him? Anyone who wasn't intimidated by him or even scared of him? Was there any time he got to simply be himself instead of the duke?

She could give him one of those times now. Turning her body so that she was fully facing the family portrait, she scrunched her nose. "You can't tell me there weren't times you'd have traded the annoyance of younger siblings for a playmate your own age."

He was silent long enough that she turned her head to look at him, only to find one eyebrow raised and his attention on her instead of the painting. "But Miss St. Claire is older than you."

Air hissed through Isabella's teeth. This was what happened when one let her guard down in the middle of a sea of lies.

His other eyebrow lifted as well. "Isn't she?"

"I have to go." Isabella ran suddenly sweaty palms down her skirt. "I should take this time to rest before dinner."

She spun and walked quickly back down the gallery, reminding herself constantly not to look back and see if he was watching her or not, making herself walk away. Alone.

Chapter 14

They'd only just been called into dinner, and already Griffith was exhausted. When he'd confronted his mother about the party, he'd surprised her by not forbidding it. He'd taken advantage of that surprise by informing her that the reasons he was going to Riverton still existed and he was going to have to take some time away from the party to deal with that business.

Unfortunately, that meant when he wasn't seeing to that business he was required to be present in the festivities and drooled over by a pack of would-be duchesses.

This first dinner was, of course, an elaborate affair to set the tone for the party. Griffith resigned himself to ten courses of torturous conversation when he saw who else had been seated nearest his place at the head of the table. Lady Alethea, to whom he had never spoken more than a passing greeting but whom society seemed to love, and Miss St. Claire, whom he'd yet to manage exchanging more than pleasantries with but had expressed a marked interest in to his family. The seating arrangements couldn't have been more obvious than if Mother had tied a sign around his chair that said *Unmarried Duke, Ripe for the Picking.*

His eyes traveled down the table to where Miss Breckenridge was seated. Surrounded by matrons and married older gentlemen, she was smiling and talking quietly, looking happy. Wasn't she missing her doting swains and her besotted admirers?

"Your Grace, I can't tell you how refreshing a mid-Season house party is. Should I be fortunate enough to marry someone with an estate so close to London, I shall have to consider doing one myself from time to time." Lady Alethea tilted her head and smiled at Griffith before ducking her head demurely to pay attention to her soup.

Griffith cleared his throat. "I'm sure the populace of London will be grateful for your generosity. I'm afraid this gathering is all my mother's doing, though. I've never seen the point of a country house party in the middle of the Season, when we're all seeing each other four and five times a week as it is."

She had the good grace to blush, but in Griffith's mind she deserved the embarrassment. Her comment had been much too forward, and given that he still had seven more days to spend confined in the same house, he wanted to set her straight from the beginning. Even if he turned away from Miss St. Claire, Lady Alethea would not be his next choice. It was doubtful she'd even be his tenth.

His attention wandered down the table again to where Miss Breckenridge sat quietly, a soft smile on her face as she listened to Lord Oakmere tell a story. The interminably long story of the time he caught a rabbit in his kitchens, if the hand motions were anything to go by.

"How was your journey to the country, Your Grace?" Miss St. Claire leaned back as her soup bowl was removed. "Our journey was ever so much easier than I anticipated. The roads have been much improved since the last time I traveled north."

Griffith fought the urge to sigh as he resigned himself to

another evening of the most inane chatter society could muster up. If he'd had any doubt before, being bored to tears in his own home was enough to finally convince him. Miss St. Claire had been a mistake.

~

Isabella's intention of quietly returning to her room after dinner was greatly hindered by the duke's sister, the Duchess of Marshington. Her Grace was at Isabella's side the moment they stood to remove from the dining table, hooking their arms together and leading Isabella into the music room with the rest of the ladies.

Leaving now would be incredibly rude, so instead Isabella made her way to a corner. One thing she'd learned during her weeks in London was that things didn't go well for her when only the ladies were present. Not that she blamed them. Isabella was quite purposefully attracting as many men as she could, particularly the titled ones—an effort that was not going to make her any friends among the ladies.

The ladies milled around, with the duke's sister and mother roaming from group to group, ensuring that everyone was having a good time and, at least once that Isabella noticed, quashing a bit of disgruntled gossip about the time away from London and the lack of top-tier marriage candidates in attendance. Lady Blackstone had disarmed all the girls in the room by baldly stating she had no intention of making her son uncomfortable by having to compete in his own home. If any of them wished to entertain other ideas, they were welcome to return to London.

Like all the rooms in Riverton, the music room was large. There was plenty of space for the few dozen people who had been invited to the house party to move around, which meant plenty of places where Isabella could get out of everyone's way.

"We could move this furniture and have dancing." Lady Alethea performed a small hop step in the space between the two rose-emblazoned sofas. "We could take turns playing the pianoforte."

"Dance at the duke's house party? You can't be serious." Miss Susan Newberry lowered herself onto one of the sofas. "He'd never join."

"Whyever not? There's going to be a ball at the end of the week. Surely he will dance at his own ball."

Several other girls came and joined the group. Isabella pressed herself deeper into the corner next to an enormous red-and-gold vase.

Lady Hannah, daughter of the Earl of Oakmere, sat beside Miss Newberry. "I'm sure he will dance, though I'd be surprised if he took a turn with anyone other than his sisters. To do anything else would practically be an announcement of engagement."

Lady Alethea smiled. "Precisely. And why else do you think we're all here? The duke is selecting a bride. And I think he intends to dance with her at the ball at the end of the week."

"Then we might as well start kissing Miss Breckenridge's feet. That's the only woman whose company he's been seen in this Season, and even that didn't look much like a flirtation," Miss Abigail Ledwell said.

"No, he has also spent time with Miss St. Claire." Lady Hannah tapped a finger to her lips in thought.

All four girls looked across the room to where Frederica was speaking amiably to Lady Blackstone and Lady Alethea's mother. They then sought the rest of the room as one, obviously seeking out Isabella. She absolutely did not want to be found listening in on their semi-private conversation, so she hunkered down and slipped around the vase and a scattering of potted plants to be nearer the pianoforte, where she accidentally caught Lady Alethea's eye.

"I'm sure Miss Breckenridge would be more than happy to play for us tonight if we wanted to dance." Lady Alethea's voice rang out across the room just as the men started entering.

"What's this?" Mr. Crenshaw asked. "There's going to be dancing? Fabulous. We'll just move these sofas aside, then, shall we?"

Isabella swallowed as she looked at the glossy black-and-white keys on the gorgeous instrument in front of her. She could play decently but was by no means an accomplished pianist such as these women were accustomed to. She'd made a point of not exhibiting, something Lady Alethea had probably noticed.

Then the duke was there, holding out the chair and bowing her into it. Somehow she found the gesture encouraging, and she settled her skirts about her and ran her fingers along the gold casing trim on the gorgeous instrument before laying her fingers against the keys.

"I believe you are almost as delighted with this turn of events as I am." His low chuckle reached her ears as he pulled a stack of music from a nearby table and spread it across the green-painted surface of the grand piano.

"They can't make you dance, you know," she whispered back.

One of his eyebrows lifted as he leaned forward in a conspiratorial manner, a piece of music in his hand. "Believe me. I know."

Then he nodded at her and crossed the room to a group of men talking in the corner.

The ladies practically pouted as they paired off with the men interested in dancing with them. Two of the ladies graciously stood up together, obviously recognizing that the duke had no intention of joining the festivities.

Isabella began to play, noting that the duke had chosen a simple but lively piece that nearly every girl in England had learned to play in the past few years. It was easy enough to play through several times as the couples established their dance and moved their way up and down the room. Lady Alethea had, of course, chosen the top position in the dance, claiming the right to tell everyone how the dance was going to go.

To Isabella's surprise, Frederica had joined the line, though she was all the way at the bottom. It would be several times through the steps before she got to join in the dancing. Lady Alethea chose an intricate, breathtaking combination, and Isabella was thankful that she got to sit this one out behind the pianoforte.

Of course, a wicked little part of her was tempted to slowly speed up the song until even Lady Alethea was tripping over her own feet to accomplish the steps she'd set forward. The woman had never been very nice, and Isabella hadn't liked the way she'd been talking about the duke. Since he was the only man who'd taken any time to get to know who Isabella really was—enough to be able to see that she hadn't wanted to play for these people—she hoped he would eventually marry someone who would treat him well.

Which wasn't any of the girls here. Aside from Isabella and Frederica, there was only one other girl in the room whom Isabella had heard say one nice word to anyone. It was as if Lady Blackstone had deliberately chosen the worst girls in the *ton* to bring to her son's home. What had his mother been thinking?

⌒

What had his mother been thinking? Griffith slid out of the house as the first light of dawn broke the horizon. The grooms probably weren't up yet, expecting the house party to keep to city hours. Griffith didn't care. He'd saddle his own horse if that was what was required to get him away before anyone else ventured forth.

Only a handful of guests had attended services with him yesterday, though it had been enough to fill the little parish church to capacity. He'd had a hard time paying attention to the sermon instead of watching Miss Breckenridge. The afternoon had been an endless sea of idle socializing, until he'd known it was either escape or lose his patience with the lot of them.

His mother was scheming, and Griffith didn't want any part of it. Could she actually want him to marry any of those women? Or was she trying to point out what an excellent choice Miss St. Claire actually was? The expectation that he intended to pick a bride and practically announce his engagement at the end of the week was ludicrous. Almost as ludicrous as the fact that his mother had planned a ball for the end of the week, and come Friday their little house party was going to explode into an absolute frenzy. It didn't matter that it was a ludicrous distance to travel for a single evening's entertainment—people were going to do it because no one wanted to be the one to miss out on the duke having a dance.

Maybe he'd travel to London so his mother could have one more bed to stick people in.

He knew he wouldn't. But he also wouldn't dance. Not even with Miranda. It would be his way of making a statement to the manipulative women inside his home right now, including his mother.

Fortunately the grooms were already up and tending the horses. Within moments his mount had been saddled and he was pounding across the fields behind his house, breathing the fresh air and, for a while, claiming the freedom everyone thought his title granted him.

After a decent ride he turned his mount toward the tenant cottages. He'd made the rounds before going to London for the Season, but if he was going to stay out of his house all day, it was the best use of his time. And if anything did need seeing to, it would give him an even better excuse to stay out and about.

By the time the sun had baked off the morning dew, he'd overseen the repairing of a fence, met a new baby, and been impressed by the number of young sheep one tenant had brought safely into the flock. Today was going to be a good day.

"He's here."

Isabella looked up from her breakfast plate as Frederica slipped into the chair beside her. Had her cousin finally lost her mind? Perhaps Uncle Percy's obsession was actually rooted in some form of hysteria and Frederica had inherited the malady.

Frederica clutched a paper closer to her chest. "We should go for a walk."

After swallowing her bite of toast, Isabella asked, "Walk where?"

Freddie glanced at the piece of paper in her hand. "There's a grove of trees about a mile past the southwest corner of the lake."

"And you know this how?"

Freddie grinned. "Because Arthur asked me to meet him there."

Isabella was very glad she hadn't taken another bite. "Arthur is here?"

Freddie nodded. "Eat quickly so we can depart. No one will miss us. It's all shooting and archery today."

"I'm rather good at archery."

Freddie rolled her eyes. "All the more reason to abstain. Do you really want to give these vipers another reason to dislike you? I do wish Lady Blackstone had invited some different ladies. You wouldn't know it from looking around this room, but there are actually a few nice ladies in London, once you get to know them."

In the end, Isabella's curiosity outweighed her good sense, and she agreed to go with Freddie to meet Arthur.

An hour later she wished she hadn't.

"Back to France?" Tears were already streaming down Frederica's cheeks. "For how long?"

"As long as it takes." Arthur lifted a hand and brushed a thumb against Freddie's cheek. It was an intimate moment, and Isabella felt rude intruding on it, but she couldn't leave Freddie out here alone, could she?

Freddie gripped the lapels of Arthur's uniform. "You will come back when it's over. Do you understand me? Because I'm waiting. Until your ghost comes back to tell me you are dead, I'm waiting."

"I've asked my colonel to tell you personally should I . . . should anything happen to me."

Freddie swung her head back and forth, making the hastily created curls bounce against her cheeks. "No. You're coming back."

"I'm coming back," he finally agreed. "And if I have to visit your father every day after I do, I'll find a way to gain his approval."

"Do you really have to leave soon? Couldn't you delay another few days? We could try to get Father to agree to a special license."

Isabella dropped against a tree. The implications of a special license before the man went off to war could ruin Freddie's reputation. Could Arthur even do such a thing and retain his post? Uncle Percy would demand that his superiors punish him, regardless of the fact that doing so would also punish his daughter. He'd disown Freddie before she'd even waved good-bye.

"I won't act like we've something to be ashamed of," Arthur said.

Isabella breathed a sigh of relief. At least one of them was thinking clearly.

He cleared his throat and pulled their joined hands in to his chest. "I brought a picnic. The post coach doesn't come back through the village for another two hours. I know it's early, but I was hoping you'd share it with me."

Arthur smiled at Freddie, and Isabella's heart broke.

This man—who was so in love with her cousin, made her cousin light up with life and laughter—was leaving with the tide in two days. And he might not come back. This could be Freddie's last memory of Arthur.

And she didn't need Isabella intruding on it.

Isabella trusted Arthur, possibly more than she trusted Freddie in this situation, and she was just going to have to believe that what she was about to do was the right thing. Because if Arthur didn't come home, Freddie was going to need this moment. A private moment. Even if Arthur did come back, it could be months. It could be another two years.

As quietly as she could, Isabella slipped back into the trees. She'd walk the grove for a while and then come back so Freddie wouldn't have to return alone. She'd get some fresh air, and no one back at the house would be any the wiser.

She walked out of the grove and across a field into another cluster of trees, this one thicker than the one she'd just left. The grounds of Riverton were gorgeous, and she could easily lose herself there for the entirety of the week. In fact, she just might.

On the other side of the trees sat a lone cottage. Brick and timber sides were topped with a thick thatch roof. Movement to one side of the roof indicated someone was attempting to fix something near the chimney, his pounding hammer echoing through the glen. Instead of a proper scaffolding, he'd propped one foot on a tall ladder and the other was braced against the stone chimney. Isabella hoped he wouldn't fall through the roof and make the hole he was repairing even larger.

A private garden surrounded the small house, and a goat roamed in front of a lean-to. A horse was tied up near a patch of grass on the far side of the house. It was an idyllic setting, similar to many Isabella had seen back home. Her eyes wandered back up to the man working on the roof as the pounding stopped and he stood to inspect his work.

Isabella's feet stumbled to a halt, and the breath froze in her lungs.

The man on the roof was the duke.

Chapter 15

His mother would be furious if she knew he'd left a house full of people to see to the maintenance needs of one of his tenants. Whether she'd be more worried about him leaving his guests to amuse themselves or them discovering he was doing menial labor would be a tight race, but he needed the space, the air, and the physical activity to sort through the ramifications of what he was thinking, what he was feeling.

Was he really going to start over on his search for a wife? And if he was, did his mother really think the women who'd frolicked through his music room last night were the best options?

Miss Breckenridge came to mind, the way she'd stood beside him in the gallery, trying to take away his loneliness or at least give him hope that it could be better.

He pounded the thoughts away with his hammer, determined to think about it later. Right now all that mattered was the fact that Mrs. Ingham would have a tough time feeding her three boys next time it rained if there was a gaping hole in the roof of her kitchen. He stripped the thatch away from the edges of the hole that had formed around the chimney and set about laying in and nailing new ribs. It wasn't the best work he'd ever done, since he wasn't about to rip the whole roof off and re-rib it, but it would keep the kitchen dry, and that was all Mrs. Ingham and her boys needed.

The sun was high in the sky, beating down upon his neck and back, which were poorly protected from the heat by the white lawn shirt he wore. The steady crack of pounding nails kept him engaged in what he was doing, even as his mind wandered.

As he reached for the first bundle of thatching, he asked himself the question, if not Miss St. Claire, then who? Immediately images of Miss Breckenridge swam into his mind. Again. Her enthusiasm over the bark of a tree. Her homesickness. Her good humor about playing the pianoforte despite the fact that she was without question not the most accomplished player in the room.

He jabbed the second bundle of thatching into the hole and nearly lost his balance as the ladder under his left foot shifted. It had been foolish to climb atop a thatched roof without building a proper scaffold, but the leak was small. He only needed to thread three more bundles into place and the riskiest of the work would be done.

The last bundle was a tight fit, as it should be. He placed both hands on the thatching needle and shoved the bound end of the reeds into place.

And pushed his ladder out of place.

Falling straight onto the roof would have caused a disaster larger than the original leak, so he pushed off with the leg braced against the chimney and threw himself onto the unstable ladder, wrapping his arms tightly around the upper rungs. The disaster *that* could have caused didn't occur to him until he'd already done it, and panic seized his muscles until the ladder rocked back against the overhang of the house, smashing his left arm into the thatching needle he still held in his right hand.

The hook that moments ago had efficiently stabbed the bundles of reeds into place now worked its way through his shirt and into his arm with fiery agony. Griffith instinctively pushed away from it, forgetting that he really had nowhere to go but down. And down he went, his ribs and shoulder banging into the rungs of the ladder and his thatching needle catching everything in its path until Griffith thought his entire arm had been slashed into ribbons.

Slamming into the ground was almost a relief.

Over his own groan of pain he heard a shout and the pounding of running feet. Air hissed through his teeth as he tried to comprehend what had just happened and assess the damage so he could decide what to do next.

The damage was that his arm hurt.

A lot.

"Your Grace! Your Grace!" The light feminine voice didn't seem right. Mrs. Ingham's voice had an odd catch to it. The result of years of hard work and cooking over an open fire.

After taking two more deep breaths, which only served to point out how many things other than his arm were currently sore, he managed to open one eye and decided he'd apparently hit his head along with everything else—because he thought he was looking straight into the face of Miss Isabella Breckenridge.

When Mrs. Ingham's lined and craggy face pushed into his vision as well, he decided Miss Breckenridge was real, because Griffith didn't want to think about how addlebrained he'd have to be to choose to imagine Mrs. Ingham.

Long-fingered hands encased in soft gloves slid against his temples and cupped his face. "Your Grace?"

"I believe"—Griffith paused to cough as his lungs reaccustomed themselves to having air in them—"under the circumstances you could call me Riverton."

Crooked white teeth sank into her lower lip, making Griffith want to grin. It was nice to know everything about his angel wasn't perfect. *His* angel? Despite the blistering pain, and really even because of it, he knew he wasn't dead. Although when he did die, if the angels weren't at least as beautiful as Miss Breckenridge, he was going to be disappointed.

And great blazes, his arm hurt.

Mrs. Ingham whipped off her apron and pressed it against his arm, making Griffith yell out in pain. The older woman ignored his yelp and wrapped her hands tightly around his arm. "Unless you want old Bessie using her tongue to clean you up, you're going to have to help us here, Your Grace. We need to get you inside."

Isabella wasn't sure she took another breath until they'd managed to maneuver the duke into the small cottage, groaning and hissing the entire way. Already the bunched-up apron was showing red. If they didn't stop the bleeding soon, the duke would be in trouble.

They took him to the large, rough wooden table in the middle of the kitchen. But instead of laying atop it, Riverton dropped onto the bench that ran beside the long end of the table. He propped his injured arm on the table and took three steadying breaths.

Isabella bit her lip as she leaned over and pressed the now-ruined apron to the wound. "You're going to need stitches."

Riverton nodded, his face looking dangerously white.

"We'll need to clean it first."

He nodded again, the tendons in his neck becoming more prevalent as his jaw tightened.

Mrs. Ingham, who'd introduced herself as they'd led Riverton into the house, brought out a nearly full bottle of whisky. "I'm sure it's not what you're used to, Your Grace, but the boys say it's the best in the village."

The frown that darkened the duke's pale face told Isabella he wasn't about to take a swig from that bottle. Did he think himself too good for his tenant's whisky? Considering that mere moments ago he'd been crawling around on the same tenant's roof, his reluctance didn't make sense.

Isabella stepped forward. "I'll take that, Mrs. Ingham. Do you have a needle and some thread? I believe we're managing the bleeding right now, but it won't work for long, and we certainly won't be able to move him."

She took the bottle as Mrs. Ingham scurried into the bedroom.

Riverton wrapped his hand around hers. "Miss Breckenridge, if you intend to stick a needle into my flesh, I prefer you do so in complete control of your faculties."

The heat in his gaze and the burn of his hand on hers distracted her more than a finger of the whisky would have. Isabella swallowed hard and yanked her hand and the bottle from his grasp. "It's to cleanse the wound. I've no intention of drinking it. Though you should rethink your decision not to take a swallow or two. This is going to hurt. A lot. I've heard the whisky helps."

One dark blond eyebrow lifted, the arrogant expression at odds with the pain-induced pallor and tension in his face. "You've done this before, then?"

"Twice."

He continued to stare at her in silence.

"And both of them survived." Her father's arm and her brother Thomas's leg didn't wear the prettiest-looking scars, but both had healed without problem or infection.

Mrs. Ingham entered with her sewing box and set it on the table before wringing her hands, anxiety obvious in every move she made. It couldn't be easy having a peer of the realm bleed all over your kitchen.

One large hand reached toward the whisky bottle once more, but this time the fingers wrapped around the neck and brought the cork to his mouth. Strong, even teeth bit into the cork as he yanked the bottle with a twist to pull the cork from the top with a loud *pop*. He spat the cork onto the table before extending the bottle in her direction and placing it on the table. "Let us hope I do the same, then."

Isabella swallowed hard as she lifted the red-stained cloth and took in the long, straight line of the cut. It wasn't too deep, but the length was concerning, and the flesh was gaping. Flakes of leaves and bark stuck to the bloodied flesh. Even the torn shirt edges appeared embedded in the wound. "I should probably flush this with water first if we don't want to use up all her whisky."

The duke gritted his teeth. "Fine," he growled. He nodded to a bucket on the hearth. "I hauled that up for her before I got on the roof."

Mrs. Ingham looked relieved to have something to do as she scooped a bowl from the table and ran to the bucket. Water sloshed over the edges as she brought the bowl to Isabella.

Isabella took a deep breath, letting her gaze connect with the duke's. He gave her a slight nod, and she tipped the bowl.

⌒

Griffith told himself not to watch the rush of clear water flood the wound, blending with the blood and dirt to soak his shirt sleeve and then run off, becoming a murky puddle seeping through the cracks in the old house's floorboards, but he couldn't look away, as if watching it happen would somehow give him a measure of control over the situation.

He had the vague thought that they should have done this outside, and then the shrieking pain stabbed him in the back of the neck. The shout ripped from his chest, and some corner of his brain was absolutely convinced that she had just ripped his arm from his body.

And that was just the water.

As his chest heaved, trying to breathe enough to work through the pain, he opened his eyes to stare at the whisky bottle. How much worse was that going to hurt? It would feel like she was cleansing the wound with a fiery knife.

"I'm so sorry, but you have to relax."

Soft fingers smoothed along his shoulder, and the sweet words seemed to burrow their way through the blood rushing through his ears.

"When you get tense it makes you bleed more."

The pain was draining down to a more tolerable level, but he knew it wouldn't last. He wouldn't last.

"Don't let me do anything foolish," he whispered before tilting the bottle of whisky to his lips and taking four long draws, trying to pour the liquid down his throat before he could taste it.

He slammed the bottle back on the table, the level of amber liquid sloshing around visibly lower, and both Miss Breckenridge and Mrs. Ingham rushed to catch the bottle before he slid it across the table.

Fire ate through his mouth, throat, and belly. What had he done? He'd let them convince him to poison himself. Even breathing seemed to hurt as the air hit the back of his tortured throat.

Miss Breckenridge gave a little cough to clear her throat. "Well, that should do the trick."

"It will take a few moments to have an effect." Mrs. Ingham wrung her hands some more.

Griffith hated what he was putting the poor woman through, and he hadn't even managed to finish fixing her roof.

The burning was subsiding, leaving a pleasant warmth in its wake. If port created a similar sort of warmth, perhaps he should reconsider his stance on the common after-dinner drink. There was something agreeable about the glow in the pit of his stomach.

Unfortunately he didn't think it was going to have any effect on the pain in his arm. He didn't feel any different, other than knowing he'd ripped up his insides with the quick swallows of liquid fire.

And it smelled odd.

He stuck his hand in front of his face and gave a heavy open-mouthed exhale. The pungent smell of alcohol made his nose wrinkle in disgust.

A light snicker drew his attention to the lovely Miss Breckenridge. Isabella, standing at his side, clutching the bottle of whisky and waiting to stitch him up and make him whole again.

Her eyes widened, and Griffith suddenly realized he'd made that observation out loud. What was he thinking? He shouldn't be telling her she was lovely. Every other man in Britain was telling her how beautiful she was.

"I think the whisky's having an effect." Isabella's smile was tight as her amusement seemed to war with her concern. She looked at the wound with a frown and then traded the bottle of whisky for a pair of wicked-looking scissors, which she used to attack his sleeve. Worry and concentration worked deep grooves into her forehead.

"You shouldn't worry." Griffith blinked. It had taken him longer than it should have to say *shouldn't*. Shhhhouldn't.

"Why not?" Isabella exchanged the scissors for the bottle and held it up to his wound. Taking a deep breath, she tipped it to send a river of amber liquid over the same path the water had taken moments ago.

Air hissed between Griffith's teeth again as pain lanced through his chest once more, angling off to travel all the way to his toes, making his foot stomp on the floor in protest.

"That hurt!"

A small smile touched her lips as she poured some more of the drink over the needle and thread she'd selected from Mrs. Ingham's sewing box. "Yes, but you didn't tense up again, so I think that's progress."

"I didn't?" Griffith frowned at his arm. She'd better not sew any of those hairs into the wound when she stitched him up. "Must be because you're an angel."

"An angel, am I?"

"Yes. An angel sent to test me. My very own thorny temptation."

Isabella frowned as she lined the needle up with the wound. "I'm no danger to you, Your Grace."

The tip of the needle sank into his skin and it hurt, but he didn't care. Suddenly the only thing that mattered was that Isabella come to understand what she did to him and explain how he could make it stop. It was a foolish conversation that he would sorely regret in the morning, but even one more second of holding it in would cause him great agitation.

Which might cause problems with the helpful work Isabella was trying to do with precision.

"You threaten everything. I had a plan, and you keep getting in the way of it."

She gave him a quick glance before devoting her attention back to his arm.

He stared at her face. It was much more interesting than watching his arm. Besides, he could feel every pierce of the needle and the slow pull of the thread. He didn't need to watch it too.

"I was going to marry Frederica."

She cleared her throat. "I don't think she's very interested in that."

He shrugged, making her squeal before giving him a sharp reprimand to be still. She was charming when she was frustrated.

"I am not charming. I'm trying to save you from bleeding to death."

Griffith frowned. He must have made his observation out loud. Again. Funny how he didn't remember actually speaking the words. He brought his free hand up to his jaw to see if it was still moving without his consent. It wasn't. He kept his hand close to make sure that his next sentence actually came out.

"I can't. I didn't know that before, but I can't."

She frowned, adding an adorable wrinkle between her eyebrows, just above the straight, narrow nose. "Can't what?"

"Marry Frederica."

"Yes, we've established that," she mumbled.

Now it was Griffith's turn to frown. Weren't women supposed to be insanely curious about things of a personal nature? Not that he wanted her to gossip about his plans, but shouldn't she want to know so that she could gossip about them? "Don't you want to know why?"

"Other than the fact that Freddie doesn't want to marry you, no, I don't particularly care for your reasons to drop your suit." She paused with the needle poised just above his arm. Her wide-eyed gaze jerked to meet his. "Only you shouldn't drop your suit just yet."

Griffith looked at the whisky bottle, the edges of which were the slightest bit blurry. Had she drunk some of the stuff too? Or was it simply his inebriated state making her difficult to understand? This was why he didn't drink. Although he probably should consider doing it more often, because he hadn't realized just how important Isabella's opinion was before. How could he have missed that while sober? "It doesn't matter if she changes her mind. I can't marry her. Not anymore."

"She doesn't want to change her mind. But you can't stop coming by the house yet."

Griffith narrowed his eyes, trying to make the features of her lovely face become clear again. "Why not? Are you hoping my attentions will shift to you?"

⁓

Isabella nearly dropped the needle. For a moment, but only a moment, she allowed herself to entertain the idea that a man such as the duke would be truly interested in her. It wasn't his title so much as what she'd seen him do with it. He was arrogant, yes, but not condescending. His status was very important to him, but mostly because of the power it gave him to change the world for the better or at least try to. He was a good, kind, honorable man who fixed roofs for widows.

Which was why he should never want to have anything to do with her.

She poked the needle into his arm again. "I assure you that I harbor no intentions of trying to secure your attentions."

He snorted. "Intentions, attentions. They rhyme."

Her answering grin was on her face before she'd even realized he'd inspired one. She quickly sucked in her cheeks to regain her composure.

"You already have, you know."

She was only halfway done sealing the long gash in his arm,

184

and if sewing a duke's flesh wasn't uncomfortable enough, the frank conversation they were having was positively excruciating. "Have what?"

"Gained my attention. I'm curious about you." Riverton leaned over his braced, injured arm and peered closely at her face. "You don't make sense. And I like things in my world to make sense."

She cleared her throat. "I assure you, I'm nothing out of the ordinary."

The bark of laughter sent him leaning back, nearly pulling the needle from her fingers. "If only every girl were as ordinary as you. Even your hair is extraordinary. Did you know it changes color? It does. It looks nearly blond in the candlelit ballrooms, but when we walk outside, the sun burns it away and it looks almost red. How do you do that? I'm sure many scientists would be fascinated to know."

"I don't . . . Well, that is I—"

"And your eyes. Have you seen your eyes? Of course you haven't. Not in person. A looking glass couldn't possibly do them justice. They pierce me. I want to drown in them. I have a lake near my home that exact shade of blue. I had a rowboat when I was a kid, and I would row across to pick strawberries. That's you, you know. I wish to row across your eyes and pick strawberries from your hair."

She tried not to laugh. Truly she did. But her shoulders were trembling so much with her contained mirth that she had to pause her ministrations. Only an inch or so left to go and she could see to getting the duke back to the house. A deep breath in helped to settle her composure. But then he started talking again.

"I love watching you dance. No one else moves the way you do. Is it because you grew up near Scotland? Do you know the Scottish dances? I'm amazed when I watch Scottish people dance. So much life and energy. I want to dance with you."

Her needle froze for an entirely different reason, as she couldn't help herself from connecting her gaze with his once more. He wanted to dance with her? "You can't be serious."

"Oh, but I am." The duke tilted his head and looked at the half-full bottle of whisky. With a frown he lifted it to his lips and took another long pull before slamming the bottle back onto the table. "Gah! That is disgusting. Works, though. I couldn't care less what you're doing to my arm. Are you sewing it to my shirt?"

He turned his head to stare at his arm, and his intense glare pulled another chuckle from her lips as she set about knotting off her string.

"No, I haven't sewn you to your shirt. We cut the sleeve away, remember?"

"Ah, yes. So we did."

He became blessedly silent while she finished. Mrs. Ingham fluttered nervously nearby but never offered assistance. What must she think of the conversation they were having? Was she of a mind to tell everyone? If it got back to the house party, her uncle would have her sent back to Northumberland in utter ruin before the sun set.

"I believe that does it. You'll have to be careful not to strain it, though. It's quite a long gash. I doubt it would take much to make it bleed again." Even now blood was welling against her stitches, forming a dark red crust against the neat little lines. "We should bandage it."

"I have a clean sheet." Mrs. Ingham scurried from the room once more and brought the sheet out, already tearing the rough muslin into strips.

"Thank you." Isabella took a wide strip and began wrapping it around the duke's arm. "I'm sure the duke will replace it."

"'Course I will." He swung his right arm in the direction of the whisky bottle, nearly sending it rolling across the table again. "This stuff too." He frowned. "Didn't I tell you to call me Riverton? Now that you've stitched me up you might as well call me Griffith. You've earned it."

He waved an arm in Mrs. Ingham's direction. "And your roof. I didn't finish the roof." He looked up at Isabella, snaring her in his green gaze. "Are we finished?"

She knotted the bandage and stepped back with arms spread wide. "Finished. Now the question is how to get you back to the house."

"I ride, of course." He pushed up from the table, took one step toward the door . . .

And fell.

Chapter 16

"My coat." Isabella tried not to laugh as Griffith plopped his hat onto his head and looked around the room with a frown. He managed to get back to his feet with little help from her and Mrs. Ingham, but he'd yet to appear steady.

Mrs. Ingham pulled the garment from the back of a chair and held it up. "Here it is, Your Grace."

A wide grin spread across his face, displaying both teeth and dimples. "Excellent."

He took the coat in his right hand and then frowned down at his left.

"Why don't I carry it?" Isabella slid the coat from his fingers, trying not to smile at the mountain of a man looking like a little boy who'd been denied a puppy.

"A gentleman needs his coat." His frown darkened until he looked less like a boy and more like a disgruntled duke.

A compromise was definitely in order here. "Perhaps we could drape it around your shoulders?"

One haughty eyebrow lifted, but the imperious glare was interrupted by a hiccup. "What good would that do?"

"Er . . ." Isabella looked to Mrs. Ingham for help, but the

older woman simply stared at the duke with wide, disbelieving eyes. There would be no assistance from that direction. With a serene smile pasted on her face, Isabella turned back to the duke. "It would get your coat home while covering most of your, um, dishevelment."

He frowned down at himself as if just now realizing that he no longer looked like he'd come fresh from his valet. "I haven't a sleeve."

"Well, no." Isabella wasn't sure what else she was supposed to say, particularly since he had lifted his head at that moment and looked at her as if she were the one missing the obvious.

"Therefore I need my coat."

Isabella managed to restrain the groan, but not the sigh of despair that rushed through her pursed lips in a gust of dread. They were going to have to put on the coat.

With great care she eased the sleeve over his injured arm. Now that he was getting what he wanted, Griffith was the model of patience, saying nothing when it became apparent that even Isabella's greater-than-average height wasn't going to be enough to smooth the coat across his shoulder without jarring his injured arm.

She gave him a stern look, or as much of one as she could manage in the face of his unfocused eyes and drunken grin. "Must we wear the coat?"

"I am a gentleman."

And that was as much of an answer as she was going to get. With any luck he wouldn't remember this tomorrow. Isabella climbed up onto the bench he'd sat on earlier. It would have been easier to have him sit back down, but she was afraid she wouldn't be able to get him back up.

It was certainly strange, looking down on the duke's upturned face. She was probably the only lady in England who'd ever had such a privilege. His shoulders seemed even broader from above as she held the fabric wide and tried to maneuver his good arm into the other sleeve. The hat he'd already placed upon his head kept knocking her in the face as she tried to adjust the coat.

They must make the most ridiculous-looking pair.

A hiss escaped him as the coat pulled tight, but no other sound emerged. She smoothed the coat into place along his shoulders, trying not to think about the fact that two layers of cloth weren't enough to stem his heat or disguise the strength and resiliency of his muscles. She remembered him poised on the roof, swinging a hammer and jamming reeds into the thatch.

Definitely not a typical aristocrat.

Warmth curled through her belly, and she snatched her hands back before jumping from the bench with an overly generous smile. "All set, then?"

Her smile dimmed as she saw that the duke looked even paler now than he had before.

"Perhaps a bit more whisky?" Mrs. Ingham held the nearly empty bottle up.

"That might not be a bad idea. The journey back to Riverton isn't going to be easy." Isabella clasped her hands together. Could she catch him if he toppled over? More likely they'd both end up sprawled across Mrs. Ingham's floor, and the poor woman's eyes would widen until they actually fell out of her head.

"It was for stitches." He shook his head as if to clear it and then stumbled sideways before catching himself. "If I drink any more, Ryland will make me spread bat guano."

Now there was a story she wished she could pull from him one day. "At least let me go for a wagon, then."

"I'll look weak in a wagon."

Isabella sighed. "You are weak. I just stitched up a four-inch gash in your arm."

He shook his head again, slower this time. "Can't look weak. Dukes make decisions."

"But, Your Grace, you . . ." Mrs. Ingham's voice stuttered to a halt as Griffith snatched the bottle and took one more slug.

"Foul stuff," he muttered before staggering his way out the door.

Isabella ran to catch up, hoping Mrs. Ingham wouldn't mind their poor manners. Given everything else she'd seen today, Isabella rather thought their lack of good-byes was the least of the woman's concerns.

Griffith was stopped by the ladder he'd fallen from. He placed his right hand on the rungs. "I didn't finish the roof."

"Oh, no you don't!" Isabella rushed forward, not knowing what she would do but knowing she couldn't let the man put one foot on that ladder. She threw her arms around his middle, thankfully remembering to avoid grabbing his injured arm.

"It won't take long. Just need to trim the reeds."

She planted her feet wide and pulled him back with all her might. With her face plastered against his back, the smell of cedar and grass meshed with the whisky for a very heady combination. It was better to think about that than the fact that her hands were pressed once more against parts of his body no woman had ever touched. No woman other than his wife should know how hard and strong his midsection was or how it felt to nestle into the dip along the center of his back.

One more sin to blacken Isabella's scoreboard. At least this one had a bit of enjoyment to it.

Despite using all her strength, she couldn't budge the duke. Even inebriated, he had a strength to match that of his will. Thankfully the same couldn't be said for his coordination. He placed a foot on the bottom rung and it slid right off.

"We'll leave the blade for her son to finish the reeds." Isabella grunted with the effort to keep the duke on the ground and not hit his injured arm, which he'd yet to use in his ladder-climbing endeavor. Did that mean it was more injured than she thought? Had there been some internal damage that rendered it useless?

"If any of her sons could do it I wouldn't have been up there in the first place. None of them can swing a tool straight, unless you smash them between two walls."

Isabella smothered a laugh against his back. She even heard a chuckle from Mrs. Ingham. Griffith would be beside himself tomorrow if he remembered issuing such a bold insult.

"Perhaps . . ." Isabella took a deep breath to calm the chuckles that still wanted to escape. "Perhaps you could return later in the week, then, when your arm is better?" And when he wasn't drunk.

He swung away from the ladder, flinging her in a circle until her hip bumped the ladder and sent it sliding along the edge of the roof to topple harmlessly into the garden.

At least now he couldn't try to climb it.

The reluctance that accompanied the release of Isabella's grip around his middle surprised her. She should have been ready to step away, anxious to avoid such an impropriety, but she wasn't. It had been such a nice moment, and her life had far too few nice moments lately.

Griffith turned again until he was facing her. "You'll return with me?"

"Oh, er, yes?" It was more of a question than an answer, and Isabella would never hold him to such an invitation, but it was rather thrilling that, even drunk, he wanted to spend time with her.

"Exshellt . . . Eggsell . . ." He coughed. "Good."

They collected his horse and started the slow walk back to Riverton. The horse plodded along behind them, its reins loosely clasped in Griffith's right hand, and Isabella walked on the duke's left to make sure nothing accidentally bumped his arm. As they rounded the trees, Isabella bit her lip. Should they take the straight path back to Riverton or go by the place she'd left Frederica? It had been well over an hour since Isabella had left her and Arthur. Odds were that he had secured another way back to the house for her when Isabella hadn't returned.

At least, Isabella hoped that was true. Because she didn't think the duke was drunk enough not to notice if Frederica joined their little party, and Freddie wasn't likely to thank Isabella for putting her in such a compromising situation. It was bad enough that the duke was likely to question Isabella's lone wanderings.

The duke seemed to know where he was going, despite his inebriated state. That or the horse was leading the way. Isabella was going to have to leave Freddie to fend for herself and hope Arthur was the man both girls thought him to be.

"And what brought you to London, Miss Breckenridge?"

Isabella smiled at the thickening of his voice and the slight slur on the word *Miss*. "I believe, under the circumstances, you may call me Isabella. Or Bella if the *s* troubles you."

"Isssa . . . Itha . . . Bella it is." He ran his tongue over his teeth and grimaced.

"I came to London for the reason most young ladies come to London." She looked out over the field they were crossing, not wanting him to see the lie in her face.

"Not enough society in . . . Where are you from?"

"Northumberland." She'd already told him once, so it didn't hurt if she repeated it, even though her uncle had started telling everyone her father's estate was in the more acceptable county of Yorkshire. "And no. There aren't a lot of people there at all." Which was the main reason her family had been able to hold on to the farm for as long as they had. Even as they plummeted into debt, there were few people who wanted to live in the craggy loneliness of the northernmost English county.

"I didn't know about you."

She raised a hand to his back to guide him around a collection of rocks in the middle of their path. "I would be surprised if you had."

"But I checked. I researched your cousin for a year. And then you showed up."

"Freddie is very private. I doubt she mentioned me to many people. We're very close, though." Closer than sisters in some ways. Even when Uncle Percy forbade Freddie's visits, the letters had continued.

Writing to Bella was one privilege Uncle Percy never took from his daughter, even allowing Freddie to send money to cover Bella's quills, ink, and paper. It was an extravagant use of the money as things became harder, but writing to Freddie had been her only escape, the only place where she could truly talk about everything she feared and felt.

"I can tell. I never see you apart." He frowned and turned to look at her, dislodging his top hat until it slid a bit down his forehead. "'Cept now. Where is Missss . . . Mithh . . . Freddie?"

That was a very good question. Isabella dearly hoped that her cousin had made it back to the house. The bigger question was how was she doing. Was she crying herself sick over Arthur's fate or worried about Isabella's? Either way, the duke didn't need to know they'd both gone wandering off from the party. "She wasn't feeling well."

"You intend to marry, then?"

It took Isabella a minute to realize Griffith had returned to his previous question of why Isabella was in London. She opened her mouth to lie to him but made the mistake of turning to look at him. He'd pulled his horse forward and draped his good arm around the brown steed's neck so he could lean on the horse. It made his walk a bit strange, but it kept him upright.

And allowed him to look directly at her.

Isabella stumbled.

Griffith reached his arm out to catch her but winced and stopped as she righted herself. "You should ride Abacus."

Isabella scoffed. "I think not."

"He's a wonderful horse."

"And he's not wearing a proper saddle. Not for me, anyway."

Griffith frowned. "I suppose not. Whom do you intend to marry?"

Was there no distracting this man? Of all the things for the whisky to affect, his tenacity couldn't be one of them? "Why does it matter?"

He shrugged his right shoulder. "Because I'm not going to marry Freddie. But you want me to."

"I don't want you to marry Freddie."

"You want me to court her."

"I want you to pretend to court her."

Griffith stopped and waited until Isabella had turned to face him. "You are not what I wanted in a wife. You are much too popular and far more beautiful than I planned. But you care. And you like trees. I find myself thinking about you when I shouldn't be."

Isabella sucked a deep breath in through her nose but could think of nothing to say that would stop his confession. If he remembered this in the morning he was sure to hate himself. And her.

"And I find myself wondering why a girl would come all the way to London, capture the attention of a duke, and then try to direct it elsewhere. You are a puzzle, dear Bella, and I find myself wanting to solve it."

He was really, really going to hate that he'd revealed this. She needed to stop him before he said anything else. "I'm flattered, truly. I just don't want to hurt Freddie."

"But Freddie loves Lieutenant Arthur Saunderson. He's alive, you know. Ryland told me last night. I had him check." He started walking again, but it was a few moments before Isabella could get her feet to move again, and she had to rush to catch up.

"You checked?"

"Of course." Griffith frowned. "Miranda said I could never compete with a dead man, so I had to learn about the dead man. Only he isn't dead."

The top spires of Riverton became visible above the trees, glinting in the sun. Fortunately her uncle would not question her making excuses about coming down to dinner. With all this new information about the duke, the headache she would soon be pleading was likely to be quite real. She already felt a bit dizzy.

"He's a good man, you know. A lieutenant in the Dragoons." Griffith tilted his head in Isabella's direction, and his hat toppled clean off the mop of twisted blond waves.

Isabella reached out to catch it and ended up smashing it against her chest. "Oh dear."

Griffith shrugged. "Just pop it back out."

A giggle escaped as Isabella tried to reshape it as best she could. It still looked like a squashed top hat, but Griffith set it back upon his head anyway, causing her to give up on restraining the giggles and laugh outright.

"You should laugh more often."

Bella shook her head as the laugh subsided into a wide smile. "It shows my teeth."

"Ah." He looked toward the last band of trees separating them from the manicured grounds around the house. "You wouldn't want to mar perfection."

They lapsed into silence as they made their way through the trees to the banks of a small lake that was, indeed, the color of Isabella's eyes.

"Don't trust him." Griffith broke the silence as a shout rang out from across the lake and a groom started running toward them.

"Who?"

"Your uncle. He tried to get Arthur commissioned into the regulars. That's why everyone thought he was dead. That troop was going into a battle that everyone knew was likely to kill them."

Isabella didn't know what to say. She'd known Uncle Percy hadn't wanted Freddie to marry an officer, but to try to send a man to his doom over it?

"Don't trust him," he said again as the groom got closer. "I don't think I like your uncle."

Isabella swallowed and followed sedately along behind the group now collecting around the duke. That made two of them.

⁓

He wasn't so far into his cups that he didn't notice the shock riding the approaching grooms' faces like a jockey at Ascot. Their wide eyes jumped from Griffith's head to his feet and back again. They barely glanced at Isabella, which was good. He would have had to dismiss them if they'd said anything untoward about her.

He stumbled to a halt and blinked. What a strange thing to think. Had he ever threatened his servants with dismissal before, even in his mind?

"Your Grace?" The head groom shifted on his feet. "May we be of assistance?"

"Yes," Griffith said, hopefully with some authority. "No one is to tell my mother."

The grooms looked at each other, and a muffled giggle came from Griffith's left.

"Of course, Your Grace." The groom reached for the horse's bridle. "Should we fetch a physician?"

Griffith frowned down at his arm. He'd been injured, but Isabella had patched him up. Did he really need to call the physician and risk having his mother learn of the incident?

"It wouldn't hurt," Isabella said softly.

With a sigh, Griffith nodded. The presence of a doctor increased the chances of the news of his injury getting out, but if Isabella would feel better having her ministrations checked by a doctor, then Griffith would have him summoned. "Bring him in the back and up the servant stairs. Don't tell anyone you don't have to tell. Including my mother."

A small smile tilted the head groom's lips. "Of course, Your Grace."

Griffith nodded and allowed the men to help him the rest of the way to the house. He slipped in the back entrance and up the stairs, Isabella at his side. After they'd climbed the stairs to the first floor, he knew they had to part ways, as her bedchamber and his were on opposite sides of the house. He was surprised at his reluctance to do so. Even as he felt the effects of the alcohol begin to wane from his system, he knew that he would not allow himself to be this intimate with Isabella ever again. And he already mourned the loss.

"I should go." Isabella backed away from him, moving toward the guest chambers. "Take care of your arm."

Griffith nodded, reaching his good arm out to the wall to brace himself as the movement made the corridor spin.

He stumbled into his room and dropped into a chair by the fireplace to await the physician. Moments later his door opened, admitting his valet and a servant carrying a steaming tea tray.

The earthy scent of willow bark tea made his mouth dry. He'd never cared for it, but if he was going to get through this week without letting anyone learn of his injury, he was going to have to drink buckets of the stuff.

He was halfway through the pot when the physician came in. His valet had managed to remove all of the torn and dirty clothing, and Griffith had managed not to say too many ridiculous things. Thankfully, he'd hired servants with discretion he could count on. At least he hoped he could. He'd never explicitly given instructions to hide something from his mother before.

"Whoever stitched you up did a fine job," the old physician said after doing a thorough inspection of Griffith's arm. "It's likely to itch for a while, and have someone come to me if it turns red or swells."

The man removed a bottle from his bag and set it on the table. He looked at the cooling pot of willow bark tea with a curled lip. "This should actually take care of the pain."

Griffith recognized the laudanum bottle but saw no reason to tell the doctor he wouldn't touch it unless he was on the verge of dying. He'd sooner go back and find Mrs. Ingham's bottle of whisky.

The doctor looked at Griffith with a slight smile. "That would work as well, Your Grace."

A groan ripped from Griffith's chest as he dropped his head back against his chair. He was never drinking alcohol again.

Chapter 17

The sun had been up for three hours. He'd been sitting at his desk for two. He hadn't growled at anyone in at least one. If he'd needed another reason to avoid imbibing in spirits, besides its apparent loosening of his lips, he certainly had it now. A subtle ache remained in the center of his head, and he couldn't seem to drink enough water. Between that and the tea he kept drinking, his stomach felt like it sloshed with every move he made.

The tea was working, though. While everything felt stiff and his arm radiated with a dull pain and pinched when he moved it, the physical effects of his misadventure were minimal.

It was the other, less tangible effects that were sure to linger and make his life miserable.

The fact that he had not fallen so deeply into the bottle as to impair his memory could be seen as both a blessing and a very unfortunate condition. Regardless of its benefits or lack thereof, his memory remained intact, if a little fuzzy around the edges. The things he'd said to Miss Breckenridge—Isabella— they could never be taken back.

Did he really want them to be?

For as much as he never wanted to be as lacking in control as he'd been in the cottage the day before, he also couldn't bring himself to regret the wall that had been removed between him and Isabella. He was now almost obligated to pursue her.

Except she wanted him to keep pursuing Miss St. Claire. But not really. Something was definitely going on with those two women, and simply thinking about it made his head hurt.

Well, made his head hurt more.

He closed his eyes and pressed his fingers to his temples, hoping and praying the pressure would stop some of the throbbing. The tension the pressing created in his arm made him groan and give up applying the pain-relieving pressure.

The quiet shift of the study door being pushed open stabbed through his brain, as if someone had shouted in his ear. He waited, bracing himself for more mind-piercing noises, but none came. It was a servant, then, come to see to the breakfast tray he'd ordered and then abandoned after his stomach clenched on the first bite of ham.

The scrape of the drapery rings hit him right before the sunlight did, making it impossible to restrain his groan of agony. "Close them."

The rustle of fabric and jangling of metal rings against the curtain rod indicated the servant was still beside the window, but his order was not being followed.

The anomaly sent a spark of concern through Griffith's addled mind. Was something wrong? He'd skipped dinner last night and managed to avoid almost everyone this morning while slipping into his study to suffer in private, but if a true emergency had arisen, surely his staff wouldn't think twice about interrupting him.

Using a large hand to shield his eyes from the blinding light, he eased one eyelid up enough to make out the silhouette of the person by the window.

With a sigh he let his eye fall shut again and folded his arms on his desk before allowing his head to drop onto them. It wasn't a servant.

It was his mother.

"I trust you intend to grace us with your presence today."

He groaned. There was no holding it back, even though the grating noise made it feel as if his head were splitting open. The idea of smiling at a bunch of ladies desperate to win his hand—because that was, in actuality, who his mother wanted graced with Griffith's presence—caused a more revolting reaction in his stomach than the ham had.

Except Isabella would be among them, and that made the prospect much more appealing.

He traced every step his mother took from the window to the desk by the clear swish of her skirt. Had women's skirts always made so much noise?

He felt the light pressure of her hand on his shoulder. "Are you unwell?"

That was putting it mildly. And yet not correctly at the same time. How could one be unwell when the illness was brought on by his own actions? And while he couldn't regret the initial swallows that had brought blessed numbness and allowed Isabella to stitch up the gash on his arm, he shouldn't have continued to drink the fiery liquid.

He'd liked the results, though. At least, at the time he had. There was no denying that part of him rejoiced in the confessing of his thoughts about Isabella and how she'd sent his plans to marry her cousin off course. This morning, though, that confession made him almost as uncomfortable as his pounding head.

"I'm going to have Watkins send a man for the doctor."

And have the man laugh himself silly at being called to nurse the aftereffects of the duke's drunkenness while knowing the duke had also kept his injury from his mother? "No, Mother, I am well."

The lie stuck in his throat, but he swallowed it. The injury was healing, his head would mend, and she had more than enough to worry about keeping a houseful of guests happy when they weren't getting the entertainment they'd been hoping for, namely his selection of a bride.

He lifted his head and forced his eyes to open. Fortunately he didn't have to look right into the bright windows in order to look in his mother's direction now. "'Tis only a headache. Have them bring me some tea and a bit of headache powder and I shall be ready to face the inquisition."

The thought of even more willow bark tea made his stomach roil all over again. He swallowed, hoping to keep the tea he'd already drunk in place.

Apparently assured that her son was indeed well, his mother straightened and lifted one golden eyebrow in displeasure. "Inquisition? Really, Griffith, if you'd simply shown a bit of interest in settling down before now I wouldn't have resorted to such measures. You have a responsibility, though, and given your father's early . . ."

Her words stumbled to a choking halt as she visibly worked to reclaim her composure.

Griffith felt like a reprehensible lout. He'd never considered what his delay was doing to his mother. She never spoke of it, had seemed to understand his desire to have everyone settled before he threw his own life into upheaval with a wife and family. Perhaps she did understand it, but that didn't mean it hadn't caused her more than a moment or two of worry.

Justified worry. His father had been frightfully young when he died in his bed of a sudden heart condition.

"Mother, I—"

"You can't leave these things to chance, Griffith. I've been more than patient with you, but it's time you take a wife."

"I agree." What else could he say? He did agree—or at least he had—that it was time for him to wed. He still thought it was time, though his person of choice was shifting.

Mother's eyes narrowed. "You do?"

Griffith considered nodding but then thought better of it. "I do. It's time."

"No."

He knew his head was pounding and that everything seemed to be working a little slower this morning, but as of yet he hadn't been hallucinating. That was the only explanation he could come up with for his mother seeming to contradict herself in a matter of moments. "I beg your pardon?"

"You are not to choose a wife as you would choose a horse. We've a tradition in this family. You're to uphold it."

One side of Griffith's mouth quirked up. "Are you ordering me to fall in love?"

"No." She sniffed. "That would be ridiculous. I'm ordering you to go find it."

She spun around, her skirt swishing against the desk, and glided toward the door. "We're bowling on the lawn in an hour. You will be there or I will know why."

Griffith winced as the door closed behind her, hoping she'd remember to send the footman with the headache powder. Griffith hated the stuff, often feeling that the slight wooziness of the treatment was worse than the malady itself. He'd take it today, though, because there was no way he was going to make it through a morning of noisy, physical outdoor activity without a little help.

There were many things the aristocracy loved that Isabella had never done. Lawn bowls, however, wasn't one of them.

While it was true that no one in her village was wealthy enough to afford the license to maintain a lawn bowling green, there were no such restrictions across the border at her grandmother's house. It had been several years since she'd played the game, but she occasionally still amused herself by throwing rocks at acorns and seeing how close she could get them. It was nearly the same principle, except the rocks never rolled as well as a lawn bowling ball would.

She cast a glance from Uncle Percy to the house and back again as the group of houseguests crossed the grounds to the strip of manicured lawn where the rack of balls had already been placed. She'd made a show of wanting to stay inside, but most of it had been for Uncle Percy's sake. She dearly wanted to join in on this particular event.

And not only because it had been such a long time since she had played lawn bowls.

She wanted to see Griffith again. It didn't matter how bad an idea it was or how much she knew it would displease her uncle, the urge was overwhelming to see if the changes that occurred during their intimate conversation the day before continued in the light of a new day.

Assuming he even remembered them. There was every possibility he intended to avoid her entirely.

And what would she do if he didn't? Gambling that a courtship with the duke would be successful and that he wouldn't care about being lied to and then that he'd be willing to pay a large sum of money to help her family would be the height of foolishness, considering everything else she'd already done to secure her family's future. He was far too upright a man to do either.

That didn't stop her from wondering, though. What would it mean if she enjoyed his company today? If his attentions were directed at her instead of her cousin or one of the other attractive, titled young ladies now strolling across the cropped grass?

Unease trickled down her spine as she glanced back at Uncle Percy's narrowed gaze.

Nothing. It would mean nothing. Because she couldn't let it.

But Griffith didn't know that. He'd begun to suspect, but she'd never actually told him why he needed to leave his attentions on Frederica. He was a duke, used to doing and getting whatever he wished. If he decided he wanted to refocus his attentions, there'd be nothing she could do to stop him.

A large figure emerged from a side door, and his long legs ate up the distance from the house to the lawn bowling green at a rate that caused her heart to speed up and match it. As he came closer, his features became more defined—the thick brows, the small dip in the middle of his chin, and the wave of his hair styled to perfection and dropping forward to cover his ears. Her gaze met his, and she felt every bit as awed as she had stumbling across the fields, talking more openly with the drunken duke than she ever had with anyone other than Frederica.

Her uncle was going to have a fit.

Breaking the connection, Isabella turned and strolled as calmly as she could to Frederica's side. At least now, if Griffith carried through on the seeming promise in his eyes, they could make it appear as though he'd crossed the lawn to approach Frederica instead of herself. Perhaps it would be enough to fool Uncle Percy.

"Finally decided to speak to me this morning?" Frederica tried to look stern, but the curved corners of her lips said otherwise.

Isabella closed her eyes on a sigh. "I'm so sorry."

With a shrug, Frederica shifted her gaze from Isabella to the rapidly approaching duke. "Think nothing of it. A group of ladies had taken a jaunt to the village. Arthur escorted me to them and I joined their party on the way back." Her brown eyes narrowed in Isabella's direction. "I have a feeling, though, that your story isn't so simple."

Isabella opened her mouth to answer, but the looming sensation of someone approaching stayed her tongue.

"Good morning."

"Good morning, Your Grace," Isabella and Frederica said at the same time, though Bella's was little more than a murmur. As they curtsied, she flicked her eyes up to look at Griffith through her lashes. He was smiling at her. A real smile. Despite the fact that alcohol could in no way still be impeding his faculties.

Frederica straightened and looked back and forth between Bella and the duke, a small curve coming to her lips. She cleared her throat and turned to the duke. "My cousin and I were just saying how lovely your bowling green is."

Isabella's gaze narrowed in her cousin's direction. They'd been saying no such thing. Why would Frederica protect her that way? It was by far the most personal thing Freddie had said to the duke in weeks. Could she tell that something had changed between Isabella and the duke? She'd made no secret about not liking Isabella's working with Uncle Percy, but she'd been supportive up to now. If Freddie thought her cousin could actually make a love match, though—and a very advantageous one, at that—there would be no way to stop her from encouraging the attraction in every possible way.

"I'm glad you approve." Griffith's deep voice rolled over Isabella, clear and free from all slurs but still maintaining the smooth tone and quality. "I don't take as much time to indulge in it as I should. I'm glad we're making use of it today."

Frederica bounced twice on her toes. "Isabella is quite accomplished, you know."

Isabella gasped through slightly parted lips and gritted teeth, causing the sucked-in air to hiss as she allowed her eyes to seek out Griffith's green gaze.

"Is that so?" He stared at her with an unwavering look that anyone who was paying any attention at all would know was not directed in Frederica's direction.

"I was when I was a child." Isabella swallowed. How could she direct his attention elsewhere? He'd admitted yesterday that she was a puzzle, and she could already see him trying to put this new information together with what he remembered from before. Could he guess she came from a less-than-aristocratic background? Had he a suspicion of anything else? "My skills have probably faded over the years. In fact, I've the intention of sitting out this first game so that I can remember how it's played. I wouldn't want to impede anyone."

One golden brow lifted as his lips twisted in an expression of disbelief and amusement. "Given that a significant portion of the game's intent is to impede another player, I believe you might stumble your way into a victory."

Isabella didn't know what to say to that, but it wouldn't have mattered if she had, because their small group was soon overrun with the other unmarried young ladies who had been invited to the country house. Their mothers were also in the group, and soon the conversation fell into a competition of who could say the most remarkable thing about how much they were enjoying the house party and how much they were looking forward to being able to show His Grace how very enchanted they were to have a chance to play the illustrious game on such fine turf. One girl even went so far as to say it was finer than the lawn bowling green in Windsor.

"How fortunate we are to be among ladies who are so accomplished at lawn bowling. I've always admired a lady who could apply herself to challenging activities." Griffith nodded at each of the young ladies as they rushed to tell him how often they'd played and how much time they'd devoted to it.

"Wonderful." He stepped away from the clinging horde and positioned himself between Isabella and Frederica. "As Miss Breckenridge and Miss St. Claire were just telling me that they hadn't been able to play in many years, I shall play this first set with them and remind them of the rules and strategies. Hopefully it will return to them quickly and we can all enjoy a second game on a more level playing field."

Isabella lifted her gloved hand to cover her mouth, inhaling deeply of the leather to give her anything to ground herself with so she wouldn't laugh at the disgruntled faces before her.

Drunken Griffith was enlightening, but sober Griffith was fascinating. He'd maneuvered an entire house party of people into the exact places he wanted them and had done it in such a way that kept Frederica in his company. Since Uncle Percy had all but set Isabella and Frederica up as each other's chaperons for the Season, he would have no way of finding fault in the situation. Rather, Frederica was Isabella's chaperon. He hadn't foreseen this development.

As everyone divided into teams to play, Griffith made a great show of describing the lawn and the rules to the cousins.

"And this"—he held up one of the small, earth-colored balls in his right hand—"is the type of ball we will roll toward the jack, the small white ball that's been tossed down the green."

Frederica sighed. "I don't think we need to get that basic. It's only been eleven years since we played." She scrunched her nose and turned toward Isabella. "That's correct, isn't it? Your nanna died when you were thirteen?"

Isabella's heart dropped to her toes as she cut her eyes to view Griffith through her lashes. Had he caught the slip? Done the math? Would he have one more question to add to the mystery that was Isabella?

Griffith was staring straight at her. "Eleven years, hmmm?"

She swallowed. "Yes."

"How fortunate to have a companion so near to one's age while growing up." Griffith's eyes narrowed, but his lips curved with the knowledge that he'd confirmed one of her lies.

It was time to retreat. She plucked the ball from his outstretched hand. "I think I'm ready to try."

Not wanting to make Griffith look like a fool for helping the two inexperienced women, she deliberately made her ball swing wide around the jack and roll a good ways beyond the target.

"A bit long." He dropped his right shoulder so he could angle his head closer to hers. "Perhaps you shouldn't try so hard next time."

"My turn," Frederica chirped. She grabbed a ball from the rack and launched it. Right into her father's stomach.

⁓

If Isabella had harbored any hopes of the ladies at the house party coming to like her, she abandoned them over the next hour.

Once Frederica had quite cleverly gotten her father to retreat back to the house while perpetuating the tale that both she and Isabella were terrible at lawn bowls, the game became decidedly more relaxed. Isabella felt considerably freer without her uncle watching her every interaction with the duke.

Griffith did eventually move on to play in other groups, keeping his injured arm tucked close to his side while he launched the balls with his right, but he always seemed to know when

Isabella or Frederica had thrown, paying them equal compliments on their progress.

As he rolled balls with Lady Alethea, Isabella fought back the bitter bile of jealousy. For the past month people had been debating which of the two girls was the most beautiful in London. Normally Isabella's paler coloring and delicate features won out, but occasionally someone preferred Lady Alethea's darker hair and broader face. It had never bothered Isabella. The people she needed to like her liked her, and everyone else didn't matter.

Except now it mattered, and Isabella couldn't help but wonder which one Griffith preferred. He'd called her beautiful and said she intrigued him, but was she just that? A puzzle to be solved before he moved on to finding someone who fit his requirements? In all the things he'd said yesterday, he hadn't said what he was looking for. Only that Isabella didn't fit it.

"He's being promoted."

Isabella dragged her gaze from where Griffith was discussing the best trajectories with Lady Alethea. "Who?"

"Arthur. He's a captain now."

"That's wonderful." She thought about what Griffith had said about Uncle Percy trying to have Arthur moved. This would make a difference. Wouldn't it? "Surely your father can't object to that."

"He can when there's a duke as the seeming alternative." Frederica reached up to jab a loose pin back into her curls.

Bella picked at a thread on her skirt. It wasn't loose, but a tiny loop stuck up above the other stitches. She ran her finger over it, back and forth, letting the seam of her glove catch against the raised thread. "I could try to redirect the duke."

Frederica turned her brown eyes in Bella's direction and grinned, hands clasped to her chest. "I knew it."

"You know nothing."

"You don't know what I know."

Isabella huffed. "Oh, I know what it is you think you know, but I also know that what you think you know isn't nearly everything."

Frederica stared at Bella. "Was that a sentence?"

"Yes." Isabella stuck her nose in the air. "It was simply a very convoluted one."

"Regardless, you won't convince me that you don't like him. I told you with all the flirting you were going to have to do you'd eventually find a man you actually fell for."

Isabella gestured toward the bowling green. "I believe it's our turn. And I have not fallen in love with the man." She picked up a bowling ball. "I hardly know him."

"But you'd like to."

"I'd also like to go home and never have a thing to do with your father again. I'd like for my own father to have never gotten hurt. I'd like a lot of things, but that doesn't mean I'm going to get them." She jabbed the ball forward, all delight in Frederica's potential good fortune lost to her own maudlin melancholy.

Frederica took the ball and positioned herself at the edge of the green. Lady Alethea's giggle rolled through the air, making Frederica frown. "Are you certain you wouldn't rather go again? You've got better aim than I do."

Had God ever created anyone as sweet as Freddie? Even though that sweetness was looking a bit violent at the moment, Isabella couldn't help but appreciate her cousin's attempts at raising Isabella's spirits. "Are you sure?"

Freddie handed the ball over, and Isabella contemplated her ball and the giggling girl in the pale pink gown before letting it roll, sending girls and mamas alike scattering across the lawn.

Chapter 18

Two days of careful activity brought the pain in Griffith's arm down to a dull ache. As long as he didn't jerk it, he could manage most things without appearing the slightest bit injured. He tightened his fist experimentally and was pleased when there was no sharpness to the pain that radiated down to his wrist. That meant he was better than yesterday, and the pot after pot of willow bark tea was doing its job. He was soon going to have to send the groundskeeper out for more at the rate he was drinking the vile liquid. Still, it was better than the numbness brought about by taking laudanum.

Although a bit of numbness in his ears might be appreciated with all the feminine chatter he'd been forced to put up with. Unlike most house parties where a man could escape the skirt-wearing portion of the guests for part of the day, his mother had scheduled events from breakfast to dinner and on until bedtime. He'd managed to make his excuses twice more, but with his injury there was very little he could do, physically speaking. He couldn't ride, couldn't help with the farm work or the animals. He was already lying to his mother about the arm. He wasn't about to add to it by lying to her about what he was doing with his time as well.

And that was the only reason why he was now standing in the doorway to the drawing room, where a game of charades had been scheduled at the ridiculous hour of ten in the morning. He cast a glance over the assembled group, but a specific head of red-gold hair was noticeably absent. It had been absent quite a bit since the lawn bowling. Whereas his excuses had been shot down by his mother's marksman-like guilt trips, Isabella's had obviously been readily accepted.

Of course, she was a guest and he was the host, but if the point of this week was for him to fall in love, he needed the woman he was most interested in to be around for him to do so.

He approached Miss St. Claire, the next best alternative to spending time with Isabella. He was fairly certain the cousin was on his side, because she would happily answer any question he asked about Isabella without skewering him with an accusatory look or asking him why he wanted to know.

"Miss St. Claire." He bowed in greeting and sat in the armchair next to her. "Are you finding your rooms to your liking?"

"Yes." One side of her mouth kicked up. "They are most comfortable. But the lighting is terrible if one wants to read in the mornings."

As Miss St. Claire had spent all of the past mornings engaging in whatever activity his mother had arranged, her statement must have been a reference to Isabella. This was the first she'd offered as to where her cousin was when she wasn't with the group.

Griffith cleared his throat and tried to look relaxed. "And have you discovered the best location to read that may have proper lighting?"

"The small drawing room on the second floor. Near the nursery. It's eastward facing and has an excellent window seat."

Griffith dropped back in his seat, stunned. When was the last time he'd even been up to the second floor? Not since he and his siblings had grown old enough to have rooms on the first, probably. No wonder she felt safe retreating up there. She'd be able to disappear for hours with no chance of running into anyone else.

He had to find a way out of this room.

Mother clapped her hands in the center of the drawing room. "Her Grace, the Duchess of Marshington, had the most wonderful idea last night."

A glance in Miranda's direction found her looking quite pleased with herself. As Miranda had made no qualms about telling Griffith whom he should bestow his attentions on, her smug grin gave him a bit of hope.

"We've decided to delay charades until after dinner this evening. This morning we're going to do a treasure hunt!"

A low murmur drifted across the room, and heads began to swivel until all the eyes of the unmarried ladies were settled on him. He immediately hooked his arm through Miss St. Claire's, prompting her to giggle behind her hand. It wasn't the annoying sort of giggle designed to garner attention but the sort born of genuine humor.

It had been gratifying to learn over the past few days that his instincts about Miss St. Claire had been correct. Once he'd gotten to know her, without the distraction of an attempted romance between them, he'd found her to be a charming and engaging young lady. That her heart was already given and his was inclined toward another made it easy for them to be friends, something he sorely needed in this dreadful house party.

"We will pair off, two couples per group. I've a list for each of you. We'll meet back here in an hour to see who has been the most successful."

Griffith sprang to his feet, hauling Miss St. Claire out of her chair and across the room to Miranda's side. "You are joining us."

She grinned. "But I thought I might relax somewhere. Perhaps put my feet up like one of those decadent Egyptian women in paintings."

Griffith lifted an eyebrow and stared her down.

"Oh, very well. Ryland and I will join you."

Griffith turned to find more than one disappointed face turned in his direction at Miranda's announcement. If his mother was trying to alienate him from some of the most sought-after ladies of the Season she was doing a very good job. By the end of this week they'd be ready to hoist him into the stocks outside Newgate.

Ryland held up a piece of paper. "I've got our list. I do think it's a bit unfair having two people who grew up in this house on one team."

"Since when has it ever bothered you to have an advantage?" Griffith took the paper and looked it over.

The other man shrugged. "Never. It just seemed like the sort of thing that should be noted."

"Acknowledged." He handed the list to Miss St. Claire. "I believe we should start on the second floor."

"But there's nothing on the second floor." Miranda scrunched her face up as she looked at the list over Miss St. Claire's shoulder. "I believe Mother would like to keep most everyone here on the ground floor."

Ryland looked from Griffith to Miss St. Claire and back again. "I have a feeling something very important might be on the second floor."

"We won't know until we check, will we?" Griffith turned to

find his mother frowning at him. He simply smiled and patted a hand on Miss St. Claire's arm trapped snugly against his side.

One side of Mother's mouth picked up. "As an added incentive," she called over the bustling crowd, "one lady from the winning group will be granted her choice of partners for the first dance of tomorrow night's ball." She speared her son with a glare. "Any partner."

Griffith pressed his mouth into a grim line.

His mother was going to make him dance.

Miranda was already breathing hard by the time they reached the first floor. She dropped a shoulder against the wall and pressed one hand to her middle. "Give me the list. You go up and see what you can find on the second floor. Ryland and I will gather what we can from this one."

As the first floor was mainly bedrooms, most of the guests were avoiding it. Few items on the list were things that someone would have packed, and no one was going to be rude enough to search another guest's bedroom. Miranda had access to the family rooms, though, where at least three or four of the ten items listed might be found.

It was a sound strategy and one that had kept anyone from questioning why the group had headed for the stairs instead of the ground-floor rooms like everyone else.

Griffith wasn't about to wait for her to offer twice.

He headed for the stairs at the end of the passage, the quick patter of slippers telling him he'd forgotten to adjust his pace for Miss St. Claire's shorter stride. At the stairs he had to grip the railing until his knuckles turned white.

"Go ahead. I'll be right behind you."

Griffith heard the laughter in her words but didn't blame her.

When he'd thought through whom he should marry, ticking off qualities like he would an estate improvement, he'd been able to move sedately, with patience. Now the urge to hurry rushed under his skin. He paused at the top of the stairs, breath rushing and heart pounding. Was this what his brother and friends had felt? The roiling emotion that caused them to make such blundering, foolish decisions?

Griffith leaned a hand on the wall and forced his brain to catch up with his instincts. He was chasing after a woman who had deliberately hid. She was avoiding him while they were in a place where more private conversations could be held than anywhere else in the Season. And she was reading in a forgotten drawing room intended for use by the upstairs servants while the children were taking a nap or doing lessons.

Obviously her emotions were not inclined in the same direction as his were.

Why hadn't he seen that before? He didn't remember everything of their countryside walk after his injury, but he clearly remembered telling her things he shouldn't have about how he felt about her. And he didn't remember her reciprocating. If her actions were anything to go by, she didn't.

"What are you doing?"

Griffith had forgotten about Miss St. Claire coming up the stairs behind him. "Reconsidering."

Her brows pulled together, bringing even more attention to her nose. "Whyever would you do that? She's just around the corner."

"Obviously she doesn't want to be found or she wouldn't be up here." He kept his voice lowered, knowing that if Isabella heard them she'd either run or come investigate, and he would once again be at a disadvantage in her presence.

"You know nothing about what she wants." Miss St. Claire rolled her eyes.

"Miss St. Claire, I—"

"Frederica. If we're going to sneak around your house to-gether, I think it's safe for you to call me by my given name."

"Er, thank you, I suppose. . . ."

"And I shall call you Riverton."

He sighed, thankful that she wasn't hoping for the same intimacy he'd recklessly given to Isabella. "Frederica, I have no wish to chase your cousin if she desires to be alone."

"Hmmph. She doesn't know what she desires. Come along."

Frederica grabbed his hand and hauled him around the corner into a small drawing room he had vague memories of sitting in with his nanny while she read stories to them. Isabella was curled in the window seat, a book open on her lap as she traced designs on the windowpane with her finger.

Her head snapped around as Frederica cleared her throat. Red flooded her cheeks as she met Griffith's eyes.

"You haven't joined us," Griffith said. "There was quite a rousing game of piquet after lunch yesterday. Emotions ran so high, cards were almost bent."

The corners of her mouth lifted slightly. "I'm sorry I missed it."

Griffith stepped forward. "Why did you? I see you at din-ner but never before or after. Your book is obviously not that interesting."

Isabella ran her finger along the edge of the pages. "No. It isn't. I'm not even sure which one I brought up here with me."

Foolish or not, the urgency under his skin propelled him to do something, so he sat on the window seat beside her curled-up legs, the toes of her slippers pressed against his leg as he reached over and wrapped his hand around hers. The long lines of her ungloved fingers felt cool against his palm, and he wrapped his grip more firmly around her hand. "Why are you avoiding me?"

"My life is complicated," she whispered.

"I'm a duke. I'm rather good with complicated."

They stared at each other for a moment. She didn't look nearly as comforted as he'd hoped she would.

"I don't know if I love you." The words came out in a rush, her eyes widening as if she hadn't even known what she was going to say. As soon as they'd cleared her lips, though, a measure of calm came over her. The slight trembling he'd felt in her fingers ceased, even as a suspicious wet gleam formed along the bottom edge of her eyes.

"I don't know if I love you," she repeated. "I don't know if I can. I have problems. You could solve them, I know, but what then? What if we're both trapped in a marriage we discover we don't want with no way out? What if you learn my secrets and don't like them? If I stay on the path I'm on, I'll be able to walk away when it's over. I'll have my life ahead of me. But if you . . . If I let you . . . I'll be trapped. We'll be trapped."

And this was what it would have felt like if that thatching needle had caught him in the chest instead of the arm. His brother had been right. His friends had been right. Love didn't play by any logical rules. It was an ever-changing maze. A monster that chewed you up and spit you out and made you fight for your happiness or die trying.

She took a trembling breath, and a single tear spilled out to slide down her perfect, smooth cheek. "I don't want to hurt you. Please go."

The gentleman in him was standing even as part of him screamed in his head not to leave until he'd changed her mind. But it was becoming clear that he was fighting a foe he didn't understand, didn't even know about. And love was just going to have to join forces with his brain if he wanted to figure it out.

He stepped away, letting her fingers trail slowly through his.

He looked up and saw Frederica still standing in the doorway, hands cupped to her face and eyes rimmed with red. There was certainly more here than he knew.

Halfway across the floor he turned and looked at Isabella. She'd curled her legs in tighter and tucked her face into her knees. There was no way she could convince him she felt nothing. A small sob escaped her curled form, and Frederica's quiet cry answered it. Emotion was as thick in this room as the dust that had been allowed to settle while the house was prepared for company. Griffith didn't do emotion and never had, and this was why. It was uncontrollable and messy.

He rubbed a hand against his aching chest. Emotion was also very real and powerful. More so than he ever realized.

But Griffith was a problem solver. That was something he'd been since he was little, stomping around the fields with his father in boots that were a touch too big because they were the smallest the cobbler had that matched his father's, and he'd been unwilling to wait for the man to make more.

He tore his gaze from Isabella. Simply looking at her muddled his thoughts, but watching her cry quietly churned them like trodden mud. He looked at the window, the floor, the ceiling, searching his brain for a promise he could make to her, to let her know that just because he was leaving this room he wasn't giving up on her.

A collection of small white figurines on the table by the door caught his eye. He picked up a porcelain couple—arms linked in the steps of some sort of dance—and held it in his palm, a dozen thoughts whipping through his mind as he watched the light glint on the clean, white surface. He grabbed on to the most important notion at the moment and held tightly to it.

"I want to dance with you."

Isabella's head snapped up, and Frederica gasped.

"Everywhere you go, every ball and soiree, I will be there, and I will ask you. I want you to be the next person I dance with."

Frederica sniffled. "But the ball. Your mother promised the winning lady her choice."

He looked at the figurine in his hand once more and then at Frederica. "I suppose we need to win, then."

⌒

Thirty minutes later he strolled into the drawing room with Frederica on his arm and Miranda and Ryland trailing behind them. Miranda placed their bag of items on the table. Mother dutifully sorted through them, then looked up with a triumphant smile on her face. "I'm afraid Lady Alethea's was the first group to return, and they also had nine of the items."

Griffith tilted his head and smiled back at his mother while he reached into his pocket and pulled out the dancing figurine he'd picked up in the second-floor drawing room. A figurine that had sat with its sisters on a table in the front hall his entire life.

He set it gently among the circle of items on the table before returning to stand to his full height.

"Miranda will open the ball with Ryland."

He bowed, trying not to feel guilty over his mother's grim expression, then turned and walked from the room.

Chapter 19

His house was full of people. After he'd set the figurine in front of his mother yesterday, he'd disappeared, hibernating in his study like the wounded bear he felt like. No one ventured into this area of the house, but the voices of the many newcomers drifted through the small gap between the door and the frame, infringing on his solitude until he considered getting up to close the door completely.

All afternoon yesterday carriages pulled down the lane, people tramped up and down the stairs, and servants rushed to and fro, trying to see to the needs of more people than this house had seen in their entire tenure.

It was ridiculous that so many people had loaded up their carriages or hired ones to drive them a long day's ride out into the country for a single day of activities followed by a ball in the evening. Tomorrow they would all be making the long trek back to London. It was entirely too much hassle for a single day of frivolity, but he was a duke. A rather solitary duke with an obligation to marry.

He frowned.

He didn't want his wife to be an obligation. Both he and

Isabella or Frederica or whoever his wife happened to be deserved more than that. She should be more than that. She deserved to be wanted, and he had enough obligations in his life without adding her to the list. Obtaining a wife might be an obligation, but the wife herself shouldn't be.

Which meant the selection of his wife could not be taken lightly. He'd known that, had always known that, and that was why he'd taken such care to think through everything so meticulously.

And now he was going to have to admit he'd been wrong.

Not just once, but twice. He'd been wrong about his ability to control his feelings, and then he'd been wrong about Isabella's feelings for him. Was he also incorrect about his feelings for her? What if he wasn't actually in love with her? What if he was only infatuated with her incredible beauty? What if his logical brain was obsessed with figuring out the intrigue around her, and once the mystery was solved she would lose the grip she appeared to have on him?

He sat back in his chair and rubbed his finger against his thumb.

The door swung open without a knock. Griffith tensed but maintained his position in the chair as he looked toward the door with a deliberately arrogant and powerful expression.

Only to find himself being laughed at.

Ryland and Anthony slid into the room and shut the door behind them.

"I can't thank you enough for volunteering me to dance the first dance." Ryland crossed to the desk to look over the notes Griffith had spread across the surface. It was mostly notes on the spring planting for his estate in Cornwall. Shafts of sunlight speared through the window to cut across the words.

"It's a bright, sunny day." Griffith pulled a paper toward him and tried to look preoccupied. "Shouldn't you be out fishing or whatever else my mother has planned? I know she intended for people to spend a good portion of the day outside."

"I don't know." Ryland flicked the paper in Griffith's hand. "Shouldn't you?"

Probably. But he'd come to the country to figure things out, and it was time he did. "I'm busy."

The two men shifted around the room, but Griffith kept his gaze resolutely on the paper in front of him, making himself read words that he'd forgotten by the time he reached the end of the sentence.

"We're busy too," Ryland finally said.

Griffith looked up to see both men settled deeply into chairs, as if they had no intention of budging from this room until he did.

Sometimes friends you couldn't intimidate were a staggering inconvenience.

He looked back at the paper.

"For goodness' sake, Griffith." Ryland moaned. "There are three sentences on that paper. They think the western-most field should be left fallow for the year because last year's crop yield was less than adequate."

Griffith made an extra effort to retain the information on the letter in his hand. Ryland was correct. Trying to look casual and confident, he slid the paper onto the desk. "Leaving an entire field empty for the year is a decision that shouldn't be taken lightly. People need food."

"And you need a wife." As Anthony's first contribution to the conversation, it was direct and to the point of the real reason the men had invaded his study. "So why are you in here instead of joining the expedition to the ruins?"

"I've seen the ruins."

"As have I. Which is why I know that in spite of the fact that you cleaned up all of the dangerous parts last summer, there are plenty of rocks and ditches for ladies to be helped over."

Ryland cleared his throat. "Ladies such as Miss Breckenridge."

"Miss Breckenridge hasn't joined in on an event in days. Why would she be going to the ruins?" But he knew why. Isabella adored seeing where and how things grew. She wouldn't miss the chance to see how the plants had taken over the old stones and piles of rotten wood.

"How should I know? But I assume that the blond curls in the middle of the cluster of gentlemen surrounded by pouting ladies belongs to your beautiful obsession." Ryland shrugged and settled farther into his chair.

"I'm not obsessed."

Anthony laughed.

Ryland pursed his lips and raised his brow.

"I'm not. Not with Isa . . ." He cleared his throat. "Miss Breckenridge."

The twin smirks on the other side of his desk proved both men had heard him slip on her name. Errors such as that were not common for him. He didn't say anything he didn't mean to say, didn't allow anyone to catch him at a disadvantage. At least, he hadn't until Isabella had come into his life.

Ryland was the first to break the silence. "I told you Miss St. Claire was the wrong woman for you."

The word *wrong* made Griffith wince and started a throbbing in the back of his head. He flexed his injured arm out of habit, even though the ache and tension wasn't coming from there at the moment.

"Who is to say," he said slowly, thinking through every word with deliberate care. He couldn't afford for his two friends to misunderstand his question. Mostly because he wasn't sure he'd get the nerve to ask it again. "Who is to say if I'll ever be able to make the correct decision? If I've already made the wrong decision twice, how can I trust that I'll ever be able to discern the woman God wants me to marry?"

"Twice? You've abandoned your pursuit of Miss Breckenridge already?" Ryland's forehead scrunched into a wrinkle so deep his dark eyebrows were nearly touching.

Had he abandoned it? Had he ever even truly started pursuing her? "Obviously, she is not inclined to find my suit favorable, so it stands to reason that she is not the woman God prepared for me."

"I don't think it works that way." Anthony pushed up from the chair and crossed to the window.

"Of course it does. Proverbs. 'In all thy ways acknowledge him, and he shall direct thy paths.'"

Ryland laughed. "You think that means He's going to tell you whom to marry?"

"Why wouldn't it?" Griffith was torn between having this conversation because he knew it was the right thing to do and tossing his two closest friends out on their ears. Or he could leave them here and join the rest of the guests at the ruins. Where at this very moment Isabella was surrounded by suitors.

This was the very reason Griffith hadn't wanted to pursue a Diamond.

Leaning forward to prop his elbows on his knees, Ryland's grey eyes pinned Griffith in his chair. It was the same gaze that had skewered many a Frenchman into giving up his secrets. Griffith had to admit it was fairly effective.

"Sometimes, I think God lets you choose."

"Why would He do that?" Griffith rolled the thought over in his mind, but he honestly couldn't fathom it. If Griffith had that sort of omniscience and power, he would certainly be telling people where they needed to be. Sometimes he did it even though he wasn't omniscient.

Ryland lifted one shoulder and let it fall again, the close tailoring of his dark grey jacket falling right back into place. "I think sometimes He likes to give us a choice. Life's pretty bleak if you only ever do what you're told. If you make your choice with an aim to honor God, then He will honor that."

"And if I make the wrong one?"

Anthony leaned against the window, his attention gliding back and forth from Griffith to something outside. "Whatever choice you make, you work within the boundaries God laid out in the Bible. If you had married Miss St. Claire, would you have treated her the way the Bible says to treat your wife?"

"Of course." Griffith crossed his arms over his chest. Picturing the stilted breakfast conversations the two of them would probably have had didn't thrill him, but if he had made the commitment, he would have put everything he had into doing it right.

"And if you married Miss Breckenridge?"

The vision that ran through his head this time was considerably more pleasant, imagining him and Isabella riding through the countryside, visiting tenants together or just enjoying the land. "Yes."

"Then, I think it might be safe to assume that God will let you marry whichever lady you choose as long as you honor Him once you've done it." Anthony tapped the glass with one long finger. "And if you think you might want that choice to be Miss Breckenridge, you might want to venture outside. It's hard to see since they're going over the rise, but I think Lord Ivonbrook is holding her parasol."

Chapter 20

Griffith strode through the house and snagged his greatcoat from the hook by the door near the kitchen. It was the coat he used when he was going out to work, but it would have to do for now. He wasn't going to wait for his valet to retrieve his good one. It was a thirty-minute walk to the ruins—twenty, if he pushed himself—and the group had probably gotten there five minutes ago. He had a lot of ground to make up.

Wind pulled at his hair, sending the blond strands into his face to catch on his eyelashes. The sun beat down on him, making him wish he'd left the greatcoat behind entirely. It was difficult to know what the weather was going to do this time of year, but this was yet another thing he'd gotten wrong.

And if he was going to develop anxiety over decisions as small as whether or not to wear a coat, his life was about to become very miserable indeed.

There had to be some sort of way to avoid second-guessing everything he did and to have the ability and confidence to weather a few errors in judgment. A very few. And only on things that didn't matter a great deal. And were within the boundaries of God's set expectations.

He shoved a hand through his disheveled hair. If he'd known opening his mind to the idea of marriage would cause this much frustration, he'd have simply informed Trent he should be prepared to inherit. Did men without titles have this much trouble?

The excited chatter of the group drifted to him on the wind, and he slowed his hurried pace. He didn't want to storm up to the ruins appearing winded, after all, and his near run across the fields had left him in such a state. He slowed to a stroll and focused on steadying his breathing and calming his heart.

A group of servants gathered to the side under a copse of trees, where they served lemonade and small, iced cakes to the strolling masses. Griffith shrugged out of his greatcoat and dropped it into the wagon behind them before working his way down to the bottom set of ruins.

The old keep was half buried in the side of the hill, its stones nearly covered by hundreds of strands of climbing vines. The plants had been cut away from old windows and doors, rickety piles of stones had been scattered, and rotten wood had been cleared away to prevent the risk of an accident, making the ruins a safe and enjoyable place for a group outing.

It also meant there were many places where a couple wanting a touch of privacy could slip away unnoticed.

Guests greeted him and pulled him into conversation after conversation, preventing him from scouring the maze of old arches and rooms for Isabella. He'd used up his quotient of rudeness by not greeting them as they'd arrived, so he made himself take the time to talk to everyone as he moved through.

He talked weather and war, politics and scandal. He encouraged everyone to stay in the more stable section of the keep instead of the former great hall, from which several of the doorways and passages had crumbled. Everyone seemed to be greatly enjoying the outing, which would make his mother happy.

Familiar laughter wrapped around a corner and slammed into his gut. It had an edge, as if she were forcing it. Of course, more often than not people's laughter had that edge to it in this setting. Hearing Isabella push herself into fake enjoyment bothered him more, for some reason. Anyone who suffered from as much despair as she seemed to in private should at least actually enjoy their merriment.

"Lord Naworth, you're too much. Whatever made you think that bird would stand still while you tried to catch it?"

Griffith rolled his eyes. He wanted to stroll around the corner and rescue Isabella from the man who had obviously used the ploy of wildlife to get her alone. But he wanted to gauge the situation before he strolled into it. Were more people with them? Did the situation call for an amiable duke or an intimidating one?

"Ah, well, I shall just have to try again when the bird returns. It is the most elusive ones that are worth the effort."

"Whyever would you wish to catch it in the first place?"

"To cherish the beauty and show it to the world, of course." The man cleared his throat. "Much as I'd like to do with you."

Griffith actually smirked and shook his head at the hackneyed compliment.

Isabella laughed again. "Why, Lord Naworth, I don't know what to say. I'm very flattered."

"Say you'll let me court you. Let me enter a room with you on my arm. Take you riding in the park so everyone will know."

Griffith frowned, willing Isabella to give the forward man the cut direct. To tell him no and walk away. After this week, after Griffith's declaration of wanting to dance with her, she had to know he intended to pursue her. Even though he hadn't fully committed to it himself until somewhere between the house and the ruins.

"I had no idea you felt this way, Lord Naworth. I haven't even spoken to my uncle about you, and I value his opinion highly on matters such as this."

"How wise you are to seek counsel about your future, Miss Breckenridge. I will gladly approach your uncle and discuss the matter with him so that he can assure you that I am in earnest." He cleared his throat. "Perhaps he can relay more details about your situation. And your dowry?"

Griffith's frown darkened, deepened. Why was she letting him talk to her that way? Yes, the rumors of Isabella had been vague. Even he had heard them. But while many large dowries were practically public knowledge, it was not out of the ordinary for someone to keep the particulars of the situation private. The Isabella he knew was not a simpering miss, dependent upon the counsel of her uncle. In fact, he'd gotten the impression she thought the man was rather revolting. She shouldn't have any problem telling this man to redirect his attentions.

Unless she didn't want him to.

He considered moving round the corner then, but what would he say? He wasn't sure he could keep the accusation from his face in such an intimate setting. It would be better to see her again once she'd rejoined the group, where the number of people would force him to remain impassive and calm. The group wasn't far. Most of them were gathered in the room Griffith and Trent had called the showroom when they were children. It had the most ornate stonework in the ruins, elaborate carvings over wide archways and faux columns carved into the walls.

It wasn't long before Isabella and Lord Naworth left their little alcove and made their way back to the group. Griffith

232

counted to one hundred before he approached them. "Lord Naworth."

"Duke. I think this may be the farthest I've ever driven to watch you not dance." The man grinned, and Griffith was forced to remember that despite his ridiculous flirting antics, the man was usually quite pleasant and someone Griffith had talked to frequently at his club. "Unless of course you intend to break your pattern tonight. I don't suppose there will be some sort of announcement?"

"I considered it." Griffith couldn't help but stare down Isabella until she blushed. "But I'm afraid the lady in question wasn't interested."

Lord Naworth was silent for a moment and then broke into laughter. "I'm never sure whether to question your sanity or mine when your wit goes beyond my understanding."

Griffith lifted a brow, wondering at the man's intelligence. There had been nothing at all witty about Griffith's veiled barb. The false flattery and forced respect left a sour taste in his mouth.

A glance at Isabella proved that she too thought the man's mirth was a little farfetched. But still she smiled and simpered in a way that seemed to indicate he was the most fascinating man on the planet.

If she were to give Griffith's suit any encouragement at all, he would be forced to question whether his feelings had been genuine or manipulated. Of course, she could be doing that on purpose, saving her less obvious attentions for the more mentally inclined.

Griffith didn't like not knowing his own mind. Always he'd been able to count on facts and things he'd thought through, contemplated. His decisions had always been supportable and evenly considered. Isabella made him question everything. Even the intentions he'd had when he joined the gathering.

It was enough to make him dizzy.

Desperate to think through what to call the feelings bubbling in his chest like a witch's cauldron in a Shakespearean play, he made his excuses and skirted around the couple to go play the happy host a bit more.

⌒

The ballroom was beautiful.

What Isabella could see of it, anyway.

At her uncle's insistence, she'd made an entrance, danced a handful of dances, and then slipped from the ballroom. Enough to make a presence, but not enough to distract anyone who might be considering Frederica.

The fact that such a problem hadn't been the slightest of concerns until the duke had visited raised Isabella's annoyance several levels.

So now she was in an upstairs parlor, clinging to the shadows and overlooking the ballroom. From here she could enjoy the music and the swirling couples. The noises that reached her were indistinct, happy noises. Laughter carried well, and it was easy to pretend that everyone down there was enjoying life.

Was everyone putting on as much of a pretense as she was?

The door opened behind her, and she whirled around, prepared to be rushed off by some servant or another. She'd had to venture into the private family wing to reach this room.

A considerably larger figure hulked in the open doorway.

"Griffith," she murmured. "How did you find me?"

He stepped in and pulled the door, leaving a hand's width gap and a sliver of pale grey light.

"I'd love to say something romantic such as I always know where you are or that God had placed an undeniable urge to come up here, but the truth is I'm simply tired of people staring at me, waiting for me to dance."

"So you came up here?"

The dark shape of him shrugged before he stepped closer to the window, and light from the ballroom below highlighted the bone structure of his face. "This is where I watched balls when I was a boy."

Picturing him as a young lad, hiding away, perhaps kneeling and peeping over the windowsill, made her heart melt in ways she couldn't afford.

"I am very sorry to have intruded upon your private space." She headed for the door but barely had time to shift her skirts before he reached out a hand to hold her elbow. "Don't leave. If you don't wish to join the festivities, this is truly the best place to watch from. Please join me?"

Isabella hesitated, wondering at the wisdom of staying with him yet unable to deny that the prospect of a few more stolen moments, out of view and hearing of everyone else, was incredibly appealing.

She stepped closer to the window so she could see the columns of dancers working their way through a quadrille. "Why don't you dance?"

"You think I have a deeper reason than not wishing to knock into everyone around me?" Griffith turned to lean his hips against a chair, directing his attention to her instead of the ball below.

"I think you have a deeper reason for everything you do."

His chuckle was low, and the dark made it feel intimate. "I suppose I do most of the time."

"And this time?" She moved to the hulking shadow of a chair set at an angle to the one he leaned against and half sat on the arm. Somehow, settling into the actual chair felt too risky, as if they would no longer be able to call this a chance encounter if they settled in to talk properly.

"That's all it was in the beginning. I learned quickly that my size threw off most dancers. My shoulders were too wide, my steps too long. The hopping steps in particular seemed to cause distress for any woman I was partnering. So I began limiting my partners to family."

"Why not refuse to dance at all?"

He tilted his head, light from the ballroom touching one side of his face, enough for her to see his surprise at the question. As if the answer were obvious. To him it probably had been, a logic he never stopped to think about because it made such perfect sense. Isabella would have dearly loved a few more moments of that sort of clarity in her life.

Fabric rustled as he shifted against the chair and crossed his arms in front of his chest. "I didn't want to lose the option. I never knew when I would need to be able to dance. Eschewing dancing entirely would have made such a thing nearly impossible without creating an incredible stir."

"Hasn't it turned out that way?"

"Perhaps."

More shifting. What was making him restless? Did he want to sit but wouldn't because she was still propped on the arm instead of seated in the chair?

He shrugged. "But it has had its advantages as well. When Trent married, for instance, his wife was not immediately accepted. Dancing with her declared her family."

Didn't he realize the protective passion in his statement? Suddenly Isabella hated that she had refused him. Hated that she couldn't afford to claim a moment of that sense of belonging for herself.

He cleared his throat. "I actually waltz rather well."

A puff of laughter breathed out of her lungs before she could stop it. "I've heard you never waltz."

"Long legs." One massive shoulder lifted and lowered. "But I danced with both of my sisters as they were learning. When I was home from school they would take turns playing the piano while I whirled the other around the room. Sometimes I lifted them up so their feet dangled above the floor."

"You enjoy waltzing." The statement was hushed, spoken into the dark like a confession, even though it wasn't her admittance to make.

"Yes." There was no hesitancy in his voice, no hint of awe or shame in the admission. "When I waltz I can go where I wish, adjusting to only one person."

He pushed off from the chair and strode to the window, leaning his shoulder against the opening. "They used to have balls here two or three times a year, when Father was alive. At Christmas they'd invite the entire village just to fill the room.

"When Father died, so did the balls. It made Mother sad, sometimes, particularly at Christmas. She would stand in that doorway over there and look across the empty room. Sometimes she hummed. Once I saw her cry."

She could imagine it, at least from Griffith's side. A boy, forced into the role of a young man, trying to be what his mother needed. It was difficult to imagine Lady Blackstone as anything resembling weak. She scared Isabella a bit, if she were being honest, but Griffith wouldn't have seen her the way Isabella did. "You would dance with her."

His head snapped in her direction as if surprised she was able to guess. "Yes. We would hum Mozart's 'Three German Dances' and I would take her across the floor. It was how I marked my growth. We danced every Christmas, our own private family ball. I don't even think the servants knew about it. Each year it'd be a little easier to guide her, until I was having to adjust my steps to her smaller ones."

Isabella couldn't stay away any more. She crossed into the square of pale, flickering light, needing to be near him and to offer whatever comfort she could without actually touching him. "Why do you deny yourself something you so obviously enjoy?"

"Because I can't only dance the waltzes. And that, down there—" he nodded to the colors swirling on the floor below— "that's not enjoyable. I step onto that floor and every eye turns my way, every tongue bears my name. I become a show, and my choice becomes all anyone wants to talk about. Who I dance with becomes more important than what I think of the latest developments in France. Speculating over whether or not I'll marry the person creates a vulnerable and socially acceptable personal interjection into any discussion."

His fingers began to fidget, rubbing against each other and causing a play of shadows across his hand. "That was a vulnerability I couldn't afford as a young duke. And then my sisters were out and I needed all the power I could retain to intimidate anyone who would take advantage of them. Now it's a habit I can't afford to break."

They fell silent as the song ended below them once more. The strains of "Three German Dances" started up, and couples paired off to waltz across the floor.

Griffith dropped his head to the ornately carved framework around the opening to the ballroom below. Isabella leaned forward to follow his gaze and could just make out the head of his mother and sister in the corner. The Duchess of Marshington looked up toward their hiding place, and Isabella ducked farther back into the shadows.

"Will you dance with me?" Griffith asked, his voice as rough as it had been after all the whisky, but this time she couldn't blame anything other than emotion for the cracked rumble.

He stepped away from the wall and approached her. When she didn't move he took her hand in his and threaded his fingers through hers, warmth seeping through the glove. "Will you go back downstairs and waltz across my ballroom with me?"

"No," she whispered.

His entire body seemed to sag, though she saw no visible change to his posture. The song wrapped around them, and she couldn't imagine the memories he had to be facing just then. He'd given up something he enjoyed for the greater good, for his family. Perhaps she could give a little of that back, though not as much as he seemed to want. "But I'll dance with you here."

Chapter 21

It wouldn't be wise. Simply being in this room with her wasn't wise. And Griffith prided himself on making the right decisions. But right now, his heart was pounding so hard, so fast, that the shrewd part of his brain seemed to be cut off from the part that made the actual decisions. Because even as he told himself that the right thing to do would be to walk away, he found himself sliding a hand around her waist and wrapping his fingers around hers.

And then they were dancing.

The space was small, and in moments his breathing was far harsher than the limited physical exertion called for. Waltzing with Isabella felt nothing like waltzing with his mother or twirling his sisters. He'd never held a woman like this before, with the curve of her waist under his hand and the heat of her body searing his palm.

Her fingers gripped his tighter as he spun her around the chair, trusting his intuition and his memory to move them around the furniture in the darkened room. The pulses of air against his throat told him that she too was affected by their dance.

Was this helping his cause or hurting it?

He stopped dancing, pulling her closer when she stumbled. "You're a lovely dancer," she whispered. "Why did you stop?"

Why had he stopped? It didn't make sense. If he was trying to ingratiate himself to her, to win her affections, shouldn't he continue when he knew she was enjoying the dance? But his mind wasn't driving his actions just then. He wasn't entirely sure what was. Somehow he was deciding what was right without putting any conscious thought to it at all.

And he knew that this dance wasn't something he could continue. Not here. It would become too much—he wanted too much.

He cupped a hand around her neck, relishing the way the fine hairs grazed his fingers even as the sensation made him feel things, want things he had no right to. And that was the dangerous part. "Come downstairs. I'll dance with you all night long."

"People will see."

"Let them."

She stepped forward, her breath still washing over him in steady pulses—a hint of the punch being served in the ballroom combined with the light scent of rosewater on her skin. "And what then?"

Her voice was stronger, and he knew reality was intruding on their dark bubble. "What do you mean?"

"What happens then? Once everyone sees, once the moment has been spoiled for you by all the prying attentions of your peers?" Her slim, gloved hand reached up to cup his cheek. "What happens when we go back to London?"

He wrapped an arm more securely around her waist to keep her as close as she'd ventured on her own. "We dance again. Everywhere. Until no one doubts that you have my full attention and all the other men fade away."

The stiffness that ran down her back radiated tension into his arm. He'd said the wrong thing. Mentioning the other men had made her pull away, mentally if not physically.

He dropped his arm and stepped back, pain slicing up his now chilled, injured arm and settling in his chest. He'd ignored the pain while he was dancing, but now it more than made itself known as it combined with emotional pain he hadn't expected. For whatever reason she wouldn't give up the other men. "That's why you won't dance with me, isn't it?"

"What?" She sounded disoriented, as if the loss of contact had scrambled her thoughts as much as it had his. But one thing was remaining clear in his mind.

"You can't make me part of your collection. I'd scare away too many suitors."

He actually heard her swallow. "That's rather arrogant of you."

"Nothing was ever gained by denying the truth."

"No, I don't suppose it was." Her fingers curled into fists, tight enough to make her shoulders shake.

Was she angry? What did she have to be angry about? She wasn't the one being denied a craving so deep it had prompted him to set aside decades of personal rules and convictions. She wasn't the one being rejected.

She took a deep breath and let it out. "Which is why I must remind you that I've already told you this will not, cannot, happen. If we can have nothing else between us, let there be truth. I'm going to walk away now, Griffith, because I have to."

"Yes. I suppose the masses of lovestruck men are waiting."

What was he doing? Was he intentionally trying to hurt her? He'd never hurt a woman in his life, had in fact gone out of his way on more than one occasion to be a gentleman. Yet there was no doubting the fact that the words spewing forth without thought were intended to strike her like a dart to a target. And if her sharp intake of breath was any indication, they had struck true.

She turned toward the door but misjudged her steps and stubbed her foot against the leg of the chair, causing her to emit a short, sharp squeal of pain.

Griffith was at her side instantly, scooping her up in his arms and setting her in the chair so he could kneel at her feet. He cupped her injured foot in his hand, ignoring the screaming protest of his arm. "Are you all right?"

"I stubbed my toe, Griffith. It's not like I fell off a roof." The humor in her voice was so much more welcome than the anger.

He smiled, even though she wouldn't be able to see it. Perhaps things could still be salvaged if he put them back on a light-hearted footing. "No need for stitches, then? I daresay whatever spirits I have in the house taste a good bit better than Mrs. Ingham's."

Her laughter made his heart break and soar at the same time. "How sad for me, then, that there is no need for me to imbibe."

His thumb traced the front of her slipper, feeling the ridges of her toes through the stiffened satin.

"It barely hurts anymore," she whispered.

Kneeling at her feet while she sat in the chair, Griffith was able to easily look into her eyes. The light from the ballroom graced her face while leaving his blanketed in the privacy of darkness, allowing him to drink her in at his leisure without her seeing whatever emotions his features might be betraying. Because he was fairly certain they were there.

As practiced as he was at not revealing what he was thinking, he'd never felt the way he felt now. His arms ached to hold her again, to dance her around the room or lift her from her feet so that she relied upon him to keep her safe. He wanted to lean forward and feel her breath in his face again, to know they were sharing the very air they needed to live.

He wanted to kiss her.

But she wasn't his to do any of those things with.

He didn't even have the right to think them.

So he stood.

He offered her his hand and waited.

How many heartbeats went by before she slid her hand into his and allowed him to help her back to her feet. Eight? Ten? Did it even matter?

She walked toward the door, her steps more careful than angry this time. She looked back once. And then she was gone.

⌒

Griffith stood at his window and watched the carriage roll down the lane. He'd follow in a few days, returning to London and the busyness of the city. First he needed to do the thinking he'd come to do in the first place.

One finger flicked the edge of a folded piece of paper in his hand. Perhaps he needed to find the answers to some of his questions first.

"You wanted to see me before we left?"

Griffith turned to see Ryland leaning against the doorframe, hat in hand and traveling coat thrown across his shoulders. "Yes."

When Griffith didn't say anything more right away, one dark eyebrow lifted as Ryland's grey eyes narrowed.

Again, Griffith slid a finger along the edge of the paper, fighting with himself over whether what he wanted to do, what he felt like he needed to do, was the right thing to do.

He looked down at the paper, at the clear, efficient strokes indicating a direction in Northumberland. With one last tap of his finger he extended the paper to Ryland. "I need one of your men to look into something for me."

Ryland took the paper and looked at the direction. "Northumberland?"

"Yes. A delivery to Isabella's family."

"Why would she give this to you? Even if her uncle refused to send it for her, her father could pay the postage on a letter to Northumberland every day for a year and not come close to the cost of the necklace she was wearing last night, even if the jewels are fake."

"She said her uncle refuses to send any letters unless he reads them first." The more Griffith learned about Lord Pontebrook, the more concerned he became for Isabella's welfare. Something wasn't right in a house where a girl couldn't even send uncensored letters to her family. "She asked if I would be willing to frank it for her."

"The letter is already franked, so I'm assuming its safe delivery is not what you are trying to secure." Ryland slid the letter into his pocket, a silent agreement to do whatever Griffith needed, even if he wasn't done asking questions yet.

Agreeing to send the letter had been the easiest part of granting her request. The number of questions that rose were what threatened his mental peace.

"It's best if the letter travels by Royal Mail." Griffith ran his hands over his face, pressing his fingers hard over eyes that hadn't closed much the night before. "There are too many rumors, Ryland, too many things that don't add up. Naworth believes her family to be from Yorkshire. Ivonbrook swears she's connected to foreign royalty. I can't go down a road that might endanger my family or put me in a position to make a choice that isn't best for my country. No matter how much I may wish to."

"Understood." Ryland crossed back to the door. "It will take a few days for my man to travel there and get what you need. What will you do in the meantime?"

Griffith lifted one large shoulder as he propped the other one on the window frame. "Pray. And perhaps do a bit of research on my own."

The first time Isabella had ridden into London, excitement and trepidation had filled her. Everything looked so big and exciting, she hadn't known what to look at next, and she'd ridden through the streets with one hand pressed to the carriage window and her face close enough for her breath to condense on the glass.

Now, rattling through the tollgate as they returned from Hertfordshire, she barely looked up. The noise outside the carriage grew until it could be heard over the rattling wheels and jangling harnesses. Smells of horses and of food from street vendors crept their way into the silent expanse while Uncle Percy dozed and Frederica read.

Isabella had a book open as well, but she hadn't turned a page in miles, too lost in her own head to even begin to focus on the words.

What was supposed to be a relaxing respite from the tension of London had done nothing but confuse her more. But it had also clarified things. Nothing could be allowed to come between her and saving her family.

It was too easy to forget how bad things had gotten, here in London with plenty of everything. Even if she was essentially Uncle Percy's prisoner with no funds of her own with which to escape, she wasn't truly wanting for anything.

What was her family doing now? Was her mother still burning dinner every night?

They'd had to dismiss the household servants soon after Father's injury, and Mother, Isabella, and her sisters had been forced to learn domestic skills they'd never thought they'd need. Scrubbing burnt food out of pots was one thing Isabella was more than happy to be away from.

They'd had to let go more than half of the farmhands in the past two years as well. And even though Isabella had learned how to sheer a sheep right alongside Hugh and Thomas, they hadn't been able to get wool to market fast enough this year, and the prices they'd had to sell for weren't going to see the family through another year.

When Isabella left, Mother had already been talking about selling things. Had they carted off the furniture? The old piano in the drawing room?

What would it do to her father, who had to spend two hours sitting for every hour he tried to walk around? If the things he sat on and among began to disappear, things he'd worked so hard to provide for her mother, would he soon follow?

Having seen and experienced the life Mother left behind in order to marry Father, Isabella could well understand the concerns she'd overheard him voicing one night. Mother had assured him then that she had no intention of leaving him, but what about when food became scarce? When there was no old piano in the corner to play hymns on? When the people in the village began to leave gifts of food on the doorstep and offered to take in the children?

Even at the height of their farm, life hadn't been anything like Isabella had experienced with Uncle Percy.

But if they could hold on for another few months, Isabella would be able to fix everything.

She'd written them from Riverton. If things were bad, then they needed hope to hold on to, hope that things would get better. Isabella was that hope now, whether anyone wanted to admit it or not. They probably thought she might marry money and at least provide something for her siblings. Sending the letter with Griffith's frank on it would probably raise their hopes to a level that would be soul-crushing to fall from, but Isabella hadn't known what else to do. Uncle Percy had given strict instructions about what she could and couldn't write home about. He didn't want her mother getting worried and finding a way to come to London.

If she were honest with herself, the decision to ask him to post it for her had also given her a reason to seek him out this morning before they left. His eyes had been so sad when they looked her way, but that had been the only indication that he felt any lingering emotional pain from the night before. Amazing how many things could change in the mere span of a week.

Was time moving as quickly for her family, or was it a phenomenon created by living with the elite of England? Did time simply move faster for them?

What would her family think when they received a letter, franked on her behalf by a duke? Mother would expect that she'd fallen in love. Father would probably worry that he'd done the wrong thing in letting her come to London but would secretly be proud that she'd made such connections. Her sisters would swoon. Her brothers would puff up their chests and ask their father if they should go to London to ensure the man's intentions.

None of them had any idea what London was really like. Even Mother seemed to have forgotten over the years.

The view of the city beyond the glass became blurry. Blurrier than the haze and speed could account for.

She let a tear roll free, not willing to alert the others in the carriage of her distress with a poorly timed sniffle or a raised hand.

When everything was over, she would explain until her family understood. Until then, whatever dreams gave them hope were good ones.

They just had to hold on a little bit longer. And so did she.

Chapter 22

Griffith had sought out more advice in the past three months than he could remember doing in the past three years. It wasn't that he thought himself better than anyone else. It was simply that he had to be careful who he let guide him, and he'd always found seeking the answers in the Bible or the writings of biblical scholars such as Philip Doddridge and Joseph Butler to be more effective.

In this case, however, he was running into a problem. It didn't feel like enough to know that God had a plan and Griffith needed to trust Him with it. It especially didn't feel like enough to know that God would let him make his own decisions on this matter. He felt like he needed to know more than how important it was to maintain his integrity and purity of thought while trying to fight for the right to court Isabella.

The questions plaguing him now didn't seem as direct. Should he continue pursuing Isabella despite the fact that she turned him down at every turn? Well, not every turn, but every time she realized what she was doing.

He pounded on the door at Ryland's house on Pall Mall, still trying to determine what he was there to ask.

The butler, Price, waved him in. "His Grace isn't here, I'm afraid. But your sister is available."

The slight grin on the butler's face let Griffith know he was recalling the last time Griffith had come by the house in an agitated state in the middle of the afternoon. He hadn't thought to bring this matter to his sister, but she'd been right last time. Perhaps it would be logical to ply a feminine mind for answers.

He could do without plying four of them again, though. "Is she alone?"

"No, Your Grace. Both of your sisters are in the nursery."

He could handle his two sisters. In some ways Georgina's mind probably more closely resembled Isabella's. "I'll see myself up."

Familiar voices grew louder as Griffith topped the stairs on the second floor. He followed them until he found his sisters sitting in the middle of a bright room with furniture catalogs strewn about the floor.

"Griffith!" Miranda rose to her feet with a groan. "That's getting more difficult every day."

Griffith lifted an eyebrow. "You could have chairs brought in here."

"That's what I said," Georgina grumbled as she pushed to her feet with a bit more elegance and grace.

Miranda frowned. "That makes it harder to visualize the furniture. And Ryland wants this room completely emptied and refurnished before we go back to the country. Even though the baby probably won't need it for a few months, he wants to be prepared."

"What else would you expect of a man who spent ten years skulking about in a war?" Georgina scooped up a paper and held it toward a wall. "This would be a darling bed. The light wouldn't be in his face when he takes a nap either."

Miranda blinked but took the paper and held it up herself. "What a clever thing to consider."

Griffith considered leaving his sisters to their room planning, but he decided to ask the question tormenting him. If he tried to leave without giving them a reason for having come in the first place, they'd hunt him down later, and the conditions might not be as private.

Trying to look less obvious in his desperation, he picked up a sheaf of papers from the floor and began to thumb through the drawings of chair options. "What would a man need to do, say, to entice a hesitant woman to marry him?"

Not exactly the question he'd thought he was going to ask, but the one he probably needed the answer to. He was still waiting to hear back from Ryland's man, but he couldn't imagine a thing he could learn about Isabella that would make her unsuitable. Of course, it was the things he couldn't imagine that were likely to cause problems. More problems than he was experiencing already. Isabella was tying him in knots, and he lived in dread that one of her other suitors would finally drum up the courage to actually propose to her. If she accepted, he would be devastated. So he might as well beat the other suitors to the asking.

Unless, of course, they'd already asked and she'd turned them all down.

"You intend to ask Miss Breckenridge, I assume?" Miranda lowered her paper and grinned at him.

"Yes." He flipped through the chair pictures again. "I find myself drawn to her, even though she's an entirely illogical choice."

Georgina coughed. "I wouldn't lead with that. It doesn't even work for fictional men."

"Agreed." Miranda shrugged. "Tell her you love her. If that doesn't do it, you don't want to marry her anyway."

252

Georgina tilted her head as she considered Griffith with far more wisdom than he was accustomed to seeing in his baby sister. "It might take more than that. Half of the unattached men in London have probably made similar infatuated statements. You need to show her that you really know who it is you claim to love. Do something different than anyone else would think to do unless they knew her extremely well."

She smiled and place a hand on his arm. "I have to ask, though—why do you want to marry her? I've never known you to do anything that didn't make complete sense, at least to you."

How to explain what he wasn't sure he even knew himself? He began to pace, an easy thing to do in a room devoid of furniture. "I can't abide the idea of her marrying anyone else. I can't think of myself married to anyone else. Whenever I consider someone who seems to make more sense, I can't imagine her in my home."

"What if she sets all the furniture in the house at odd angles to each other?" Miranda smirked. Probably remembering the time she'd done that very thing and Griffith had nearly hit the ceiling every time he walked into a new room.

He stopped pacing and tried to give careful consideration to his sister's question. Imagining Isabella shifting furniture behind his back. It was all too easy to picture her hiding behind a curtain, waiting to see his reaction so that she could laugh at his frustration before helping him put it all back. "I'd let her."

And he would. He'd let her drive him crazy every day because the reward would be her smile, her laugh.

Georgina narrowed her eyes and stepped as close as she could get and still tilt her head back to look in his face. "What if she slurped her tea?"

"She doesn't."

"Let a dog in the house?"

"The maid can clean behind it."

"Turned all the books upside down on the shelves?"

"It would help knock the dust off the top."

"Decided she wanted to go to the opera instead of a ball when you were already in the carriage?"

"It's a good thing I keep a box."

"Sang the wrong words to 'Lady of the Lake,' off-key, at the breakfast table, while drumming her finger against her plate, causing the fork to rattle, and dangling her slipper halfway off her foot."

"I can hire a music tutor."

"Marry her."

Griffith stuttered for a moment. "What?"

Georgina shook her finger at him. "She clearly is in possession of magical powers, and if you don't marry her and keep her blissfully happy she might decide to turn everyone in London into frogs."

His youngest sister spun on her heel and went back to the drawings of window dressings she'd been considering earlier.

Griffith shifted his gaze to Miranda, whose shoulders were shaking with mirth while both hands were clamped over her mouth below wide eyes. "Am I truly that bad?" he asked her.

She lowered her hands, but the wide smile remained proof of her delight in the conversation. "I wouldn't say *bad* so much as *particular*." Two steps brought her to Griffith's side, where she wrapped him in a tight hug. "Although, the fact that you've been in this room for nearly ten minutes and have yet to stack the papers is akin to a miracle. I have to agree with Georgina. Marry that woman. As soon as you possibly can."

"Special license!" Georgina chirped. "The archbishop's office is still open, if you're quick about it. You can have the whole thing secured by dinner."

If only he knew she'd say yes, he'd be taking his carriage to Doctors' Commons as fast as the traffic allowed. "What if she says no?"

Miranda wrapped her arm around his and dropped her head to rest against his bicep. "Then we find a way to turn her into a frog."

Griffith's mind was filled with the frippery of potential love until he walked into his study. Jeffreys, Ryland's valet, was waiting for him, road dust still coating his clothing.

"Ryland sent *you*?"

The wiry thin man shrugged. "He said you needed the best and the fastest."

God certainly knew what he was doing when he created friendship. Griffith couldn't be more thankful. He gestured Jeffreys into a seat. "Would you care for tea?"

"Much obliged, Your Grace. I don't have a great deal to report, though. Why would you need to know about a failing sheep farm in the wilds of Northumberland?"

"Failing, is it?" Griffith tried to keep the emotion out of his voice as he arranged for tea with the servant who answered his summons. "And the family?"

"Nice folks. A bit threadbare and living close to the bone, but nice."

Griffith tried to sit in his chair behind the desk, but the more accurate description would be that he fell into it. Isabella was dancing through London in gems and satin, riding rumors of a great dowry and powerful family connections. And her family was barely eating? "Are you sure you had the right family?"

"Yes, Your Grace. That letter you sent them caused quite a bit a noise."

The tea arrived and Griffith fell silent, watching Jeffreys quickly prepare his cup and start to guzzle it with the grace of a tavern regular. Let him have his tea. He needed to clear his parched throat of any remaining dust, because he was about to tell Griffith everything.

~

He was there. Tall and handsome, an oasis of calm in the middle of social desperation.

Isabella dragged her gaze back to the man currently talking to her. Lord Someone-or-another. It had gotten incredibly difficult to keep them all straight. As her uncle had predicted, a week away from London had done nothing but enhance her popularity. It was ridiculous, really, and didn't say much for the individual decision-making abilities of the country's leaders.

Seeing Griffith watch her but refuse to wade into the throng only made it harder. Did it mean he'd changed his mind about the things he'd said in Hertfordshire, or did he simply refuse to be one of the masses?

She escaped to the retiring room to catch her breath, wondering what she was doing in this mess. It had been difficult before, but now every dance, every dinner, every flirting smile or restrained laugh had become nearly impossible.

Miss Newberry slipped her feet back into her slippers as Isabella walked into the room.

"Enjoying the ball?" she asked.

It took a moment for Isabella to realize the other girl had been talking to her. Most of the girls didn't want much to do with her, the unknown who had waltzed into Town and stolen their men's attentions. And Miss Newberry certainly hadn't had a nice thing to say to her at the house party last week. "Er, yes. It's not too much of a crush tonight."

256

"Much to Lady Wethersfield's dismay." The girl grinned.

"Many more people and there wouldn't be room to dance."

"And everyone would talk about it for days." She shrugged. "It's the way things work."

Isabella fidgeted with the edge of her glove. "Does it ever bother you?"

"I don't let it." Miss Newberry leaned over to look in a mirror and adjusted a curl. "I have to marry, so I might as well marry as well as I can. We don't all have our pick of the top tier."

The smile she gave Isabella looked genuine but sad.

Guilt crashed through Isabella. "If you could choose, who would it be?"

A quick shake of her head sent Miss Newberry's carefully adjusted curls bouncing. "I try not to think about it. Alethea talks constantly about the merits of one man versus the other. I simply want a comfortable home and secure future. There's a lot of men here who can give me that."

"What of love?" Hypocrisy layered over the guilt until Isabella wondered if she was going to be ill.

Miss Newberry sighed and hugged herself. "I danced with Lord Ivonbrook once. He'd just come back from observing the workings of a new steam engine. I didn't have the slightest idea what he was talking about, but it was nice to see someone . . ."

"Excited?"

"Care."

Isabella had been in London for more than a month, and this was the first time someone, outside of Frederica and Griffith, had seemed like a real person, had shown any sort of vulnerability.

She wanted to ask more, but at the same time she didn't. Already she knew she'd never look at Lord Ivonbrook the same way again. Every time she danced with him, she'd wonder if

Miss Newberry was unknowingly losing her secure future for Isabella's family's future. It didn't seem like a very fair trade, especially not when someone else was making the decision for you.

The door opened, and two more girls tripped in, giggling. They looked young. Too young. Were they even eighteen? Isabella felt old, knowing these ladies thought her to be nineteen like them, but she suddenly felt ten years older instead of only five.

Any chance of conversation was lost, and Miss Newberry gave Isabella another smile, this one the practiced, cold one Isabella had seen on so many of the other faces in the ballroom. Then she rose and left the room without another glance.

If Isabella wanted a distraction, she'd certainly gotten it, but it wasn't the kind she'd been looking for.

She slipped back down the passage and into a door on the side of the ballroom.

"Will you dance with me?"

That deep voice was the last thing she needed. Even as it rolled over her, making the hairs on her skin stand up at the very idea of being the one to finally dance with him, it fed the ball of misery in the pit of her stomach. "I can't."

"Why not? You've hardly left the floor all night. And I know you don't keep a dance card." Griffith pushed away from where he'd been leaning against the wall. He angled his body so that anyone looking their way would see only his back. No one would know she'd returned. Her cream silk skirts would be visible on either side of his legs, but they probably looked like the skirts of half the other women in the room as well.

"I can't."

"You said that already."

"And it's as true now as it was five seconds ago."

"Oh."

He fell silent for a moment. Isabella could have walked away. He wasn't touching her or caging her in. He wasn't even standing all that close, but somehow she felt trapped, glued to the floor until he decided to let her go. Only, if she were honest with herself, it wasn't his will keeping her there—it was her desire that things could be different.

She stood, feeling her heart beat, focusing on keeping her breaths shallow so she wouldn't inhale too much of his cedar and grass scent.

"How about now?"

"I beg your pardon?" Her gaze flew to meet his. A mistake, as she got snagged in his deep emerald gaze.

"Is it still true?"

Despite herself she smiled. "Yes. I'm afraid it is."

"*Can't* is such an interesting word." He tilted his head but kept his eyes on hers. "So many times we confuse it with the word *won't*."

She swallowed. "Very well. I won't."

"*Won't* is also an interesting word. It means there's a chance I can change your mind."

Again she smiled, realizing she'd been neatly maneuvered but having trouble caring. "You won't." She swallowed, the curve drifting off her lips. "You can't."

One eyebrow winged upward, and for a moment he looked every inch a man capable of holding his own against anyone—up to and including the ruling monarch of the country. And she was trying to take him on in a battle of wills.

"That's a rather bold declaration. I am a duke. There isn't much I can't do."

"You can't do this. I won't let you."

A shadow slid over his face, taking away the playful glint in his eyes and the teasing crease at the side of his mouth. "You're probably the only person who could stop me. I'd like to call on you tomorrow."

"I'll tell Osborn that I'm not home."

"Then I'll call on Frederica."

"If you like." Isabella wanted to cry, to scream, to growl, to do something that would release a small bit of the frustration caused by the clashing of the light moment with her dreadful guilt and the nagging voice at the back of her head that was getting harder and harder to silence. "But she won't be home either."

If he thought to come visit her uncle, there would be nothing she could do to keep him away, but somehow she didn't think that he wanted to bring Uncle Percy into this. Her name had dripped from many a tongue, but to her knowledge, it had never been linked with the duke's in more than a cursory fashion, and he seemed to want to keep it that way. It made her wonder about his declared intentions. If he truly wanted to court her, why wasn't he doing it openly?

"Etiquette says that once you've turned someone down, you shouldn't dance the rest of the evening, lest you make him feel like you're rejecting him personally."

She pressed her lips together, trying not to laugh at his overly innocent expression even as a little bit of her heart broke at the thought of hurting this man. "I suppose I'll just have to assure you that it's personal, then. We wouldn't want anyone to walk around with erroneous assumptions."

Then she curtsied and walked around him, taking great care to not look back until she'd been swallowed up by the crowd.

Chapter 23

It was fascinating, really, the way he chose to torture himself. There were so many other ways Griffith could be spending his time. He could go to the library and play cards. Retreat to the drawing room, where refreshments had been set up. He could even go home, take off the cravat that felt like it was choking the life out of him, and get a good night's sleep.

Instead, he was holding up the wall of the ballroom, trying to ignore the fact that people were starting to stare. Speculations had only grown about what he intended to do this Season and if he would eventually select a partner for the dance floor. The amount of time he'd spent in ballrooms lately probably had something to do with it. The betting book at the club and an impromptu house party hadn't hurt.

He watched Isabella dance, remembering all too well how it felt to curve his arm around her waist, to have her trust him enough to guide her through the dark. Trust him enough to send a letter home to her family. But not trust him enough to tell the truth about what she was doing in London. Because even with all he'd learned, things weren't adding up.

Other than Ryland's contacts and the little bit of privileged information he'd received from Isabella, he'd had a difficult time tracking down the truth about her. When her mother married, she'd broken contact with everyone in the aristocracy, embracing the life of a northern county sheep farmer. Isabella and Lord Pontebrook had been able to create any sort of history they wanted, and no one in London would be able to contradict it.

Still, nothing he'd been able to find told him why she'd done it. Or had allowed it to be done. Her current situation remained shrouded in mystery.

The dancers had worked their way up and down the line, so the song would be ending soon. Where would she be escorted? It was a game he was playing with himself. Albeit a rather torturous one, but he didn't have anything better to do with his evening than plant himself within view of wherever she was when she selected her next dance partner. He'd been more than obvious that he would accept the position whenever she let him.

As the dancers moved and the song wound down, he worked his way through the crowd to a group of men in high collars and stiff cravats. Their coats ranged from the bright dandy colors to the somber black, with every shade in between. As most of her potential partners were part of the group, it was likely that corner of the room was where she would head.

He refused to join the actual group, milling about like cattle waiting to be cut from the herd. He could be close enough to see and hear, though, without actually wading in.

As he approached, it became clear that men were not the only ones in the group. More than one lady had braved the crowd in the hopes of procuring her own potential dance partner. Feathers could be seen waving over the shoulders of the men, and a few couples began to break away and move toward the floor as the current dance set broke apart.

Isabella smiled as she approached the group, but it wasn't

a real smile. Griffith wasn't an expert on such things, but real smiles didn't tend to leave people looking as if they had the beginnings of a headache swirling at their temples.

She didn't break into the middle of the group, choosing instead to stand to the side. As if what she really wanted to do was make a run for the retiring room again.

The men didn't let her remain on the fringe very long.

Ladies who hadn't yet procured a partner were deserted as the men flocked around Isabella.

The abandoned ladies didn't look happy.

Lady Alethea was among them, and the frown on her face made it plain that she no longer cared to put up with Isabella's position as queen of the ballroom.

She took a deep breath and squared her shoulders before pasting a smile on her face and wading in once more. Only she wasn't heading for any particular man. She was cutting her way through to Isabella.

Griffith stepped closer, trying to hear what was being said. He'd witnessed more than one all-too-public ballroom fight, most of them the fault of his own family. They were never very pretty and almost always ended badly.

There was too much noise in the crowded ballroom to hear the women over the cavernous echoes the rest of the revelers were making, so he pushed into the fringes of the group.

"Are you enjoying London, Miss Breckenridge?" Lady Alethea's voice was simpering and hit Griffith's ears like sludge from the Thames.

"Immensely." Isabella smiled at one of the men around her. "Never have I found myself in the midst of such enjoyable companions."

"It must be so different than . . . Where did you say you were from, again?"

Griffith tensed. There was very little chance this wouldn't go badly. He knew Isabella's shell was delicate. When poked just right, it cracked easily. And while he'd had no problems with what he found beneath the surface—in many ways even liked it—it wouldn't put Isabella in a very good position to have it revealed in the middle of a ballroom that she was the twenty-four-year-old daughter of an injured, half-Scottish farmer from Northumberland instead of the nineteen-year-old heiress of a landed gentleman in Yorkshire.

While the answers Griffith had learned from Jeffreys weren't enough to make him drop his pursuit of her, they were enough to destroy her reputation here in Town, and likely Miss St. Claire's and Lord Pontebrook's along with it.

"The north," Isabella said quietly.

"Ah yes. Yorkshire, so I've heard. How far you must have traveled!" Lady Alethea fluttered her fan and, to most, probably looked as if she were avidly curious about Isabella's life. And she probably was, but not in the congenial way she was implying.

"The drive is long."

"Did you come from your father's estate, or did you winter with Lord Pontebrook? Winters must be so cold up there. It's practically in Scotland, after all."

Griffith stepped closer, trying to catch Isabella's eye and give her a way out of the current conversation. He wasn't above using uncomfortable circumstances to attain his goal, as long as he was innocent of the creation of such circumstances.

"Yorkshire isn't that close to Scotland. We do keep the fires burning all night in the heart of the winter, though." Isabella's smile looked even tighter. Was she about to crack?

Finally she met his gaze. He lifted a brow and tilted his head toward the dance floor. None of the other men were moving toward it, as if they'd just realized that they didn't actually know much about Isabella's father or background. Everyone had associated her with Lord Pontebrook, as if she were simply another daughter he'd kept hidden away. But she wasn't. And they'd all just been reminded of that fact.

Isabella's gaze flitted from face to face, pain and indecision in her eyes. Then she turned to the man nearest her. "We have a lovely winter dance every year. All of the gentry come. The Duke of Northumberland even came down and made an appearance last year."

She was so set against dancing with him where others could see that she was going to allow this to continue.

Lady Alethea's lashes fluttered. "I've never met the Duke of Northumberland."

If Isabella's expression was anything to go by, she hadn't either.

Griffith could not allow this to continue.

He allowed his arm to bump into Lady Alethea's. He inclined his head with a bow. "My humble pardons, my lady."

She smiled and dropped into a slight curtsy. "Not at all, Your Grace."

"I was simply taking the shortest path to the terrace. I find myself in need of air." And with that statement he'd marked himself the veriest dolt to anyone who was actually thinking about what he was hearing. While going through this pack of people might have been the most direct path from wherever he stood, five steps to the right would have taken him around it much more expeditiously.

Fortunately, most people didn't listen too closely at a ball.

"The crush is dreadful tonight." She fluttered her fan and looked up through her lashes.

It was no such thing, but Griffith wasn't going to correct her. "Are you in need of air as well? Shall I escort you to the terrace?"

She glanced at the lines forming on the dance floor, people setting up to start the next set. Griffith wasn't about to make that offer unless the danger to Isabella grew significantly.

Lady Alethea said nothing about the dance, though, and set her hand on his arm. "I would be honored, Your Grace."

As Griffith led the brunette viper out of the circle, he looked at Isabella. With the altercation over, men were jostling each other once more for the chance to claim her for the dance, but Isabella was watching Griffith, her expression unreadable. Griffith turned away, too afraid that if he looked much longer he'd attribute feelings he wished her to have instead of things that were evident.

Near the doors, spring air rushed to greet them, comforting despite its warmth.

Lady Alethea's grip on his arm tightened as they approached the door. "Are you sure you wouldn't rather dance?"

Griffith looked from the lady to the very long string of dancers lining up on the floor. Isabella and her partner had taken the spot at the head of the dance. She would be determining the pattern for the dance unless someone of greater social power took the head in the next moment or two.

Should he choose to approach the floor, he could no doubt claim that spot for himself and his partner. It was what Lady Alethea obviously wanted, and Griffith couldn't help wanting to maneuver her into as uncomfortable a position as she was trying to pin Isabella in. "I could perhaps consider taking up the foot of the lines."

Her eyes widened and her mouth went slack. "But it stretches the entire length of the ballroom. It could be ten minutes before it reaches the foot."

"Yes." He squeezed his eyebrows together and looked over the dancers. "How dreadful it would be to wait. Especially if your partner was too absorbed in ensuring he knew the steps to speak while you waited."

Obviously the potential embarrassment of having him stand up with her at the foot of the dance only to ignore her was stronger than the hope of actually being the first unrelated female to dance with him, because Lady Alethea cleared her throat and stepped out onto the terrace.

He let her go, stepping onto the terrace enough to say he stepped through the door, but making sure he maintained a non-gossip-inducing distance between him and the lady. A scattering of other people stood on the terrace. None of them were paying attention to the newest couple to wander outside.

How long did they have to linger outside before returning to the ballroom? Was his fix permanent, or would she return to trying to diminish Isabella's reputation?

Her smile looked shy as she turned to look at Griffith over her shoulder. The woman really was beautiful. She would make a lovely subject for a painting, but Griffith had always found her rather irritating. The fact that he had just committed himself to several minutes in her company proved that Isabella had motivated his tolerance of certain annoyances to change.

"Are we to be silent while we take the air, then?"

Griffith bowed his head in her direction. How insolent could he be and still claim to be a gentleman? He didn't want to abandon Lady Alethea, but he didn't want her getting any ideas either. "Of what do you wish to speak?"

She looked a little bit startled, but recovered quickly and took two steps closer to him. "We could speak of the weather . . ."

"It's a pleasant night."

". . . or the ball . . ."

"One of the less crowded ones thus far this Season."

". . . or your family."

"They are well."

Lady Alethea fell silent as she turned to look into the darkness.

The terrace overlooked a paved work yard between the kitchens and the stables, so lights had only been placed on the balcony itself. Plants lined the railing, giving it the illusion of overlooking an outdoor garden, but beyond the greenery lay darkness. Even the stars had disappeared behind a thick haze.

After a few moments she stiffened her shoulders and turned his way once more. "Perhaps you should choose a topic, then."

He considered shrugging but decided it would be verging into rude instead of arrogant and eccentric. "I've nothing to discuss. We have stepped out for the air." He took an exaggerated deep breath. "Air is silent."

It was obvious that she wanted to give him a setdown, to berate him for treating her in such a way, only she had nothing to compare it to. He had, until very recently, been most elusive at social functions. A silent giant hulking around the edges, speaking at length only to those he knew well. How could she know this wasn't the way all of his conversations went? She risked insulting a duke to imply otherwise.

Music and the murmur of voices flowed out the doorway. Another group of people stepped outside and two couples stepped back inside.

The rudeness of his silence disturbed him, so he started telling her about the latest improvements made to his agricultural efforts. It was supremely boring, but at least he was talking to her.

Through it all, Lady Alethea stood there, not wanting to give up his attentions but clearly miserable in the keeping of them. It was sad, really. He enjoyed being a duke, was thankful God had blessed him with such a position, but he wasn't sure he would like it so much if he hadn't been born to the position, if everything done from the moment he first breathed hadn't been done with the knowledge that he would one day be the duke.

But why women seemed to be so desperate to become a duchess baffled him. Didn't they know how much pressure it was? His mother worked harder than anyone he'd ever seen. Of course, she had in many ways been doing the job of two, but Griffith's wife, whoever she may be, could certainly find herself in a similar position. God had not promised Griffith a long life.

He wasn't going to delude himself that he personally was the draw. As Lady Alethea had so perfectly demonstrated, most of the women didn't know him at all.

"You don't really expect a lady to know about drainage ditches and—what did you call them—fallow fields?"

Griffith lifted a brow at the sly smile and the coy tilt of her head. Pearls and feathers stood out in her brown hair, completing the delicate picture.

"My apologies. I did not see how idle discussion of topics neither of us cares about was a meaningful use of our time." His mother would have pinched his ear if she'd heard such a statement. Not because it had been overly rude to Lady Alethea but because it implied that she'd never taken the time to teach him proper social graces.

The song ended and another began.

Lady Alethea glided past him with her nose in the air. "I am stepping inside. Perhaps I can find someone more amenable to dancing."

"That shouldn't be difficult."

She frowned at his quip but moved on into the room. There were two men at her side in moments, and she was soon making her way to the dance floor.

Griffith stayed outside, watching the bodies swirl on the other side of the window. Isabella was easy to find.

Courting her wasn't going to be easy. Obviously, traditional methods weren't going to work.

He leaned against the window frame and started to think.

Chapter 24

Griffith rubbed his hands hard over his face as he stepped from the House of Lords chamber into the vestibule. It had to be nearly midnight, and he was exhausted. He'd planned to go by Lady Oakmere's musicale tonight, but given that the visiting opera singer was sure to have completed her arias by now and Griffith was so tired he was willing to consider taking a nap on one of the lobby benches, it was probably best he head home for the night.

Even if Isabella was in attendance and socializing after the musicale's completion, he wouldn't do his suit any good in his current condition. He'd spent the past week trying to come up with unique ways to win her attention, as well as attempting traditional methods, and everything had come up short.

"Your Grace!"

Griffith winced and considered not stopping. There were, after all, others in the building who could answer to the honorific. The fact that the footsteps rushing toward him indicated he was probably the intended recipient was something he could easily be convinced to overlook.

Lord Pontebrook came to his side in a rush and adjusted his pace to match Griffith's. "Your Grace."

Griffith nodded in acknowledgment but was afraid to speak lest he let out the yawn building in his throat.

"I can't thank you enough for the invitation to Riverton. Splendid week in the country."

"The party was my mother's doing. I shall pass along your regards." He wouldn't, but Lord Pontebrook would never know that.

"Splendid. Splendid." He looked at Griffith out of the corner of his eye as they crossed the lobby outside St. Stephen's Cathedral. "My daughter, Frederica, has talked of nothing else since we returned."

And that was the purpose for this uncomfortable walk through the parliamentary building. Lord Pontebrook wanted to know why Griffith wasn't visiting his little girl anymore. "I'm glad she enjoyed the trip. It was a pleasure to have all of you in attendance."

Griffith almost choked on the words. Why did they have to tell so many lies simply for the sake of social propriety? Why was it such a bad thing if he honestly told Lord Pontebrook to begone because Griffith was irritated with the entire family?

"There've been quite a few men pounding down my door this year." Lord Pontebrook laughed. "But then you know how that goes."

"Indeed." Was there a point to this? Because there was certainly a limit to his patience tonight, and he'd much rather use it on something that actually mattered.

The viscount cleared his throat. "Of course, very few of them have been by for Frederica."

Griffith highly doubted any of them had been by for Frederica this Season, aside from himself. She wasn't exactly encouraging anyone's attentions.

"Then again—" a nervous laugh preceded the man's wiping his hands along the sides of his coat—"it only takes the right man to come knocking. Not all the best ladies inspire crowds. Some palates are more refined."

Could Griffith say *indeed* again, or would that be considered rude? Did he care? "Indeed."

The nervous laughter grew tighter. "You've been by to see my girl this Season, haven't you?"

He had, though his attentions had quickly drifted elsewhere. Griffith narrowed his gaze at Lord Pontebrook and came to a stop on the outside steps of the building. Obviously, the viscount was unaware of Griffith's change in affections. It was an advantage Griffith would be a fool not to use.

"She and her cousin seem to spend a great deal of time together." Perhaps he could use Lord Pontebrook's ambitions while still satisfying his own need for complete honesty in his dealings.

"Yes, yes. Isabella's like the, uh, little sister Frederica was never blessed with. That's why I was so happy to offer my home and support for her first year out. Young hearts need guidance, you know."

Griffith arched an eyebrow, wondering what sort of guidance the other man meant. Because from what he'd seen, Lord Pontebrook's guidance had involved lying about her age, manipulating her attachments, and pushing her in uncomfortable directions. Had he ever once taken the girl to a garden for a purpose other than a garden party?

"And where are Miss St. Claire and her cousin spending their time, now that we've returned from the idylls of the country?"

Lord Pontebrook beamed, and it made Griffith's stomach roil. "They've the energy of an entire militia, I tell you. Seeing the sites of London during the day and gracing the ballrooms in the evening. Tomorrow it's the opera. Lord Ivonbrook keeps a

273

box, you know. I think they've plans to see the Royal Academy before that."

An easy enough place to while away his day as he waited to ambush his prey. "'Tis good for her to be able to see some culture after growing up so close to Scotland."

He watched Lord Pontebrook closely, looking for any sign that Isabella might be in danger from his almost negligent care. There was none. All he could see was a self-absorbed man who couldn't fathom the idea that Griffith's intent might not match Lord Pontebrook's hope.

Another man joined them then, allowing Griffith to make his good-byes and climb into his carriage to go home. Griffith didn't care overly much about art. If he saw something he liked, he put it in his home. Most of his collection had been acquired by a very art-conscious duchess a couple of generations ago. He'd commissioned portraits of the family, and his sister Georgina had added a sweeping painting of Riverton to the walls, but other than that, he'd left them as they'd hung for years.

And yet he found himself mentally rearranging his schedule for the next day. He'd look at art all day long if it meant he could spend the day with Isabella.

⌣

"Why are we here again?" Isabella trudged up the circular staircase behind Frederica, a thin booklet in her hand.

"Because if we stay home Father will make us visit with someone horrible, and if we go to a coffee shop we'll have to sit with someone horrible." Frederica reached the top of the stairs and, with a wide smile on her face, turned to watch Isabella climb. "Any of the men who are already here came to escort someone else and won't be able to approach you. It's the perfect opportunity for a bit of peace."

Isabella craned her neck back as she entered the cavernous room at the top of Somerset House. The Royal Academy had filled every possible inch of wall space with paintings. From floor to ceiling, they were so close together that the frames laid against and on top of each other.

No wonder they'd made her buy a guide book. And with more than one room similarly adorned, she and Frederica could easily spend hours looking through the artwork. The visit suddenly seemed inspired.

"Might I suggest you start with the painting of the hackney? It's remarkably uninspired, and your opinion is destined to rise from there."

Isabella spun to find Griffith standing right behind her, hands clasped against his lower back, dark brown coat topping a golden-yellow waistcoat. "What are you doing here?"

"Looking at something beautiful."

His direct green gaze focused on her and not any of the surrounding art, sending heat coursing through Isabella's cheeks. She glanced at Frederica, but her cousin seemed enthralled by a rather disturbing painting of a donkey and an old woman. She looked back at Griffith and mumbled, "Thank you."

A single brow lifted as if mocking her for assuming he meant her, even though he obviously had.

She cleared her throat. "And where is this hackney painting?"

"Over here, near the floor." He offered her his arm and then stopped by Frederica to offer his other before leading them around to a nearby section of paintings.

After inspecting the hackney, they moved on to portraits of several people no one knew, a scattering of landscapes, some of which were quite breathtaking, and even a depiction of a scene from the Bible.

They strolled around until they entered the hall of statues.

A lone artist sat in the corner sketching a statue, but the room was otherwise empty.

Frederica strolled off, looking consumed by the need to inspect a carving of Apollo shooting his bow and arrow.

Isabella wasn't sure if she wanted to thank her cousin or strangle her.

"I met with the gardener at Hawthorne House. He told me the orchids are doing quite well this year."

"You have a gardener for your city house?" Of course, there had to be gardeners somewhere in the city, but Isabella had never thought of anyone hiring them personally. Everything seemed to be so hard and paved over.

"He doesn't work only for me, but yes. There's a conservatory in Hawthorne House and a small green area behind the house."

"And he's growing orchids?" Isabella had seen orchids, though not very often. People in her area of Northumberland tended to be happy if they managed to grow enough grass for their sheep. There'd been one time she'd been in Scotland at the right time to see a massive cluster of purple orchids. She'd stayed until the sun went down, watching them sway in the breeze.

"Yes." He glanced at her and then down at his toes before fixing his gaze back on the bust of one of the generals. "They're doing rather well."

She said nothing. It wasn't as if she could invite herself over to see them. Even if he extended the invitation, would she take it? She'd never seen the inside of Hawthorne House, so had never been able to picture herself there. At Griffith's side. Starting a new life.

Perhaps she would be better off if that remained something she was unable to imagine.

She walked a bit down the room, both to separate herself from Griffith's side and to have something to do. A row of busts stretched along the wall, ranging in size from life-size to a rather enormous sculpting of His Majesty. She cocked her head to the side and looked down the row. "Do you think the rest of the body is really that much harder to carve?"

"I think it is probably more that the rest of the body is unimportant."

Isabella laughed and threw Griffith a skeptical look. "You should try to take a day and not use your legs."

"You should come by Parliament. I'll show you plenty of examples of working legs and nonfunctioning heads." Griffith looked down on her with a smirk.

The laugh Isabella couldn't contain bounced around the large room, echoing off statues and windows and relieving more than a little of the tension.

Griffith looked quite happy with himself. "Besides, the most identifiable portion of a man is his head. In both the physical and nonphysical ways, his most identifying characteristics can be found above the shoulders."

"So what you're saying is this is a collective philosophical statement and not a bunch of lazy sculptors?" Isabella pushed her lips together and squinted her eyes. "I'm not seeing it."

It was Griffith's turn to laugh. Isabella caught Frederica smiling their way, her happiness making Isabella both giddy and sad. A moment shouldn't be this pure and beautiful if a person wasn't free to enjoy it without restraint, if she couldn't accept the promises implied.

They passed a window, and for a moment Isabella could see out of their sheltered world and into the city, the busyness and the grime a stark contrast to their meandering in a bright hall of white stones. If she could choose which world to live in, this one would win. Every time.

They circled the end of the room and passed the sketching

artist with a nod. His gaze never left the enormous statue gracing the end of the room.

Her eyes drifted sideways to look at Griffith's arm, bulging against his coat as he clasped his hands behind his back. "How is your arm faring?"

"Quite well. The surgeon who inspected its healing last week informed me that the woman who'd sewn me up must have an incredible trousseau based on the precise, even stitches." One side of his mouth kicked up. "So how is it?"

"How is what?" Isabella tried not to look at the half grin, made more boyish by the lock of hair that had drifted down to frame his face.

"Your trousseau."

A blush sped up her neck and to her cheeks as her gaze plummeted back to the floor. She picked up her pace so that he was no longer immediately beside her. She blew out a breath, trying to aim it so that the gust could somewhat cool her cheeks. Her trousseau was nothing like what his sisters had probably taken to their marriages. There was a trunk in her room at home, lovingly packed with a set of linens and a few handkerchiefs. She hadn't had time in recent years to add to it, with all the work she'd done to help keep the farm going.

Perhaps if he knew more about her actual background instead of the one everyone assumed and Uncle Percy encouraged, he would stop pursuing her.

"It isn't very large," she said, her voice soft and quiet. "I'm sure it's nothing like your sisters'."

"Most of my sisters' trousseaux were purchased, so I hardly think we can hold them up as the example for what every lady should have." His step faltered for a moment, as if he'd been thinking of something else to the point that he forgot he was walking. "I'm perfectly capable of purchasing another one, if need be. I've no need for my future wife to come with an abundance of ready linens. If I did, I'd be courting the haberdasher's daughter."

That image brought a giggle and allowed her cheeks to cool somewhat.

They circled around to Frederica, who was still standing in front of the same statue. By now she'd probably learned how to carve it herself.

"Beautiful, isn't it?" Her voice was overly bright, in part due to the enormous grin splitting her features. She was obviously happy with the way the day was going.

Isabella looked at the statue. It was rather marvelous. "I'm afraid we've seen all there is to see today."

Frederica frowned and looked from Isabella to Griffith and back again. "We're leaving?"

Yes should have been such an easy thing for Isabella to say, but she couldn't. The word stuck in her throat like a too dry biscuit.

Beside her, Griffith rocked onto his toes and cleared his throat. "Unless you'd like to come see the orchids."

Chapter 25

He liked the way she looked in his house.

Griffith led Isabella and Miss St. Claire on a basic tour of the house while they made their way to the conservatory. Never could he remember finding so much to say about the surroundings that had simply been home to him for many years. The house hadn't held a significant entertainment since his mother remarried, so seeing a woman strolling through the passages was a bit jarring.

It was also wonderful.

If he couldn't get her to say yes, this memory would haunt him for a long time to come.

Her simply being in his home was an indication that she was changing her mind, wasn't it? She wouldn't have come, wouldn't have been that cruel.

The conservatory was bursting with color, having one of its best years in recent memory. A little bit of a helping hand from God? Griffith wasn't about to turn it down if it was.

"Look!" Isabella surged across the room, ladylike decorum all but forgotten. "You have chrysanthemums."

"Do I?" Griffith strolled over to look over her shoulder at the flower. Its thin spiky petals were rather beautiful. "I've never taken the time to learn what they are."

She narrowed her eyes into accusatory blue slits. "Then how do you know the orchids are good this year?"

Griffith leaned in like he was telling a secret, inhaling deep of the scent of lemongrass that clung to her skin. "Because the gardener told me."

Accusations faded into humor. "Then you don't actually know where the orchids are in this room?"

"I can guess, but you are probably much more qualified to find them than I am."

"Brave of you to admit it."

He'd admit almost anything if it allowed him to keep looking into her eyes this way. "I've no problem admitting my shortcomings. They are so few, after all."

She laughed, as he'd hoped she would, and took his hand, hauling him around the conservatory until she was once more gasping over a collection of delicately curling blooms in a variety of colors.

Miss St. Claire trailed behind them. Occasionally she grazed a plant with a finger. Mostly she smiled at them, her silence a better encouragement to Griffith than anything she could have said.

"That's not possible." Isabella squatted down to stare at a plant in the long, low bed. Moss covered the expanse of dirt, and a purple conical flower folded out of the tall, elegant stem.

Griffith sat on his heels beside her. "Now, that I do know about. It's a lady's slipper."

"But . . . how? I've never seen one. Not the real thing."

"He transplanted it. Saw it growing in the wild through the fence at Green Park and requested that I get special permission for him to move it before it was trampled underfoot. Now here it is."

"It's beautiful. And so very interesting. Did you know that the moss feeds the seed and then the adult flower feeds the moss?" She looked at him over her shoulder with eyes widened by the thrill of knowledge.

Griffith was captivated.

Eventually there were no more flowers to ooh and aah over. Griffith didn't want her to leave now that she was in his home, where he felt she belonged. "May I give you tea? We've done quite a bit of walking this afternoon."

Miss St. Claire gripped her hands together, excitement pouring off of her as she nearly trembled. "Can we have it in the white drawing room?"

Griffith winced. The best thing about his sisters marrying and moving out of the house had been that he no longer had to use that drawing room. Every surface from the chairs to the wall to the floor and the fireplace was white with gold accents.

Well, it had been until recently.

He ordered tea be brought to the drawing room and led the ladies in that direction. As they entered the famous room, Isabella began to laugh, and Miss St. Claire actually pouted, though with her mouth edges curled up a bit as if she were trying not to laugh.

In the center of the room was a large, sturdy peacock-colored sofa. When Griffith had ordered it in an effort to make some sort of ridiculous point about the house being his home, he hadn't realized how badly something could clash with white. He didn't know who he was making the point to, but changing the room that had been so much his mother's and sisters' had felt good. It had made the room a bit less terrifying now that he had a piece of furniture he could sit on without worrying it would break. But it also made it more than a bit uglier, with the bright sofa somehow making the rest of the room seem unstable.

Isabella perched on the sofa with a delighted laugh, and Miss St. Claire sat next to her. They had taken the only seat in the room built for his frame, leaving only the delicate chairs for him to sit in. He didn't mind, though. It was worth it to watch Isabella enjoy his home.

Tea arrived and Isabella offered to pour.

His hand shook as he accepted a cup from her. He'd drunk thousands of cups of tea poured from this same pot, but this one felt significant. She'd poured this one. Assuming the role of lady of the house.

He drank, filling his mouth with tea so he didn't declare himself right then and there.

It was going to happen soon, though. She was comfortable with him, laughing and joking. Talking about a myriad of things. Whatever her troubles, she had to know he would help her solve them. Once she had the assurance that he wanted to marry her, she would understand that and be willing.

He hoped.

"Will you walk with me tomorrow?" He set his cup aside before he could drop it.

"Walk where?"

"Green Park. Have you been?"

She shook her head and then scrunched her nose before turning to her cousin. "That's not the one with the strange pagoda in it, is it?"

Miss St. Claire shook her head. "No, that was Kew Gardens. We attended that outdoor musicale there."

"Oh yes." Isabella turned back to Griffith with a smile. "I've never been to Green Park. What do they have?"

"Maple trees, though none as fascinating as the ones in Berkeley Square. Lime trees. A lot of green things." Griffith grinned at his own mild joke.

Isabella grinned back. "I suppose I could take the afternoon to see another park."

"Lord Vernham is making hints that he intends to propose soon." Uncle Percy adjusted his waistcoat and sent Isabella an accusatory stare.

What did he expect her to do about it? A proposal was the customary conclusion to a bout of courting. She was pulling them in, convincing them the way to her side was through Uncle Percy. What else did Uncle Percy want her to do?

She stared at him, leaving her fingers resting silently on the piano keys in front of her. He would get to the point eventually, even if she never said anything. Probably faster. Ever since the house party, she'd found herself less inclined to talk to her uncle, less inclined to do his bidding, less inclined to even stay in his home.

Especially now that he was ruining her lovely, lovely day. She had actually enjoyed herself today. She had smiled, she had laughed, she had blossomed like the lady slipper under the obvious affection in Griffith's eyes and voice. And now, when she was tired and wanted only to bask in her memories, her uncle was ruining it.

If she had a place to go, she'd run there.

"You'll have to discourage him. There's a good bit of discussion around the Apothecary Act, but it hasn't even been officially read in the House of Lords. I can't have the men proposing until the vote is imminent."

"And how would you have me do that?" Did he really think she was that manipulative? So capable of leading men around by the nose that she could manage the expectations of individual men at will? If she could do that, why was Griffith still popping up in every corner of her life? Why couldn't she discourage him? Though, after today, did she really want to?

He humphed. "How should I know? Just do a little less of whatever it is that got him to this point to begin with."

Gladly. "Very well. I'll inform my maid that I shall be staying in tonight."

Red tinged his cheeks as he blustered. "What? No! You have to go. Lord Kennard is going to be there, and he's seated on the cross benches with the rest of the uncommitted lords. I need his vote."

Isabella pushed her way to her feet, her fingers slamming out a discordant chord as she rose. "Perhaps you should try convincing them of the merit of the act, then, instead of luring them in with false promises of my affections and I don't even want to know what else."

"Watch your tongue, young lady."

"Or you'll do what? Send me home? Please do! I'll be happy to not even pack. I'll change and be on the next mail coach to Northumberland." Isabella was so tired of it all. So tired of the lies, the hurt, the guilt. She should never have come here, never have done this. She'd known God wouldn't be happy, and now she wasn't happy either. Even Uncle Percy wasn't happy, and if this situation left him in the doldrums, then what point was there in continuing?

"You will see this through," he growled through gritted teeth, deep grooves marring the edges of his pointy chin.

She crossed her arms and forced herself to keep staring into Uncle Percy's beady brown eyes. Her insides trembled, but she squeezed everything together until her body stayed firm. Uncle Percy could not see any weakness. "I will not."

"And what will you do? Marry the Duke of Riverton?" A look of smug satisfaction crossed his face. "The man gave his first attentions to Frederica—though I've no idea why—so he obviously isn't inclined to marry a woman such as yourself. You could, of course, turn his head if you chose. That's why we've made our arrangement, after all."

He leaned in until his nose was inches from hers and she could smell the sour whisky on his breath. "But what do you think will happen when he finds out you are not only the daughter of a farmer but you actually work the farm and didn't even have a maid until I got you one? What will happen when he discovers the Scottish blood running through your veins?"

What would happen? She had to believe he was interested in what he knew of the real her, not the stories Uncle Percy had told about her supposedly influential and wealthy family, about her dowry and her land. She had to believe that, had to believe that there was one man in all of London who saw the real her and liked her. "He won't care."

"Has he offered to marry you?"

Oh, how she wanted to lie, but that was what had gotten her here in the first place. "No."

"No offer of marriage. No public attentions. Doesn't sound like a man who intends to be there forever."

This conversation had to end now, before she gave in to the urge to cry in front of Uncle Percy. "What do you want?"

"I want you to keep our original deal. Keep them guessing, keep them wanting, but keep them far enough away that no one proposes."

"And then you'll pay off the debts and take care of my brothers' schooling?"

"Of course." Uncle Percy's grin crawled across his face.

"And if I don't?"

He frowned, his face scrunching into a menacing dagger. "I'll finish ruining your father once and for all. Theft should do the trick. Just one of those necklaces you're so careless with, found in his possession, could be enough to get him transported."

The floor seemed to sink from beneath Isabella's feet. She'd been so close to walking out the door, secure in the knowledge that if her family was together they could make something work. But this new threat was too much to risk. "You wouldn't."

"I would." His cruel smile returned. "But I'm also willing to throw a little more in to sweeten the deal and show you what a generous man I am."

"Oh?" What could he possibly think would make up for threatening her father?

"I'll throw in Frederica."

What did he mean? Isabella narrowed her gaze and waited.

"You finish the job, and Frederica can marry her officer. Free and clear and with my blessing."

Chapter 26

Isabella had known better than to agree to go on a walk with him. But she was weak, craving whatever bit of attention he was still willing to give her. The fact that he still spoke to her at all rather amazed her. She'd done everything she could to discourage him. Or at least she had when she'd thought about it. Too often she forgot what her goal was when she was around him.

And so here she was, strolling down the street with him, her maid four paces behind, and more than a few speculative glances turning their way.

"Where are we going again?" Isabella asked, turning her face up to catch the sun.

"Green Park. You said you haven't been there yet?" Griffith rested his hands at the small of his back and looked down at her with an excited grin.

"No, I haven't been to Green Park yet." Isabella couldn't help but laugh. "Is it your intention to show me every park in London before the Season is through?"

He smiled and faced forward again. "Of course. Vauxhall Gardens is next, the source of your infamous trees."

She laughed. "I've already been there, Your Grace."

He stopped and faced her, forcing her to do the same. The seriousness in his teasing eyes made her shiver. "Not with me."

And with that she lost the ability to breathe whatsoever.

He gestured to an open gate behind her. "Green Park, my lady."

"I'm not a lady, you know. My mother was the daughter of a viscount, but my father is only a gentleman." She winced. "Sort of."

He lifted a brow as he offered her his arm. "I doubt you will ever hold the title of lady, but that doesn't mean you aren't worthy of the honor and respect bestowed upon them."

For a moment she felt a pang at his assumption she would never gain a title. Not that she wanted one, except for perhaps his. Understanding hit her with enough force to send her stumbling if she weren't holding on to his arm. Marrying him wouldn't make her a lady. She'd be a duchess. Her Grace. That couldn't be what he was thinking about when he made his comment. She'd told him no too many times.

And yet here they were, together once more.

They strolled through the park, looking at flowers and trees and admiring the long stretches of empty lawn.

He led her up a small rise, away from the scatterings of other people enjoying the park and into the middle of a small copse of shade trees.

"At Riverton you said you didn't know if you loved me. And it made me think, made me question myself in ways I never had." Griffith knelt before her, among the birds and the trees and the nature he knew she loved, and took both of her hands in his own, stealing what little breath she had left along with the final pieces of her heart. "I had to ask myself if I loved you, or if I simply loved the challenging puzzle you presented. My sisters tell me that's a horrible thing to admit to a woman, but if you're going to marry me you should know that I think about everything."

"Oh, Griffith." Isabella freed one of her hands so she could reach out and cup his face, running a thumb along his cheek. She should stop him. This wasn't going to end well. But she selfishly craved the memory.

"I thought I knew what I wanted in a wife, so when my heart kept turning back to you, I fought it. I considered myself infatuated with your beauty or mesmerized by the mystery around you. I couldn't be in love with you, because you went against everything I'd thought through so carefully."

Another woman might think his declaration insensitive and unromantic, but Isabella had come to understand Griffith a bit, and she knew what he was saying, what it was costing him to say those words. And the more he spoke the more ill she became. His love she could accept, but not his understanding.

"Griffith, I—"

"Please." He took a deep, shuddering breath. "I need to say it all. It turns out that my heart is perhaps a bit smarter than my mind, because it never beat for Frederica. It never whispered her name to me at odd moments of the day. And I thought that made her the smarter choice. She would fit into my life and everything would remain in its logical, thought-out place.

"You turn my world upside down. I've told you things I never thought to share with anyone. I've changed my plans for you. I've danced with you." He grinned. "Or at least tried to."

Isabella couldn't take any more. She wanted to run from the park crying and screaming, wanted to rail at God for the unfairness of it all. Why, why when she had begged His forgiveness, when she had resigned herself to the consequences of her actions, had He allowed something like this to happen?

She knew where this was going. Despite Griffith's claim that she made him illogical, he was not a man who would make such a speech without intending to ask for her hand at the end of it.

"Isabella, my love"—Griffith swallowed—"will you do me the honor of marrying me? Of challenging the rest of what I thought I knew of life? Will you take up the challenge of reminding me daily that God created the heart as well as the mind?"

Pain stabbed Isabella from her chest to her feet. Had any woman ever received such a beautiful request? The sincerity and thought behind it amazed her. That this brilliant man had looked at all the angles and then decided that he wanted to spend his life with her anyway.

She tried to look away from him, tried desperately not to soak in every detail in his handsome and eager face. The evidence of love and hope that seemed to burn right through her, threatening to overwhelm the hope of her family's solid future that she'd carried in her heart.

She couldn't do it. Couldn't leave Frederica to live with the consequences of Isabella's actions. Couldn't risk her uncle carrying through on his threat against her father. Couldn't ask Griffith to wait while she continued to build her reputation as London's most indiscriminate flirt. Couldn't ask him to take on her family's debts, her brothers' education, and who knew what other problems her uncle would cause. Eventually Griffith's logical mind would realize that she'd brought more misery into his life than joy, and she'd have to watch the light burning in his emerald gaze die.

And she couldn't do it.

"I can't," she whispered.

Griffith rose slowly from his kneeling position, his fingers still wrapped tightly around her own. She should take her hand back, but she knew the moment she did she'd be ripping her own heart out, because it was his and she had no way of claiming it back. Nor did she want to. If she was going to cause the torment gathering in his emerald eyes, then she deserved to feel heartbreak of her own.

"Bella, I—"

"No." A sob cut off anything else she'd been going to say. Hearing the shortened version of her name, the one used by those she cared so much about, spoken in his deep, gentle voice was too much.

So she ran. Down the gentle slope of the hill and around the line of trees, along the street where peddlers and hack drivers yelled at her. Whether it was a bid for her business or an admonishment to get out of the way, she didn't care. She simply ran. Her skirt kicked up in a wildly scandalous manner, which would probably make the papers the next day. Somewhere behind her she heard the huffing and scrambling of her maid trying to keep up.

Her side was aching by the time she slammed into the front door of her uncle's town house. The pain didn't subside when she pressed a hand tightly to her ribs, but part of her didn't want it to. There should be physical pain when one's heart broke. Maybe she'd die from it and her uncle would fulfill his promises out of sympathy and her mourning family would never have to know what she'd done.

She'd said no.

There was no denying that the word had come out of her mouth. Just that word. Not even a string of platitudes had followed it before she'd fled from the scene, giving him no time to form a rebuttal. And he would have had a rebuttal. Eventually. After he got over the shock of being so very wrong about how she felt about him.

Again.

He still wasn't over the shock, though, so it was probably a good thing she'd gone home. They'd have both caught colds or some other dreadful ailment standing in the wind for five hours.

Quiet pressed in on him as he stood at a back window, looking out over the small but immaculately manicured garden that passed for grounds in the city. Roses danced in the breeze to a tune only God knew, but the one he heard was of a decidedly more earthbound, if still angelic, source. The pianoforte was behind him, a solid, hulking presence in the darkening music room. Now it lay silent and still, but he could almost hear her plunking away the notes of the Scottish ballad he'd caught her singing one afternoon in the country. Could imagine her escaping to the keys to avoid her uncle's displeasure over Griffith's attentions. He had no trouble remembering the small grin she'd given him when the pompous Lady Hannah had derided her for playing someone as plebeian as Hummel when she had in fact been playing a lesser-known piece by Mozart.

Why had she turned him down?

Griffith sat at the pianoforte, running his fingers over the keys, sending a disjointed clash of notes careening around the room. It broke the quiet but didn't ease the oppressive feeling of it. For the first time, living alone in his large London house felt lonely. Why now? His family had been out of the house for nearly two years.

He'd never been lonely, during that time, because he'd never expected them to stay. Isabella was someone different entirely. There wasn't a room in the house he couldn't see her living in, imagine her bringing a bit of life to, even if it looked a touch more chaotic than he'd like.

With a last slam of the keys, Griffith jerked to his feet and stomped out of the room to seek a haven in the only place he could think of. His study should still be solidly his own, as Isabella would have no reason to be in there even if she were his wife.

The house was quiet as the servants went about finishing their work elsewhere in the house. The silence felt heavy and thick. Even his clothing seemed to feel the tension, forcing him to roll his shoulders and undo his cravat in an effort to ease the tightness.

He walked into the study and eased the door into its customary position, leaving a three-inch gap between the door and the frame. After a moment he reconsidered and pushed the thing closed until the latch clicked.

A curl of peace worked its way through his midsection. This was the room he did his best thinking in, was the most comfortable, and usually solved whatever problem he was facing. He'd always loved this study, even when he'd spent most of his time away at school. As he'd gotten older he frequently took his school breaks in London just to absorb the energy in this room. Despite the fact that most of the time spent with his father had occurred in the country, this was the room that felt as if it had received the old duke's mark the most. Griffith had changed very little of it in the eighteen years since it had become his.

He wandered the room, grazing a hand idly over a standing globe, running a thumb along a shelf filled with gilded and leather-bound volumes. His thoughts shifted far from the room, trying to decide what he was going to do now that the woman he'd fallen in love with refused to marry him.

Could he marry someone he didn't love, knowing that Isabella was out there somewhere? No, he couldn't. Not until she had married first, removing any hope he had of making her his bride. He would have to become even more of a social hermit, because he couldn't bear to see her with the man she and her uncle eventually chose.

Why not him? As beautiful as Isabella was, she came with pitifully little in dowry and connections. His suit should have

294

been accepted with glee by anyone seeking to advance their family's status and station in life. With what he knew of her family's situation, she should have jumped at the chance to marry him. She wasn't going to get a better offer.

His mind mulled the problem until he suddenly blinked the room back into focus, reality stunning him out of his musings with an abrupt crash. He was sitting in a wing chair, feet extended toward the cold fireplace. It wasn't an unusual position to find himself in, but never before had he sat just so while also swirling a glass of amber liquid in his hand.

When had he poured it? He couldn't even remember going over to the sideboard he kept stocked for gentlemen who came to discuss business. With a shaky hand he lifted the glass to his nose and sniffed. He didn't even know what he'd poured. Scotch? There was a certain amount of irony in that choice of drink that he could imagine himself subconsciously choosing.

He ran his tongue over his teeth to see if he had not only poured the drink without thought but also drunk it without noticing.

Nothing felt thick and dry like he remembered it feeling after his accident in the country. He tested his breath. Only the normal staleness of a long day met his nose.

He set the thankfully untouched glass of spirits down on the table beside him.

This wasn't him. This moping around like a brooding dandy whose lovesick poetry hadn't been well received by society's darling. He was the Duke of Riverton, and while he was now ready to admit that his plan to control and plot his journey to a loving marriage had been doomed to failure almost from the first, he was not ready to say that love should not have a measure of such logic applied to it.

Isabella denying his suit was illogical.

But it still hurt.

Chapter 27

Isabella slept late the next morning.

When she woke, Frederica was sitting in a chair by the window, reading a book. She glanced over when she heard Isabella moving but said nothing and turned her attention back to her book.

Isabella pushed up into a sitting position and waited until Frederica flipped a page, curious to see if her cousin was actually reading or simply trying not to look at her.

"Why didn't you wake me?"

Frederica huffed a sound that could have been termed a short laugh if it weren't coated in sadness. "When a woman cries until well past three in the morning, you let her sleep."

With a groan, Isabella flopped back onto her pillows. "I didn't realize I was so loud."

Another page turned. "Do remember that our beds back up to the same wall. It doesn't take much." She closed the book and looked at Bella with a blank expression. "What happened?"

For a few seconds Isabella considered lying. Would Freddie understand why she'd said no? Why she had to say no? Poor Frederica was waiting to find out whether or not the love of her life was even going to survive to be able to propose, while Isabella was walking away from the man who had declared his love for her and had so sweetly asked her to be his wife. Would Frederica understand that more was riding on Isabella's success than ever before? That Freddie's own happiness was at stake?

"He proposed."

In the ensuing silence, Isabella couldn't look at Frederica. She heard her cousin rise and cross the room to yank the bell pull.

"And you said no, I'm assuming. Otherwise we'd have been up all night celebrating."

"I couldn't, Freddie. Not with so much at stake. My father was a proud man before the accident. When I left he was barely holding on, working himself to exhaustion every day to accomplish a small fraction of what needed to be done. He'd sit before the fire at night, looking older than I'd ever seen him. How could he survive being indebted to my husband? Relying on a Peer of the Realm to care for his family, his children? It would break him, Frederica. And that would break me. And I know Griffith would blame himself for my unhappiness."

Frederica drummed her fingers against her book. "I don't think," she said slowly, "that your father would be all that pleased with your making decisions for him."

"Of course he wouldn't. Which is why I won't tell him." Isabella got up from the bed and began to pace. "When I go home at the end of the Season, we'll say I wasn't successful. Uncle Percy agreed to pretend to help out of sympathy."

"Leaving your father indebted to his wife's brother instead of his daughter's husband. I'm not sure that's any better. Personally I think His Grace would be considerably less annoying and condescending about it than my father will be."

Isabella frowned. "Maybe, but at least then I'd be there to suffer alongside them. Not off in my shiny new castle, living life without a care while they scrape by knowing everything they've got is from the hands of another."

"It seems a rather impossible situation."

"Yes."

A maid arrived then, carrying a tray. The cousins waited until she'd left again before returning to their conversation.

"Are you going to be ill today?" Frederica set about pouring and fixing the tea the way Isabella normally took it. "I wouldn't blame you. But Father's expecting people to stop by this afternoon and informed me he expects us to be available. The House of Commons approved the draft of the bill. Now it only needs the approval of the House of Lords."

Isabella sat at the dressing table and wrapped her hands around the cup of tea, taking a deep breath of the fragrant steam. "So it's almost over, then? He said the Lords would vote on it once the Commons had."

"It's almost over. He wants you to make a final case for him, though." Freddie frowned as if trying to remember something important. "Assuming, of course, they stop picking over it and vote on the thing. You'll be happy to know that even though all these men want to vote on it to make the path to your side a little smoother, they're not voting blindly. All the changes have Father worried. Of course he's never thought it strict enough. If he had his way the apothecaries would be nothing more than chemists, able to do nothing without the oversight of a fully educated physician."

Isabella well understood her uncle's frustration. This Apothecary Act had been something of a burden for him for years. She just couldn't bring herself to care. "How did you find out about all of this? He's barely talked to me about what's going on. Just tells me to get more men. As if they were flowers I could walk around a ballroom and pick at will."

Frederica shrugged. "The bedroom wall isn't the only one that's thin."

"I'll be ready." Isabella made herself take a bite of fluffy pastry even though it sat on her tongue like cotton stuffing. She swallowed hard. "I still have to see this through, and the sooner we finish it the better."

Frederica nodded and then pulled a folded white square from her book. "I almost forgot. A letter arrived for you yesterday, but you'd already closed yourself away in here. I assumed it could wait."

Who could possibly be sending her a letter? Had her mother sent another note?

Isabella's hand trembled as she reached for the paper. Perhaps a word from home was just the motivation she needed to see this through, to bear the cold stares in another ballroom, to ignore the papers one more day, to resist the urge to tell her uncle what a conniving manipulator he was and leave London in her dust.

Her mother's handwriting looped across the front of the paper, bringing a smile to Isabella's lips.

Frederica reached down and hugged Isabella. "I'll leave you to your letter and your breakfast, then."

Isabella was already breaking the seal when the door latched behind Frederica.

But the words did not bring solidifying motivation. A cry wrenched from Isabella's lips as she read the note.

They were selling the farm. Not all of it, of course, but enough to pay off the debts and send Hugh to school. There would even be enough for a small dowry for Isabella and her sisters. They wouldn't have to rely on her uncle's generosity anymore.

That sentiment brought tears to Isabella's eyes.

Her mother continued by saying that once the girls married, the small farm would be more than enough to support Isabella's parents, especially as her father had become exceptionally good at leather work during his convalescence. They'd taken his leather goods to Dumfries and made almost as much as they'd made with the farm the previous year.

Mother sounded so happy. Isabella could do nothing but cry.

It was so clear now. She'd made the wrong choice. She'd given up everything, telling herself it didn't matter because at least she'd be saving her family. She could deal with her own unhappiness to know that they were safe and taken care of.

But she shouldn't have.

Everywhere she looked she saw reminders of everything she'd given up, everything she'd done. Flowers from men she'd flirted with. Dresses and jewelry purchased by her uncle as an investment in her success, left strewn about the room because she so frequently dismissed her maid. The grandeur of the room itself, under a roof she'd never been allowed to visit until she'd become useful and malleable. All of it made her sick to her stomach.

Closing her eyes didn't help. Because then all she could see was Griffith's face when she told him no. The hurt and surprise that he couldn't hide because he'd laid himself bare in his bid for her hand. And she'd wanted to say yes. Oh, how she'd wanted to.

But he didn't know. And she couldn't tell him. Because as difficult as it was to see him hurt by her hand, how much worse would it be to see his caring fade? To see his regard slide into disgust when he, who valued his integrity above all else, learned that she'd been willing to sell her honor?

Either way she was destined to lose everything she'd come to care about. At least now, when she slunk home to marry a

300

local merchant with no ties to London and no knowledge of Town gossip, she'd be able to carry with her the knowledge that a man as wonderful and amazing as Griffith had loved her.

In time, he would love another, which was why she would never be able to accept the suit of any of the other men vying for her attention. She would never return to London, would never run the risk of seeing Griffith with someone else.

Would never again roam the rolling fields of Northumberland, safe in the feeling that at least there, she belonged. Because she didn't anymore. And not just because her family had sold those precious fields, but because she had changed. Whether London had changed her or the pressure and subterfuge had done it didn't matter. Perhaps it was both or neither, in some strange combination with the way she felt around Griffith.

A tear welled in her eye. She tried to blink it away, but it spilled down her cheek anyway. With an angry swipe of her hand she pushed it away. What right did she have to cry? She'd made her decisions, had foolishly believed that there was no other way out for her family and only her bravery and sacrifice could save her sisters and brothers from a life of drudgery and her parents from ruin. Now she had to live with that foolishness, the complete lack of trust in God, and the repercussions of it, with no one to blame but herself.

The letter had crumpled in her frustrated fist. For a moment she considered lighting a candle and holding the paper up to the flickering flame, erasing forever the inked proof of her folly. But she couldn't. Her family was all she had now, and burning the precious words her mother had scraped together the time to write wouldn't change the truth.

That didn't mean she had to look at it, though.

She crossed the room and flipped open her jewelry box, empty save the precious memories she'd collected in London and her mother's forgotten jewelry. At the bottom lay the only other letter her mother had been able to send. But it wasn't the folded parchment that sparked a trembling in Bella's lower lip and a burning in the corner of her eye.

The quaich Griffith had bought her and the scrap of thread she'd found clinging to her skirt after sewing up his arm lay across the letter. Traces of sunlight played over the piece of plane tree bark nestled beside them. Whomever she married would likely be a working man, without the time or inclination to take her around to examine strange trees and plants. Even reading about such plants was probably lost to her, as being the wife of a working man and raising a family would require every bit of her time and attention.

And while it was entirely possible she'd find the need to stitch him up at some point, she doubted the ensuing conversation would be half as enjoyable.

She would not cry. Not now. Now she would be strong. There was no denying that her lack of trust and deliberate choice of a path God wouldn't have led her to had brought nothing but destruction. A warning about that was probably in the Bible somewhere, but she'd never paid much attention to memorizing verses unless her grandmother or parents made her.

Yet another thing to be mad at herself over. She should have taken more time. Studied Scripture instead of horticulture.

With angry swipes she scooped up all the carelessly discarded jewelry and hurled it into the box on top of all the things she'd foolishly thought to treasure. The splintering sound of the delicate piece of bark broke the dam holding back her tears, and as she slid the jewelry box lid closed, she let them come.

The trickle turned into a flood, and she found herself weeping in a heap on the floor, her hip pressed into the sturdy leg at the foot of her bed.

She cried until nothing remained but a headache and an overwhelming weakness. Too tired to climb up into the bed again, she snagged the corner of the coverlet and pulled until she could wrap the covering around her on the floor.

Chapter 28

Griffith shifted against the red upholstered bench and leaned his head back until it was supported by the wall behind him. He didn't often choose to sit on the back bench, since it was usually occupied by those who simply couldn't be bothered to care, but considering he'd actually contemplated not even showing up to Parliament that day, sitting on the back row was a decent compromise.

Ryland climbed the steps and slid onto the bench next to him. "Why are we being backbenchers today? Is there a division I don't know about?"

The ministers in the front row didn't look very anxious, so Griffith had to assume there wasn't an exciting vote planned for the day. "I hope not. I doubt I'll hear much of the debate."

Ryland crossed his arms and settled against the bench. "Things didn't go well yesterday, I take it. Did you tell her what an illogical choice she was?"

A heavy sigh accompanied the closing of Griffith's eyes. He was never telling his sister anything ever again.

A bump to his shoulder caused Griffith's back to slide against

the seat, scraping his head against the tapestry-covered wall.
He lifted it and opened his eyes to glare at his friend.

Ryland looked at him for a moment. "She really turned you
down?"

"Yes." That was all the explanation Griffith felt like giving.
Of course, it was all the explanation he'd been given, so he
couldn't give Ryland much more even if he wanted to.

Anthony slid onto the bench on Griffith's other side. "Why
are we sitting back here? Do we have something against Irish
priests now?"

Ryland leaned forward to look at Anthony across Griffith.
"Is that what we're talking about today?"

"How is it you don't know? Last week you told me not only
which days we'd be discussing the foreign ally treaty but who
was prepared to make statements and whether or not Prinny
was inclined to get involved."

Ryland shrugged. "I care about the treaty. Roman Catholics
in Ireland don't really concern me."

"I'm going to have to side with Ryland on this one." Griffith
grunted, thankful that today's debate was one he didn't really
care about. He'd happily sit with the other disinterested men
when it came time to call for a division. Assuming they were
even voting on it today. He let his eyes fall shut once more and
debated leaving the hall entirely.

"What's his problem?"

Ryland laughed. "He's fallen prey to the illogical upheaval
of love, I'm afraid."

Anthony's mouth went slack. "She turned him down?"

Griffith glared at the marquis. "Your wife wasn't even there
when I talked to my sisters."

He shrugged. "No, but Miranda and Ryland came to dinner
last week."

"It was a couples thing." Ryland grinned. "I'd say you should join us next time, but that would require you actually settling on a woman to marry." He angled his shoulders and ducked his head, as if afraid Griffith would attack him for the dig.

Griffith thought about it, but it wasn't worth the effort. "I apologize for every comment I made at your expense, gentlemen. I am now convinced love turns a man into an idiot."

"Are we back to making logical choices about who we marry?" Ryland shook his head. "Please tell me Miss St. Claire hasn't returned to the top of the list."

"That would put him in too close a proximity to the idiocy-inducing Miss Breckenridge." Anthony tapped one finger against his chin, eyes squinted in exaggerated thought. "He needs a lady who will take him in a different social direction entirely."

"You can save your energy." Griffith shifted against the seat again. The benches had never been overly comfortable due to his long legs, but today they felt like torture devices. "I've decided to abandon the idea of marriage for a while."

His friends looked at each other and then back at him.

"You can't be serious," Anthony said.

"You're really going to give up?" Ryland rubbed a hand over his face before sitting back to stare in shock at Griffith.

Griffith's gaze fell to the other side of the chamber, where Lord Pontebrook was blustering, so angry his face was turning red and spittle flew from his mouth as he gestured toward the open chamber doors. "She needs help, and I can't be the one to help her."

An inelegant, scoffing snort came from Ryland. "You're a duke. If you can't help her, who can?"

"I don't know." Griffith shrugged. "She won't tell me the problem."

The other two men were silent for a long time, longer than

Griffith had expected. He'd rather hoped that they would have some advice on how he should proceed, given their own difficult paths to happiness.

"That's it?" Anthony finally asked. "That's the reason you're moping on the back bench?"

Griffith frowned. "I'm not moping."

"You are, but that's hardly the point." Ryland crossed his arms. "If you want to fix her problem, the first thing you have to do is discover what it is."

It was such a simple concept, the next logical step. Why on earth couldn't he have thought of it? He'd investigated her background but obviously not enough of her present. "You see?" He looked from Anthony to Ryland before gesturing to himself. "Idiot."

He leaned forward and placed his elbows on his knees, pressing his hands together and balancing his chin on top of his fingers. His mind began to leave the familiar surroundings of the House of Lords once more, but this time he welcomed the disconnection as he stepped into the equally familiar activity of problem solving. He wasn't giving Isabella up without a fight. Something strange had been going on with her all Season, and there was no reason to think whatever it was had gone away.

Which meant it was time for Griffith to shift this emotion to the side and let his mind save the day once again.

And he would start with her uncle.

⌒

They weren't supposed to be nice.

Isabella smiled at Sir Richard over the top of yet another bouquet of flowers. This one hadn't come with over-the-top poetry or ridiculous compliments. It had been honestly handed over as the sentiment of wishing to come by and see her was expressed. She'd tried not to keep a record, even a mental one, of the men who visited her, but she remembered him. She was fairly certain he'd been by three or four times before.

He had been pleasant to talk to and seemed genuinely interested in what she had to say. They would speak for a while and he would take his leave, promising to seek her out when next they were at the same event.

Today was no different. As his visit came to a close, he remarked upon the weather they appeared to be headed toward for the next day or so. He always closed with the weather. After they danced at a ball or shared a cup of punch at a musicale, the last thing he mentioned was always the weather.

It was a rather refreshing change from it being the first thing mentioned, but it was a strange habit.

And it made her feel a bit guilty.

Because not only was he nice, but he wasn't even one of the men her uncle wished to convince to his way of thinking. Sir Richard didn't have a vote. He was a baronet, doomed to live on the line between peerage and gentry. As far as she could tell he had no real political aspirations. He was simply a nice man who had come to London to socialize with his peers and perhaps find a wife while he was at it.

And Isabella didn't know how to tell him that she wasn't going to be that wife. If she started discouraging any of her suitors, she would start discouraging them all. If she ever gave leave to the words screaming inside her head, she was afraid they would never stop.

Even though she wasn't sure what the point was anymore.

Her family didn't need her to sacrifice herself. They'd been saved through other means, through another plan. One she hadn't been patient enough or confident enough to wait on. Even though her mother would look to the sky every night and say how glad she was that the Lord was in control, Isabella had always thought it more of a hollow statement that kept her mother from admitting how bad things really were. But what Isabella had thought was a weakness was actually evidence of a faith stronger than she could have imagined.

And God had come through. Not as Isabella had hoped, not the way she'd asked for in the early days after her father's accident, but in a way that had left everyone in her family better off.

Everyone except her. But she couldn't blame God's unusual plan for that one. She'd done this to herself.

She wasn't sure what she'd said, but her smiles had been bright enough and her conversation witty enough, because Sir Richard looked as pleased as ever as he made his good-byes and predicted that the dreary grey in the sky would not give way to rain for another two days.

If only it would rain now. Pour down in sheets and buckets so she would have a reason to curl up in her bed for the foreseeable future.

Frederica came walking in, her quick breathing and flushed cheeks proving she'd run through the house to get to the drawing room even though she was walking sedately when she came through the door.

She looked around the room, eyes wide. "He already departed?"

"Of course. They visit, I smile, they leave. We've been doing this for a while now." Isabella dropped her eyes to the flowers, lying bright and vibrant against the oldest skirt in her wardrobe. It had been the nicest dress she owned before her uncle had swooped in and told her he had a way to fix everything.

"But he just got here! Osborn sent a maid to get me, and I ran all the way down here. It couldn't have taken more than five minutes."

Perhaps Isabella hadn't been as sparkling a conversationalist as she thought.

Freddie sat on the sofa next to Isabella. "Why didn't you tell me you were coming downstairs?"

Because she was afraid she'd lose the will to come downstairs at all if she didn't come straight from her room.

Frederica ran a hand over Isabella's skirt where it fanned out over part of the seat. "Is your family well?"

"Yes. Very well." Isabella looked up into Frederica's concerned face. Her cousin had been there through everything. She shouldn't have to suffer for Isabella's sin. That was the consequence, then. She could and would beg God for forgiveness, but she would still have to follow through for Frederica's sake.

"Have you heard from Arthur?"

"No." Frederica lifted one shoulder and tipped her head down, a sad smile on her lips. "But that's not surprising. He didn't know if they'd be riding straight into battle or making camp somewhere. Even if he could send a letter, it could be tied up for weeks before they clear it of any secret communications."

"He'll come home, Freddie."

She looked up with a smile, but tears clung to her eyelashes. "I'm praying he will." A deep, shuddering breath lifted her shoulders. "Either way I'm thankful that God let me see him again, let me know that I wasn't mistaken to continue loving him. And this time, his colonel promised to find me personally should anything . . . Well, this time I'll know for certain. I'm grateful for that blessing."

If anyone deserved to question God's plan, it was Frederica. She'd lost her mother and brother to taking the wrong medicine. Her father had all but tossed her aside as useless after telling her the man she loved was dead, but he'd lauded her cousin as worthwhile simply because she was pretty. And now, after

310

finally being reunited with the man she'd stayed loyal to, he'd been sent off to war again. Yet still she had faith.

It was enough to make Isabella wish to run upstairs and curl up beneath her coverlet.

The butler knocked once upon the open drawing room door. "My ladies, Mr. Emerson is here to see Lord Pontebrook. As his lordship is not home yet, would you like me to show him in here?"

No. No she most certainly would not. "Yes, of course. Send him in and have tea brought directly."

Osborn bowed and retreated.

Isabella slid her hand across the sofa until she could grip Frederica's. This was for her and her future happiness. A few more weeks of smiles weren't going to hurt anyone. And maybe, when everything was over, she could throw her future into God's hands and see if Griffith could possibly forgive her for everything.

The idea that she may not have to walk away from Griffith after all lifted her spirits like nothing else. As Freddie had said, it all might not turn out well in the end, but she could have faith and do what needed to be done to know for sure that God had closed that door. Perhaps something good could come of Isabella's folly.

Mr. Emerson bowed at the door before entering and sitting in the armchair across from the cousins.

The smile Isabella gave him was real—possibly a bit too wide for the occasion, but she didn't care. The last time Mr. Emerson had come to the house, the Apothecary Act had been approved by the House of Commons the day before. So far the man had brought nothing but good news to her uncle.

Perhaps this would all be over soon.

Tea arrived, and they chatted the same conversation Isabella had held countless times as they sipped tea and nibbled on strawberry tarts. She could almost speak this conversation in her sleep. The names of the events changed and occasionally she switched up her choice of words that indicated how lovely she was finding London, but by and large it was always the same, barely scratching the surface.

Uncle Percy joined them in the middle of a debate over the current opera that was actually quite interesting.

"Good afternoon, Mr. Emerson. Come to brighten your day with my niece?" He glanced their way. "And daughter?"

Freddie rolled her eyes and tipped up her teacup.

Mr. Emerson rose. "It's always a pleasure to visit with your family, my lord, even when it was not my original intention to do so. I merely came to bring you a piece of news. You've been so interested in how the House of Commons was viewing the Apothecary Act that I thought I would do you the courtesy of delivering the news myself."

Uncle Percy rocked up onto his toes and patted his midsection with a wide grin on his face. "Well, I have to say I appreciate that. Shall we adjourn to my study, then?"

The two men exited and went up to her uncle's study. Mr. Emerson was back down the stairs in less than ten minutes.

"Good afternoon, ladies. Always a pleasure."

"That can't be good." Frederica set a half-eaten tart down on the tray.

"Why not?" Isabella picked at her skirt.

"Because he didn't stay long. If it had been good news, Father would have convinced him to celebrate with a toast at the very least."

Isabella swallowed hard. "Perhaps they drank it quickly."

The girls waited, all but holding their breath.

When the clock in the hall struck the hour, they both jumped, stunned to find they'd been sitting in silence for nearly half an hour.

"Should we check on him?" Isabella whispered.

Freddie turned wide eyes on her cousin. "Why would we do that? If it's bad news he'll take it out on us eventually. Probably by saying we've wandered down Bond Street a few too many times and then cutting my pin money for a month."

There was a good deal of truth to Freddie's statement. If something had gone wrong with the Apothecary Act, Uncle Percy had no reason to keep Isabella in Town any longer. And no reason to let Freddie marry Arthur.

Aside, of course, from that fact that it would make him a good father.

Isabella stood and smoothed her skirt, finding comfort in the brightly patterned silk that was highly unfashionable here in London but was admired by many back home in Northumberland. "We'll just walk by. If he calls us in to share his news, then we'll know. If he's drowning his sorrows, then we can just keep walking."

"I suppose it wouldn't hurt to walk up the stairs." Freddie stood, though she was considerably slower to straighten. "Quietly."

"Of course." Isabella agreed, though Freddie had no way of stopping her if she decided to stomp on the top two stairs to let her uncle know they were there.

They moved toward the stairs as if a monster lurked at the top, waiting to devour them.

As they neared the top of the stairs, Isabella elected to go with Frederica's plan for quiet and placed her foot gently on the next tread. At the top of the stairs they walked through the passage, winding their way to the next staircase that led up to the bedchambers.

Their feet had touched the first stair when a voice boomed out from the open study door they'd slipped past.

"Isabella!"

She swallowed, the bravery of downstairs drowned out by the panicked thudding of her heart.

Dear Lord, give me strength.

Her heart didn't stop trying to pound its way out through her ears, but a calm came over her in other ways. She was still scared, but there was an innate sense that everything was going to work out. It was amazing how quickly God was willing to take her back after she'd spent months doing things her own way.

She took a deep breath. "Yes, Uncle?"

"Come in here. The Apothecary Act has been abandoned, and I need you to save it."

Chapter 29

Was it unethical to sell jewelry that didn't actually belong to her? Of course, she couldn't risk doing so because her uncle had threatened to blame the loss of the jewelry on her father.

Was anyone buying used gowns? Isabella hadn't understood how very trapped she was until she realized that she didn't even have enough money to buy a seat on the mail coach home.

Of course, her mother would be livid if Isabella crossed the entire country by herself in a mail coach, but what else was Isabella going to do? She certainly couldn't obey her uncle's wishes.

The Apothecary Act was dead. While Uncle Percy had been doing his best to gather votes in the House of Lords, the House of Commons had washed their hands of it. After the numerous small changes the House of Lords had made and the amount of time they'd delayed the vote, the elected men had given up on the bill. Uncle Percy was livid. He'd spent the past seven years of his life trying to change things, trying to restrict the power of the people he felt were at fault for the death of his wife and son.

And now it was going to slip through his fingers.

Isabella admitted to feeling a bit of sympathy for that, but it wasn't enough to make her hurt Freddie, the one person she cared about that she hadn't yet lied to or manipulated in some way.

Freddie charged into Isabella's room without knocking and closed the door behind her. "What did he say?"

"The bill is dead. He said the only way to revive it would be for someone powerful to rewrite it and propose it again."

"Someone powerful?" Freddie sank onto Bella's bed. "Someone like the Duke of Riverton?"

"Someone exactly like the Duke of Riverton." Isabella paced from the window to the bed and back again. "He wants me to convince Griffith to throw his weight behind a new bill. He's even prepared to marry me off to him in order to make it happen."

Freddie's brows drew together. "But don't you want to marry the duke? You were just crying over—"

"Not like this! Never like this. I can't do it, Freddie. I can't use him like that."

"Why not?" She twisted her fingers together in her lap. "You used everyone else."

Sometimes truth hurt. And Isabella was glad Freddie was willing to tell her the truth even as she resented the uttering of it. "It's different."

There was silence for a moment as Isabella stopped her pacing and leaned her head against the window, the sun-warmed glass doing nothing to ease her frustration. "He's different."

"Because you love him."

"Yes," Isabella whispered. "I've hurt everyone I love over this business. I don't want to hurt him too."

"Haven't you already hurt him?"

Freddie's quiet voice called forth the memory Isabella had been repressing of Griffith rising to his feet, shock and pain on his face after she'd turned down his proposal. "Not like this would. He'd come to resent me, Freddie. I'd be the thing he traded his honor for."

"Unless he supports the bill."

"If he does, then he'll revive it on his own. I won't be the one to force him to make that choice."

Freddie crossed the room and wrapped her arms around Isabella, who dropped her head onto her cousin's shoulder in abject defeat. She couldn't even cry right now. It was as if she was so numb, so far removed from what was really happening, that she couldn't call forth the tears in the midst of her misery.

"Well, look at it this way, then," Freddie said, rocking Isabella back and forth. "You haven't hurt me yet. Did you know I've gone out to more events this year than the past two combined? I've been invited to absolutely everything."

Isabella sighed and buried her face in Frederica's hair. "How could I have forgotten? Freddie, what am I going to do?"

Freddie pulled back and tried to tilt her head to look Isabella in the eye. "What?"

"He won't let you marry Arthur." Bella pushed away from Freddie and began to pace again, hands pressed over her cheeks and temples as if she could somehow reach in and calm the tumultuous thoughts in her head. "I can't do this to Griffith, but if I don't, your father won't let you marry Arthur. He made it a condition when I threatened to go home after the house party." The tears that had so far been absent rushed forth with a vengeance, sending a raw sob up Isabella's throat. "Oh, Freddie, I'm so sorry!"

Freddie laughed.

It stunned Isabella into silence. She froze, hands falling limply to her side, tracks of pain still rolling slowly over her cheeks. Her voice was a raw whisper. "Freddie?"

317

"Bella, I'm three-and-twenty. Father can't stop me from marrying whomever I wish to." She shrugged. "Arthur and I sent messages to our home parishes before he left. They've been read three times by now. We'll be able to marry as soon as he comes home."

"You didn't." Isabella blinked. When Frederica decided to grow a backbone, she went for one made of iron. "But your dowry, your inheritance."

"All of it came from Mother. It was stipulated in her marriage contract, so there's nothing Father can do about it. Not really. I'm sure he'll bluster and fuss, but it's not his to deny. He's already told me the rest of it will go with the estate. He doesn't want Godfrey, or whatever his name is, to have any trouble retaining the glory of the viscountcy." Freddie rolled her eyes at the last bit, but her wide smile remained.

"So I'm not ruining things for you?" A small ray of hope poked through the shadows crowding Isabella's vision.

"I won't deny that it would be nice if Father supported my marriage, but I've lived the last ten years in this house, watching myself fade along with my mother's memory and, quite possibly, my father's grip on reality. I'll not keep fading away until I'm nothing but a shell."

"I wish I had your courage, Freddie."

"Where do you think I got it from?" Freddie brushed a final tear from Bella's face. "Anyone who comes clear across the country with the confidence that she can ensnare an entire population of powerful men isn't lacking in courage. Even if it is a bit misplaced."

Both girls sank back onto the edge of the bed, the swirl of fast-changing emotions draining their energy.

"I want to go home, Freddie."

Freddie frowned. "Are you sure that's the best idea? Father

318

can't make you say anything to Griffith about the Apothecary Act, even if you do change your mind about the proposal. You could go be a duchess, and there isn't a thing Father can do about it."

"You think Uncle Percy wouldn't say anything? The moment he could lay claim to any family connection to Griffith, he would be on the doorstep, hat in hand. And Griffith would know that I'd come to him with another agenda, whether I wanted to or not. Not to mention I still have to tell him that everything he knows about me is a lie. That would be enough to convince anyone that I'm colluding with Uncle Percy on this business. But by then he'd be committed and he would feel obligated because that's what he does. He'd do anything for his family."

A small wrinkle appeared across the bridge of Freddie's nose as she allowed an impish grin to cut through the melancholy. "Except dance."

Isabella laughed. "Except dance."

And he'd even been willing to do that with her. Anxious to, even.

With a sigh Isabella dropped her head onto Frederica's shoulder. "That is probably my biggest regret, Freddie. He asked me so many times and I never said yes."

⌒

"Tell me again why I'm here?"

Frederica straightened her glove and moved to join the flow of people entering Lady Farnsworth's home. "Aside from saying yes to a dance should the duke ask again?" She grinned at Isabella over her shoulder. "You are here because I am not about to let you sit in the house until you become a piece of furniture. It's bad enough that Father has hardly moved from the lounge in his room. I'll not have you become a living ghost."

"I admit, getting dressed and leaving the house is a good thing. But did it have to be here?" Isabella trailed Frederica up the stairs and through the receiving line. She'd done her best to appear less ornate tonight, but there was only so much she could do without taking a set of shears and hacking off a few pounds of flounce and trim. Uncle Percy had bought her a wardrobe to be noticed, and leaving off the ostentatious jewelry and doing her hair up in a simple cluster of curls—all hers tonight, no fake hair or milled starch—wasn't going to detract from a gown created to draw attention.

They greeted their hostess and slid into the ballroom, Isabella doing her best to stay shielded behind Frederica.

"If you wish to hide, my skirts would probably be the worst choice you can make. My nose is like a beacon pointing people in your direction. We've rarely been less than five feet apart all spring, unless you were on the dance floor." Freddie nudged Isabella with her hip until she straightened and moved to stand next to her.

"Your nose isn't that big," Isabella mumbled. It was a ridiculous, and rather untrue, thing to say, but Isabella couldn't bring herself to address anything else around her this evening, so she might as well attempt to bolster Frederica's courage. Although Frederica hadn't seemed to need any such encouragement of late.

"We both know it's half the size of Yorkshire." She shrugged. "It is what it is. It keeps me from drowning in the rain, and Arthur doesn't seem to mind it, so why should I?"

They stayed to the edges of the ballroom, working their way toward the corner where all the spinsters were gathering. Isabella doubted they'd welcome her into their circles. Ladies hadn't been very excited to see Isabella in the past few weeks, but the spinster corner was the best place for a woman to hide if she didn't want to be noticed.

She never quite made it.

"Miss Breckenridge! So nice to see you again."

Isabella smiled at Sir Richard. "And you as well."

"Would you care to dance?"

No. Not unless it was Griffith asking her again.

She opened her mouth to decline, but then thought back to when she'd finally faced her fears and opened her grandmother's Bible this afternoon to read Psalm 23. It had been peaceful and comforting, but one thing she'd noticed was all but one of the verses talked about moving along with God. If she was going to leave the consequences of her bad decisions behind and move forward to whatever God had in store for her, she wasn't going to be able to do it holding up the ballroom wall.

It didn't mean she had to accept everyone who asked her. Some of the men she'd been flirting with were rather unpleasant. At least Sir Richard was nice.

She smiled and dipped her head. "The honor would be mine."

As they lined up with the other couples on the floor, Isabella had to make herself pay attention to the formations patterned by the couples at the top of the rows. Her mind kept wandering back to the idea of moving forward. Finding a future. She glanced at Sir Richard. He would be a good provider and spent most of his year in the country. If she remembered correctly, he lived in one of the northern counties, though not nearly as far north as her family. All things considered, there were considerably worse futures God could give her than the one Sir Richard could offer.

But she couldn't marry him.

At least not any time soon. The very idea of giving serious contemplation to such a union made her skin feel too tight, and she'd never been so thankful for a dance pattern to have worked its way down to her before.

They joined the formations, and Isabella's smile came a bit easier as they chasséd across the line and changed places with the couple above them. There was something freeing in learning what one wouldn't do. It was almost as helpful as knowing what she would do with her future.

Unease still settled heavy in her belly, because if she wasn't going to marry . . . what was she going to do? Father was a businessman now, anticipating lowering the number of people in his house that he had to care for.

And Sir Richard was saying something to her that she was missing completely.

Isabella smiled. It had worked for her for nearly three months now. Smiling when she didn't know what to say or couldn't say what she'd wanted to say.

It worked again. Sir Richard smiled in answer and continued to speak.

Isabella took a deep breath and let it out through her smiling teeth. Freddie was determined to keep dragging her to these things until she was sure Isabella was fine. Which meant Isabella was going to do everything in her power to make it look like she always had before or drive herself unconscious trying.

Chapter 30

When a man wanted information that he didn't already have, he had to go to sources he had as of yet not visited. The problem was, when it came to learning more about Isabella, the only people Griffith hadn't yet asked were her collection of doting suitors. To this point, he'd done everything he could to pretend the group of unattached, powerful young men hadn't existed.

But seeing as how that hadn't aided his cause any, it was time to try a different strategy.

"Tell me again what I'm doing here?" Colin McCrae, Georgina's husband and a man who somehow seemed to know nearly everything about everyone in London, adjusted the sleeve of his jacket and looked around the edges of the ballroom. "I could be dancing with my wife."

"If you'd known the information I need, I'd have been happy to let you dance with your wife." Griffith rubbed his forefinger against his thumb and angled his shoulders to avoid brushing into too many people as they made their way to their target.

"My apologies for not seeing anything strange about a bunch of powerful men swarming around the most popular woman of the Season. It happens every year, you know." Colin put a hand on Griffith's arm and brought them to a halt. "Seriously, Griffith, what do you expect me to do?"

Griffith lifted an eyebrow and tried not to look upset. When he'd realized that he had no way of finding out what he wanted to know without somehow becoming someone he'd never been, or at least hadn't been in so many years that it no longer mattered, frustration like he'd never known had eaten away at his composure. Colin's striding in the door with Georgina on his arm had been a godsend. "You're going to gossip."

"Gossip."

"Yes."

The two men stared at each other, Colin's blue eyes boring into Griffith's, unintimidated despite the vast disparity in social class.

Griffith sighed. "That is what you do, isn't it? Gossip and listen and get people to tell you things they had no intention of telling you?"

"While your confidence in my abilities is rather flattering, I hate to tell you that my vast knowledge is more the result of observation and patience than any actual ferreting out of information." Colin ran a hand behind his neck. "What exactly are you wanting me to find out?"

"Something or someone was encouraging these men to keep pursuing Isabella."

Colin coughed. "Are you sure it wasn't Isab . . . er, Miss Breckenridge herself? Women have been known to simply enjoy a great swarm of admirers."

"No."

Neither spoke for a few moments, and only the swell of orchestra music and the occasionally overloud comment from someone nearby broke the silence.

Colin coughed. "No, you aren't sure, or no, it wasn't her?"

"Colin, nearly every single man of any significance has spent time paying court to the woman I love."

Colin choked on air and went wide-eyed.

Griffith didn't stop to let his shocking announcement sink in. "They're a competitive lot, but they wouldn't all have stayed in the game unless they thought they had some sort of advantage. I want to know what it was."

"Was?"

He wasn't even going to dignify that comment with an answer. Right now Griffith was expending a great deal of time and energy to figure out what, exactly, was going on with Isabella. Everything he knew about her family situation in Northumberland would have pointed to her acting in a different manner than she was. Something was going on in her uncle's house to change that. He had to focus on that part of the problem. Because if he actually began to consider the fact that he might not eventually be the one to win her hand, his brain would become overrun by the ensuing emotional panic.

"May we keep walking now?"

Colin inclined his head and took a large leading step toward a group of three young lords. "To gossip we go." He stopped again. "And why can't you go gossip without me?"

"Because I'm not any good at it," Griffith growled between gritted teeth, knowing what was coming next.

Colin grinned. "I know. I just wanted to hear you say it."

A moment later Colin stopped again. This time within an arm's breadth of the first man Griffith had wanted to talk to.

"Why are we stopping now?" Griffith whispered.

"Because I'm not a septuagenarian matron with a cane who can bust in and take over any conversation she wishes."

Griffith had to concede that point and was gratified to know he'd made the right decision bringing Colin in on this fact-finding mission. Griffith dealt very well with people as long as honesty was the most essential element in the communication. Unfortunately he was as awkward with social dances as he was with real ones.

"We should talk about something," Colin murmured.

"Like what?"

"Anything."

"I assume you mean we should talk about anything besides the need to be talking about something."

Colin rolled his eyes to the ceiling. "What would you normally be talking about at a thing like this?"

He'd normally be holing up in a corner until he'd made enough of a presence to get out of a place so full and confining that he could barely breathe without having to apologize for bumping into someone. Which, come to think of it, was a rather brilliant way to start a conversation.

A grin touched his lips as he shifted sideways. "We don't need a conversation. We need his attention." A slight angling on his feet and half a step to the left and Griffith was bumping his shoulder into the other man's back the way he had done to countless other people in countless other ballrooms.

"I beg your pardon, Lord Ivonbrook. I'm afraid I misstepped in the crush."

The younger man clapped Griffith on the back and made him wince. Not from any sort of pain but from the sheer discomfort of the conversation he was about to enter. "Do you intend to step out onto the dance floor with those moves tonight?"

As the other man laughed at his own joke, Griffith tried to muster a self-deprecating smile. He must have been fairly successful, because the man didn't turn and walk awkwardly away.

"Have you met my sister's husband, Mr. Colin McCrae?" Griffith gestured toward Colin, and the two men inclined heads in acknowledging bows.

326

"Ah, yes, Mr. McCrae. You married Lady Georgina two years ago?"

Colin sighed and smoothed a hand over his waistcoat. "Indeed I did."

Lord Ivonbrook smirked. "She's a very beautiful woman."

"That she is. A beautiful wife is quite a prize for a man."

If Griffith didn't know that Colin was hopelessly in love with his sister, he would have been tempted to deck the man right there in the ballroom. Without actually saying anything insulting, he'd reduced Georgina to little more than a pretty vase to be displayed in the front hall to impress visitors.

"A prize such as any man can hope to gain." Lord Ivonbrook lifted his glass of punch in a toast to the sentiment.

"Oh?" Colin rocked back on his heels. "You have plans of joining the privileged set anytime soon?"

"I do. Though my path just got a bit more difficult." Lord Ivonbrook turned to Griffith. "Did you torture him with preconditions and stipulations before he married Lady Georgina? The hassle of marrying off such a popular woman must have had some gains."

Griffith tried to take Colin's lead and smile at the barb, but he didn't know what to say.

Colin saved him with a groan. "You've no idea what I went through. Is the lady's father putting you through your paces?"

"Uncle." The man shrugged. "He's a bit out of his tree about it, but it's a simple thing to do, or at least it should have been. Politics can be a brutal mistress."

"I've often thought it would be so," Colin replied.

"Are you into politics, Mr. McCrae?" Lord Ivonbrook inclined his head in Griffith's direction. "You've a good chance at the House of Commons if you choose to make a run for it."

"That would certainly be something to consider. Those green

benches are a far cry from the red ones in the House of Lords, though." Colin gave a self-deprecating laugh.

"Indeed." Lord Ivonbrook leaned in. "We recently abandoned a bill they'd passed up to us. All sorts of holes and problems with it. Nearly half the peers had a change to make to the bill before we tabled it. Shame."

"Were you in great favor of it, then?"

The man shrugged, and his gaze began to wander away from Colin to drift over the heads of the rest of the room. "It had some merit. Mostly, its passing would have been convenient."

"I have to know," Colin dropped his voice, as if he were the one imparting a secret, "are you saying there was an additional perk attached to this bill?"

"Only favor with a certain lady's family." Lord Ivonbrook laughed. "Nothing more. I've still got my eye on the prize. I just have to find another way to get there."

Griffith's hands curled into fists at the leer that crossed Lord Ivonbrook's face, but he forced himself to stay silent. Watching Colin was like watching a master artist sculpt clay. A little nudge here, a trim or a cut there, and then you were getting exactly what you wanted.

Colin shook his head, eyes wide in awe as he turned a bit to the side, angling his shoulder so the three of them weren't as closed off as they had been before. "That's a lot to keep track of."

Lord Ivonbrook stiffened his shoulders. "That's why we were born to it."

"God knows what He's doing," Colin murmured.

"Indeed He does." Lord Ivonbrook's attention was caught by something beyond Colin's shoulder. "Mr. Harrop, how did your horse do at the race last weekend?"

Griffith and Colin stepped slowly from the new conversation before setting off in search of the next man Griffith had seen being rather persistent about clinging to Isabella's skirts.

"What bill was he referring to?" Colin whispered.

"We've tabled a few recently, but only one with that much discussion. The Apothecary Act was abandoned not too long ago." Griffith knew Lord Pontebrook had been a very vocal proponent of the act. But would he have actually made it a condition of Ivonbrook's suit?

They approached the next man and Colin worked his charms all over again. And with two men after that. The answers they got were forming a disturbing pattern.

The Apothecary Act had been a hotly contested bill for many years, going back and forth between all the parties involved. For the most part the lords had stayed out of it, waiting on the physicians, druggists, and apothecaries to come to their own agreement. The number of men showing a vested interest in it over the past two and a half months had been rather surprising.

Griffith looked at the men grouped around Isabella.

Most of them were young. Nearly all of them were peers.

Practically the entirety of the unmarried portion of the House of Lords, save himself, was plying her with punch and begging to take her onto the dance floor.

Colin, who had approached the most recent target on his own, sidled up to Griffith's side. "That makes five men who've hinted that a political loss has made their pursuit of a particular woman more difficult."

Griffith didn't like the idea that was forming in his head. But as he worked every encounter, every conversation, every piece of gossip through the filter of this new information, one conclusion seemed to rise up above all the others. And it nearly made him ill.

Chapter 31

"Your Grace." Gibson, Griffith's butler, knocked on the wide-open study door with hesitation and a wrinkle of confusion on his forehead. He cleared his throat, and his face dropped back into the stoic lines of a duke's butler. "Your Grace, there is a woman here to see you. A Miss St. Claire."

Griffith surged from his seat, concern for Isabella sending him to the door before his quill had even finished rolling off the edge of the ledger book he'd dropped it on. Despite his resolve, he hadn't been able to gain any information about why Isabella had turned away from him. All anyone really knew about Lord Pontebrook was that he was a major proponent of the Apothecary Act, which nearly everyone had chosen to abandon.

Had the loss driven the man to do something unspeakable?

Griffith's long legs ate up the passageway between his study and the front hall. He was fairly certain now that Isabella had been brought to London for the express purpose of gaining Lord Pontebrook an audience with men he otherwise wouldn't have been able to convince. Now that the bill was dead, had he sent Isabella home? Had Miss St. Claire come to tell him if he wanted Isabella he was going to have to chase her to Northumberland?

It was a logical enough consideration, and he almost ordered his carriage made ready as he crossed to the drawing room.

On the other hand, he might have simply been another conquest. His steps faltered. What if Isabella was as masterful as Colin, knowing exactly what her target needed to hear in order to do her bidding?

He pushed open the door with a bit more trepidation, but with less concern that something had happened to Isabella. He was more concerned that, in addition to a broken heart, his pride was about to be shattered as well.

"Miss St. Claire."

She stood, hands clasped tightly in front of her, lips pressed into a thin line. "Your Grace." She cleared her throat. "Isabella doesn't know I'm here. In fact she'd be rather furious at me if she knew I'd come. But I've had a lot of decisions made for me in the name of protection, and I didn't like it. I like even less seeing Bella hurting. I've come so that you can make your own decision."

One eyebrow winged upward. Make his own decision? Hadn't he done that when he asked Isabella to marry him? What other decision did she need him to make?

Miss St. Claire shifted on her feet. "My father is a rather obsessed man."

"I'm aware." Griffith crossed his arms over his chest and braced his feet apart. Perhaps Isabella's cousin was making mountains out of molehills, but her wariness was making Griffith concerned that whatever he was about to hear he wasn't going to like.

"My mother and brother died of putrid fever. We were out in Somerset. There wasn't a physician in the area. Just an apothecary whose position had been passed down for several generations. The medicine he gave them made them worse. By the time the physician could be brought in from Glastonbury, it was too late."

331

This was information Griffith had already been able to learn. The tragic tale was one of the first things he'd uncovered when he actually started asking around about Lord Pontebrook. Sadly, it wasn't the only tale of such tragedies—which was why the act had gone as far as it had. Of course, there were equally as many stories of people who would have died waiting for a physician to be brought.

It was easy, however, to see the man's motivation. But not how it affected Isabella or why it mattered now, ten years after the fact.

He said nothing.

Miss St. Claire swallowed, and her hands gripped together tighter.

"Apothecary reform became my father's life work. He brought us to London. Stopped letting me spend the summers with my cousin because he couldn't bear to have me staying in an area so far from a proper doctor. When he started, I think there was actually something noble in his intentions."

"And then it became about winning?"

She shrugged and cast a glance at her maid, who was sitting quietly in the corner with a lump of knitting in her lap. Miss St. Claire's voice dropped. "I don't know if it was winning or simply surviving. If he wasn't working toward reform, he didn't have a reason to work for anything."

"And now?"

"We're lucky if he eats."

Griffith's lips pressed into a thin line, and he fought the urge to pace. Whatever had driven Miss St. Claire to come to him, it wasn't so he could be overrun by his emotions. There was a problem, and she expected him to fix it.

It was the story of his life.

And he did it very well.

"At what point did he decide that Isabella was the perfect bait to lure the necessary votes in the House of Lords?"

Miss St. Claire's mouth dropped open in silent question, her eyes widening until he could see traces of white around the brown centers. "You . . . but when . . . ?"

"Only recently, I assure you." He fought back the bile that threatened to rise in his throat as his suspicions were confirmed. Griffith inclined his head toward the corner a bit farther from the maid, and Miss St. Claire slowly moved in that direction. "More than one man seemed to think your father was holding out for proof that they cared about Isabella's well-being enough to ensure she had proper medical care no matter where she was."

"Is that what he was telling them?" She shook her head. "We never knew."

Griffith couldn't help but feel a bit betrayed as he faced the fact he'd been trying to ignore—that Lord Pontebrook might have been the creator of the scheme, but Isabella had willingly and actively gone along with it. "What *did* you know?"

The question came out harsher than Griffith had intended. Perhaps he wasn't quite able to remove himself from his emotions in this instance. Still, it was a valid question, and one he felt he deserved to know the answer to, even if it had no bearing on the problem Miss St. Claire wanted him to solve. The problem she'd yet to actually state.

Miss St. Claire frowned. "Whatever the outcome, I assure you Isabella's motives were good, Your Grace. She is the eldest of five, and despite her gender she felt a need to protect them when it seemed her father couldn't. The offer from my father was too good to refuse—paying off her father's debts and sending her brothers to school."

Both things that Griffith could have done for her as well, and would have done without hesitation. The logical thing to do would have been to run from the risk of her uncle's promise, which hinged on the passing of a bill, to the security of Griffith's proposal. He understood, even though he didn't like it, why she'd felt she couldn't come to him with such a request.

"Why wait? Isabella is four and twenty, not the nineteen your father tried to pass her off as. Why now? He could have used her years ago to convince someone powerful to help push the creation of the bill along."

"Father hadn't seen her in nearly ten years. But then we passed through Northumberland on our way to the medical college of Edinburgh to try to build support for some of the new adjustments to the bill. We stopped at their farm again on the way home, and four hours later Isabella left with us. Father bought her clothes, jewelry, everything she'd need to be the Season's most sought-after debutante."

It all made a sad sort of sense. Less than four hours for a spirit such as Isabella to make such a monumental decision. Save her family for the price of her reputation. At least her reputation in London, a town she'd never been in and probably never intended to come to again. Even the coldest of people would be enticed by a trade that seemed to cost them so little.

"I appreciate your honesty." And he did. Just having answers for the questions that had been building in his head seemed to ease the discomfort in his chest a bit. In some ways, though, the pain dug deeper. "I fail to see, however, your intention in coming here. The act is dead. With the stakes gone, Isabella could have come to me. I proposed to her mere days ago. She can't believe my feelings for her would change so swiftly."

"Isabella used a lot of men this Season, Your Grace. She regrets it but cannot change what has been done. You, however, are different. She refuses to trade on your feelings for her. And if she came to you, even with the best of intentions, she would. Because she loves me, and my father knows it."

Griffith waited, knowing that Miss St. Claire would continue, because no one could possibly think that explanation sufficient on its own. The twisted mass unraveling before him boggled the mind. How could a man become so entangled in a single mission that his entire being, his every thought and motive, wrapped itself around it like a tree growing around a hatchet that had been left embedded in its trunk?

"You are a powerful man, Your Grace. If you chose to, you could revive the Apothecary Act. My father knows this. He told Isabella that if she could get you to do so, he would let me marry the man I love when he returns from war, despite the fact that he is an officer."

Griffith lifted a brow. "Having you become a spinster is preferable to having you marry an officer?"

One shoulder lifted and settled as the lines around Miss St. Claire's mouth grew deeper. "War is dangerous. Who's to say I wouldn't become one of the camp followers if I married an officer of war? Father is terrified I'll join the wives who travel with the camps and put myself in the line of fire." She cleared her throat. "I'm not here on my behalf, Your Grace. I intend to marry Arthur with or without my father's blessing. There isn't much he can do about it. But Isabella can't quite understand that I gave up craving my father's attention long ago and contented myself with the fact that he wanted me to remain safe."

She stepped away from Griffith and started for the door. "But you deserved to know, Your Grace."

That was it? Griffith gave in to the frustration churning through him and ran a hand over his face. "How is she?" The question came out rough and broken, ripped from him without permission. Because, while all of the things Miss St. Claire had told him were things he wanted to know, all he really cared about was whether or not Isabella was happy.

Miss St. Claire stopped in the doorway to the room. Her maid stood awkwardly behind her, eyes cast downward for the most part but sneaking occasional glances up at her mistress and then Griffith. "She is trying to rediscover who she is, I suppose. She cried a lot, those first days, but the plants calm her. She goes to the park a lot."

"Which park?"

Miss St. Claire glanced over her shoulder. "All of them."

Chapter 32

A splash of color near Isabella's feet caught her eye, and she squatted to see a clump of bright red flowers marching around the base of a sprawling bush. Had she seen flowers like this in the garden area? She probably wouldn't have noticed them if she had. The formally laid-out portion of Kensington Gardens was a beautiful riot of color and pattern. As a whole it was absolutely breathtaking. It was difficult to look at any of the plants individually, though.

But here, in the wilder area of the gardens, the little red flowers stood out, allowing her to easily see the softness of the stem and the silkiness of the petals. In contrast, the bush limb jutting out over the cluster of flowers was rough and hard, the green leaves looking harsh. That both could exist in nearly the same place was one of the things Isabella found so fascinating about plants.

The murmur of voices reached her from a distance, and she took a last longing look at the little red flowers.

She slid her hands to her knees, prepared to push herself up to a more respectable standing position. As she stood, her gaze rose until she could see over the top of the bush.

Then she immediately dropped back down so she was sitting on her heels. When did Griffith find time to take a stroll through Kensington Gardens? And though she'd yet to meet him, the man with him looked similar enough to be identified as his younger brother, Lord Trent Hawthorne.

As much as she didn't want to see Griffith, she couldn't take the chance that he would turn down this particular path and find her hunched over in front of a bush.

It was possible, if she moved quickly, that she could get around the next bend and start making her way to where she'd told the carriage to meet her. Armed with a plan, she stood again and felt a sharp tug before hearing a series of small cracks. The jutting limb, which had earlier made such an interesting juxtaposition to the little red flowers, had several skinny twigs branching off it. Twigs that tangled easily in curls that brushed against it.

She turned to her maid, who stood three feet away looking bored but resigned. It was the same expression she'd worn through every other park, garden, and square Isabella had dragged her to.

"How bad is it?" she asked.

The maid cocked her head to the side, showing the first sign of real interest she'd shown in a while. "It's an unusual look, miss. If you're wanting to really claim the effect, I'd suggest adding a few more. Perhaps one or two with a leaf attached."

It was hard to tell if the maid was joking or not, but the picture she'd painted inspired a sputtered laugh from Isabella. "We'll just walk on, shall we?"

But she'd neglected to realize how much ground two energetic, long-legged men could cover in a short amount of time. Griffith and his brother had not only seen her but were standing within easy speaking distance.

"Isabella."

She'd missed his voice, resonating from his broad chest and wrapping around her like a blanket. "Your Grace."

His eyes widened, and she could see the hurt her deliberate use of his honorific had caused. But she didn't have the right to call him Griffith anymore. Not when she'd walked away from him so completely the last time she'd seen him.

"Miss Breckenridge." His voice had roughened. "May I present my brother, Lord Trent Hawthorne."

She gave a curtsy. The other man, who looked like a smaller, more carefree version of Griffith, grinned at her. "Miss Breckenridge. I've heard a lot about you. May I say that the tales haven't done you justice? You've no need for ornamentation, but I've rarely seen a woman wear it so well."

Heat rushed to her cheeks, and Isabella fought the urge to start yanking at her hair to get the twigs out of it.

"Isabella." Griffith stepped forward. "How have you been? I haven't seen you around."

"I'm socializing with trees these days." She gestured to her nature-enhanced hair. "As you can see."

"It's a good look for you." He reached forward and pinched one curl between his fingers and let it slide through. "I like the red. And the earrings."

She hadn't powdered her hair since the Apothecary Act had been abandoned. Her mother's jewelry had also been dug from the bottom of the drawer where it had been stashed. It had been nice seeing her natural hair in the mirror. It felt even nicer that he approved of the color as well.

It felt too nice.

He dropped his arm. "I won't ask if you've reconsidered, though should you ever decide to, my request stands. But you don't need to confine yourself. I would like to see you. I would like to dance with you. But should you wish me to refrain from attending any event so that you may attend in peace, you need only send word and I will send my regrets."

And this was exactly why she couldn't let him know of Uncle Percy's plans. Already he was trying to sacrifice for her. And she couldn't live a life with him knowing their entire marriage had been based on a similar sacrifice.

Why, oh why, had she thought all aristocrats were cold and unfeeling people she could use and leave at her will? Hadn't her loving mother come from the same group of people? Tears threatened to choke her, and the last thing she needed was for him to see her cry.

"If you would excuse me."

She whirled and fled down the path, her maid scurrying behind her. She didn't know which way she was going, but it was away from Griffith, and that was all she needed at the moment.

By the time she stopped to get her bearings, she could see nothing but trees and grass, meandering paths, and a scattered handful of fashionably dressed people strolling along. Until she saw something she recognized, she was just going to have to walk and try to look as if she knew what she was doing.

Light sparkling through the trees told her she was nearing some sort of water. If it was the Serpentine, she'd gone a long way in the wrong direction. Clear into Hyde Park instead of back to the carriage at the edge of Kensington Gardens. She was near the edge of the water, and it would be a simple thing to skirt the edge of it and enter the expanse of Hyde Park. The area was devoid of London's elite. All she could see were sheep. And a few deer at the edge of the forest.

Throwing propriety to the wind, she crossed to a large tree and sank down to sit at the base of it.

Her maid squeaked but didn't say anything. Isabella thought

about telling the other woman she might as well sit down and get comfortable because Isabella didn't intend to leave anytime soon. This spot, this moment, felt more like home than anything she'd felt in a long, long time. Not since her week in Hertfordshire had she felt anything resembling the peace she did now.

The peace went beyond the idyllic setting. It was bone deep, heart deep. Sometime during the last few days, strolling through parks and quietly slipping into various squares, she'd accepted that God forgave her for what she'd done. That knowledge and acceptance had brought the overwhelming peace only Jesus could bring.

It hadn't brought happiness, though.

But she deserved to be unhappy, didn't she? Who could say how much unhappiness she'd caused? Had any of those men actually developed feelings for her? It was hard to say, since she'd never let herself consider them much beyond whether or not she could get them to keep visiting her.

And then there were the ladies. Like Lady Alethea and Miss Newberry. What had she done to their futures? Their happiness?

But if she were forgiven, if she truly accepted that Jesus had taken her sin as far as the east was from the west, that meant it could no longer impact what God decided she did or did not deserve.

It didn't mean she was happy. It didn't mean she'd be happy anytime in the near future, because the fact was that what she'd done had consequences, and they made her sad.

But as she looked across the field of happily grazing sheep she knew that one day she'd be fine, and eventually, she might even be good.

⁓

Griffith leaned his shoulder against a tree. She'd been sitting there watching the sheep for nearly half an hour. What was she thinking about? He couldn't see her face, but she seemed peaceful, like a country milkmaid taking a break in the middle of the day.

"I've seen more trees today than in the rest of my life combined." Trent leaned his back against another tree trunk and crossed his ankles as he watched Griffith watch Isabella.

"Your talent for exaggeration has developed well." Griffith didn't bother reminding him that they'd grown up in the wooded hills of Hertfordshire.

"What are you going to do now?"

"Wait until she leaves and make sure she gets to her carriage safely."

Trent laid his head back against the tree. "Does that mean tomorrow we'll be scouring the parks again?"

"I don't know." It was a fair question, but not one Griffith could answer. Ever since he'd learned what was really keeping them apart, he'd been conflicted.

"I've got one chance left, Trent, and it's something I might not be able to accomplish."

His brother scoffed. "What does she want? Napoleon's crown jewels? Talk to Prinny. He may loan them to you when they get here from France. I've heard the treasures are coming out of Paris by the boatload."

"I don't think she wants *anything*." And that was the problem. If she wanted something from him, he could do it. Buy it, make it, trade for it—whatever it took. But she didn't actually want anything except for him to be free of her uncle's potential schemes.

"*Nothing* is pretty easily obtained." Trent held out his empty hand, palm out. "You can borrow mine if you need to."

One side of Griffith's mouth kicked up. "Thanks. I'll keep that in mind."

342

"Have you prayed about it?"

"Every day." Every moment. Griffith wasn't sure there was an hour he'd been awake when some part of him hadn't been crying out to God for a way to fix this dull ache in the middle of his chest that refused to go away as long as there was a chance that Isabella could be his.

Trent shrugged. "Then do the next thing and let God take care of the rest."

Such a simple concept, but so very difficult in practice, even if Griffith knew his brother was right.

"If I marry her, we'll probably have children," Griffith murmured.

"That's the natural order of things." Trent laid an arm around Griffith's shoulders and turned him back up the path.

"Your chances of becoming a duke will decline."

Trent grinned. "All the more reason to get busy doing what you've got to do."

Griffith let his gaze linger on Isabella as his mind wandered. He was fairly certain that he knew everything now, or at least enough to approach Isabella about whatever concerns were keeping her away. But it wouldn't do to simply make things right for a day. He needed to make sure that every last bit of this situation was settled so that they could move past it and never return.

"All right, then." Griffith adjusted his coat and rolled his head back and forth, trying to relieve the tension in his neck. It was time to take a more active role in this whole apothecary business and learn what politics were really taking place. Only then could he make sure it went away. "Let's go see a doctor."

Chapter 33

"We're going out tonight."

Isabella pulled a twig from her hair and frowned at her cousin in the mirror. Her day had not been going well, and the last thing she wanted to do was get dressed back up and go see the same people who had witnessed her strolling back through Kensington Gardens with twigs in her hair. From now on she would be staying with the public parks, despite the fact that they made her maid nervous.

"You are free to go wherever you wish." Isabella yanked at another twig, wincing when it didn't dislodge from the coiffure as easily as the first had.

Frederica crossed her arms and frowned. "No. You're going with me. I had my maid prepare your dress so you've nothing to do but get cleaned up and then drop the gown over your head."

It was going to take a little more effort than that, but Isabella was impressed with Freddie's initiative. She sighed and began plucking the pins from her head. If she was going to go out, they were going to have to start over on her hair. "Where are we going?"

"A ball."

"No."

Isabella would do many things for her cousin, had in fact agreed that two people wasting away in the house was two too many. And since she could do nothing to rouse her uncle—or at least wasn't willing to do the one thing that would rouse her uncle— Isabella had agreed that she would get out of the house every day and attend at least two events a week with Freddie.

She wasn't doing a ball, though.

"Mr. Boehm is a merchant." Frederica picked up the brush and began stroking it through Isabella's hair. "What are the chances that you'll see any of your former suitors there? Balls are fun, and you need to remember that or you'll needlessly avoid them forever."

Balls were fun. When she wasn't having to spend the whole evening being calculating and manipulative, she enjoyed the dancing and the energy that could only be found at a ball. And a ball given by a merchant? Obviously the attendees would all be rich and powerful men, but would the aristocracy come out in great numbers for a merchant's ball?

Isabella allowed a small smile to tilt her lips and crease the corners of her eyes. It felt strange on her face, but good. "Very well, then. We'll go to a ball."

⁓

"Mr. Boehm must be a very rich merchant," Isabella growled.

Freddie had the grace to look a bit ashamed at having tricked her into coming to one of the most attended and exclusive balls of the entire Season.

Isabella drained her glass of punch in a single swallow before glaring at her cousin. "I just saw the prince regent on the other side of the room."

"He looks nothing like you thought he would, does he?"

He didn't. And Isabella had actually been a little surprised, given the types of events her uncle had been dragging her to, that this was the first time she'd seen the country's acting ruler. But she was seeing him now. Along with several hundred of his closest titled and wealthy friends.

"Perhaps I'll go outside." Isabella cast a glance out the wide windows. "St. James's Square probably looks lovely in the moonlight."

"And you'd look lovely to any lingering robbers." Frederica hooked her arm with Isabella's. "No, I'm afraid I must insist that you stay with me until it's time to leave."

Isabella sighed. "Very well. But I'm not dancing."

With a shrug, Freddie took the last sip of her punch. "That is your choice."

So far none of her old pursuers had asked her to dance, even though many of them were in attendance. It could have something to do with Isabella clinging uncustomarily to a shadowed corner.

As she put down her punch cup, Freddie said, "We should at least say hello to Miss Newberry."

"Why?" Other than Frederica and possibly Griffith's sisters, there hadn't been a female in London who seemed inclined to actually befriend her. Granted there had been a few, Miss Newberry included, who had been nice when removed from the rest of their friends, but none had gone out of their way to do more than that.

Freddie sighed and stepped forward, her arm still linked with Isabella's. "Because it will get you out of this corner. Come along."

They greeted Miss Newberry and exchanged pleasantries, but polite topics were quickly used up and the woman moved on, leaving Frederica and Isabella exposed to the rest of the party attendees.

"Miss Breckenridge!"

Before she could stop herself, Isabella was turning to acknowledge the young man with a soft smile on her lips. Weeks
of near solitude, visiting every park and green space London
had to offer should have been long enough to break an unwanted
habit of three months, but apparently it was not.

"Lord Naworth." Isabella gave the smallest of curtsies.

"The ballrooms of London have been devastated by the loss
of your lovely face. How fortunate we are that I chose to attend
when you chose to grace us with your presence again."

"Thank you, my lord. You are more than gracious." He was
also pompous, empty-headed, and smelled a bit of linseed oil.

"Might I have the honor of this dance?"

She was about to decline. The excuses were readily available
on her tongue. Her lips had parted to say the word *no*.

And then she saw him.

Griffith was standing on the other side of the ballroom. His
height allowed him to see over the sea of people between them,
and her height gave him a clear view of where she stood.

He started making his way toward her.

Retreat. She couldn't leave, but she could retreat. And hide.
And what better place than the one place Griffith avoided if he
could at all help it?

Praying God would forgive her for using this man one more
time, she smiled up at Lord Naworth. "The honor would be mine."

⁓

Once she'd stepped onto the dance floor, there didn't seem to
be a polite way to leave it again. Despite her uncle's insistence
that the men would forget about her without constant encouragement, most of her suitors still seemed inclined to give her
their attentions. While they weren't as insistent or outrageous
as they once had been, they were still plentiful.

And all of them wanted to dance.

Any guilt she'd felt disappeared partway through the first set of dances. Even though she was dancing with the men, her demeanor had changed. The flirting statements and the coy glances she'd worked so hard to include were thankfully left behind, and she found herself actually enjoying it.

Until her feet began to hurt.

And her throat became scratchy from talking and exerting herself for so long.

But after every dance, there was someone waiting to ask her hand for the next one. And every time she saw Griffith waiting to the side, eyes sad and hopeful at the same time, and before she could think it through, fear would prompt her to accept the invitation to dance, and she would once more find herself taking her place in the lines of dancers.

She found herself praying that God would do something to get her off the dance floor.

It wasn't the type of prayer she really expected God to answer, but as she said a mental *amen*, a loud boom echoed through the ballroom, bringing the music and the dancing to a blessed halt.

All eyes swung to the entrance of the ballroom, where one of the heavy, ornate doors had been thrown back hard enough to slam against the wall, causing the echoing crack.

A soldier stood in the doorway, his uniform sporting more red than usual. He strode in and people scattered, exclaiming at the blood and dirt that marred his wrinkled and torn uniform. The man looked around the room and made his way in the prince regent's direction. As he went the crowd parted, until Isabella was able to see he held objects in his hands. Golden eagles. The kind Napoleon had bestowed upon his army regiments with the command that they protect these standards with their lives.

And this soldier was carrying two of them.

And then he was kneeling, laying the golden eagles on the ground at the feet of the prince regent.

No one moved. Isabella wasn't even sure anyone was breathing.

"Your Royal Highness. I come bearing news from His Grace, the Duke of Wellington." The man lifted his bowed head. "Napoleon has been defeated."

Never before had a drawing room seen so much agitated gossip. Despite the fact that none of them knew a thing, the ladies—who had been removed from the ballroom and placed into every other available public room in the house—were speculating wildly on what the men were hearing in the ballroom as the official dispatch was being read aloud.

"What do you think is going on in there?" Isabella shifted her weight onto one leg and shook out one of her already tired feet. The seats in the room had respectfully been granted to the elder ladies, and if the waiting went on much longer, Isabella was giving serious consideration to sitting on the floor.

"I don't care."

Isabella looked at her cousin in surprise.

"What?" Freddie shrugged. "I don't. Considering whatever official declaration being read in there won't tell me what I really need to know, all that matters right now is that the war is over."

Isabella inclined her head to acknowledge the truth. It didn't matter. Curiosity still kept her from suggesting they make their way home. History was being read in that ballroom, and it was rather thrilling to be so close to it.

Then a cry rang out through the house, indicating the ballroom doors had been reopened. The ladies surged, a tidal wave of silk and satin.

Freddie and Bella flattened themselves to the wall to avoid the trample of curious ladies who were doomed to remain disappointed for the time being. Even the men who would be willing to share some of the details with their wives or daughters weren't going to do so here.

Isabella and Frederica trailed the last of the ladies out of the drawing room. Some of the men were talking excitedly in passages and alcoves, and others were seeking out their ladies to escort them home or back to the ballroom.

Griffith was standing atop the staircase leading up to the ballroom, his glance bouncing from group to group until it landed on her.

As the ladies clustered, a more somber attitude rolled through their ranks. Isabella's heart threatened to choke her with its rushed, heavy beating, and a sense of numbness covered her as she took in the whispered news being passed back along the crowd. The prince regent was crying. The victory had come with a great loss. At least thirty thousand dead. Countless more wounded.

A tight squeeze of her hand broke through Isabella's numbness. She looked at Frederica's pale face, the stark white of her skin making her nose appear larger.

With hope and dread battling in her chest, Isabella swung her gaze back to Griffith. Did he know anything? Had the dispatch contained the names of officers lost?

Griffith continued slowly down the stairs. It was a beautiful thing to watch him cut his way through the crowd, going against the flow with ease. When the man wasn't hemmed in by dancing couples he was actually rather graceful.

Isabella held her breath and her position. To move forward would bring her to meet him on the stairs. To move back would leave her trapped in the now private emptiness of the drawing room. As much as she wanted—no, needed—to know what he knew, simply seeing him this close was making her heart hurt. Speaking with him would be agony.

He came closer, and Isabella caught her breath as she drank in the handsome lines of his face. He looked tired. There were shadows under his green eyes that she hadn't noticed as he descended the stairs but became clear as he stopped in front of them.

"Miss Breckenridge. Miss St. Claire. Perhaps you would both like to step into the drawing room for a moment?"

No. No, she most certainly would not like to step back into the drawing room, but next to her she heard Frederica suck in a harsh breath. Isabella's heart pounded at the possible implications. Unless Griffith had lost all sense of logic and propriety, he wasn't about to take this moment to renew his pursuit of her or seek to ask her to explain her refusal to marry him or even see him.

It was more likely that the communication that had just been read in the ballroom actually mentioned Arthur. And if it did, it probably wasn't good news.

Isabella gripped her cousin's arm as she nodded and quietly pulled Frederica back into the drawing room.

Griffith followed, his face giving no indication of what he was going to share. His eyes seemed to drink in Isabella, though, the same way she'd absorbed his presence earlier.

Once they were in the drawing room, the noise from the hall, stairs, and ballroom faded into a distant, indistinct roar. It was easily conversed over—assuming one knew what to say, of course.

Griffith turned to Frederica. "Arthur Saunderson is alive."

Isabella had to wrap a steadying arm around Frederica as she wilted with her first indrawn breath. A few tears slipped down her cheeks to ride the grooves made by her sudden smile.

Griffith returned her smile with one of his own, and Isabella considered joining her cousin in a boneless heap. How could she have forgotten how dear and handsome his smiles were? The large, honest ones like he wore now were so rare, and the dark sadness that had been wrapped around Isabella's heart cracked at the sight of it.

His smile faded a notch, possibly considering the number of men who would not have such a simple, hopeful statement said about them.

His green eyes locked on Isabella's. "I've been trying all night to approach you. The ball is over now. I don't think anyone is sure if we should celebrate or mourn. That will change soon, and there will be victory balls all over London. Will you dance with me at one of them?"

Isabella's mouth dropped open in shock. "You bring news like this and then ask me to dance with you without giving us any details?"

He shrugged. "I have your attention now. I don't want to waste it."

"I won't dance with you," she said quietly. "I won't allow you to align your name with mine only to have everyone think you're one more man I toyed with before deserting London. Please don't ask me to do that to you."

He said nothing as his eyes roamed her face. His lips pressed into a grim line before he redirected his attention to Frederica. Once more his mouth softened into a curve of joy.

"Not only is he alive," he continued, as if he'd never requested Isabella dance with him, "but he is coming home a hero. He led his squadron around the back to cut right through the 105th regiment, capture the standard, and send it back to the rear while he kept charging through. You should be proud of him."

A sob and a laugh escaped Frederica, and she turned to Isabella to throw her arms around her. The resulting hug was so tight, it drew a laugh from Isabella even as she tried to breathe.

"I've missed your laugh," Griffith said quietly.

Though the statement wasn't enough to bury all of the merriment in the drawing room, it was enough to quiet their celebration.

Frederica pulled back, her lips still curved and her eyes still bright with happy tears. She looked from Isabella to Griffith and back again. "I'm going to see if the front hall has a little more air."

The statement was ridiculous, and all of them knew it, but that didn't stop Frederica from positioning herself at the door. Enough in the room to say the couple hadn't been left alone, but giving them as much privacy as was possible in a house bursting with several hundred people.

Griffith reached out a hand and cupped her cheek. "I've missed you. I came to see you."

"I know." Isabella almost choked on the words. She should have found a way to go home to Northumberland, found a way to convince Frederica that she didn't want to come tonight. Had she secretly been hoping that something like this would happen? Had she been so hungry for the mere sight of Griffith that she'd been ready to break her heart all over again?

"I love you, Isabella. And I don't believe there is anything between us that can't be overcome."

She lowered her lashes down over her eyes, blocking his earnest face from her sight. "Sometimes life blocks our paths because God has a different plan."

She had to believe that. Had to believe that God still had something good planned for her, despite her earlier disobedience. And she was going to do her best to walk in His path from now on. Even if it hurt.

"This isn't one of those times."

"How do you know?"

"Because if God wanted to turn the paths of two people seeking to honor Him, He'd have made the problem immovable. And this barricade can be overcome."

As a duke he probably hadn't come across many obstacles that he couldn't overcome. But this one—she didn't even think he knew what it was. And there wasn't any way he could change the past three months. "I wish that were true, Griffith. But it isn't. There is nothing that can be done. I shouldn't have stayed. I'll find a way to be on the next coach to Northumberland."

Griffith reached out, gripped her shoulders. "No." A single word, but it had sounded almost panicked, dripping with emotion.

Slowly, his hands slid down her arms until he held her fingers loosely in his. He leaned forward, his forehead rested against hers.

"I know more than you think, Isabella, enough that we could go forth from here. But I want no lingering doubts between us. Let me take care of all your trepidations. Give me a chance to prove you wrong."

Chapter 34

"This is a mess." Ryland tossed the sheaf of papers onto Griffith's desk and leaned back. "And everyone's happy with it?"

Griffith leaned one hip against his desk and ran a thumb along the edge of a blue dart. "That's how it ended up so convoluted. All of the pertinent parts of the old proposal are there. I simply adjusted the contested parts and maneuvered them around a bit."

"A bit?" Anthony extended his red dart and poked at the discarded papers. "It's eleven pages long. Half of them aren't going to read it."

"As long as they leave the room to vote, I don't care. It took me nearly two weeks to write that and get the required support." Griffith cocked his head to the side and shrugged one shoulder before straightening from the desk and lining up his dart to toss at the board on the far wall of his study. "It does the job."

The men fell silent as Griffith took aim and launched his dart at the target. Once the thunk of metal into cork had faded, Ryland leaned forward in his chair and propped his forearms on the edge of the desk. "I don't understand. What about the concerns you had last time? That some of the villages in your

355

territories would be left without any options for medical care? The College of Physicians is growing, but there are not many of them wanting to move out to Cornwall and set up on the cliffs."

"There's nothing in there that says a town can't still have a practicing apothecary—only that he must be trained." Griffith threw another dart. "We're learning more about medicine every day. The more I looked into it, the more I saw the value in some form of standard training. So I'll pay to have them trained."

No one spoke as the last blue dart left Griffith's hand and sank into the center of the board.

He turned, not knowing what he expected to see on the faces of the men he'd turned to for counsel and camaraderie in his adult years.

Ryland's grey stare was leveled in Griffith's direction. Unblinking, unwavering, and unreadable.

Anthony's blue gaze was a little bit easier to read, but the underlying humor Griffith saw there made him turn away.

The marquis laughed and moved into position to throw his own darts. "It's nice to know that love can fell even the largest of men."

"Does she know you've done this?" Ryland asked.

Not wanting to look at either man and discover he'd done something foolish despite his careful considerations, Griffith kept his eyes on Anthony's flying darts, soaring across the room in considerably quicker succession than Griffith's had.

"No," he said into the quiet stillness after the last dart had been thrown.

"It was read officially for the first time today." Anthony strode across the room and began pulling the darts from the board. "Someone's bound to have gone by Lord Pontebrook's house and informed him."

Griffith knew this, had even contemplated going by and telling the man himself, but he knew the next time he saw Isabella's uncle he was going to be laying down some very specific expectations on the man.

Most of the time Griffith tried not to think about the fact that what he wanted was almost as good as law for most people. It was a heady and somewhat terrifying power to wield, and Griffith didn't take it lightly. Sometimes, though, it was good to be a few steps below the king.

"Are you going to go see her?" Ryland's voice matched his unchanged gaze.

"No." Griffith had lost a great deal of sleep last night wondering the same thing. "Not until it's done. She walked away from me because she didn't want the apothecary measures to come between us. I'm making sure they're out of the way before I approach her again."

Anthony stopped at Griffith's shoulder. "And if she comes to you?"

"She's always had that option."

"I'll pay for mine as well."

Ryland's declaration cut into Griffith's suddenly maudlin thoughts, and it took a few moments for Griffith to grasp what he was talking about. "Your apothecaries?"

The other duke nodded. "It's a good solution. Better for my people all the way around."

"Then, I can count on you if debate gets too heavy tomorrow?"

Ryland let out a bark of laughter and picked up his copy of the bill once more. "If? With the way this thing is written I think we're looking much more at *when*."

"Never have I seen such a bungling bill, not even from the bunglers over in the House of Commons!"

Ryland bumped his shoulder into Griffith's. "See? Even Earl Stanhope agrees with me."

"Can you name a bill Earl Stanhope hasn't had an objection to lately?" Griffith whispered back. He was once again sitting in the back row in the House of Lords. The vote would occur tomorrow, assuming this debate didn't get the third reading pushed back even further, but the bill's fate would really be decided today. He waited to see who else would have an objection.

"I think this an honest and worthwhile topic," the earl continued, "but should we really be smuggling through such a potentially oppressive act at such a pace?"

Griffith bit back a groan. He was trying to be as uninvolved in the proceedings as possible, not wanting this reform to become synonymous with his name. Because the new bill was actually a massive edit of the old one, he could pretend he hadn't written it. He had, however, vocally thrown his support behind the revision, along with explaining his intentions for making sure his people didn't suffer.

A few nods around the room made Griffith think the bill was about to be tabled once again. But then the lord chancellor's voice replaced Earl Stanhope's. "Granted, this is not as perfect as it might be, but the changes have been calculated to do much good. In all honesty, my lord, given the amount of time and money and effort that has been put into this bill already, your objections hardly seem valid enough to merit tabling it until a later date."

Griffith held his breath as it was finally decided that the third reading and vote would take place the next day.

He was one step closer to removing the last obstacle between himself and Isabella.

Isabella approached the house feeling a touch lighter if not any happier. The last threat her uncle held over her was gone, and now she had only to live with the consequences of her choices. On her way to Richmond Park she'd stopped by the jeweler whose name was stamped in the box and returned all of the rented jewelry. He'd been surprised, saying her uncle had paid the rent full through for another month, but Isabella had insisted that he take them back now. Chances were her uncle wouldn't carry through on a threat against her father that could color himself in such a poor light as well, but returning the jewels made her feel better, and precious little else did that these days.

Even the fabulous view of the Thames from Richmond Park hadn't lifted her spirits today, and she had to drag herself up the stairs and through the front door.

Servants scurried back and forth across the front hall. Loud laughter rolled out the open drawing room door.

Isabella paused with her hand on the door. This was nothing like the house she'd left that morning. When she and her maid had slipped out the door after breakfast, the house had been cold and somber. The servants crept about as quietly as they could, and only Frederica dared disturb the silence. Eventually she would pull Isabella into her frivolity, but it had felt out of place and discordant with the house's temperament.

Of course, Freddie had every reason to be happy. Arthur would be returning as a hero any day now. And with her father so distraught he couldn't bring himself to rise from his bed, Frederica wasn't likely to get much of a protest from him when she married her officer.

But the laughter coming from the drawing room wasn't

Freddie's. It was distinctly male. The difference in the house was so great Isabella actually stepped back out onto the front step to make sure she'd entered the correct house.

She had.

Easing back into the hall and shutting the door behind her, Isabella debated whether to try to find out what was going on or simply retreat to her room. The very last thing she wanted to do was paste on a fake smile and deal with a roomful of men. She'd done enough of that to last her a lifetime. She didn't think she had it in her today, especially. Not when she'd received word that Parliament had closed out its session today. Somehow that made everything feel more final. She'd been brought to London to convince the men in Parliament to do one thing. She'd failed, which didn't sadden her all that much, but somehow that failure hadn't felt final until now—knowing that Parliament was closed and London would soon empty.

Soon she would have to return home and somehow tell her mother that she'd been a rousing success but hadn't gotten married.

Before Isabella could make good on her intentions to retreat to her room, Freddie rushed out of the drawing room, an enormous smile spread across her face. "Bella! Come join us. There's quite the celebration going on."

Isabella handed her bonnet and gloves to her maid, the change in the house suddenly making more sense. A small smile of her own appeared as she responded to the happiness in Frederica's entire being. The woman was actually bouncing on her toes in excitement. "Has Arthur arrived home, then?"

Her smile fell into a brief pucker of confusion, a deep line appearing between her brows. "What?" The confusion cleared. "Oh. No. They marched on to Paris after the battle at Waterloo. Another officer reached the shores yesterday, though, and sent word that Arthur was supposed to be on a ship arriving within the week."

The wide smile returned, and it was Isabella's turn to be confused. She had no time to ask for more details, though, as Frederica grabbed her hand and hauled her into the drawing room.

In the middle of the room stood Uncle Percy, dressed and groomed to perfection for the first time in nearly six weeks.

Three other men stood around the room, but Isabella only recognized one of them. Mr. Emerson looked at Isabella over Uncle Percy's head and raised his small fluted glass in her direction with a smile.

Frederica pressed a similar glass into Isabella's hand.

She lifted the glass to see what was in it, then watched a tiny bubble pop on the surface of the splash of golden liquid resting in the small bowl of the glass. Champagne. They were drinking champagne when everyone else in London would be partaking of tea.

"What—"

"It's a celebration, my girl!" Uncle Percy threw one arm out, thankfully not the one holding his glass of champagne. "We've done it!"

"Done it?" Isabella had very purposefully done nothing of late.

"It passed," Frederica whispered in Bella's ear.

"What did?"

Mr. Emerson strolled over. "The Apothecary Act."

It had passed? But how? A hundred questions flitted through Isabella's mind, but she couldn't manage to utter any of them. Her mouth opened and shut with a repeated clank of her teeth.

Uncle Percy emptied his glass and set it on a nearby table. "Earl Stanhope's pretty speech tried to table the thing, but the lord chancellor knew what was best for this country and led the final charge."

"Two dukes pushing from behind didn't hurt," Mr. Emerson murmured.

Isabella put her glass down, her hand suddenly shaking so badly that she was afraid she'd spill it if she held it any longer. *Two dukes?*

Uncle Percy continued his jolly tale as if Mr. Emerson had never spoken. "We had to sacrifice a few points, men, but those are the casualties of victory! Today will go down in history as the day we saved England's wives and children!"

Having only weeks ago been present when the dispatch had interrupted Madame Boehm's party, hearing her uncle equate his parliamentary mission to a battle made Isabella a bit uncomfortable. It was probably as close to one as the man had ever gotten, though, so she supposed she had to give him a bit of latitude.

Mr. Emerson looked at Isabella. "I've always thought it a bit ridiculous when the lords temporal begin debating between their scarlet benches about what the common man needs, but from everything I've heard, the speech given with this last proposal was a thing of beauty."

"Oh?"

"When one of the most powerful men in the land challenges the other lords to put their money to better use and pay for the training of their apothecaries whether the proposal passes or not, I have to respect him. It was bold. And one of the shortest speeches ever made upon a bill's first reading."

He'd pushed the Apothecary Act through. Isabella swallowed. And he'd made it personal. He'd made it about more than a law. Many of those men would never follow through on such a nonlucrative investment of money, but she knew Griffith would. Every apothecary under his authority would be given the best opportunities available.

Had he done it for her? Had he known?

"Give me a chance to prove you wrong."

Isabella felt strange as her gaze found Frederica's. She felt a little ill, a little light-headed, perhaps even a bit faint. It took more than a few heartbeats to recognize what was happening to her.

She felt happy. For the first time in months.

And maybe, just maybe, God was telling her that she should do something to stay that way.

Chapter 35

Isabella was nearly shaking as she watched the door to the drawing room. The doors to all of the rooms on this floor had been opened up to allow guests to move freely about the area, but still Isabella didn't see the man she was looking for.

Lady Georgina had assured her that Griffith would be in attendance.

Of course, she hadn't offered that information until Isabella had shared the entirety of her plan.

It had been a bit disconcerting when Frederica had introduced her to Lady Georgina. When she lived on the farm, Isabella hadn't thought much of how she looked, but since she'd been in London she'd been forced to consider it almost daily. Was the awe Isabella had felt coming face-to-face with Lady Georgina anything like what other people felt when they met her?

She pushed the unsettling thought out of her mind, but it was sure to come back and plague her when she tried to sleep tonight.

At the moment, she had much more pressing concerns. Such as whether or not Griffith was going to make an appearance at his sister's card party.

There were disadvantages to standing head and shoulders above everyone. It was impossible to enter a room with any sort of discretion, no matter how careful he was; he banged into things simply because the space was not intended for his size; and he'd found very few tailors who could actually do an acceptable job sewing clothing his size.

He almost hadn't come tonight, but Georgina entertained so rarely that he'd felt obligated. Besides, the chances of her allowing Isabella in the door after she'd so thoroughly broken Griffith's heart were very low.

Word of the passing of the Apothecary Act had arrived at Lord Pontebrook's house as soon as Parliament had closed. Griffith had made sure of it.

But she hadn't come. He'd spent the entire day walking through the conservatory, waiting to hear from her. He'd sent footmen to wait in Green Park and Berkeley Square in case she looked for him there. Nothing. Silence. He had lost his gamble.

Even knowing Georgina would never torture him with Isabella's presence, his eyes sought her as soon as he entered the room. His gaze flitted over the heads of people playing cards or talking in groups, looking for a tumble of red-gold curls.

And then he found it. His eyes drifted down and then back up over her patterned yellow silk evening gown that had seen some wear, past the curls that looked more red than blond, over the simple pendant necklace, the unadorned ears, and the creamy skin of her neck and shoulders until he once again looked into the most beautiful eyes in all of England.

His broken heart flew in two directions, plummeting to his toes and lodging in his throat at the same time.

She was there.

And she'd never looked more beautiful.

And she was looking right at him.

———

Isabella swallowed hard. If things went wrong in the next five minutes she was going to have to run very quickly. She'd be able to get quite a good start, because, at Isabella's request, Georgina had left a large section of open space in the middle of the room.

A few people turned their heads when Griffith walked into the room, but the attention was minimal and conversations hadn't stopped.

She intended to change that.

All Season long she'd been attracting attention she didn't want, publicly leading on more men than any one woman should ever flirt with. Her entire relationship with Griffith had been in secret, though. As if he were her hidden indulgence. And while this party wasn't the crush many of the others she'd attended had been, it was filled with people Griffith cared about. Friends—or at least friendly acquaintances—and family were scattered at the tables.

If things didn't go well, Frederica would be Isabella's only ally.

Isabella tore her gaze from Griffith's to track down her cousin. Frederica was already moving along the wall, making her way to the pianoforte sitting just inside the next room.

As she began to play a few people turned to look, but there was nothing of note in her quiet playing. A few women swayed in their seats or where they were standing, feeling out the timing of the waltz, but card play continued.

Isabella's heart was pounding. What she was about to do made no sense. It was a public declaration of intent, a very bold laying out of her private emotions. But Griffith deserved no less.

He stepped toward her, confusion giving way to concern as he worked through what she was doing. She would have to be quick or he would move to save her from doing something so scandalous. But she didn't want to be saved this time. She wanted people to talk about this, wanted everyone in London— in England—to know that this was not a match being made for power. It was a match made in love.

So she crossed the open area to meet him at the edge of the card tables.

Before she lost her nerve, she dropped into a deep curtsy. "Your Grace."

"Isabella." His voice was tight, breathy, as if his heart was just possibly pounding as hard as hers was.

She lifted her head and looked up, very far up from her lowered position. "May I have this dance?"

A gasp rolled over the tables around them, and whispers rushed soon after, as word spread out of the room and across the passageways.

Griffith extended one hand to help her rise but didn't let her go once she'd reached her feet. Instead he pulled her closer and wrapped his other arm about her waist. His smile stretched wide, wider than she could remember seeing in a very long time. "It would be my honor."

The low rumble of words, spoken as quietly as possible so that only she would hear them, washed over her until she was shaking within the circle of his arms. He swirled her and guided her, dodging people and chairs and tables with a grace that probably marveled everyone in the room.

It was so much like the last time, but so very different as well.

This time she wasn't burdened by guilt. In fact she felt lighter than air, held to earth only by the grip of Griffith's arm around her waist.

This time she could see his handsome face, could see the joy and the love shining there. The joy caught her a bit by surprise—she had a sneaking suspicion it wasn't all because of her.

"You enjoy dancing," she murmured.

"I enjoy waltzing," he corrected. "But I particularly enjoy waltzing with you." He guided her in an intricate step that almost had her tripping up but didn't even make him blink. He leaned his head down until the rumble of his voice fell straight into her ear. "I have a rule, you know."

"What is it?" she whispered.

"I only dance with family." He spun her in a quick circle that stole her breath all over again. "That means you'll have to marry me."

The last notes faded into a thunderous applause from everyone around them. They were swarmed with well-wishers and congratulations, as if they all assumed what Griffith had requested.

But she hadn't answered. And a brief look at the concern in Griffith's eyes even as he smiled and joked with the people around him showed that he was well aware she hadn't answered.

Eventually the excitement died down enough for her to make her way back to his side, and he maneuvered them through the room as only a duke could. In moments they were standing on a small balcony, the noise of the party behind them and the press of the evening summer heat around them.

"You didn't answer."

She snuck a sideways look at him. "You didn't ask."

A short laugh escaped as he shook his head. She placed a finger against his smiling lips before he could utter the question. "You should know something first."

He pulled her hand from his face and dropped a light kiss on her knuckles that sent shivers up Isabella's arm. But he didn't speak. Simply stared at her with his earnest, intelligent green eyes, tilting his body to block the slight wind that caused the lengths of his hair to fall alongside his ears.

Isabella took a deep breath and plunged ahead before she could stop herself. "I didn't come tonight because you made the Apothecary Act happen. I want you to know that. When you said you wanted a chance to prove me wrong—"

"I love you."

Isabella's words stumbled to a halt. "I . . . what?"

Griffith grinned. "I love you. There isn't a person on this balcony who hasn't made a bad decision before. But don't tell anyone I acknowledged that. I have a reputation to uphold."

Laughter sputtered from her lips even as tears welled to cling to her eyelashes.

"I may not have all the details, but I know enough. Your cousin is quite talkative when she wants to be."

Frederica had talked to him? When? They were going to have a very long conversation when they got home. But for now Isabella couldn't quite believe that moving on was going to be this easy. "You don't care?"

"Oh, I care. I care a great deal." He wrapped his arms around her waist and pulled her a bit closer, then left one arm there so the other could nudge her chin up and keep her looking him in the eye. "I care that the rest of your life you never go a day thinking you have to handle things alone. I care that you are reminded of God's forgiveness every day until you learn to accept it. I care that the world has an opportunity to see you for who you really are instead of just a beautiful face. I care that you get a chance to see every plant in England."

Isabella could barely see him through the stream of tears falling from her eyes. No one, not even her parents, had ever made her feel so very personally important.

His thumb grazed her cheek as he slid the tears away. "I care that another day doesn't go by that I don't get to say I love you."

She sniffed. "I love you too."

"Will you marry me?"

"Yes!" She threw her arms around his neck, stretching onto her tiptoes to reach as far over his broad shoulders as she could. "Yes, I will."

His smile was wide, showing his teeth in the moonlight. "Perfect. I believe Father Winstead is in attendance."

"What?" Isabella felt dizzy.

Griffith looked down at her, that annoying and endearing eyebrow lifted into the edges of the hair that had been disheveled by the breeze. "We're getting married. You agreed."

"But it's eight o'clock at night," Isabella sputtered. "On Thursday."

He shrugged. "I obtained a special license." He leaned in until his nose was even with hers. His grin returned, and the happy excitement in his eyes was infectious. "Now, are you going to marry me or not?"

Epilogue

Griffith watched Isabella stroll through the manicured gardens of Regent's Park, marveling at the orderly flower beds and the bright colors. The summer heat had taken a significant toll on the gardens, and most of the plants had lost their luster. He'd have to bring her back next spring.

"Please tell me you didn't buy a house on Regent's Square just so we could have access to this garden."

Griffith shrugged. "It was the only garden in London you hadn't tramped through yet."

She gasped, her head flying around until she was staring him down, mouth dropped open in an exaggerated gasp of indignation. "I do not tramp."

He laughed as he scooped her up in his arms, causing her to squeal before falling into giggles. As he set her down, he couldn't help the smile that split his face until his cheeks hurt. He'd been smiling a lot lately.

Nearly every time he looked at his wife, in fact.

His wife. They'd been married for a week and he still said the phrase over and over in his head. As if he couldn't quite believe it. But every morning she was there, smiling and teasing him at the breakfast table, awing him once more with her incredible beauty and her generous heart.

He'd come so close to losing her, to having never found her in the first place. And now he couldn't imagine his life without her.

"I did not buy another house," he admitted, sliding her hand into the crook of his elbow as he led her deeper into the park. "I'm a duke. I merely asked permission."

"From whom?" she asked, looking around at the fashionable houses that bordered the gardens, claiming the grounds for their personal use.

Griffith considered throwing out a nonchalant reference to asking Prinny for permission, mostly to see the adorable glare she got when he was being presumptuous and arrogant, but they'd promised on their wedding night never to lie to each other again. "I've an old school friend who lives in that house over there." He pointed to the east. "We're his personal guests."

She bit her lip. "Will he let us come back? I'd love to see this in the spring."

"Sure you don't want me to buy a house so you can see it whenever you'd like?"

With a laugh, she ducked her head and burrowed it into his arm, her bonnet scraping against his shoulder.

They walked farther into the park lands, enjoying the sun and the breeze. He had work waiting for him at home, and soon he'd have to admit that he couldn't spend every day strolling through parks and gardens with his wife on his arm, but there was balance in his life now. Balance he hadn't even realized he needed.

He pulled Isabella to a stop and looked down into her face. "I don't believe I ever thanked you."

"For what?" A small crease appeared between her eyebrows. He smoothed it away with his finger.

What could he tell her? That he was thankful she'd shown him that the heart was as important as the mind? For teaching him how to laugh at himself? For removing the constraints he hadn't even realized he'd put on himself?

"For being you" he finally settled on. "I have a surprise for you."

She laughed. "Another one? I'm not sure I can take much more."

"You'll like it. One of my traveling coaches should be arriving in Northumberland today."

He watched her closely, saw the exact moment she realized what he'd said.

Her mouth dropped open, her eyes glistened. "You did?"

Griffith nodded, feeling a bit choked with emotion himself. "I even sent men to watch over the farm. If everything goes smoothly, they'll meet us in Hertfordshire within a week or so. And I've already arranged for Hugh to start school at Harrow in the fall."

She sobbed through her smile, drawing a laugh from him at the mix of emotions she wore so well.

"Griffith, it's too much."

"No, it isn't. I love you. Whatever matters to you, matters to me." He pulled her tightly to him. "And I take care of what matters to me." He grinned and lifted his eyebrow in as haughty a look as he could manage, given how happy he was at the moment. "Haven't you heard? I'm a duke."

Then he leaned down and settled his lips against hers. His heart pounded and his fingers tightened their grip in instinct before he tilted his head to change the kiss in a way he knew she loved. Her sigh brushed his lips as she wrapped her arms around his waist.

And he was home.

Author's Note

One of the interesting things about writing historical fiction is choosing how to fit your fictional story in with what really happened. Quite a bit of history was used in *An Inconvenient Beauty*, though literary license was taken.

The prank with the bat guano that the boys pulled in the prologue is actually inspired by a prank pulled at Oxford in 1790. William Buckland did use bat guano to spell out a word on the field, and it was a very long time before that word disappeared. At the time, however, guano wasn't widely used as a fertilizer in England, so Buckland was also introducing a bit of science into his prank.

While the Apothecary Act was a real bill and the timeline of its journey to law was similar to the way it was portrayed in the book, the motivations behind the people involved are entirely fictional. The timing of Napoleon's return to Paris and the battle at Waterloo are also accurate.

The French Eagle that Arthur Saunderson is given credit for retrieving was retrieved by the 1st Royal Dragoon during the battle at Waterloo. Captain Alexander Clark led his cavalry troops charging through, though there is some dispute over whether or not he was the one to actually snag the golden eagle. The hero's welcome Arthur is predicted to receive was actually granted to Corporal F. Stiles who returned the eagle to the rear. The account of the eagles coming to the prince regent is based on the way it actually happened, though a few adjustments were made for story purposes.

The trees in Berkeley Square are real, as are all the pieces of art described in the Royal Academy, though they weren't necessarily laid out in the order described.

For more details about the actual history behind the book, look in the bonus materials section on www.kristiannhunter .com.

Acknowledgments

When I signed my contract for the HAWTHORNE HOUSE series, the day you would hold this book in your hand felt really far away. I'm still not sure I believe it's here. The Hawthorne family has come to mean so very much to me, it's hard to believe it is good-bye. Or at least good-bye for now.

I'm very happy too, because in sharing this fictional family, I've gained another real-life one: the readers who have gone on this journey with me and will continue on to the next, the incredible team at Bethany House that makes the magic happen and takes it from manuscript to finished book, and the other writers who have come alongside me and offered brainstorming help and support along the way.

Thanking every single one of them would take forever, but there are a few who need a little share of the limelight, because this book wouldn't have happened without them.

First of all, if you enjoyed this book you have no idea how much thanks you owe my family. *Supportive* doesn't even begin to describe them—the word is too small. It needs more syllables. Like supercalisupportivelistic.

Thankful is also an inadequate word when it comes to letting God know what it means to me that He lets me ride this incredible ride. I am truly living my dream.

You probably knew about those two, though. So here are a few people you might not have known played a part in making this book.

Acknowledgments forever to Regina Jennings, who taught me how to Save the Cat and therefore led me to a plotting method that finally made sense to me. My writing will never be the same.

To my sister-in-law, who not only makes sure my books make sense but also is one of the prettiest women I've ever met—yet somehow manages to be so nice you can't hate her for it. She proves it's possible for Isabella to actually exist.

Thank you to the Internet, for having a home for some of the most obscure information imaginable. And thanks to Google for helping me find it. I now know how much Chris Hemsworth weighed when he was playing Thor.

Though I shall not call you by name, thank you to my friends who told me what it was like to be drunk. There are some things I'm not willing to experience in the name of research.

And finally, though he has no idea he did anything for me, I'd like to thank Jon Acuff and the 30 Days of Hustle Challenge for helping bring some sanity into my schedule. It is partly because of this that the books will continue coming. Jon, if by some strange meeting of worlds you ever actually read this acknowledgments page, I hope you post an Instagram picture of a llama with a bear, if for no other reason than it would be funny. And because *llama* is a fun word.

Kristi Ann Hunter graduated from Georgia Tech with a degree in computer science but always knew she wanted to write. Kristi is an RWA Rita Award–winning author and a finalist for the Christy Award and the Georgia Romance Writers Maggie Award for Excellence. She lives with her husband and three children in Georgia. Find her online at www.kristiannhunter.com.

Sign Up for Kristi's Newsletter!

Keep up to date with Kristi's news on book releases and events by signing up for her email list at kristiannhunter.com.

More from Kristi Ann Hunter

When Lady Adelaide Bell and Lord Trent Hawthorne are stranded together and then forced to marry for propriety's sake, is there any hope for love after such *an uncommon courtship*?

An Uncommon Courtship
HAWTHORNE HOUSE

◊ BETHANY HOUSE

You May Also Like . . .

After being unjustly imprisoned, Julianne Chevalier trades her life sentence for marriage and exile to the French colony of Louisiana in 1720. But soon she must find her own way in this dangerous new land while bearing the brand of a criminal.

The Mark of the King by Jocelyn Green
jocelyngreen.com

When unfortunate circumstances leave Rosalyn penniless in 1880s London, she takes a job backstage at a theater and dreams of a career in the spotlight. Injured soldier Nate Moran is also working behind the scenes, but he can't wait to return to his regiment—until he meets Rosalyn.

The Captain's Daughter by Jennifer Delamere
LONDON BEGINNINGS #1, jenniferdelamere.com

When a financial crisis leaves orphan Elise Neumann and her sisters destitute, Elise seeks work out west through the Children's Aid Society. On the rails, she meets Thornton Quincy, who suddenly must work for his inheritance. From different worlds, can they help each other find their way?

With You Always by Jody Hedlund
ORPHAN TRAIN #1, jodyhedlund.com

When Grace Mallory learns that the villain who killed her father is closing in, she has no choice but to run. She is waylaid, however, by Amos Bledsoe, who hopes to continue their telegraph courtship in person. With Grace's life on the line, can he become the hero she requires?

Heart on the Line by Karen Witemeyer
karenwitemeyer.com

⧫ BETHANYHOUSE

More Historical Fiction

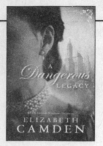

Lucy is determined to keep working as a telegraph operator at a news agency, even though the arrival of Sir Colin Beckwith threatens her position. When she discovers Colin's shocking secret, she agrees to assist him if he helps her find her family's stolen inheritance—not realizing that the trail leads into a web of treachery, danger, and conspiracy.

A Dangerous Legacy by Elizabeth Camden
elizabethcamden.com

On the eve of WWI, a client hires Rosemary Gresham to determine whether a friend of the king is loyal to Britain or Germany—and she's in for the challenge of a lifetime.

A Name Unknown by Roseanna M. White
SHADOWS OVER ENGLAND #1, roseannawhite.com

When a British plane crashes in the park in Brussels, English nurse and resistance spy Evelyn Marche must act quickly to protect the injured soldier, who has top-secret orders and a target on his back.

High as the Heavens by Kate Breslin
katebreslin.com

After her family is killed by the Hebrews, a Canaanite woman enters the battle herself—not intending to survive. But when a Hebrew warrior finds her unconscious among the dead, he brings her to a healer—and together, they must find a way to live with the consequences.

Wings of the Wind by Connilyn Cossette
OUT FROM EGYPT #3, connilyncossette.com

◊BETHANYHOUSE